# SHADOWRUN:
# DARK RESONANCE

## PHAEDRA WELDON

This is a work of fiction. Names, characters, places and incidents either are the products of the author's imagination or are used fictitiously, and any resemblance to actual persons, living or dead, business establishments, events or locales is entirely coincidental. The publisher does not have any control over and does not assume any responsibility for author or third-party Web sites or their content.

If you purchased this book without a cover you should be aware that this book is stolen property. It was reported as "unsold and destroyed" to the publisher and neither the author nor the publisher has received any payment for this "stripped book."

The scanning, uploading and distribution of this book via the Internet or via any other means without the permission of the publisher is illegal and punishable by law. Please purchase only authorized electronic editions, and do not participate in or encourage electronic piracy of copyrighted materials. Your support of the authors' rights is appreciated.

SHADOWRUN: DARK RESONANCE
Cover art by Victor Manuel Leza Moreno
Design by Matt Heerdt

©2014 The Topps Company, Inc. All Rights Reserved. Shadowrun & Matrix are registered trademarks and/or trademarks of The Topps Company, Inc., in the United States and/or other countries. Catalyst Game Labs and the Catalyst Game Labs logo are trademarks of InMediaRes Productions LLC. No part of this work may be reproduced, stored in a retrieval system, or transmitted in any form or by any means, without the prior permission in writing of the Copyright Owner, nor be otherwise circulated in any form other than that in which it is published.

Published by Catalyst Game Labs,
an imprint of InMediaRes Productions, LLC
PMB 202 • 303 91st Ave NE • E502 • Lake Stevens, WA 98258

## DEDICATION

I want to thank all the wonderful people at Catalyst Game Labs for their hard work and dedication to the game. Without them and the players, we wouldn't have our Sixth World. I'd also like to thank my closest friends who've heard about this book for five years (I can't wait to see the looks on their faces!).

But most of all, I want to give a full-hearted thank you to the ones that never gave up on it and never let it go. To John Helfers, Jason Hardy, and Loren Coleman.

# PROLOGUE

Justin Stonewater crouched in the shallow shelter made by the ruined wall, a remnant of a brick and mortar building. Others huddled close to him in an attempt to share their pain, their fear, their isolation.

He knew the sensations enveloping him—pain, cold, exhaustion, hunger—weren't real; they couldn't be. That's what his subconscious insisted, day after day...because there was no night here. No reprieve from the endless sun above them. No relief from the harsh, unceasing wind. No rescue from the twisting, iridescent band that stretched from one end of the sky to the other. Something he had once believed would bring him out of this nightmare.

Now it just twinkled and laughed at him. At all of them.

No one knew where they were or how they got there. Only that the world was a scorched wasteland. His stomach yearned for food, but there wasn't any. No food. No water.

But no death.

In the dim light, he stared dully at the half-formed avatars around him. Some still looked human, or at least closer to their living personas. But those were the newer arrivals. The ones that had arrived with hope in their eyes who-knew-how-long ago were now hunched into fetal positions, scattered around the hull of what could have been a brick building.

Justin held up his skeletal hand. It no longer possessed muscles or veins. No bloodied nails to bite or fingertips to scrape against the sharp rock walls that kept them in their pen. His other hand was only half-deteriorated, as were his feet and part of his torso.

He knew what his eventual fate was. He'd seen a dozen of his comrades turn to dust as their life gave out. More and more vanished into the sands each time after the Old Man came and blocked out the sun. The routine was the same. To exist in this hell until He called for them.

And then the pain began. Wrenching, tearing, knotting pain as it twisted his soul into blackness. It was the only relief any of them knew any more. That dark, dark, cavernous nothing.

But each time, he woke afterward to the endless hell still around him—just with more pieces of his flesh removed. One day, he wouldn't wake up at all.

Justin looked up at the twisting pool of energy he wasn't allowed to touch. Just like he and the others weren't allowed to go near the only other building in their pen. It was a large metal building, seemingly untouched by the scorching sun and heat. Light pulsed from its roof as the Old Man's ladder wound its way upward. From where he sat Justin thought it looked as if the ladder had almost reached it. And if he could climb the ladder...he could touch it!

Rising on stick legs and bony feet, he stumbled over the half-corroded group toward the warehouse. His thinking was that the Old Man wasn't around...in fact, he hadn't shown himself in...well, a long time now. Justin knew if he could just touch that energy—it had a name, one that danced at the edge of his memory, but he couldn't remember it any more. All he knew was that if he touched it, he could finally go home.

Home that felt like a long-lost dream. A life in...somewhere else...with...his family? His...wife and...son...?

The warehouse loomed over him as others reached out to stop him, whispering on the constant wind. "Don't go! You can't go in there! If you go in there, you'll die!"

And what was this? Life?

Justin wrenched at the building's double door. Its metal surface was cool against his skin, almost comforting, and he felt a vibration. A stirring he hadn't felt since waking up in this nightmare.

He pressed on the doors. One of them gave a little. He pressed harder as others followed him when they saw he wasn't destroyed. Some argued against opening the doors, while others tried to help him. Eventually, the door was wrested all the way open, but Justin was the only one willing to step into the darkness inside.

The cool temperature soothed his aching body and chilled the sweat on his brow. He took a few more steps inside, and the door closed behind him. Silence. He couldn't see anything for a few seconds, until his eyes adjusted. A light up ahead grew brighter, and he trudged toward it.

Thunder rolled outside, and the cool, smooth floor shook as he got closer to that light. *Is that it? Is that...the base of the ladder?* It had to be. The closer he got, the more detail he could make out.

Yes! It was the ladder! Only—

This time the thunder shook the building to its very foundation as Justin slowed his pace. What he saw couldn't be possible. Yes it was a ladder...a wide, heavy ladder that reached up through a hole in the ceiling.

***"YOU DARE DEFY ME!"*** a voice boomed, so loud that it shattered the warehouse walls.

The ceaseless wind howled into a gale around Justin as he ducked down, slamming his skinless hand against the hard floor. Without the walls, he could see the rest of the pen now, scattering before the Old Man in a futile attempt to escape the inescapable.

A black tornado swept up everyone inside of it, including him as he tried to run. He crashed into flying debris, possibly the rest of the ruins. Rocks, bricks, and thin pieces of the warehouse walls and roof hurtled at him. He screamed as he was struck repeatedly, and saw others flailing in the gusting storm beside him.

He lost his legs first, neatly severed by a warehouse wall that blurred by. Next, flying rocks tore his hands off his helpless limbs. A brick smashed into his face, crushing bone and muscle as he caromed out of the tornado and into the void, where the pen no longer existed.

There he fell in a silent scream until everything stopped.

Forever.

# CHAPTER ONE

## 4 MONTHS AGO

Kazuma Tetsu gasped when the host around him revealed a ravaged world.

At first, he wasn't sure he was in the right place—it looked like a battlefield. There were no trees or grass under a hazy sky of gold and dark smoke. Jagged, silver tiers of once familiar buildings rose up like broken bones sticking up through charred, blackened skin.

"Wow, chummer...nice pajamas."

He turned to see a standard, out-of-the-box avatar of a man with dark hair, squared jaw, scruffy chin, and long, dark coat. Yep, generic P.I. from a gaming box.

Kazuma smiled. "Dirk. Nice Dick Tracy motif." He stepped over a puddle of oily water to take the man's offered hand. "Interesting choice. This an art piece?"

Dirk shook his head. "Not really. This is a replica made from another host—one a bunch of technomancers nearly died in. They created this to show what almost killed them. But it's just a representation. If you were really on the host right now, you'd become deathly ill."

"Sick from a host?"

"A host totally corrupted, *omae*. I wanted to meet you here so you could see what's creeping along the periphery of your realms. Take a good look at this, Kaz, and don't ever get caught in it. The artists for this call it dark resonance. And that description isn't far off. Memorize, and know it's real." He stepped closer. "Your sister's missing again."

"Yes, I know," Kazuma answered, but he kept looking around. "But I don't think she's submerging this time. I think she's in trouble."

"I think you're right." Dirk reached out and put his hand on Kazuma's arm. "There's not a lot more I can do for you. You're going to have to look for her on your own. But there are a few things I can advise you to do, and you should get quicker results."

He had Kazuma's full attention.

"Even after you let me know that Hitori had showed up a few weeks after the fun at Cup O' Sin, I kept doing research because a name kept coming up. Caliban."

"You mean like *The Tempest*?"

"Yeah. Like that. Do two things." He moved in close, so Kazuma could see every painted cell of the comic book icon. "I need you to change your online handle from Dancer to Soldat. Got that, *omae*?"

"Soldat?"

"It means soldier."

"Yeah, yeah."

"It's better than Dancer. That's a drek name. Then I want you to refine your searches to include the name Caliban. Just keep Hitori's name and add Caliban. Got it?"

"Yeah..."

"Good." Dirk stood back. "That's good. Do those two things and you should be reunited with her soon. Or if not, you'll definitely attract some interesting company."

# CHAPTER TWO

### GiTm0

Welcome back to GiTm0, *omae*; your last connection was 13 hours, 9 minutes, 22 seconds ago.

### BOLOs

Just a reminder—this board's got less than six hours before it terminates in your comms. Send your sprites out twenty-four hours after that for the new link.

New shadowrunner handles to look out for: Mangle, Blackwater, blessie89, and DongleSave. Full list available [Link][Guest], but don't read the list online. And don't forget, these runners are out for the nuyen, and they don't give a damn about us.

Remember, GOD is always watching.

### NeW oNLiNE

*Twenty more known technomancers vanish from Novatech Arcology. No trace. Families won't even acknowledge they're missing. [Link]

* Saw in an early morning feed that Contagion Games' latest MMORPG, TechnoHack, crashed another host early this morning, toppling several regions of play and causing a semi-brownout with a Matrix gateway near Seattle. CEO Ferdinand Bellex held a press conference apologizing for the downtime, and promptly blamed the failure on the resurgence of decking units not syncing with the hosts. He also made a few odd comments about technomancers attacking their mainframe, and is in negotiations with

Knight Errant for tighter security to prevent this type of breach again. Bellex also announced a new UV host opening within the week that should relieve traffic to their home host and prevent any more grid inconveniences once Knight Errant's got their systems firmly in place. Anyone in here played this game? We need reasons why Bellex even brought us up. [Link][Review Posts]

    * A breach in security at an Ares facility in Lower Los Angeles has the Pueblo CC buzzing around with hi-tech might—though the local corps spokesperson insists nothing was stolen or tampered with. This is the fifth in a series of random glitches plaguing the company two days after an employee in the personnel department was fired. Coincidence? [Link]

    * In a similar thread, Cup O' Sin coffee house—whose name was in the news cycles a few years ago when it was attacked by hackers—is back in the news. One day after the firing of the above-mentioned Ares employee, the shop experienced the same glitches with the establishment's PAN. When an espresso machine exploded in an employee's face, she blamed it on one of the shop's regular customers—that customer was identified as the same employee fired from Ares the day before. When no commlink was found on him, the man was beaten to death. During his autopsy, they found an internal comm. Things are not happy out there for us, people. Always have a commlink or decking unit visible. If you got jacks, use 'em for show.

**EYES OPEN**
\>\>\>\>Open Thread/Subhost221.322.1
\>\>\>\>Thread Access Restrictions: <Yes/**No**>
\>\>\>\>Format: <**Open Post**/Comment Only/Read Only>
\>\>\>\>File Attachment: <Yes/**No**>
\>\>\>\>Thread Descriptor: **Denial**
\>\>\>\>Thread Posted By User: Shyammo

- Hey Shyammo! Thanks for finding that article on the missing Novatech employees. I noticed there hasn't been any comment at all except a blip on a late night vid-squawk. In fact, when I saw the story carried only once, and then it wasn't carried over to the other networks—I started to wonder if I'd seen it at all.
- 404Flames

- Not sure they were all employees. Read the article. Says most were employees, and the others were just members of employee families. What kind of harsh piece of drek do you have to be to deny your family member is missing?
- MoonShine

- We need to look deeper into joint ventures. Corporations working in tandem on projects involving technomancers. Look for tags like electronic magic, hacking research, dark waters or caliban.
- Soldat

- Hey Sol, where you been? It's been ages since you posted.
- HipOldGuy

- Did that bit of intel you were checking help, Soldat? Did you find her?
- 404Flames

- I didn't find her, but I found something that might help. Which is why I'm throwing the suggestion on those tags out there. We need to watch for the corps working together. Possibly forming hush-hush covenants when it comes to technomancers.
- Soldat

- What did you find, Soldat? You sound like you saw or read something.
- Netcat

- I'll get on that, Sol. I've already started looking into Contagion Games and their issues. I wasn't happy old Bellex felt the need to bring us into his problems. If the guy's team can't build a decent game, take responsibility. Don't go slinging mud. I'll see if anything pops up.
- HipOldGuy

- I don't want to say yet, Netcat. I've got Silk working on a few things. I'll post when there's more. It's just that...have any of you felt something weird? And I mean weird while in AR or the streams?
- Soldat

- Thanks ahead of time on that, Hip. I always like to make sure you guys know how much you're appreciated out there. I was happy I didn't have to report any of us missing this week. Last week's number took a toll.
- RoxJohn

- Hey Hip, been doing a little grade work for Contagion. I'll check out the game. Been a little curious myself. Might be a little more nuyen to be made if they keep breaking the Matrix like that.
- Venerator

- Sol, what do you mean weird? I'm asking because last time I submerged, I did run across something. It wasn't in the streams, but it was there waiting when I left. And I had the feeling I was being watched.
- Netcat

- Yeah...Ten gone in a matter of a week. Rox, did you find out anything more about their disappearance? Like did they all work for a corp, or were they even connected?
- EasterBunnyun

- That's close to what I felt, Netcat. Almost like something's on the edge in there, on the outside looking in. I'll make sure to get back when I know more.
- Soldat

- You know I can't give out that information on the board, Easter. But if you click this [Link] I can give it to you.
- RoxJohn

# CHAPTER THREE

## HORIZON ARCHIVE ANNEX
## LOS ANGELES
## RETIRED DS HOST
## THURSDAY EVENING

Kazuma Tetsu's living persona, a red-headed, black-clad ninja, stood within the drab, gray-walled virtual reality of the Horizon host, sword held in front of him. An antique desk with a worn, leather briefcase visible in the open lower drawer stood between him and his opponent. He raised his weapon as the blade reflected his opponent's icon.

The icon, a simple, snarling, drooling white wolf, looked like one of those out-of-the-box personas Kazuma had seen with the resurgence of decking units.

He didn't have time to linger and fight the persona of whoever this was. He needed to do a bit of technomancer hand-waving. A diversion—something with enough power and strength behind it to distract and detain this bastard long enough for him to grab the information and get out.

The use of his skin-linking echo was draining, but not enough to alarm him just yet. Kazuma hadn't planned on compiling, given that it would require a bit more of his stamina than he could afford. If he hadn't physically been next to the host and accessed it remotely, perhaps a fight would be justified. But not right now.

He moved his sword up and around and slowly re-sheathed it on his back. The white wolf roared and drooled as it showed its teeth and pushed its back end up as its front went down. Drek—it was going to attack within seconds. *Have to be a fast compile...*

With his hands now free, Kazuma held them out from his sides, palms up, and opened his senses to the whisper and buzz of the Matrix around him. The space between them abruptly swirled with wisps of incandescent smoke filled with 1s and 0s of data. With his arms held out, he inhaled and drew those wisps to him, bringing his imagination to bear and thoughts into sharp focus as he spoke to the datasphere, gave it purpose, and asked it to stand in the enemy's way.

The Matrix answered him with action as the wisps formed ribbons of colors that spun and danced before him. The 1s and 0s wrote themselves into existence as he called forth its form...that of a Bengal tiger. Twice the size of the wolf-hacker and for a brief time, far more clever. Kazuma liked to give his sprites the freedom of imagination. This decker might think he knew what he was up against, but he would be wrong.

Feeling the drain impact his physical body, Kazuma took a step back as his newly compiled Paladin Sprite roared in the face of the white wolf.

The white wolf answered with an attack. It vaulted upward, claws extended as the user's voice came through: *"I'm gonna take you down!"*

Kazuma's Paladin sprang forward and intercepted the wolf. Both beasts crashed into a side wall, then the tiger burst into a cloud of small, iridescent, yet iron-clad butterflies that flew into the wolf's face, knocking chunks off it.

While the two programs tangled, Kazuma grabbed the briefcase, turned, and ran. The Paladin would fight long enough for him to disengage from the host, and its essence would return to the web-like whispers of the datasphere.

Weaving his way through the endless maze of corridors, Kazuma used his katana to cut away the lingering ghosts of previous security protocols, now too weak to be useful. While slicing and dicing, he considered his options. Before Big, Ugly, and Drooly had showed up, he'd planned to open the briefcase and gather only the information he found that referred to his sister and the name Caliban. He hadn't counted on anyone else being here—much less wanting what looked like discarded files. But there wasn't time for that now, so he decided to get the briefcase as far away as possible. It would be simple to compile a courier sprite and have it squirrel the briefcase away to a secure location in the Matrix, where he could retrieve it later.

Unfortunately—this host wasn't connected to any grid. No outside connections to the Matrix itself.

But there was a wireless signal nearby that allowed *him* access.

*Boss!*

Ponsu, Kazuma's registered sprite, appeared beside him as a large, golden origami swan. She was his first sprite—a creature born and nurtured within the Matrix. She contained information from both himself and from the resonance streams that pulsed like rivers around him. She—and he called her a *she* because she spoke to him in a soft, feminine voice (not the voice he'd purposely given her either)—had been with him for more than two years, his constant companion in the Matrix.

Kazuma shoved the briefcase into her beak. The host itself wasn't connected to the Matrix—but Kazuma was. He'd never tried it before—but it stood to reason that *he* could be the conduit between the two. "Get this away from here—just hide it safely in the Matrix somewhere. I'll get it later."

*You want me to leave you alone? I can't do that–have you noticed that big, ugly wolf back there?*

"Yeah, that's kinda why I'm running." Kazuma glanced back, sensing the dissipation of the Paladin. It hadn't lasted as long as he'd liked. The wolf might look generic, but its strength wasn't.

He looked back at Ponsu. "Just get it out of here. I've got this guy mad enough to follow me."

But the sprite was looking down the corridor behind them. *Let me take care of the fool. I can–*

"Ponsu! *Please!*"

She gave him a lingering look with iridescent eyes before vanishing.

"YOU GIVE ME THAT BACK, YOU ASSHOLE!" shouted the wolf as it charged into the hall.

Running along his escape route, Kazuma jumped out of VR and back into the disorienting world of reality. The wolf-hacker would have to leave by his own way in—most likely via a deck. Kazuma assumed they were close by. *Physically* close by. The wolf's user had to be *in* the Annex and physically wired to the host in order to be inside—and they weren't a technomancer. That much Kazuma knew.

Before attempting this harebrained idea, Kazuma had disabled the two other terminals in the building that had been daisy-chained to the host he needed. But somehow the jackass had managed to fix the sabotage. Should have made sure they couldn't be fixed—but he hadn't wanted to draw attention to himself in case another tech took a look.

*Hindsight. Twenty-twenty. All that. Damn it.*

Coming out of VR hot was always a bit of a disaster for Kazuma—re-orientation took a few minutes as he stumbled blindly from where he'd propped his body in an office chair. Compiling that paladin had cost him a bit, not to mention Ponsu's escape to the Matrix. The dim room grew dimmer as he took his hand from the host's outer shell and took several deep, stabilizing breaths. He needed to get himself and his gear out of the Annex before the idiot wolf-hacker tripped a security wire he hadn't disabled.

The deck was still packed in the small bag, but he kept his commlink visible. His datajack was still prominently positioned on his temple, and he kept his hair pulled back to emphasize its presence. He wouldn't let anyone—especially his employer—know he was a technomancer. Not exactly an advertisable skill nowadays. More like a curse that could get him killed, or vanished.

Like so many others.

He carried a Fairlight headset, the very first commlink he'd bought. But if anyone took a hard look at it, they'd find the thing was factory-modeled. Just like the deck. No upgrades. Not even an app for the most mundane tasks of being a KE tech. His partner, Silk, called his bluff all the time—hammered home that he needed to at least pay for the upgrades and have them visible.

"If you're going to live the lie, then live it right," was her constant advice.

But he didn't need them. Which was a major plus when it came to expenses.

Kazuma had the commlink connection set in place on his wrist, but not turned on. He managed to stumble back into the chair in front of the desk when the door to the terminal room burst open.

He turned, genuinely startled, as an ork in a Horizon Security uniform came in, weapon drawn. Clearing his throat, he presented the guard with his best smile. "Sir—"

"Show me some I.D.!" the ork barked.

Kazuma nodded quickly, taking in the security officer's yellowed tusks protruding up from his jaw over his upper lip. The ork's jaw was built forward, allowing for the added weight and space for the powerful teeth. His small, pointed ears twitched, and Kazuma could smell his fear. Something was wrong within the building itself. And whatever that was had this security guard spooked.

*Damn that wolf hacker!*

Kazuma transmitted his SIN to the ork. The guard kept his weapon trained on Kazuma as the information popped up in his AR. Though Kazuma could see the virtual window in the guard's PAN, he already knew what it would show.

*Morimoto Toshi, Human, Knight Errant Supervisor, Birthplace: Chiba, Japan.* The image would be that of an older human. Kazuma had used nano-paste to change his face and hid the arching points of his ears beneath a bushy gray wig.

The ork appeared to be satisfied and handed his wallet back. "Sorry, Mr. Morimoto, but the silent alarm got tripped—over on the south side of the building. We suspect there's a hacker in the host. Luckily, this is an off-grid system. We've got people looking around the building for them."

Damn it. The hacker *had* tripped the alarm. *Baka.* He nodded as he carefully made a show of unhooking his deck from the terminal. "That's quite all right, sir. Are you here to escort an old man out of here for safety?"

The ork was about to answer when the door opened and a human dressed in the same uniform as the ork stepped inside. "Brigg," the smaller man said with a narrowing glance at Kazuma. "Got anything?"

"No," the ork named Brigg said. "This is Mr. Morimoto—he was here working on the security system for KE." He leaned in close to give a hoarse but audible whisper. "I think he was in the system when the alarm got tripped. He doesn't look so good."

The human moved past Brigg and glared harder at what he perceived to be an elderly Asian man. "You need a CrashCart, old man?"

"No, no." Kazuma shook his head. "It's just—your friend is right. I wasn't prepared for the tertiary failing of subsidiary drives, causing a cascading failure that—"

The human guard put up his hand. "I got it, I got it."

Kazuma smiled inwardly. It was always better to baffle them with bullshit. The key was to know *who* and *when* to bullshit. Coming off as a tech-head security flunkie could be disarming enough.

"I am sorry to be so much trouble." He smiled for real as he finished packing his gear into his bag and stood.

Ponsu was back, hovering just inside of Kazuma's peripheral vision within his own AR. She gave him a nod to let him know the briefcase was hidden. Nothing to see here—and nothing to find in his deck or his commlink.

The human nodded at the terminal. "You finished? 'Cause we think the autodial's already contacted your people's security unit—that happens in a time like this. You want to wait for them?"

No, he did not want to meet them at all. Fooling these two had been easy—but fooling a Knight Errant officer? Or worse, GOD, in case Ponsu had triggered the attention of the Grid Overwatch Division spiders. Kazuma wasn't ready to test his skills at disguise just yet. "Yes—I would very much like to be here when they arrive. May I gather my things and meet them at the front—"

But as he spoke, the room fell into total darkness. Though the host itself wasn't on the grid, the Annex's security system was. Kazuma unconsciously tapped into the faint wireless signal, asking Ponsu to check on the blackout. Within seconds the swan appeared in a new AR window to his left.

*Boss—all the power's still on—otherwise the network wouldn't be viable. The lights are still in operation.*

He cursed under his breath. It was dark, but the power was still on. In theory, the lights were on as well—only none of them could see. That meant the blindness was *magically* induced. And there was no telling how far the range went, or if the hacker himself was immune. But Kazuma was sure the wolf-hacker was still in the building, waiting for him.

A single shot echoed outside the small room's darkness. Kazuma didn't need sight to know both guards had drawn their weapons.

"They've cut the power," the ork said. There was a *click*. "Mullens, this is Brigg. We heard gunfire."

Another pause, then static before, "Yeah, we're in the dark here—you?"

"Yeah, us too. We're in the center basement. Mr. Morimoto is here from KE doing work—we're gonna try and find the shooter."

"Copy. We'll advance along the south ring. You go north."

"Roger."

Kazuma winced at the exchange. They'd used *open* communication—voice activated. Any hacker worth his cybereyes would have already had taps on bus to bus. Basically, they'd just given out their plan to the shooter. Unless it was code for something else. But he didn't really believe that.

A small light appeared in the ork's palm, illuminating the room in a greenish glow. Whether the ork knew he was countering magic with magic was uncertain—but it was enough. Kazuma could see their faces—prints in shadows and emerald. "That's about as big as I can make it, Chief."

"That's good," said Chief, the human. "Mr. Morimoto, I need you to stay here. This room has a steel door. Once Briggs and I step out, I want you to lock it and just stay calm. I'm sure the KE cops will be here in a few seconds. Can you do that?"

"*So ka,*" he said.

"Do you have a weapon?" Briggs asked.

"*Ee-ae,*" he lied. "I'll be fine."

Once the two were outside, Kazuma touched his watch. He could see the glow in the dark. The magic had only affected the environment, which meant it had vulnerabilities. Like the ork's light and the illumination from an electronic device. Using the watch as a flashlight, he found a utility drawer, and in it a small, battery-powered light.

He pulled up a minimized window with a chewing gum-smacking blonde inside it. **<You get all that?>**

<Yeah,> she said as her persona blinked. Her gaze looked to be tracking something Kazuma couldn't see. <*Wolf dude pulled the fire alarm in the south slde.*>

Fire alarm? Kazuma moaned. **<So KE isn't coming?>**

<Oh, they're coming all right. I'm just making sure a few red lights stay red long enough. Your car's where you parked it. I found a rigger nearby–she's a few tables over from me. Seems I picked the right place.>

**<She with this wolf-hacker?>**

<That's my guess. I'll draw their attention away. Ponsu's got the strategy. Take care, and remember the GODs are watching.> Her window disappeared.

After surveying the area one more time to make sure he hadn't left anything visible that could be traced back to him, Kazuma opened the door carefully, wincing when it made a *click* that resounded throughout the darkened corridor. Hooking his bag around his shoulder, he decided the flashlight would bring too much attention. Since the blackout was magic, then a camera should see just fine.

Mentally reaching out to the closest datasphere whisper, he

opened the back door of the building's security network—which he'd helped install, of course. A new window appeared in his AR—giving him a fully lit corridor on both sides. The angle was going to throw him off, since he would see himself coming down a hallway instead of what was directly in front of him. "Ponsu—you got the strategy?"

*Right, Boss.*

A grid of the building's corridors, rooms, and exits appeared in a window to his left. He noted the flashing red dot telling him where he was. The basement. One level up to street side. There were three possible exits out of the Annex—but he didn't see any vehicles nearby that might belong to the wolf-hacker. Unfortunately, he hadn't made a contingency plan—never considered anyone else would want the information. Another fact Silk was going to yell at him for.

As he trotted toward the stairs, one of the cameras overhead detected a movement near the door to the basement. Kazuma assumed it wasn't a security guard, but the wolf-hacker coming to look for him.

Retracing his escape route on the grid, he found another exit open upstairs—rarely used—on the opposite side of the building facing a one-way street. Boulevard Avenue, NE. It wasn't a usual route for transports to follow, as half of the street on that side had caved in and was under construction. But then, *most* of this side of town was under construction. If he could get a ride there—

Ponsu rustled in front of him, visible in all the AR windows.

As Kazuma neared the stairs, he heard the telltale sound of boots descending. Moving as quickly as he could, given the constant fatigue pounding at the back of his eyes, he ducked behind the stairs, the spaces between the steps visible. Kazuma moved the AR windows aside except for the single camera that gave him a bird's eye view of the staircase. He waited for the hacker to appear.

It didn't take long. As the boots hit the appropriate steps he reached out, grabbed just above the ankles, and pulled with everything he had. The booted man yelled in surprise as he tumbled down the rest of the steps.

Kazuma bolted around him, using the basement cameras to watch himself sidestep the man as he scrambled to get back up. Taking the stairs two at a time, the technomancer reached the top just as the man below raised his pistol and fired.

# CHAPTER FOUR

## OUTSIDE THE HORIZON ARCHIVE ANNEX

Mackenzie Fenrir Schmetzer—Mack to his runners, and anyone else he chose to associate with—stood in the shadows of the warehouse across the street from the Annex building of Horizon's Los Angeles offices. He'd boosted his cybereyes' vision magnification up by x4, enough to see the tool marks on the Annex's windowless wall. Traffic was nil this late at night, with the Annex located in a less than desirable area of the city—farthest away from the glitter and lights of the main thoroughfares, and smack in the center of construction. In fact, the entire place was scheduled for demolition.

Most of the street lights here were dark—busted by rocks and bullets long ago. City politicians felt it was a waste of resources to constantly replace them, only to have them knocked out at the next opportunity.

There was one bulb that burned bright enough close to where Mack stood. He liked the light—without light there couldn't be shadow. And without shadow—there was no run.

And with no run—no nuyen.

Even in today's economy, Mack was doing pretty good for himself. He owned two successful clubs in the Los Angeles area, a bar in Seattle, and a stash of private homes. Not much else was known about him, except for his ability to complete runs. Not always successfully, but he was fair. As long as the Johnson was fair.

And that wasn't often.

Mack believed in honor among thieves. Or at least he believed in honoring the deal.

His Los Angeles runners had gone nearly a month with no good jobs until this one. And even this job seemed simple. So simple that Mack was monitoring it personally. He didn't know why—he just had a feeling that something wasn't right.

First off, why would a corp like Horizon have an Annex with active hosts that weren't on the grid? And second, why would anyone store something important on one of them?

Mack considered the recent bad public opinion regarding Horizon, and thought it would be a brilliant place to hide things they didn't want easily found. The security in the building impressed him, especially the fact they were employing Knight Errant when the PCC police was closer, and probably cheaper. But this fact also set off warning signs all over the place. Five guards for a three-story building that covered maybe an eighth of the block? Excessive was a thin word.

He knew whatever they were extracting off that host was important. Or volatile. And then—in hindsight—maybe this place was the best when it came to disguising something higher up on the food chain?

As he pondered that idea, he felt as well as heard the *pop* in his speaker—it was a sound he'd committed to memory decades ago in a former life. The sound of a gun being fired.

"Damn," he muttered as he held up his hand, the rings on his fingers activating his AR. The building's grid appeared, an electric wire-frame of the first and second floors, as well as his team's markers. He only had two runners in the building—his hacker and his magic backup. Cole Blackwater was the best money could buy when it came to retrieving information of any kind. His programs and gear were bought out of Mack's club Worldwide. Blackwater was a man on his game. He was good. Damn good.

And he had the ego to go with it. That was a flaw. And it was a *fucking* whopper.

Maria Venzuella was a shaman. One of her specialties was security dampening—which Mack had chosen to use on this run.

And it had appeared to be working—until someone got capped.

Mack narrowed his eyes at the markers—he could make out Blackwater's pulsing red star near the center of the building. But Maria's wasn't there.

Moving, twisting, flipping and finally closing the map, Mack broke one of his own rules—using verbal communication during a run. Usually he preferred everything be communicated via one of Blackwater's texting protocols, but he didn't have time to text *<What the fuck?>*.

Instead, his commlink picked up his lowered voice. "What the hell's going on in there?"

Several seconds passed before Blackwater answered. Mack tapped a small grid icon in the lower left of his vision, bringing the map back up. He overlaid it onto his view of the building. "I got company—fucker was already in there getting the fucking file. Had to cap a security guard."

Mack swore under his breath. "Cole—you and Maria—"

"I'm on it—I can see where he is. I'll get the shit from him."

Swearing again, Mack swiped the map aside and a keyboard appeared in the air, projected by his AR. He typed in a few directory commands for the building's security system, and was able to tap a few of the cameras. "Visual's still up. Only a few cameras out. Why isn't Maria's spell working?"

There was an uncomfortable pause.

The hairs on the back of Mack's neck stood up. "Cole—where is Maria?"

"She's moving just ahead of me. I'll call when I get the bastard—"

"No, you get out of there *now*," Mack interrupted. "If you've tripped something, those guards will already have called KE—and I do not want to tangle with them." And if GOD showed up—that wasn't a level of trouble he needed. When Blackwater didn't answer, Mack switched channels. "Shayla, you been monitoring?"

"No sweat," she said, perky as always—which never really fit the way she looked. Shayla was a changeling, a partial transformation into a troll. And she was the best rigger he'd ever hired. On his best friend's recommendation, of course. "GMC's already in position. Got a bead on the Knight Errant boys—about two minutes out."

"Any sign of GOD?"

"Not yet. Might not have caught their attention."

*Yet.* Mack refocused his attention on the physical world. He started jogging down the street. The GMC Shayla usually used for runs should be parked just outside the exit for a quick dive and squeal. He'd worn his soft shoes tonight—no noise on the concrete.

As he reached the block corner, he glanced down the street and saw the GMC parked inconspicuously along the opposite street, complete with a legal parking pass and record. All he, Maria, and Blackwater had to do was run to the van and get in.

Mack took in a deep breath, looked both ways, and crossed the road in a leisurely jog. To any passerby, he would look like any other middle-aged human working on his health.

Only he was doing it at night—in a not-so-friendly area of town.

Mack stopped halfway across the intersection as the GMC's horn began squawking and its lights blinked on and off. *What the—*

"Boss!" Shayla's voice was loud and unhappy over his link. "Someone's hacked my RCC."

*What?* Still in the street, Mack closed the distance to the annex's corner. "Shayla—you're telling me *you* were hacked?"

"My deck was. Gotta be someone in here with me. I can't—*drek*—it's gonna take me a few to reboot—"

"Shayla—what are you saying?"

"I'm saying KE's less than two minutes away, and I don't have control of the GMC."

Mack moved away from the squawking van. Damn thing was going to draw attention. "Shayla, you gotta shut that thing down!"

"I'm *trying*—but I have to wait for the RCC to reboot. Gimme a minute!"

Mack stood halfway down the side of the building's wall. *Fuck.* He took off toward the GMC. If she couldn't do it remotely, he'd do it physically.

# CHAPTER FIVE

## CONTAGION GAMES
## MAIN GAME HOST, LOGIN WELCOME CENTER
## THURSDAY EVENING

HipOldGuy read through the game rules as his living persona paced inside the Welcome Center. The environment alone made him uneasy. Whoever designed the landing platform had thought it would be a great idea to create an invisible floor and then surround the whole thing with a constantly swirling iridescent coiling of white and silver.

*This is not what the Realms look like,* he thought to himself as he glanced down between his boots. Not having a visible floor... don't like that.

"Oh. Wow. This is awesome."

Hip glanced over at the new player as they rezzed on the platform. Young female—or the persona was female, at least. No telling what the Matrix user was. Didn't matter to him. She was shapely, with great legs, white hair, bright blue eyes and ample breasts. She was dressed in camo shorts, combat boots, and a tight-fitting top. She had some serious artillery strapped to her hips and what looked like goggles perched on her forehead. He didn't say anything, and went back to reading the rules.

"Hey mister...does this game really make you feel like a technomancer?"

Was that a trick question? Hip looked back at her again. "How would I know?"

"Just askin'. So, how do we start?"

"You read the rules."

"I hate rules."

"Don't we all." But he continued to read and sort of watched her out of the corner of his eye. She grabbed the booklet with the game rules and sort of skipped through them. But she wasn't actually looking at them. Finally she skipped ahead to character creation and he watched her make a technomancer street samurai (*Seriously?*) and buy up all her points in gear.

"Miss," he said, and she turned to stare blankly at him. "If you're a technomancer, you don't need all that gear."

"Oh please, Mister. Technomancers are just couch potatoes. Can't actually fight. And I'm not gonna get ganked my first hour out. I want the gear." She finished and jumped on the pad to teleport her into the game host.

Hip sighed and finished reading the rules. But what she said bugged him. Yeah, it was becoming common knowledge that technomancers were weak physically—but wouldn't that be true of anyone who spent too much time in the Matrix and not enough in physical life? So why couldn't a Matrix user also be healthy? There wasn't a law against it. Then he thought about his own old and plump body kicked back in his recliner. Not moving. Not exercising.

*Yeah, well...stereotypes be damned.*

The game wasn't that far off from present day—the player could choose to be a shadowrunner, a wageslave, though the game called them corporate executives. The point of the game was to slip in and become part of the roleplay. Submersive playing. He'd seen this type of game before—and he'd also known players who forgot to leave this kind of game to tend to the meat suit, and either died while online or got really sick. He pulled up a timer on his AR and set it to remind him to pull out in one hour. Should be enough time for him to at least look around the host, map it out, and see if he could use the information Rox sent him on where the deaths took place.

Of course, no one else but he and Rox knew there were deaths—the media was still reporting them as blackouts. Even the boards said Bellex had come out and apologized for the host crashing—and taking out nearby ones as well. But closer digging by Shyammo had revealed an interoffice memo at Lone Star about the deaths during that blackout. Twenty-seven of them. And not all on the Contagion host, but on the other crashed hosts. Hip was out to get more intel so they could upload the truth to GiTm0.

Hip made his character a KE Agent, complete with the latest commlink, and chose his apps carefully. Before he became a technomancer, he'd been a pretty damn good hacker, so even after he found he didn't need all the gear, he still kept up with the latest versions and bug fixes. Still gave verisimilitude to his continued work as a hacker.

Once he had the map downloaded and the NPC players, group leaders, and storytellers per faction, he jumped on the landing pad and teleported to the host.

Though the Welcome Center hadn't impressed him, the build overcompensated to a point where Hip had to double check where he was. It was the most detailed duplication of Denver he'd ever seen. Down to the latest street name changes. Hip walked around for a bit, his OOC (out of character) tag on so as not to interfere with any ongoing game play. And again, the immersion was incredible, down to the smell. He was actually smelling Denver at street level. Hip had only been there once as a boy, but he remembered. "Profound" was the word he used later in life.

He took a detour to Genesee Park and stood outside the park's fence. He pulled up the information on his AR, double checked his encryption and then checked the deaths again, each of them showing up as red dots. A cluster of three dots showed several meters ahead of him.

With a quick glance around, he moved to the left and entered the park, then continued to follow the red dots—

"Help! Someone!"

He and two other players nearby stopped and moved out of character as they looked at each other. Hip was pretty sure the others were thinking the same thing he was—*is that a real cry for help, or part of the game?*

"*Somebodeeeee!*"

The voice sounded familiar.

Hip and one of the other players, an ork, took off in the direction of the voice—straight ahead. Right where the dots had shown up on his AR. This couldn't be a coincidence.

He recognized the technomancer samurai from the welcome center. What he didn't recognize was what she was half-submerged in. It looked like one of the old tar pits—but this stuff wasn't just thick and viscous. It looked like it, or something *inside* it, was...*moving*.

"Mister!" She reached out to him. "Pull me out of this!"

"Oh wow. That is some messed up code," the other player

who ran with Hip said as he moved past him to offer her a hand. "I swear, this game's got one glitch after the other."

Messed up code? Hip looked from the kid to the black tar, and then grabbed the kid's shoulder. "Tell me what you see."

"Where? Hey look, we need to pull her out."

"I know—but tell me what you see."

"I see a hot chick stuck in pixelated lag. It's a glitch. Haven't you been watching the vids? This host's been having all kinds of trouble." He pulled his hand away. "I say we get her out and then leave before it goes down again. I was here when it went out last time, and I still have a headache." He leaned forward to help her out.

Everything in Hip's head said *LEAVE!* Everything. "You don't see her stuck in a tar pit?"

The guy shook his head as he reached out to grab her hand. "Naw, man. I see bad resolution."

*If I see one thing, and he sees something else—*

Realization dawned on Hip just a second too late as he watched in horror. Something resembling an oily, dark tentacle slid out of that blackness and wrapped around the kid's arm. He yelled as it dragged him forward, his feet pushing grass and dirt up in an attempt to stop himself.

"Hey, old man!" came another voice behind him. "Why're you just standing there?"

Another player, also an ork, ran past him and tried to help them out as well—but more of those tentacles lashed out and wrapped around him. He drew a sword and hacked at it, cutting it off, but more came and wrapped around the ork's waist, hips, arms, neck, and face. Hip watched as those same tentacles encircled the girl and the first boy who'd come to her rescue.

Their screams brought more attention, and more would-be rescuers.

Hip took several steps back. He had no experience to compare—no way of knowing what it was he was seeing. He broke his own protocol, compiled a recording sprite and told it to record everything in front of him. Every person that tried to help was pulled into that pit of thick black ichor. He watched as their mouths filled with it, blocking their screams, suffocating them until—

Someone put a hand on his shoulder. He assumed it was another player, giving him shit about not helping. But when he turned to face them—

The man was tall, with pale skin. He wore a shiny black trench coat and a skirt that puddled on the ground like the ichor. On his face he wore a gas mask that looked fused to his skin. The moving ichor of his skirt slid up his body, down his arm and over his hand onto Hip's shoulder.

"*There you are,*" he said as the spreading gunk wrapped itself around Hip's head. It blanked out his eyes and filled his mouth so he couldn't see or speak. Icy fingers pinned his arms to his body as the ichor traveled down his back to his legs, until he was completely trapped in a cocoon of ice and darkness.

His last coherent thought—just as his AR alarm went off—was to tell the sprite to find Soldat.

And then, despite the black ooze filling his mouth, he screamed.

# CHAPTER SIX

## HORIZON ARCHIVE ANNEX

Kazuma was able to get the basement door closed and locked. But that wasn't going to stop the wolf-hacker, just delay him and annoy the hell out of him at the same time. Before he could get far enough away, the wolf-hacker started shooting at the door from the other side. Making a *lot* of noise and large bullet holes. Whatever this guy was shooting with was actually coming *through* the door.

Kazuma stumbled backward, only barely aware he could see again without the need for the camera link. The spell was finished. With his bag securely draped around his neck and shoulder, he pressed himself up against the opposite wall, his breathing fast, his heart beating even faster.

*Shit...*

*Boss?*

Closing his eyes for a second, Kazuma blinked a few times to try and clear the fog that threatened to pull him down before mentally reaching out to retrieve the grid again. He was fading fast. A red line appeared over the blueprints, starting from where he was and leading to the south end and then through the closest exit. He tried to steady his breathing even as he reached around and put pressure against his right side, just below his ribcage.

*Boss? What happened? Your vitals are dropping.*

Kazuma's mouth tightened to a thin line as he dared to move his hand to look down. It was hard to see the blood against the black KE uniform, but he knew it was there. And if he wasn't careful, he'd start leaving blood drops all over the floor. A DNA trail to find. "I'm hit...I think it's just a graze."

*Boss!*

"I'm fine, Ponsu. I just need to use a slap-patch."

*Boss—those things are dangerous.*

"I don't have a choice—just make sure to get my ass out of here. Got that?" Kazuma managed to keep himself upright as he reached into his bag and pulled out a homemade slap-patch. It was a stimulant mostly used by runners, but he'd managed to learn the technology after reading *ShadowSea* and created a small set of them.

He peeled the backing away, grunting as he shoved the plastic into his pants pocket, and then hissed as he opened up his shirt and slapped the patch on his bare skin. Instantly the stimulant, absorbed through his pores, sent a burst of energy into his nervous system.

He was up with no dizziness. But it wouldn't last. When the drugs faded—

So would he.

Orienting himself with the grid and where he was, as well as checking the position of the other security guards, he turned and ran down the corridor. But even as he headed to the corridor's end, he heard the thunder of footsteps and stopped, pressing his back against the wall on the corner. "Ponsu—"

*I see them. Recalculating.*

"Ponsu—this slap-patch is only gonna last eight more minutes before I fall on my ass."

Even as he spoke, the grid on the map shifted several times, Ponsu doing calculations faster than he could blink. The grid reappeared, the route glowing bright white this time.

*Take this path. I calculate you should get there with one minute to spare—starting—now!*

Kazuma pulled the Fichetti Security 600 from the concealed holster at his back. He checked the chamber. Loaded. Holding it in his left hand, barrel pointed down, he followed the grid overlay to the right and then down a corridor, another abrupt turn right and then—

He'd been so fixated on the route and the timer in the upper left of his AR window that he hadn't been watching in front of him. He tripped spectacularly over something solid and unforgiving. Kazuma landed squarely on his right hip, jarring his wound so hard he saw stars through the stimulant's effects. The Fichetti and his bag skittered across the dingy tile floor, the bag popping open and spilling his gear everywhere.

Cursing, he righted himself, taking in air through gritted teeth, and opened his eyes—

A pair of sightless, dark brown eyes met his.

With a sharp hiss he realized he was on the floor, face to face with a dead body.

She had a bullet hole between her open, staring eyes.

Kazuma scrambled back, grunting at the fire in his side, pushing himself along the dusty floor, leaving a smeared trail of blood behind. Using the heels of his shoes, he distanced himself from the body. He could see it was a female. Human. Dark hair, dark eyes, skirts and shawls. There were tattoos on her upper arms and along her neck.

*Shaman? Mage?*

He didn't know enough about magic to know which—he only knew that sometimes tattoos could be the effect of magic. But had he read that somewhere?

But magic hadn't put that bullet into her head. Had it been the security guards? A look around, and he spotted two more bodies—the two guards he'd spoken to before. The ork and the human. Both lay in pools of blood.

What the hell? Had the wolf-hacker done this? Was he insane? This kind of body count was going to draw a lot of attention!

Kazuma's vision tunneled, and he braced himself against the floor, willing himself to stay conscious. What had he been thinking? For months he'd been so careful, using his abilities to just search here and there. Three submersions to coincide with his vacations. Refining his abilities. And everything brought him to this host. He didn't think it was a setup—no one knew who he was. Not in the living world. In the Matrix, his name had gained a bit of notoriety among the other technomancers, primarily because of the information he brought them.

Working for a security company, he should have realized seeing that kind of data hidden on a closed host wasn't a fluke. It had been *put* there by someone. Deliberately. And now that someone had come to collect it. Was it just fate that it happened to be the same night he'd chosen?

But who was this girl? And why had someone killed her?

Ponsu appeared in a subdued color to his left within his ever-present AR. In fact...his entire virtual desktop was a bit dim.

*Boss,* Ponsu said. *The patch isn't working. Your vitals are dropping. I need to call a CrashCart.*

*Well, it's not an exact science now, is it?* "No—no CrashCart. Understand?" Kazuma was still staring at the body, but was able to stagger into a somewhat standing position. His event horizon was totally fucked up, and the floor looked closer than he knew it was. "I need to get to my car."

*Just outside the door. It's parked and the door's open. Just...hurry.*

*What?* Kazuma narrowed his eyes as he stumbled to retrieve his Fichetti. He grabbed things and shoved them back inside the bag.

*Boss...now!*

Kazuma picked up the pace and followed the quickly dimming directional guidance from his sprite, but nothing was stopping the perspiration streaming from his body; a side effect of the stimulant—or the effect of shock and blood loss. "Ponsu...you can't move a car..."

<No, but I can. Get your ass out here now!>

Silk.

He could see the exit at the end of the corridor—a light beckoning him—and he pushed himself to move toward that light. He burst through it and saw his car at the curb, the passenger door open, and Silk at the wheel.

# CHAPTER SEVEN

## OUTSIDE THE HORIZON ARCHIVE ANNEX

Mack kicked the now silent GMC's tire. It wasn't a bright thing to do—and it hurt like hell. But the pain sharpened his senses, and he stood unnaturally still as he listened to the night around him. *There...* He heard the gentle purr of a high-performance car nearby.

Pursing his lips, he took off at a dead run, backtracking the same path he'd used before, just on the opposite side of the street. Once he got to the corner—the one across from where he'd been hiding in the shadows—he turned to his right.

There sat a beautiful Lexus sedan. Its right two wheels were *on* the sidewalk—its passenger door open right in front of the Annex's side door.

*What the—*

As he started toward it, the building's door slammed open. He saw an older man in a long coat stumble out onto the pavement. He had a messenger bag over his shoulder—and he didn't look well.

Breaking into a run, he shouted at the man. "Hey!"

The stranger turned, but Mack couldn't see his face. And then—

Something moved in front of him, blocking his view. It was brilliant, and had a familiar shape—something he remembered from his childhood. A bird. A stork? And that shape was in front of him, blinding his cybereyes and causing painful feedback into his neural sensors that was the equivalent of a blow to his forehead. Clapping his hands to his eyes, he cursed as he stopped just a few meters from the car. He could hear the car door shut, and was able to regain enough sight to see it hauling ass down the road.

He ran to the open door of the building and bulled inside. He didn't see Blackwater anywhere. But he smelled blood, and pulled his Ares Predator V from its holster as he walked farther in.

Mack followed the building's blueprints on his AR and came to the corridor where Maria and two security guards lay motionless. There was blood everywhere, smeared on the floor as if someone had tripped in it, and then tracked it down the hallway toward the door he'd just entered.

"Mack! Blackwater's in the GMC! We gotta roll!" came Shayla's more than stressed voice.

"Maria's dead—"

"I know. He told me. We can't do anything right now."

"I can't just leave her—"

"Mack," Blackwater interrupted. "You get out here now, or we're leaving—and I'm taking your club while you're in jail."

That was enough to kick Mack in the ass, and the hacker knew it. With a last, sad look at the dead shaman, he spotted a commlink by her foot and assumed it belonged to one of the dead security guards. Cursing under his breath, he retraced the same route out and headed to the GMC.

Just as the wail of approaching KE sirens broke through the night.

# CHAPTER EIGHT

## HORIZON ARCOLOGY, LUXURY LEVEL
## LOS ANGELES
## FRIDAY MORNING

Artus Wagner, soon-to-be-retiring Horizon Personnel Manager for the Los Angeles Home Office, did not enjoy being awakened at six in the morning by the authorities. It had been a long evening downtown—Wagner's people entertaining the Vice President and his associates for their first night in Los Angeles. Everything had gone so smoothly—

Except for the Vice President's guest, an irritating dwarf named Powell and his mongrel dog—a large, black animal with a haunting stare. He had spent most of the evening in the shadows, drinking very little and keeping part of his attention focused through the monocle on his left eye. Wagner knew the monocle was the dwarf's AR connection—and he knew the dwarf was someone the Vice President held in high regard. But Wagner had no idea what the man's purpose was. The Vice President never revealed his position in the company—or whether he worked for Horizon at all.

But putting that aside—it had been a very productive evening.

Until his personal assistant had called. Charis Monogue was a tall, slender, leggy elf. He hadn't hired her for her organizational skills—but because the woman could shoot a hole through a moving target's left eye socket. Ork, human, elf, dwarf, or troll. She was the best weapons specialist he had on retainer.

Her call was a heads-up about a little "incident" at the lower Annex building on Boulevard Avenue.

"What do you mean by 'incident'?" he asked as he rose from his bed. The house environment raised the bedroom lights a degree at a time until his eyes adjusted. Holo-vids activated, and the room filled with a chorus of voices as the world stock reports came online, as well as smaller windows searching the local news stations for pertinent information culled 24/7 for Consensus.

Charis had already uploaded the information to his agent, but she answered him anyway. "Apparently there was a break-in last night. The thieves left two dead security officers and a dead girl."

Wagner stopped in his tracks—his robe half on his shoulders. He turned and looked at the single screen, Charis' perfectly proportioned face staring back at him. "Thieves? Dead bodies? You did say this was at the Annex?"

She nodded. "Fortunately, your PCC friend arrived in the building first, so the media didn't get wind of the girl's body—just the security officers. But of course no one knows why she was there—"

"What was stolen?"

She paused, her expression, which was usually cool and collected, darkened just a shade with irritation. "Nothing. I mean, that Annex is scheduled for demolition tomorrow. The host's cleared out. It's not connected. It's just a redundant system. There was—*is*—nothing there to steal. I triple-checked the host's last diagnostic, along with its manifest."

"Who ran the last manifest?"

"Knight Errant, during the decommission protocols."

Wagner narrowed his eyes. "KE? Since when do they work security on, like you said, a redundant system?"

Charis looked down at her desk and moved a few things around. "Since Las Vegas. Remember, we've sustained a number of brute hacks ever since, even with a closed host like that. They won the contract to securely destroy the host. I think contracting them was a good move due to Horizon's—perceived indiscretions."

Funny how Charis used the word *perceived*. Wagner knew the truths behind many of the corporation's rumored side projects. Was it possible she did too? Or was she just being suspicious because he paid her to be?

She shook her head. "They even had an employee working last night during the break-in."

"Oh?" Wagner's shoulders stiffened. "Knight Errant had a tech at the facility?"

"Yes. One of the retired consultants—a Mr. Toshi Morimoto. He specializes in erasures and reformatting."

The name didn't sound familiar to Wagner. "I need a copy of that work order and who issued it."

"Yes, sir."

"I'll be there in a half-hour."

"Yes, sir. Half-kaf-soy or a non-fat whip sugar-free mocha?"

"Both," he said as he disconnected, canceled the house systems and went to a wall safe, hidden behind the main holo-vids. Pulling out a wrist commlink, he inserted the earbuds, slipped on the image shades, and logged in through his neighbor's secured PAN. It was a stunning deal Wagner had set up with Charles Hockenberry, having Wagner's IT man set up a secure network for the neighbor.

And leaving Wagner his own back door.

In the commlink's AR, he contacted a preset number and waited. There was a pause before the handshake and then a new window opened up. The familiar Matrix persona of Cole Blackwater appeared in the window. Usually Blackwater preferred to parade around as a large, white wolf. But this image was human, a heroic male figure right out of a romance trid. Full pecs; long, flowing blond hair; and electric blue eyes. Wagner knew the real Blackwater looked nothing like this.

The persona looked anything but happy to see his meal ticket. "Not now."

"Yes, *now*. Did you kill the guards and the girl?"

"How'd you already know that?" The persona actually looked impressed. "The guards walked in on me, so I had to cap 'em. They were just rent-a-cops anyway." Blackwater looked around. "I can't talk right now. Mack's on the warpath. That other hacker somehow nixed our rigger's RCC. I've got Mack thinking *he* was the one that killed Maria and the guards."

"I really don't care what your boss thinks." Wagner summoned several news reports his agent had compiled. "Do you realize how easy it's going to be to ID that girl and track her back to you, and then back to me? How could you be so stupidly careless?"

Blackwater's persona made an obscene gesture. "No one can track her real ID—I'm not even sure I could. About the only person that might know it would be Mack Schmetzer."

Schmetzer. Schmetzer. Why was that name familiar? It wasn't that Wagner didn't already know his hired gun worked for a face named Schmetzer. It was just that every time he heard it there was a slight tremor—a distant memory of the name he couldn't quite make clear. "What is this about another hacker? Did you get the data?"

Blackwater's persona rolled its eyes in frustration. "I put some serious hurt on the guy before he got away."

Wagner closed his eyes. "Did you get the data I hired you to retrieve?"

There was a pause. It was all the answer Wagner needed. "You failed."

"I'm gonna get it back. I just told you, Shayla and I are looking for him. I shot him."

"Who is this person? And why are they after *my* data? I put it there. No one else knew it was there, except for you."

The persona held up both hands. "I'm gonna find him and get the stuff back."

Wagner held up the right hand of his own icon, a stately man with ashen skin and an ork's protruding jaw. He wasn't an ork, but they were a race of beings not usually screwed with. In the Matrix, one could be anything they wanted. He paused, remembering what Charis had said about the Knight Errant tech working on the system. "Did you get a look at him? Was he Asian?"

The persona shrugged. "I got a glimpse of someone—some old dude in the basement. All I could see was his back—gray hair. I did see his Matrix persona—it was some red-headed dude with a katana."

"Get that data back, Blackwater." Wagner disconnected and removed his commlink, shades, and gloves. He stood very still for a moment. *Katana...* Was it possible the thief was the same Morimoto who had the work order? And if this hacker had successfully fabricated a work order and managed to pass the Horizon System's sentinels, and then stolen the intel right out of Blackwater's hand—he had skills to rival the hacker's.

Stowing the gear back to its hiding place, Wagner readied himself to see Charis.

# CHAPTER NINE

## KNIGHT ERRANT ARCOLOGY
## LOS ANGELES

"You haven't rested enough."

"I'm fine," he called from the bathroom.

"You look like hammered shit."

"I said I'm fine." Kazuma stepped out and smiled at the lithe, mocha-skinned beauty lounging in his bed, the sheets barely covering her assets. His gaze lingered on the dark blue tattoos along her arms and thighs, and he sighed. "They don't care what I look like, just as long as I show up and do my job. And I can't *not* go in. After last night—they're going to be looking hard at anyone who doesn't show up today."

"You used Morimoto's ID, not to mention his face—that's what they're going to look for. And once they realize he's dead—"

"How are they going to connect me to him?" He walked back into the bathroom to finish dressing. The face in the mirror still showed a bit of the effects of fading. Silk was right—he looked bad. Dark circles hung under his eyes, and he was paler than usual. The fading had hit fast after the slap-patch wore off. He had no memory of the drive home, or of getting into his apartment. Silk had taken care of everything.

As she had ever since their first meeting.

Kazuma and his sister had been online, exploring an art host and talking about their upcoming trip to see their family in Chiba, Japan, when the Crash of 2064 hit the Matrix. The last thing Kazuma remembered was sharp pain, and then nothing.

A long, long time of nothing.

Thousands had died at their decks, and many of the survivors were found in comas. He and Hitori languished in this state for nine months. Hitori awoke first, claiming to hear voices, whispers, to see things out of the corner of her eye. She was diagnosed with AIPS— Artificially Induced Psychotropic Schizophrenia—and locked up for a while before she figured out what had happened to her.

She was released when Kazuma woke and helped him as he dealt with his own symptoms of AIPS. Though his wasn't as severe as Hitori's, he suffered from horrific nightmares of being trapped in darkness when he slept, and intense migraines when awake.

Where Kazuma fought the terrifying changes, Hitori embraced them. Kazuma refused to use them at first. Hitori honed her skills at technomancy and achieved two submersions before Kazuma attempted his first, and the nightmares and migraines disappeared.

She'd disappeared during her first one—and Kazuma had hired a private detective to find her. It wasn't until after the event at the coffee ship near Knight Errant that she showed up again. Different. Calmer. And determined more than before to help others like themselves.

Hitori talked him into and helped him through his first submersion. The thought of releasing himself fully into the Matrix terrified him, but she was able to help him relax and try to accept the changes his body and mind were going through.

When he returned feeling, seeing, hearing things a little different, Hitori introduced him to Silk, the one who had guided her into her second submersion into the Resonance Realms, a place inside the Matrix that only technomancers could go when submerged. When they faced these realms, they increased their connection to the Matrix resonance and increased their abilities.

Silk was something most technomancers were not; physically active. Her parents were street fighters, and her life had been mired in gangs outside of Chicago. When her mother was killed in a fight, her father sent her to live in Seattle with her aunt—not so much out of love, but because he couldn't be bothered with raising a child who seemed more interested in the Matrix than in physical prowess.

Silk told him she felt as if she'd lost both her parents. And as her own special brand of revenge, she trained in several physical skills and rejected the cyberware her parents and the culture she'd left depended on. Her aunt showed her books that spoke about a time before the upgrades, where men and women honed their physical bodies as art. She fell in love with the tattoos of the Maori tribes, and had her body adorned in tribute, a new tattoo for each skill she'd mastered.

And all the while, she had still learned the Matrix and became fascinated with machinery. And through it all she never had a datajack installed. Refused to even think of adding cyberware. But she had used trodes to explore VR.

And then the Crash came. At the time, Silk had been online along with so many others—and her world had changed forever.

Silk had been the one to teach Hitori how to fight physically— and taught her how to run when her opponent was too cyberized to defeat. There was always a choice in survival. And when Kazuma had been mugged one night, it was Silk staying nearby who had saved him from having his throat slashed. Since then she made sure he exercised every day, and kept his physical strength up. She'd also had him reinvent himself in the Matrix. He refined his online persona, making the red-headed ninja more realistic to fit his new online name, Soldat.

Silk appeared beside his reflection in the bathroom mirror. She was nude, and her dark, thick hair cascaded over her shoulders. "Your name is still connected to his, idiot. He was your supervisor. And he was a technomancer."

"But not for very long." He ran his fingers through his hair. "He only lived a few years past the Crash. But what he taught me about KE was invaluable."

She wrapped her arms around his waist. "Stay home. Call in sick. You never miss work."

He leaned into her and placed his hands on hers. "And *that's* why I have to go in. That fact alone will make it look weird if I don't show up this morning." He turned and wrapped his arms around hers. "It's Friday. I'll get my work done, be home on time, and then you and I can head out for the weekend."

"You plan on retrieving the data?"

He looked down into her amber eyes. "That's part of the plan. But I have to make sure it's not marked or got some sort of tracer on it. So, waiting a little while might be a good idea."

"I could transfer it into a drone." Silk smiled. "Send it into storage somewhere. No one'll think to look in there. And stop—hear me out," she said, putting a finger on his lips. "If I'm right and your name does show up, hiding it anywhere within your sphere of family would be dangerous." Her eyes widened. "Oh shit….tell me you didn't put it *there*."

"I told Ponsu to hide it. I didn't tell her to specifically hide it there, but I'm pretty sure that's where she put it."

Silk pulled back. "In your grandmother's host. Kaz—"

"Wait, wait. I'm not sure, okay? And it's encrypted so tight now that only Ponsu can open it."

But his partner wasn't having any of it. She pulled away and he watched her backside as she left the bathroom. He followed her and shrugged on his black KE suit jacket as she put on clothes as well. "Silk…don't be mad."

"I'm not mad. You just don't get it, do you?" She turned an angry face on him, and he stopped what he was doing. "Kazuma… our people are dying out there. They're having their brains cut open, and no one gives a damn. Is this all a game to you?"

"No it's not a game—"

"Then wake up already!" She pulled her vest on and zipped it up. "Hitori is missing—*really* missing this time—and you're fooling yourself if you think you're going to find her alive. I can only tell you that so many times."

"But I would *know* if she were dead, Silk. We're twins. I would *know*."

She looked at him for a while, and her expression became sad. "How many times have you submerged, Kazuma?"

"Three."

"You need two more. You're right about the data, that it needs to be left alone for now. But it's not safe where it's at. Tell Ponsu to meet me in your grandmother's host. Do I still have admin access?"

He nodded.

"Good. Then I'm going to hide it in a better place. Then you and I are taking a long weekend with friends, and you're going to submerge again."

Kazuma frowned as he turned to the wall facing his bed. He touched the surface, connected with the apartment's AR, and the wall broke into three panels. The one in front of him opened and he stepped inside to look for pants.

"Kazuma?" Silk followed him inside and watched as he picked a pair from the dozens hanging on the wall. "Is it that thing again? Is that why you're afraid? Why you don't want to?"

"It's nothing."

"Don't shut me out. I'm listening."

Anger flared, and he kicked a pile of clothing aside before he faced her. "No, you're not. No one's listening to me. No one's paying attention to it. Not even on the boards. What's the use of those things if no one's looking?"

"Wait, calm down," Silk reached out and put her hand on his arm. "You're talking about that shadow again, aren't you?"

"It's not just the shadow." He put a hand to his forehead and stared at the row of pressed shirts and suit jackets. "It's a pressure. A weight. It's exactly what Dirk said it would be." He chewed on his lower lip. "It scared the shit out of him, Silk. And when I feel it...it scares me like that, too. But it's there, just on the edge of the resonance. Like it's...waiting."

She rolled her eyes. "Dirk Montgomery is a recluse and an old man. I wouldn't take much stock in what he says about the Matrix. He's not exactly wired."

"He was right about the information. It was right where he said it was. And I saw the word Caliban. It's the first time I've seen that word in relation to Horizon since Vegas. It's important. And we both think it's got something to do with whatever's out there."

"In the Resonance Realms."

"Yeah, and I told you and I told Gomer, but no one paid attention. I've had nightmares about a man-eating tree...and black. Everything goes black. And things are twisted and bent and covered in...evil and rot." He had to admit that sounded a bit out there when he said it out loud. But it didn't stop the dreams, or the images of Los Angeles being swallowed whole, and the laughter. The incessant laughter that followed him out of sleep.

"Hip did say you might have experienced a touch of dissonance when you left the resonance stream. That is a possibility, since both dissonant and resonant beings—us included—use them."

Kazuma lowered his hand and looked at her. "That's true. I just...with Hitori missing, and now this thing in the realms that I can't shake...I'm on edge."

"Get dressed. I'll make some breakfast." She went up on her toes and kissed his cheek. "Always remember to fuel the meat."

He watched her leave the closet before he went to the waist high chest to his right. He opened the top drawer and retrieved the KE pin there, the one that acted as his ID and his SIN, and clipped it onto his lapel.

No matter what the other technomancers thought or believed or wanted to see...there was something there. Something in the resonance.

And it was dark...

*Very* dark.

# CHAPTER TEN

## HORIZON HOME OFFICE
## LOS ANGELES

Charis was at the front doors of the Horizon Building, drinks in hand, when Wagner stepped through. He took one of them, sipped it. Perfect, as always. She ran through the day's calendar as usual. Even though he was there several hours early, Charis was still efficient.

"—and there's someone in your office."

Something in her tone caused him to stop just outside his office door. "Who?"

She lowered her shoulders and sneered. "It's *him*."

"Him?"

The doors opened at that moment, and the all-too-familiar visage of the dwarf, Mr. Powell, poked out. He looked from left to right, and then up at Wagner, his expression breaking into a garish smile. "Ah—Mr. Wagner! So nice of you to see me so early. Please come in—we have so much to discuss."

Before Wagner could complain the dwarf was gone, the door to his office closing.

He whirled and glared at Charis. "No one is ever supposed to be in my office."

"I know that, sir. But he was already *in* there when I arrived. Him and that—wolf."

Wagner frowned. "He brought that dog?"

Charis looked at him under lowered brows, her hand on her hip. "If that's a dog, I'm an ork. That creature is a wolf. And it's a damned scary one."

Shaking his head, Wagner looked at the clock in the upper

right side of his shades, the company's AR always active once he walked through the doors. "Just page me in a half-hour. Do you have that work order? The one the Knight Errant employee had?"

She grimaced. "I requested it. But he—" She pointed at the door. "—intercepted it."

"Fine, fine." He waved at her to go, and then stepped into his office. He'd half expected to see Powell in his chair behind his desk. But the interloper was in the guest chair, sitting patiently, the dog—wolf—sitting resolutely by his side.

Wagner set his briefcase by his desk and removed his suit jacket before settling into his chair. With controlled impatience, he leaned forward and interlaced his fingers as he placed them on the desktop. "Mr. Powell, what can I do for you?"

Powell pursed his lips. "Do you know what I do, Wagner?"

Wagner shrugged. "I have no idea."

"I procure...assets."

Wagner leaned his head to his right. "Assets?"

"Yes." The dwarf smiled. "I work for a group of entities who seek and use...individuals with *special* abilities."

The wolf made a noise—almost a small *woof*.

Wagner sighed. "Ah, I see. You're looking for technomancers. Mr. Powell, you've come to the wrong office. I'm afraid I don't have the information you seek."

Powell jumped down off the chair and put his hands behind his back. The wolf stayed put—watching Wagner. Powell was just over a meter tall—with short, cropped red hair and a thin beard that outlined a strong jaw. His skin was olive, and he was perfectly proportioned in every way. To Wagner he looked like a small human—except for the thick, pointed ears. "Late last night—or early this morning—an Annex owned by Horizon and scheduled for demolition tomorrow was broken into. Three bodies were found inside, but according to the intel I have, nothing was taken."

There was nothing stopping the quicker beat of Wagner's heart in his chest. He had thought Powell little more than a nuisance. But there was something here that just became very dangerous. Not to mention the almost intelligent light in the wolf's eyes as he watched both Wagner and Powell unnerved him. "The work order your assistant retrieved—at your behest—says that a Knight Errant employee was scheduled to double-check the erasure of an off-grid host within the building. Supposedly, this was a redundant system—something the corp used for archiving and encrypting. I believe that was the purpose for the Annex in the first place. It was shut down after the Vegas incident, and the hosts removed. All except three. From what little information I've been able to access, the remaining hosts were empty."

"I'm sorry—I'm not following you."

"Oh, I believe you are, Mr. Wagner." He started to pace very slowly, and then stopped next to the wolf. "This is Hyde. Hyde—please say hello to Mr. Wagner."

The wolf dipped his head in what Wagner could only assume was a bow. "Powell—"

But Powell turned and walked to stand in front of the desk. "Hyde is a special creature, Mr. Wagner. He is a technomancer."

The laugh escaped his lips before he could stop it. Wagner shook his head as he held out his hands. "I'm sorry—but did you just tell me this animal is a technomancer?"

"Yes. I did. This is no laughing matter, sir. technocritters—as they are called—revealed themselves a few years ago. My employer caught many of them—as one technocritter can sense another—and trained them. Trained them to hunt and identify others of their kind. They can no longer hide, Mr. Wagner. And Hyde," he glanced back at the wolf. "Can sense the more powerful ones. The...*special* ones."

Frowning, Wagner watched the wolf. "Special ones?" He had no idea where this line of discussion was going, so he made sure Charis was listening to the conversation as well.

Powell strolled back to the wolf. He scratched the animal affectionately behind the ears. "If there is one thing research has shown us so far, it's that no two technomancers are alike. They all have different specialities, abilities, strengths—as do we all." He pursed his lips. "Do you know how they increase their power, Wagner?"

Wagner leaned forward. "Can you just spell it out in plain English, Powell? Why are you in my office, going through my things?"

The dwarf smiled. "They submerge into Resonance, Mr. Wagner," he continued, as if Wagner had never interrupted him. "They develop abilities they call Echoes. One of these abilities is to connect with a host with no signal." He smiled. "Much like the host in your Annex."

Powell moved to a small bag on the floor by the door Wagner hadn't noticed until now. He retrieved something from the bag, crossed the room, and set it on Wagner's table.

"It's a commlink."

"It is." Powell smiled. "Knight Errant standard issue. Factory default."

Wagner lowered his shoulders. "Powell—"

"Think about it. If a Knight Errant tech was scheduled to double-check that host before the building was demolished, doesn't it stand to reason the tech would be outfitted with Knight Errant's best? This commlink should be loaded with apps. The memory should be full of upgrades. Alas—" Powell pushed at it. "There is nothing there. This is—as one would say—straight out of the box."

Wagner glanced at the device more closely. "You're saying this is the commlink the KE tech was using?"

"Yes. It was found near the body, along with boot prints and a lot of smeared blood. No real discernible fingerprints, but blood can be worked with." Powell put his hand on the commlink and fixed Wagner with a serious look. "Technomancers use these as a means to hide, Mr. Wagner. You have one of these visible when you access your AR or VR, and no one thinks anything of it."

Wagner finally took the commlink and looked at it. "Whose is it? I'm sure they register serial numbers to their employers?"

"This one isn't registered. It's not in the KE database. Now, let's go back to something very important I just told you." He stepped back and laced his fingers together. "The skin link. The ability to connect with a host. If a technomancer were to physically touch that host, they could spoof an ID and enter it and have this commlink visible so as to not look suspicious."

"Please, Mr. Powell. No one can hack with a commlink anymore."

"Yes. I know. He would need a deck. A technomancer doesn't even need that. But that's not where I want to direct you. A man hacks an abandoned host. So, what I have to know is—" Powell focused on Wagner's face with a frown. "Why?"

"Why?"

"Why? It's a dead host. There's nothing on it but the most basic OS, or so the Knight Errant manifest reported. So, why would anyone break into that Annex and hack *that* host?"

Wagner did not like where this conversation was going. "Mr. Powell, no one said anything about that host being hacked—"

"Of course they didn't." The dwarf smiled. "Because your friend in the PCC police didn't report it. Then again, how would she know? She and her group of armed thugs wouldn't have looked past the three dead bodies."

*How does he know this?* Wagner made a mental note to discuss his office's security with Charis. "Mr. Powell—answer this question. If this Annex has been secured since the break-in, how is it you have this information before I arrived for work? I only received word Knight Errant is looking into the building's security when I woke—and even they haven't established that the host was compromised."

Powell moved to the desk and retrieved the commlink. He spoke as he dropped it to the bag by the door and returned. "Mr. Wagner—you seem more interested in my being well informed than in the possibility that a technomancer hacked your host."

"Because the only proof you've shown me that a technomancer hacked a host is a factory default commlink. He probably had a deck. All you have is speculation." This little freak was getting on his last nerve. "We've already established this. There was nothing on the host. Now, if there isn't anything else, this pointless meeting is over."

But Powell didn't move. Neither did his wolf.

Wagner sighed and sat back. After a few minutes of staring at one another, he finally held out his hands. "Anything else?"

"Your signature is on the work order."

"What?"

"The work order for Knight Errant. The one that allowed a KE tech to be in the Annex last night."

*"What?"* Wagner said again. "I never signed any order for anyone to be in that Annex last night."

Powell gestured and a document abruptly appeared on Wagner's own AR desktop. "This is the work order you had your assistant procure this morning that I intercepted. It's for a Knight Errant technician named Toshi Morimoto. A work order by itself is usually non-suspect. But when the name on the order is that of a man who died a few years after the Crash—a dead man who somehow broke into your Annex last night, stole something, and murdered two security guards and a young girl—it becomes *very* suspect. Your name is on the work order, authorizing it."

Wagner reached up and yanked the virtual page closer,

zooming in on the signature at the bottom and the name of the employee, Toshi Morimoto. "I never signed this!"

"I'm aware of this." The horrid little dwarf laced his fingers together over his chest. "So what I'd like to know is why a technomancer broke into a host with basic programing? What was he looking for, Mr. Wagner?"

"I have no idea."

Powell steepled his fingers as Hyde growled. "I believe you do. And neither I nor my associate are leaving this office until you tell me everything you know."

# CHAPTER ELEVEN

## OUTSIDE THE HORIZON HOME OFFICES

Netcat sidestepped the fast-moving human as he bolted through the front doors of the Horizon building. She didn't care why he was in a hurry. She didn't care that he nearly ran into her. Nor did she care when he scowled at her less than professional dress. While others moved around her in the latest designer suits, complete with their built-in links and ID tags, she'd chosen to dress as she always had.

*Her* way.

That way consisted of a pair of fitted black jeans, a thigh length utili-kilt, cropped black top and a waist-length black jacket. Her thick-soled boots were adorned with silver studs, and her nails and lips were painted in iridescent black.

It was practically the nicest outfit she owned. At least it didn't have any holes in it.

And she definitely had on clean underwear.

Bag slung over her shoulder, Netcat stood just outside the cathedral-like doors, the haze filtering out the morning sun, and looked up at one of the least popular corporations in the world. Well, least popular with technomancers, anyway. Netcat couldn't speak for anyone else. She felt an overwhelming nausea intrude on her stomach when she thought about the TMs that had lost their lives in Vegas. And the ones that disappeared daily. She thought about the Renraku Tower in Manhattan, and the trail of information that had led her across the country to this hell of corporate greed.

Los Angeles.

She knew it would have been better, even safer to do this in the Matrix, but she wasn't up for extended periods online. Not with GOD watching. Not with what she planned on doing.

Which included finding the bastard that sold lists of registered technomancers to Renraku, just to name a few. The evidence she and a few others had gathered was staggering. She hoped if she could find the source of the leak, maybe even find copies of those names, she would have a better idea of where they were, what corporations had them, and maybe even some leverage to negotiate their release.

*Yeah...it's a pipe dream. But it's all I got right now.* She thought of her son and Slamm-0! back home. *What if the boy becomes a technomancer?* No one knew yet—it was too early to tell if he would develop the gift. And it was a gift. Netcat couldn't see it any other way. But what kind of life would he have if he grew up persecuted, was hunted, captured, and got dissected?

This had to stop. She might not be able to stop it by herself, but she planned to at least make one hell of a statement about it.

She just wished Slamm-0! was on board with it all. He worried about their son, too. And he'd proven to be an incredible father, never missing a minute with their little Jack.

"I don't think you should go," Pistons had said two days earlier, after Netcat had confided in her. "Getting that close to Horizon makes me nervy. Yeah they're full of drek, but they're powerful, too. You know what they've done to their security, right? I mean... even with your mad skills or Slamm-0!'s, getting into their mainframe, even a tertiary host, will be next to impossible."

"I just have to see the building. I have to put a face on it. I have to," Netcat had told her. "I have to see the face of the traitor."

And here it was. In all its glory.

As if on some ridiculous cue, the datasphere whispered to her, a warning of sorts as she detected another technomancer. She stepped to one side of the front doors and sat on a dark brown marble bench with a wage-slave, busy with his AR. Her own AR, ever-present on the edge of her peripheral vision, came to the forefront and searched IDs to find the techno.

The doors opened as a stream of people walked in, then paused and scrambled out of the way as a well-dressed dwarf and a large wolf exited. She zeroed in on the wolf with her e-sense—a technocritter. That's where the signature was coming from. And he in turn stopped and looked in her direction.

Not liking where the situation was going, and listening to her own intuitive danger alarms, Netcat hurriedly compiled a sprite to duplicate the Matrix signature of the wage-slave next to her. Hacking his PAN was a breeze, as was imitating him. It was a trick she'd learned from other technomancers on GiTm0, and it seemed to work.

The dwarf looked around at the people moving back and forth, and if he looked at her through his AR, he'd just see another person on their basic commlink having a conversation. As for the critter? She wasn't sure. The wolf didn't growl at her or stare. In fact he seemed to lose interest as he stopped, dropped, and licked himself.

She suppressed a snicker as she watched them walk away. A pain between her eyes reminded her of the sprite's presence, and she quickly released it. The headache would remain for a while—so while she had the creepy little dude in her sites, Netcat compiled a crack sprite with a cookie and sent it after the dwarf's commlink. Within seconds, she had confirmation the cookie was in place, and dismissed the sprite. The cookie would tag the dwarf's commlink and report back his activities in the Matrix. It wouldn't give her the contents of any communications, but it would tell her where he went, who he spoke with, and what applications he launched.

Why the dwarf?

Easy. Why was a dwarf with a technocritter—an obviously trained one—coming out of Horizon?

Now her head really smarted. But she remained seated, watching metahumanity come and go, and making sure the dwarf didn't come back because he registered her sprite's hack.

After ten minutes or so, she stood and strolled toward the garage where Pistons' Honda was parked. She had put a face to her nemesis—now she just needed a way in. And maybe the dwarf would be it.

# CHAPTER TWELVE

### GiTm0

Welcome back to GiTm0, *omae*; your last connection was severed: 7 hours, 22 minutes, 3 seconds ago.

### BOLOs

Just a reminder—this board's got less than six hours before it terminates in your comms. Send your sprites out twenty-four hours after that for the new link.

New handles to look out for: Wipeout, EasterBunnyun. Full list available [Link][Guest] but don't read the list online. And don't forget, these runners are out for the nuyen, and they don't give a damn about us.

Got a heads up on a host just outside of Seattle. Not sure what the subscription is on it, but it's showing red, and the two TMs that went to check it out haven't logged back in.[Link][Guest]

Remember, GOD is always watching.

### NeW oNLiNE

\* More local—both Horizon and Knight Errant were mentioned in a Los Angeles article. Three bodies were found in a Horizon Annex early this morning. The building was listed as a repository for Horizon archives, and the system inside is a dinosaur, predating 2064. Not even *on* the Matrix. The media isn't giving this much attention. But really...if the host isn't that important to Horizon—why are they paying Knight Errant for security on it? And why would anyone hack it?

\* It is with great sadness I have to report another shadowrun team has gone missing after accepting the job to infiltrate the Renraku Tower and extract the technomancers held there. Our thanks and appreciation goes out to their friends and family. We're working on clandestine compensation.

\* Got another weird story relating to Contagion Games and their gaming host. Seems Lone Star was called in to break up some sort of situation on the new host the company rolled out just last night, but no information is available. This story showed up, and not long after, several cases of what is being termed Cortex Rot were reported in three hospitals, all within the Seattle and Denver area. Coincidence?

**EYES OPEN**
\>>>>Open Thread/Subhost221.322.1
\>>>>Thread Access Restrictions: <Yes/**No**>
\>>>>Format: <**Open Post**/Comment Only/Read Only>
\>>>>File Attachment: <Yes/**No**>
\>>>>Thread Descriptor: **Closer Look**
\>>>>Thread Posted By User: Shyammo

- Need everyone to notice EasterBunnyun's been added to the BOLOs. Had him follow the link last time, and used a cookie because he was asking too many questions about our real world identities. Traitor's been looking into our handles and contacting Ares.
- RoxJohn

- No way! Not Easter! What'd you do?
- 404Flames

- Revoked his ass. Got a contact working intel on him. And it is a him. Shyammo was the one that compiled the cookie data. We'll have him soon.
- RoxJohn

- Way to go, Rox. Good to see you're protecting us behind the scenes. Also anyone find anything out on this Contagion Games? Hip, weren't you working on it?
- 404Flames

- Nothing yet. Where ever they came from and whoever's funding them is under some seriously tight security. But funny about that Cortex Rot being reported—I found a few follow up blogs from two of those treated. All of them talked about nightmares of being eaten by a tree.
- Bakersman

- Like that's not creepy.
- LongTong

- It is creepy. All of this is creepy. But we can't lose sight of getting those technomancers out of Renraku.
- Prettyboy

- Working on it, Pretty. Got a few things in place. Might need a few extra hands when I know more. Hey Sol, you know anything about that Annex?
- Netcat

- Soldat's taking a breather, Net. Don't know what you're talking about.
- Silk

- What's wrong with Soldat? He's never sick. Silk, contact me offline.
- Netcat

- Hey Rox—what do you mean we'll have him soon? You're not actually advocating using the same sort of kidnapping scenario the corps use on us, are you? Is that why we're here?
- Venerator

- I'm advocating keeping our asses our own, Ven. I don't like technomancers taking advantage of their own kind's vulnerability to make a buck. That's not why Shy and I started this board. We're here because we have to get organized. We have to fight back. And we have to be informed.
- RoxJohn

# CHAPTER THIRTEEN

## BANG BANG BOOTY CLUB
## LOS ANGELES

This was shaping up to be the worst day Mack Schmetzer could remember.

"I'm sorry, Mack," Preacher said as he stood beside his boss. "But Maria's body vanished. Their security's reviewing the surveillance tape, but it looks like someone hacked in and set it to just loop a ten-minute interval taken from earlier in the day. No one saw the body snatcher come in or leave."

Mack spit to his left, away from the troll. They stood in front of the GMC in the lowest floor of his club's basement, the former boiler room for what had once been a school, and was now his business and home. It was also a safe haven for his team, as well as freelancers that knew Mack.

"Where the fuck is Blackwater?"

Preacher shrugged. "Said he had something personal to take care of. Could be anything."

It was getting so Blackwater had a *lot* of *personal* things to take care of. And Mack was still pissed at him for leaving Maria's body in the first place.

Not that it mattered now.

Shayla had the hood up on the GMC, and all its doors open. The vehicle was hooked up to a dizzying array of wires and thick tubing.

Mack crossed his arms over his chest as he said, "But why? Why go through that much trouble to hide taking her body? Why take it at all?"

Preacher wasn't the tallest troll Mack knew, but he was wide. And he was definitely the most imposing character Mack kept on his payroll. He was also damn good at slinging a spell. "If we keep going on the theory that the hacker that out-hacked Cole was the one that killed Maria and hacked the GMC," he said, pointing at the truck with his horns, both elaborately carved with symbols Mack wasn't familiar with. "It might make sense that he's covering his tracks and disposing of the body."

"No. No one's that stupid. You don't leave a body for the authories to find and then go back for it," Mack shook his head. "This guy out-hacked Cole. I've never known anyone to out-hack him. What bothers me more is that Cole didn't even seem concerned that Maria's body was still in there. We don't leave team members behind—dead or alive. He just bolted."

"I noticed that."

Shayla emerged from the truck, her hair damp against her head. Her SURGE onset had happened late in life, and she remembered how she looked as a human. Mack had seen the pictures she kept tucked under her pillow. Though her mutations weren't as severe as some of the ones Mack had seen in his lifetime, he knew she was still touchy about the way she looked. Her neck wasn't as broad, nor was her body, though her shoulders were wide. Her hair was long and thick and the color of spun gold. Her tusks were smaller than normal, and her eyes a brilliant sapphire.

She was also very shapely, and Mack was always embarrassed for his race when men looked at her body, whistled, and then cringed at her face.

Bastards. None of 'em were good enough for his Shayla.

Right now her expression was less than happy. "Dammit," she said in her deep voice. "It's all good."

"What are you looking for?"

Preacher chuckled. "She's looking for a reason this other guy was able to hack her RCC."

Mack frowned at her. "Wouldn't you be looking at your deck?"

She nodded. "I already did. Nothing. I tried calling Blackwater to help me track this hacker down, but he hasn't gotten back to me either." She looked at the mess around her and sighed. "This is gonna be a bitch to put back together."

Preacher turned away, pulling his own monocle down over his left eye. Someone on the club's staff was calling him. Preacher was the liaison between the customers and staff. So if they were actually contacting him, it was important.

But Mack already knew what it was. "Is it the Johnson that called earlier?"

Preacher turned back to him. "Upstairs. Boss, why'd you have them come here?"

"Oh, I'm not worried about this one knowing or suspecting. They've got just as many skeletons in their closet as I do."

Preacher's expression fell.

Mack took the outside elevator, the one that opened up through a fake brick wall around the corner. The cold greeted him outside, and he pulled his jacket up around his neck as he turned the corner and walked into the *Bang Bang Booty*.

He spotted the Johnson easy enough, sitting in the farthest corner of the bar at Mack's table. The bartender handed Mack an OJ as he moved through the dancing bodies and pulled up a chair facing the woman.

Charis Monogue was well known in Horizon news as the ever-present woman behind Artus Wagner, the face the corp tacked on the Los Angeles Personnel Office. Mack had downloaded the dossier, but he'd also used his old access and downloaded a few other choice bits of information on both Charis and Artus. Namely Wagner's abrupt "promotion" within the Horizon company after the massacre in Vegas.

Charis was a tall one, with well-toned long legs, broad shoulders, and a perfectly chiseled nose. It was all accented by the delicate points of her ears as they protruded through her luxurious ripple of blonde hair. She smiled at him as he sipped his juice. "You look like hell."

"Yeah, I get that a lot." He put his elbows on the table. "Let's get to the point. We didn't get your intel last night."

"I know." Charis chewed on her lower lip. "Don't look so surprised. There's this horrible little dwarf nosing around—met him at the party Artus and I attended last night. He was all chummy with the President—"

"President Cline?"

"Oh no. The president of the department Artus and I work for. I knew about the botch at the Annex because it's set to alert me if anything happens there. Something Artus wanted set up over a year ago. I called him with the news and he agreed to come in early, then that dwarf showed up in his office this morning. He already knew what had happened at the Annex, and he knew about Artus's friend in the PCC police." She put up a red-lacquered finger before he could speak. "That's how I knew you'd failed. Someone else was in that Annex, and somehow Powell knew he'd be there."

"Powell?"

"That's the dwarf's name. Draco Powell. He's creepy and arrogant, and I don't like him. He's got a hard-on for technomancers."

Mack sat back in the chair. "Is that what this is all about? Hell, no," he said as he stood up and his chair scraped back. "I ain't getting involved with that hot rock, Charis. I told you that when you contacted me. Dammit...I shoulda known. If it deals with Horizon, then it's about the TMs. We're done. I'm keeping the retainer."

He reached down to take his OJ, but Charis grabbed his wrist. "Wait—Mack, don't do this."

"Charis, someone hacked Shayla's RCC last night and picked that guy up. I saw them leave. So it wasn't just one person—it was two."

"You saw the car? Did you get the license?"

"Yeah, and I'm running it. Privately. But I'm done with this. I don't get involved with technomancers. I don't hire them, and I sure as hell don't save them." He twisted his wrist away. "Is that what that data is? Does it have something to do with Vegas? Or something else?"

"I can't say. I didn't put it there. I told you, Wagner's the one hiding it, not me. My job is to get it away from him." She pursed her lips. "It is helpful to know there were two others there and not just one. I am sorry you lost one of your team."

"Yeah. Real nice of you to notice." He downed his OJ and stood beside the table, looking down at her. He and Charis went back a lot of years, before he decided on augmentation. Before puberty and the world took away their dreams. He knew things about her that would make his team turn and run. "She's missing."

Charis looked up at him. "Who's missing?"

"My team member. Her body's missing. Out of the morgue. We were going to retrieve her—so she couldn't be traced back to us and you—but she was already gone. Wiped from the morgue records."

"Wiped from the records? No surveillance vids?"

"My hacker said it was all clean. I know her folks, Charis. When she came to me, 'bout five years ago, she was a runaway. Took me a year to gain her trust, and I let her parents know where she was. Of course I didn't tell them she was a runner, but that she was working for me at the club. And now I have to tell them she's dead, and I got no body to give them." He toyed with his glass, wishing it was whiskey. "That bastard killed her, Charis. Whoever he is. He took your data and he killed my shaman."

"He could be a technomancer. Or the other one if there were two."

"And you think this because of Powell. Did he say he knew it was a technomancer?"

She reached into her suit jacket pocket and handed him a card. "This is what they discussed this morning. Artus likes me to monitor his office meetings." Charis frowned. "What you're going to hear is a bit...out there. And I think this Powell is right out there with it. I also suspect he's an investigator."

Mack palmed the card. "Private or Lone Star?"

"I'd say private." She grabbed her purse and her commlink and fastened it back on her wrist. "I need to get back to the office. I left before that little pissant did. I'll look into finding your shaman." She paused after she stood and put a hand on his shoulder. "Find the data, Mack. Find it. For all our sakes."

He stood there for several more minutes before he looked at the card. It was a generic orange one. Not even a Horizon logo imprinted on it. But that didn't mean it wasn't bugged. He licked his lips and thought of Maria and her family, and thought of old ghosts that seeing Charis always brought back...

*A missing body, missing data, a nervous CEO assistant, a private investigator, and a possible technomancer and friend.* "My life just got way more exciting than I can stand."

# CHAPTER FOURTEEN

## KNIGHT ERRANT OFFICE
## LOS ANGELES

Netcat followed the dwarf to Knight Errant, which was a surprise to her. He hadn't felt like a KE wageslave, or even one of their techies. And the technocritter wolf? Definitely not KE standard issue.

So what was he, and why was he going into the KE office? She parked the car in a local lot across the street and used a machine sprite to give the mechanized attendant the required creds. No currency changed hands, but the auto-attendant wasn't smart enough to know that. Once the sprite decompiled, she tossed two PainZap tablets back and washed them down with water. She knew her limits on compiling, and just how bad the headaches could get before she suffered any fading.

Netcat pulled up the technomancer equivalent to augmented reality and downloaded the information that the tag she'd placed on the dwarf had found so far. Not much, other than a few searches for street addresses. Los Angeles. A few names. Fred Jacobson, Kazuma Tetsu, and Neela Jinkins. None of them rang a bell, so she set up her own searches using a registered data sprite. She wanted to give it time, and as long as it was registered, GOD might not notice.

Might.

Netcat continued watching the building, watching the black suits go in and out. Los Angeles in the morning—not much different than Seattle. Except for the air. It was smellier and dingier here. The sooner she found a way in to Horizon, the sooner she could go home and get back to Slamm-0! and their son.

Another ten minutes, and the tag started feeding her all

kinds of information. From Netcat's perspective, this dwarf had declared an intel war on those three names. He was downloading everything from photos to blogs to subscription use—to personnel files.

She sat up straight. They were *all* Knight Errant employees. She couldn't see what was in the files—all she could see was his search history as it unfolded. She fed the information to her own data sprite as it worked in another window. Her headache eased a bit as the aspirin kicked in, but she had the sneaking suspicion it was going to get worse.

Abruptly the Annex break-in she'd seen on the vids earlier flagged in her sprite's window as it zeroed in on the name Toshi Morimoto. That window led to more windows, each of them headed up with the names in the dwarf's search. Information came in on each—none of which flagged anything. They were all employees, all of them technicians, all had A-1 ratings and all had been trained by Morimoto.

Then she saw something that made her jaw drop.

Morimoto's death certificate.

She pulled up the Annex dump file retrieved from a PCC security blotter—a KE tech had been in the building, and her sprite had found the report given by one of the security guards working inside. She cross-referenced that information with reports across the Matrix on the Annex, Morimoto, and Horizon. As the information scrolled down, she glanced at the tag's window—the dwarf was zeroed in one of the employees.

Kazuma Tetsu.

She moved the windows over and brought up what her datasprite had pulled on him. Twenty-six, elf, born in Japan, moved to the UCAS with his twin sister, Hitori Tetsu, when they were both young. Suffered a nine-month coma after the Crash, diagnosed with AIPS, then had a miraculous recovery and was recruited by Knight Errant after an incident three years ago at a local coffee shop. Tetsu prevented a group of suspected shadowrunners from using a back door in the coffee shop to hack into Horizon. He had a perfect record. No missed days. She touched the sister's name, and came up blank.

Nothing.

She pushed the sprite harder, and finally a few dribbles of information trickled out. Hitori had worked briefly as an artist for Ares. Sister to Kazuma Tetsu.

Netcat spotted a small Lone Star report. Reported missing by her brother five months ago.

The dwarf was searching through Tetsu's personal life. His family here and in Japan. His medical records, as well as his upgrade purchases–both with his account and by Knight Errant's. He's looking at Tetsu's commlink…his programs… She combed the same stores the dwarf was hitting and found nothing. Not a single upgrade.

And Tetsu has a missing sister. A twin.

*Drek!* She knew of one technomancer who was that obsessed with finding his twin. And he lived in Los Angeles.

A new window appeared. Surprised and relieved to see Silk's ID, she answered immediately. **<Hey.>**

<Hey Netcat. Sorry for the clandestine post on GiTm0, but things have been a bit crazy here.>

**<Silk, I need you to trust me like you've never trusted me before. Is this handshake secure?>**

There was a pause before her window responded. <Yeah. I just checked. What is it?>

**<I need you to answer me this as honest as you can. Is Soldat's name Kazuma Tetsu?>**

Now the pause dragged out forever. **<Silk, I really need you to answer me. This is serious.>**

<You know I can't answer that kind of question, Netcat.>

**<Then maybe you can help me understand why some dwarf with a technocritter is so interested in a Kazuma Tetsu who works at Knight Errant with a connection to Toshi Morimoto?>**

Another delay, briefer this time. <Shit! I told him that was stupid!>

**<Is he on his way to work?>**

<Yes. I tried to stop him.>

**<Can you contact him?>**

<Not while he's in the KE building. We never communicate there. Wait…are you here? In L.A.?>

**<Yes. Get down to the KE building as soon as you can.>**

<I'm too far away. Can you help him? I can pull in some favors.>

**<I'll do my best.>**

Netcat disconnected everything and pulled out of every window except the tag. She had a vague idea of what Tetsu looked like from the photos. Tall, slender, longish dark hair. He was Asian, but only half, given the look of his features. Shouldn't be hard to spot. There was no way she'd get into the building undetected.

Not enough time to plan. But there might be a way to get a warning to Tetsu—and hopefully a way out.

A new AR window popped up. She smiled at the name, and answered. *<I need your help.>*

<*It's what I'm here for, Cat.*> MoonShine's icon of a snowflake spun in its window.

# CHAPTER FIFTEEN

## KNIGHT ERRANT OFFICE

Kazuma had made it through the door at five after nine. Late, but not by too much. He wasn't sure if he'd been late by five minutes before, however, and that worried him. He knew how law enforcement worked. They scrutinized anything out of the ordinary three days before a murder and three days after. Which is why he knew he had to keep going into work and not touch that data, even though it was killing him not to.

A few coworkers nodded to him as he entered the elevator. Karl, the smallest troll he'd ever known—who still clocked in well over two meters tall—slipped into the elevator with him and smiled around his tusks. "Sorry...I'm late to a meeting. Usually I wait till the car's empty."

"*So ka.*" Kazuma managed a smile and inhaled. It wasn't that the troll took up the entire space—it was just a very real optical illusion when compared to his own, smaller body.

"You hear about that break-in last night?"

Kazuma started to nod, but paused instead. As the head security tech on several of the Horizon accounts, it would make sense that he would have been alerted—but he hadn't been. In fact, he couldn't remember getting any alerts in his AR. He reached into his bag to pull out his commlink—had to keep up appearances, even here in KE—but it wasn't there. He pulled his bag up in the cramped space and dug around. The commlink wasn't there!

"Hey, you okay?" Karl tilted his head. "You look paler than usual."

"I think I might have a cold or something."

"Wow...and you never get sick. Must be bad." Karl watched him a minute. "Something wrong?"

"My commlink...I can't believe I left it in my car."

The troll laughed and the elevator vibrated. "That's a rich one. Why would you ever take it off?"

*Think!* "Oh...Karl...I have to be in AR all day long, sometimes fifteen hours a day. When I get home, I just want to relax, shut it all down, and watch mindless vids." *Did that sound good? Does it make sense?*

"Now *that* I can understand, Tetsu." The elevator stopped, and Karl got off, sidestepping a dwarf getting on.

Once the door closed, the dwarf reached up and punched a code into the elevator panel. All the floors lit up before the dwarf said, "Personnel."

He turned and looked up at Kazuma. "Good morning, Mr. Tetsu. You and I need to have a conversation."

# CHAPTER SIXTEEN

## UNKNOWN LOCATION

HipOldGuy was awake, but he couldn't remember waking up. He didn't know where he was.

When he was.

How he was.

And the resonance was all around him.

But he wasn't alone. And he was in pain. And the pain, when it touched him, when he touched the streams, turned the beautiful, incandescent wisps black.

A tree as tall as the world and as black as night twisted itself around him. He could look down, but he couldn't look up. He was a part of the tree; a branch close to the ground, his arms and legs melted into the bark. It didn't hurt when he didn't move. But then his skin folded and wrinkled as the bark slowly devoured him and he tried to escape, and the pain would start again.

The wisps thickened and fell from the sky and pooled onto the ground below as he heard two distinct voices. One was male and the other was hard to pinpoint, but it sounded like a chorus of voices bound together to make one.

*It's still not enough.*

"I don't think there are enough technomancers in the world to do what you want," said an eerie male voice.

*Of course there are. We just haven't found them all yet.* This voice echoed in his mind.

Hearing a faint sigh nearby, Hip moved his eyes just enough to look at the branch beside him. It twisted and arched, and if he looked closely, he could see a face bent into the bark. Closed eyes and a silent scream. He heard the scream of the realms.

"Well, unless you can break into every corp and get their lists, we've just about exhausted everyone Horizon had."

*Then we should do that.*

"Are you crazy? You do realize the moment you try something like that, we'll have every corporate spider team on our location in minutes. GOD's always watching." Frustration permeated his tone.

*You sound like one of them.*

"Well, I'm *not* one of them."

Hip recognized that voice. The one that wasn't in his head. It was the same voice he remembered from the game. The gas-masked man. And with that thought, more pain came, and he screamed. Or he would have screamed if he had a voice. Or a mouth. He tried to call up his AR, and again received only pain as the bark scraped deep crevices into his flesh. His blood ran down the extended branch, dripping into the tree's gaping maw. And when he called out to his sprites...

Nothing.

So, he kept his thoughts singular. One thought. One...reoccurring command.

*Deliver it to Soldat. Deliver it to Soldat. Deliver it to Soldat. DeliverItToSoldat. DeliverItToSoldat. Deliverittosoldat. Deliverittosoldat. Deliverittosoldatdeliverittosoldat deliverittosoldatdeliverittosoldatdeliverittosoldatdeliverittosoldatdeliverittosoldat–*

*Now now, you just stop that. Once you just surrender to me, all the pain will go away. You hear the voices of the others? Just join with them! It's easy. Just let go and join them.*

Yes... Hip could hear them. All of them. A cacophony of sound, buzzing in his brain. Thousands of voices calling out...

*Deliverittosoldat.*

But the voices were so loud. They clawed at him as if he were the muddy bank they couldn't climb out of. The pain was too much. So much easier to just stay still, and let the tree take him.

*Soldat? What is Soldat? Bring what to Soldat?*

"You talking to him?" Now the male's voice sounded curious. One voice over the other...drowning out his own thought.

*Yes. He's fighting. They all fight. And eventually, they surrender. But he keeps moving around a command line.*

"What's the line?"

Screaming...

*Bring it to Soldat. What is Soldat? Bring what?*

"Cal...Soldat means Soldier. He's been commanding something to deliver something to Soldier. *The Soldier.*"

The bodiless voice in Hip's head screamed louder than the rest. Everyone was silenced.

Forever.

# CHAPTER SEVENTEEN

## HORIZON HOME OFFICE
## OFFICE OF ARTUS WAGNER

Charis made it back across town within an hour, give or take. She stopped at the coffee shop nearby and ordered Wagner his favorite morning drinks again, seeing as how his earlier enjoyment had been destroyed by that horrid little dwarf. She hoped Mack could work some of his magic. She needed to see whatever was in that data packet Artus had hid in that host. She had to know what was so important that he felt he had to hide it in the first place, and why some unknown player had stolen it.

She strode through the front doors. The security men smiled at her, and she hoped Powell was gone by now. But just to make sure: "Hey Zanth?" she addressed the ork behind the desk. "Does Mr. Wagner still have company? Did Mr. Powell leave?"

"Oh yes, ma'am," Zanth answered in his deep, rumbling voice. She always loved that voice. "But a Knight Errant officer went in about a half hour ago. Haven't seen him come out yet."

Knight Errant? Her conversation with Mack fresh in her mind, not to mention what she'd overheard in the office between Powell and Wagner, Charis narrowed her eyes. "What did he look like?"

"Young. Elf. Longish, dark hair. Didn't really see his face."

Charis handed Zanth one of the coffees, winked, and strode toward the office. Once at her desk she put her things away, took her desk PAN off AWAY, and picked up the coffee before knocking twice and then opening the door. "Sorry sir, but I need to speak with you about—"

The smell hit her first, before the scene. It was thick and coppery. She'd smelled it plenty of times before.

Artus was laid out on his desk, his pants around his ankles. His eyes, open and staring.

And his mouth...his mouth was stuffed with his—

Charis set the cup of coffee down before approaching for a closer look, hands on her hips. "Well damn, Artus. I don't know what pisses me off more; that I'm looking at a year of undercover work down the toilet, or that I really wanted to be the one to shove that into your sick little mouth."

# CHAPTER EIGHTEEN
## OUTSIDE KNIGHT ERRANT OFFICE

<*Are you sure?*>

Netcat frowned. <*Of course I'm sure. Silk told me, and that dwarf's been downloading all kinds of stuff on him since I tagged him.*>

<*And you saw him go in?*>

<*Yeah.*> Netcat stared past the ghostly AR of her datasphere as she'd been doing since MoonShine contacted her. <*Any luck?*>

<*It's Knight Errant, Net. This is not a walk in the park.*>

<*Yeah, but I figured you of all people could at least do something.*>

<*I've spoofed an ID for maintenance access–but I'm worried if I try anything further I'll poke a spider.*>

<*You're not at home, are you?*>

Not that she knew where MoonShine's home was. The two only knew each other off the GiTm0 board, but they had met up in VR once. She knew Moon was a male, he was young, and he had no augmentation at all. Not even a datajack.

<*Moon? You there?*>

<*Yeah. I just need to concentrate. Hold on.*>

She watched the front door again, wishing there was some way she could see inside, find where Tetsu was, and yank him out. One of her research sprites—a registered one she kept for legal activities in the Matrix, because researching people wasn't a crime—popped up in her AR. She had sent it out earlier to track down any information it could on this dwarf named Powell. She skimmed what came up in the Sprite's window and felt her blood run very, very cold. <*Moon?*>

<*I think I got it. There are several drones on the maintenance LTG.*>

*<MoonShine–>*
<So I figure...I could maybe grab one and toss it into a window.>
*<Moon, hold on–>*
<Unless that would send the whole place into lockdown.>
*<Moon! Stop and listen to me. I'm sending you a packet. I need you to read it as fast as you can.>*
<What is it?>

She swallowed and looked back at the door to KE. *<It's bad. Really, really bad.>*

# CHAPTER NINETEEN

## KNIGHT ERRANT OFFICE

Kazuma sat in the single chair facing Mr. Powell's impressive desk. He had been in this office only twice—both times to receive a promotion. Both had been given to him by Trajan Black, the manager who had hired him, and a longtime friend of Toshi Morimoto. Kazuma had asked several times where Mr. Black was, but Powell only raised his hand now and then as he focused on images in his AR.

Kazuma forced himself not to notice, but he could see what Powell was looking at—the dwarf didn't have the files in a protected folder, but out in the open.

Twice he saw his name. And that of Morimoto.

The gunshot wound in his side throbbed, and he felt sweat trickle down his neck, the sides of his face, past his datajack. He felt naked without his commlink. He spoofed a neutral ID from security, one he'd set up a year ago, and compiled a sprite behind it to search for anything on where Black could be, who this dwarf was, and if he'd done anything to expose himself. And Kazuma did it all while maintaining a somewhat composed visage.

Except for the sweating.

"Mr. Tetsu—are you in pain?"

The question surprised him and he blinked at the dwarf. "Oh yes. Yes I am. It's a stomach thing."

"Stomach thing?" the dwarf waved in the air, brushing his AR desktop away. "You're leaning toward your right side—and knowing physiology, your stomach is on your left. Are you sure you're not suffering from anything more serious?"

Kazuma gave him a half-smile, but his thoughts were in turmoil. *He knows I'm wounded!* Somehow this dwarf either knew he'd been shot, or he knew Kazuma was involved in last night's break-in. He brushed the building's datasphere, and knew the doors were locked. He also sensed a familiar presence nearby. Another technomancer. Only...there was a slight...*tang* to the e-sense of it. Either the TM was an animal, or it was tainted somehow.

The dwarf smiled as he laced his fingers on top of the desk. Kazuma guessed he was sitting on a booster seat. "Well. If your... stomach pain grows worse, all you have to do is request the company's services, and we can attend to it."

"Oh. No. I wouldn't trouble anyone here. I think I should go home."

"You do."

"Yes, sir. I shouldn't have come in today."

"But you did. And from your record—which is exemplary, I might add—you haven't missed a day in two years. You take regular holidays. You keep everything very neat, and very...clean."

"Mr. Black likes that."

"Yes, he does." Powell frowned for a second, and Kazuma could have sworn the man was suppressing a smile. "Last night, a host in the Horizon Annex on Boulevard was broken into. A host under your control that was scheduled to be deleted."

Kazuma kept his features calm as his sprite returned and dumped its files into a protected folder. He didn't have a moment to look at them and keep a serious conversation going, so he mentally brushed it and his AR aside. "Karl told me about it in the elevator—"

"You didn't already know? As supervisor over that area, Mr. Tetsu, I would assume you would have come straight into Black's office, or at least roused him out of bed."

*Drek!* Powell was right, and he would have done those things— *if* he'd had his commlink nearby. But he didn't know it was missing, and as a precaution to mask his abilities, he always took calls and messages relating to Knight Errant through the commlink.

"Yes, I agree. But I realized in the elevator that I must have left my commlink at home—"

Powell moved then and opened a drawer to his right. He pulled out a commlink, same make and model as Kazuma's, and set it on the desk between them. It took Kazuma a few seconds to realize it wasn't a model just like his—it was *his*. "You didn't leave it at home."

A window flashed in his AR. He brushed it aside. "That's not my commlink."

"Yes, I'm afraid it is."

"Have you checked the registration?" Kazuma compiled a crack sprite and sent it into the assets database to create a registration file for his commlink. He didn't have one, as he'd never registered the commlink he usually used. He told it to grab the serial number to the spare he kept in his apartment. It was one of the newer models, the ones with the limitations in place. He silently cursed himself for never registering either of them—but then, this could be a blessing in disguise if he could convince Powell he had a registered commlink with the company and it was in his home.

Pain bloomed behind his eyes, and he narrowed them to keep from wincing or putting his hand to his temple. Two sprites within ten minutes—he was going to pay for this. But not right now.

Ponsu appeared in the periphery. *Boss, you want me to turn it on? Have it download all the messages?*

<**Yes.**>

That same new window flashed again in his AR. He watched Powell motion for his own AR—hopefully a prelude to looking for Kazuma's registered commlink—and pulled the window up. He didn't recognize the persona—that of a black cat—but he did recognize the name.

And he was panicked that *that* name was contacting him— Kazuma Tetsu—and not his handle. Was this a joke? Or maybe a trap?

He kept an eye on Powell as he mentally ran his own security on the message and opened it. She had the GiTmo passwords.

<*You're in a drekload of danger, omae. Yes, I know who you are because Silk confided in me. Don't react to this missive, just read it and do what we tell you to do. Don't even respond just in case Draco Powell is monitoring you. And don't think he can't—he's got a technocritter nearby, and it isn't a normal one.*>

Kazuma kept his face stoic as he appeared to wait for Powell. The crack sprite reappeared with the information. It was done. And Ponsu would have the commlink on and running with a built-in history.

<*The dwarf in front of you is an investigator and he's very interested in you. This is a bad thing. His name's come up in a dozen technomancer disappearances, and now you're in his sights.*>

Powell looked less than happy as he brushed his AR away and sat back. "Apparently you do have a registered commlink. It wasn't visible before, because it was still kept in Black's files along with three other commlinks he changed out when the upgrades were activated."

By upgrades, Kazuma knew he meant the new Matrix protocols the corps had put in place. One of the reasons he didn't want to use it.

<In about two minutes, there's going to be a distraction. Take that opportunity to get out of there. I'm in a Honda across the street. It's black and a bit beat-up. Make it to me and we can disappear.>

Kazuma's thoughts churned as he got the instructions and looked at this dwarf with fear and hate. *This piece of drek was responsible for technomancer disappearances...and how he was looking at me? Was he responsible for Hitori's disappearance? Did he know anything about her?* He clamped his jaw shut just as an alarm klaxon shattered the silence. The office door automatically clicked open as an automated voice blasted through the speakers.

**"FIRE ALERT! FIRE ALERT! THIS IS NOT A DRILL! EVACUATE IMMEDIATELY!"**

*Yeah, well...that's definitely a diversion.*

Kazuma stood and headed to the door just as something growled and struck him in the small of his back. He landed on his stomach, and his wound sent up flares of pain that nearly blinded him. He felt hot breath on his neck, heard the creature growl, and felt teeth puncture skin. Yelling at the pain, he tried to push himself up.

"Now now, Mr. Tetsu," came Powell's voice to his left. "I'm sure this fire alarm is just a ruse you sent your sprites out to create so you could escape. But you see, I can't allow that. I have too many things in place, too many responsibilities I have to take care of. And you, Mr. Tetsu, have two things I want." He knelt down and put his face in Kazuma's. "One, you're a technomancer, which makes you the property of my employer, and two, he wants that data you stole."

Kazuma was panicking even as Netcat's window remained open. Her constant messages of escape helped him boost his own confidence. So did Silk's insistent need to make himself physically capable. He closed his eyes as he listened to the data-whispers of the active system in the office. The fire alert had overwritten anything Powell might have put in place, which gave him an added option of a quick hack. He needed to see where he was.

Using the same idea he'd used in the Annex, he slipped into the cameras—through the same back door he'd worked into the system months ago—and drilled down to this office. He saw himself inches from the cracked door, with Powell kneeling beside him, going through his pockets, and a huge gray wolf on his back. As if knowing what it was doing, it clamped its teeth on his neck, but didn't close its jaw.

If it did, the wolf would sever his spine.

He gathered a copy of the image, encrypted it, and sent it to Netcat.

Within seconds she would see what was happening. He heard voices outside the door, and recognized Karl's. He was making sure each of the offices were empty per the evacuation plan. Kazuma watched from the camera as Powell went to the desk, retrieved a weapon, and moved back to the door. The bastard was going to shoot him!

Anger replaced panic, and Kazuma took a deep breath as he extended himself further into the security system. He assumed he was flagging all kinds of spiders, but he was not going to let Karl get hurt or have his own head bit off—not to mention the danger Netcat was putting herself in by helping him.

*Boss! Let me do it! You take care of the dog!*

*Ponsu!* He smiled as he felt her presence. He gave her a few ideas before he pulled himself back from the system, away from the soft whispers of the datasphere, and readied himself, despite the pounding migraine behind his eyes. On cue, he heard Karl at the door, saw Powell move himself behind the door, and counted to three.

On three, the door moved on its own, bashing hard into Powell. The impact smashed the dwarf into the wall as Karl came through. The technocritter let go of Kazuma's neck as he faced down the ork.

"Karl! Help! It's a technocritter!"

The security officer brandished his weapon and fired at the wolf before it could pounce. Kazuma pushed himself up as fast as he could—though his knees gave out as he staggered to the door. Karl caught him and slipped an arm under his shoulders.

"Kaz—what happened? Why was a technocritter in Black's office?"

"There was a dwarf in there..." he said as they made their way through the lobby along with the other stragglers. He had to shout over the klaxon. "I think he killed Black. Need to check on him. He told his technocritter to kill me because I walked in on him."

"You kidding me? You think he was a technomancer too? The dwarf?"

"Could be." They reached the open door as several fire trucks and more black security vans pulled up. Netcat said she was across the street. A black Honda. He didn't spot the car, but he spotted a delicate elf with short hair, dressed in a kilt, jeans, and boots.

<Are you hurt? Did it bite you?>

He knew that was her.

"Hey...let me get you over to that DocWagon. Your neck is bleeding."

Kazuma straightened himself up and patted the ork's arm. "I'm okay, Karl. Thank you. I owe you. I really do. But I think the others could use your strength."

Karl gave Kazuma a half-smile around his tusks. "All right, *omae*. You get cleaned up. I'll tell them about the dead technocritter in the office."

He waited a beat as he watched Karl lumber away, then moved as fast as he could through the throngs of people, the newsfeed drones, and the vans to the parking lot across the street. The closer he got, the more he was certain this was Netcat.

Her eyes widened as he neared and she went to him and started tugging on his suit jacket. "Get this off. Your KE pin acts as a SIN, right?"

The pain behind his eyes hurt even worse now in the semi-bright light of the Los Angeles morning. He did as she said and watched as she wadded it up and shoved it into a nearby trash can. "Get in the car."

He got in the passenger side and managed to buckle himself in before Netcat put the car in reverse and maneuvered the old POS through the back and out a side entrance. Once on the road, they passed more trucks and people headed toward Knight Errant.

Netcat held out her hand. "It's nice to meet you, Soldat."

"Nice to meet you, Netcat." Her hand was warm and delicate. "Now...if it's okay with you...I think I'm gonna..."

And he fell over the side of the world.

# CHAPTER TWENTY

## LOCAL HIGH SCHOOL
## LOS ANGELES
## FRIDAY AFTERNOON

Blackwater mentally patted himself on the back as he tossed the last piece of Maria into the school's roaring incinerator. Luckily, none of the local PCC offices monitored the schools on the lower east side. No one cared. This was Blackwater's territory. This incinerator had been good to him over the years. Gotten rid of a lot of enemies in this little piece of hell.

The hardest part of the job had been flash-freezing her body so he could run the saw through her limbs. Luckily the morgue hadn't started the autopsy yet, which meant they hadn't taken her blood or any fluids. It was all here, going up in smoke. Other than the blood left at the Annex, there would be no other way to trace her. Getting rid of that evidence would take up the rest of his day.

The bell to switch classes sounded, and Cole sat back on the cold concrete of the school's boiler room. He turned on his commlink and easily slid into the school's PAN, only available wirelessly during the class change. There wasn't much security—the student's grades and records weren't kept on any hosts at this physical location. They were kept secure by Renraku technology.

This PAN was mostly set up as a communication device between the school board and the students. Announcements, schedules, syllabi, and e-text were kept there, available for students to pull down and use. It was their responsibility to govern their own lives, not the school's. If they wanted to learn, and get on a path to employment with a megacorp, here was the opportunity. If not, then the local Stuffer Shack a half-kilometer down the road was hiring.

If there was one thing Blackwater had been in school, it was a straight-A student. No one in his present life would ever believe that. But he'd been in the top of his class. Voted most likely to head a corporation.

Yeah.

And then the Crash happened. His only parent had gotten caught online. Turned his dad into a meat sack. And with it went his small family's income and status. There wasn't anyone left to take care of Blackwater. His mother had disappeared over a decade ago.

He'd survived the best way he knew how by using his intellect and his skills. He'd done pretty well for himself in making a name. And he'd never lost a hack, not in five years.

Until that asshole had gotten him. Appearing in the host out of nowhere like that. Blackwater hadn't even noticed him coming. Damn ghost. The only consolation he had at that moment was knowing he'd capped him good. Made him bleed.

And as Blackwater sat on that cold concrete floor, he made a deal with himself to get even with that motherfucker.

Even if it killed him.

As the last of Maria turned to ash, Blackwater logged into his AR. Several messages appeared, a few from Wagner. But it was the three from Shayla that caught his attention. Apparently Mack wanted him back as soon as possible.

*Screw him.* Blackwater logged out of his email and skimmed the news headlines to see if there had been any mention of the missing body at a local morgue.

No missing bodies—but a headline just released a few minutes ago from Reuters dropped his jaw.

**HORIZON OFFICER MURDERED. KNIGHT ERRANT TECHNOMANCER SUSPECTED.** — **Reported, Vid [Link] 2:34 (6 minutes ago)**

Blackwater turned up the volume in his earbuds and touched the link to pull up the article on his AR.

A human with little to no visible augmentation appeared on the screen. She stood in front of the Horizon offices, their glass pyramid the scene of dozens of black vans, hovering news drones, and milling metahumans. She mentally counted to one and smiled.

*"Good morning, Los Angeles. One hour ago, the body of a high ranking Horizon employee was found dead in his office, the victim of what PCC security is calling a technomancer attack. The name of the*

official hasn't been released yet to protect the family and the official's immediate staff. Knight Errant had warned the public that it was only a matter of time before technomancers would retaliate for the so-called Technomancer Massacre in Las Vegas. As you can see behind me, all efforts to identify and find the person or persons responsible for this brutal attack are underway, though at this time, no leads are forthcoming. Stay tuned for more updates."

Blackwater chewed his lower lip as he re-watched the report, then logged into a few hacker boards for information as to who the official was...even though he had a pretty good idea.

When Shayla pinged him, he took her text and opted for audio. Within seconds her online persona, a vivacious elf with long legs, big tits, and thick lips, appeared in a third window. "Hey, you *really* need to call Mack back," her persona said in a sultry voice.

He made his own persona smile. "I'm kinda busy right now."

"You looking for Maria?"

Blackwater glanced at the incinerator as the second bell sounded.

"What was that?" Shayla asked. "Sounded like a bell."

"Nothing. Yeah, I'm looking for her. What does Mack want?"

"He wants you back here. He needs a hacker he can rely on in case we get hit about who that other hacker was."

"Screw him."

"Yeah, well, he's been in a mood since he met with the Johnson this morning."

Blackwater paused. "He did? Told them we lost the data?"

"I guess. You know I don't listen in on Mack's conversations. I did get a good look at her though. Tall, blonde, and elven."

Now *that* was an interesting piece of information. "Dressed to the nines?"

"Yeah."

It would be a stretch to assume that Mack had met with Wagner's assistant directly—there were only maybe a hundred thousand blonde elves on the planet. Artus Wagner had originally contacted Blackwater to retrieve the data from the host a day before Mack got the same job. Of course, Blackwater had contacted Wagner, more than a bit put out the jack-off would hire him, and then show nil confidence and hire the same mission out to a team. The same team Blackwater ran with on occasion.

But Blackwater hadn't hired Mack. That hire was still as mysterious as the hacker who actually stole the data away from him.

Given the description, was it possible the one who hired Mack was Wagner's assistant? And if it was—why? What would that elf want with the data?

He knew the only way to get answers—and maybe a larger payday—would be to get that data.

Blackwater watched the vid again, but without the audio this time. This time he sharpened up the scene and started looking at the people in the background. "Shayla, you hear anything on the guy that got ganked at Horizon?"

"Yes and no. Mack's been in his office since we heard about it. But I don't know who it is, if that's what you're asking." Her icon laughed. "Looks like Horizon's got all kinds of problems. Couldn't happen to a nicer bunch of drekholes."

"Yeah," Blackwater replied absently. He narrowed in on a few people, tracking their movements behind the vans and the PCC cops. He spotted an interesting-looking woman in a long black dress. Which itself was a bit odd. Her dark hair hid her face and she seemed to know where the drones were at all times—and avoided letting them get a good lock on her. He captured a few images, encrypted them and sent them off to a few *omae* who might be able to identify her. He wasn't sure yet, but if the dead guy was Wagner, Blackwater had to make sure whoever ganked the asshole didn't come looking for him, too.

"Cole?"

"Yeah. Look, I got a few irons in the fire. I'll get back when I can." He disconnected the call and went back to looking at the images as the local PAN disappeared and the connection switched to the public grid. He disconnected, and after a final look at the flames in the incinerator, left the school through back doors and into an alley.

He wasn't going to sit easy 'til he knew for sure Wagner got killed. And then he still wasn't going to sit easy 'til he knew the reason for the killing wasn't the data the other hacker took. And if he found out it was—he planned on setting that guy up for the fall. Since there was a possibility of technomancers involved, he had just the muscle to pull in for a little side job.

Blackwater connected to the public grid on a spoofed ID— one only a few would recognize—and made a call. After several seconds the connection opened, but no icon showed up. Blackwater knew he was listening, though.

**<Got a job for you in Los Angeles. Hot data with a possible**

*large payday and a technomancer lookin' for a new home. Interested?>*

He walked to his ride and shut the security on it down as he got in. He cranked it, and was halfway out of the parking lot before the answer came.

*<Nuyen and technomancers? I'm there. Send me the intel and where to meet.>*

A wicked smile pulled at the side of Blackwater's mouth as he turned out into traffic, the sign-off still visible in the window.

*Clockwork.*

# CHAPTER TWENTY-ONE

## BANG BANG BOOTY CLUB

Mack liked looking at the whole picture—and if he couldn't see all of it, he at least liked to have everything up in front of him.

When he'd first started his business, long before opening the club as his haven, Mack took cues from his father, who retired as a private investigator. Jack Schmetzer had worked for three decades for Lone Star, and decided to work for himself for the last fifteen years of his life. Mack didn't know his father during his life in Lone Star, but he remembered those afternoons watching him spread everything out on the kitchen table, taking notes, putting the puzzle together.

Now, as an adult with a long and colorful life of his own, Mack used his AR desktop the same way. He connected his commlink to an interactive vid that displayed his dad's old kitchen table on the wall across from his desk. With his rings he moved images, vids, and notes around to fit the timeline. Mack had remained there since getting Charis's call about Artus Wagner's murder while a search app filtered in more news clippings, vids, and intel on the key players.

So far, the story still didn't make a hell of a lot of sense.

His door chimed, and he made a noise at it. Shayla stepped in and set a tray of food on his desk, then stood beside him and looked at the projection. "You looking for something?"

"The point." He crossed his arms over his chest. "You get in touch with Cole?"

"Yep. And he blew me off. He did ask about the murder at Horizon. Seemed real interested in who it was."

"Yeah...they're being real tight lipped on that information."

She faced him. "But you know who it was."

One nod. "I do."

"You care to share all this with me and Preacher? I mean, we are part of your team, right?"

"I can tell what I know right now...but it's not going to make any more sense to you than it does to me."

"Try me."

Mack shrugged. "Okay...the Johnson, who you know is Charis Monogue, assistant to Horizon Director Artus Wagner, hired us to retrieve data from a retired host in a building scheduled for demolition. Somebody else out-hacked Blackwater and took the data, killing Maria and two Horizon Security guards. Maria's body mysteriously disappeared from the morgue. Blackwater, who lost the data to this other hotshot, hasn't reported back in after heading out to look for Maria's body, and now you tell me he's blowing us off." He moved closer to the projected images and started pointing and moving icons. "Charis gave me the vid of one hell of a conversation between Artus Wagner and an investigator named Draco Powell. This dwarf is interested in the data and a Knight Errant employee named Tetsu, whom he believes is a technomancer. Kazuma Tetsu is also the Knight Errant supervisor in charge of the Annex's secure decommission and destruction, and has nothing in any file we can get a hold of that indicates he's anything more than a Knight Errant flunky."

"Does Powell have any proof? I mean...going off half-cocked, accusing people of being a technomancer can get them killed. Or kidnapped."

"Powell said his technocritter could sense other technomancers. But I didn't see any evidence of that on the vid. He talked about skin links with technomancers, and I think he was trying to tell Wagner that's how Tetsu got the data off the host." He moved the vids out of the way and displayed several articles on different news feeds. "Now here's the part I know and you don't—that the dead body was Artus Wagner's, and Charis found it after she left here. Within an hour, these images of a tall man in a Knight Errant uniform is seen entering Horizon with the headline *Knight Errant Technomancer Suspect Sought in Horizon Executive Murder.*"

"Yeah, but that story went away. Can't even find the images you have any more."

"Uh huh...which is why I've got these backups on our secure host here. Don't want any grid bugs coming in and getting into my personal shit to pull them out. Thing is, who removed it? Who killed the story?" He looked at Shayla. "Who leaked it in the first place, and why? And to make a point—they got Wagner's title wrong. He wasn't an executive. I still have contacts at Horizon, and they swear there wasn't any image of a tall Knight Errant employee entering the building that morning up until Charis found Wagner's body. So the only reason I can come up with—why this article showed up and then disappeared—is the killer put it out there and forces more powerful than him or her made it disappear..."

Shayla looked at the board, then back at Mack. "Or?" she prompted when it looked like he wasn't finished.

"No...no or. What if the killer put it out there to frame whoever's picture this is?"

"That's not rocket science, boss. The image looks like Tetsu. The longish dark hair? Just the hint of a pointed ear? The dark KE suit?"

"But why? Why remove it?"

"I have no idea, boss. All I know is we got a hacker out of pocket and being all mysterious and no data. We need to go after the data and find out what's in it."

"Charis said Wagner put the data in the host himself, and he hinted several times it was his own personal kill file."

"His what?"

Mack made a slow, deep shrug as he continued looking at the board. "It's a revenge thing." He turned to look at her. "Let's say you work for some unscrupulous people who tell you to do equally unscrupulous things. Things you know would land you in jail if you're caught. But you need the job, the money, or they have something on you as blackmail. So to protect your family or to reveal the truth after you're dead, you keep records. Hard copy, vids, files, clippings, recordings—anything that will implicate the people who killed you."

"Oh, wow."

"So, Charis thinks that file had a lot of dirt on Horizon in it, and she wants to get her hands on it."

"All the more reason we need to get it back first." She moved forward and pointed at a smaller file. "Whose license are you running?" Shayla turned to him. "Mack...you got the license of the other hacker's getaway car? Why didn't you say anything?"

"Because I'm still trying to put all the pieces together. The car is registered to Hitori Tetsu."

"*Tetsu*? Are you serious? Mother? Sister?"

Mack shrugged. "It's Kazuma's sister, but she's been missing for six months. Former Ares employee is about all I can find on her. Artist. In fact, she designed that billboard over on Rodeo Drive, the one with the moving panels?"

"Oh, I love that one!" Shayla put her hands together. "And she's missing?"

"Kazuma filed a report with all law enforcement agencies, even Knight Errant...but the case is cold. I got her apartment address."

"It's still active?"

"Yeah. I'm assuming her brother's keeping it paid up." Mack stepped forward and moved things around to bring up Hitori's small folder. The image was of a beautiful young Asian woman with short, cropped hair and a bright smile.

"Huh. She's not an elf like her brother."

"No. Human. Her only augmentation is a datajack, just like Kazuma." He moved Hitori's image to the side and brought up the dossier on her sibling. "Like I said, this guy's a straight arrow. No priors—except an altercation in a coffee shop a few years back. Stopped a group of hackers from entering a back door into Horizon." He chuckled. "I'm pretty sure that's why he got the job as one of the account supervisors. And get this—he's also the nephew to a Lone Star operator."

"Mack...if he's looking for his sister, and he hacked that host to get to that data...you think the two are linked?"

"I'm looking at all possibilities at this point."

"He's not really looking good for this, is he? As the one that out-hacked Blackwater?"

"No. Which is why I want to talk to him myself and ask why an investigator's got it in for him." Mack's AR flashed, and Preacher's icon appeared in the right corner. "Boss, you got a priority call coming in. It's encrypted and...it's got a California prefix."

He lowered his shoulders. *Drek.*

"Mack?" Shayla leaned forward.

"Shayla, change all the access codes we gave Blackwater, and anything he might have hacked. Get me a new hacker—just look through the boards and find one. If you know someone you trust—and he's good—bring him in. But I want him here in the morning." He ushered her out and locked the door.

With a wave of his hand, he cleared his AR desktop and settled into his desk chair. He raked his fingers through his hair a few times before he signaled the call to go through. This wasn't going to be a chat. It was a full visual.

It was how she liked it.

The familiar face came into view in his AR, the smiling, red-headed beauty from his childhood. One look at her and all the years disappeared, and he was once again a small child in her service.

Hestaby.

"You look well, Mackenzie." Her spellcrafted voice amplified over the speakers in his office, yet her lips never moved.

"So do you. I'm sorry for your loss."

A dark shadow crossed her face for a brief second. She recovered and smiled again. "I still grieve, Mackenzie. But that isn't why I called you."

He nodded. "I'm assuming it has something to do with the Horizon death?"

"It might. But what I really need to talk to you about is something more distressing." She leaned forward, and a crease formed between her brows. "What do you know about Contagion Games?"

# CHAPTER TWENTY-TWO

### GiTm0

Welcome back to GiTm0, *omae*; your last connection was 4 hours, 12 minutes, 13 seconds ago

### BOLOs

Just a reminder—this board's got less than two hours before it terminates in your comms. Send your sprites out twenty-four hours after that for the new link.

We're missing a few of our own: Cobble, NetherNet, and Wet-Paint have all been missing for more than a week. No trace of their logins. If anyone has any information on them, especially sensitive personal information, get hold of Shyammo so we can add them to the database.

No new known dangerous handles yet, but don't drop your guard.

Remember, GOD is always watching.

### NeW oNLiNE

\* Breaking News! One of Horizon's junior flunkies was killed in his office today and technomancers are being framed. From what the vids are showing, which isn't much, PCC security has little evidence, and they're in a turf war with Knight Errant, who conveniently had a fire alarm system act up at the time of the murder. Dumped everyone into the streets for nearly an hour and caused a traffic backup. We have to get on this fast and get some kind of smear campaign going against Horizon—get them to prove the guy was killed by a technomancer. Anyone can say that's what it was, but the public should ask for proof. Anyone got any details on this story? New information hasn't hit yet, but it might by the time the news cycle rolls tonight.

* Contagion Games showed up in a report this morning, but of course the news was overshadowed by the Horizon murder and KE fire. Apparently their host went down again, and Bellex announced the decision to close the game down temporarily since the new UV host crashed. At least this time he didn't finger technomancers.

**CLOSER LOOK**
>>>>Open Thread/Subhost001.445.1
>>>>Thread Access Restrictions: <Yes/**No**>
>>>>Format: <**Open Post**/Comment Only/Read Only>
>>>>File Attachment: <Yes/**No**>
>>>>Thread Descriptor: **Closer Look**
>>>>Thread Posted By User: Shyammo

- Gonna start the posting up myself with news on the Horizon murder. Got images off a drone near the building. [Link] Looks like a guy in a KE uniform. But there's nothing that says he's a technomancer.
- RoxJohn

- Seriously? That could be any tech they have, or a guy in a black suit walking in. Where is that? The front of the building?
- 404Flames

- Yeah. This has got setup written all over it. But what I don't get is why. I don't believe a technomancer killed this official—and we still don't have an ID on him. So who killed him and why?
- RoxJohn

- We're not going to get anywhere till we know the victim's name.
- 404Flames

- You guys think the murder is linked to the fire at Knight Errant?
- LongTong

- Duh? They happened within what, an hour of each other? It was organized to draw attention.
- Prettyboy

- Yeah. I agree. But away from what?
- J@zh@r@d

- Everyone—the Horizon murder victim is a guy named Atrus Wagner. He was once involved in the registration of technomancers for Horizon, and has worked in personnel for most of his career in Horizon. He was scheduled to retire in six months. Need everyone to look at this image and tell me if you have ever dealt with the dwarf beside him, and get a good look at the technocritter. I think it was dissonant. [Link]
- Silk

- Was this at a party?
- 404Flames

- Silk, I got a whole dossier on Artus Wagner. I'll upload it to the files. Maybe someone can filter through and see what's going on there.
- LongTong

- Has anyone seen HipOldGuy? I got a missive from his wife. She went with a church group to a trideo and came home to an empty house. And he hasn't come home. The guy's as dependable as the sun. I just checked his job, and they haven't seen him either.
- Venerator

- Silk, LongTong, I've encrypted the image and dossier. Anyone interested in pursuing, contact me or Shyammo for a secure download. We need to get on this asap and start stopping this before it starts.
- RoxJohn

- Venerator, the last I spoke to Hip he was going to check out the Contagion Games host. Anyone else heard from him?
- 404Flames

# CHAPTER TWENTY-THREE

## BANG BANG BOOTY CLUB

Mack sat in his office, the lights off, his door locked. It was going to be hard to do this again—to step back out there and save the world. How many times had he done this as a child?

Too many to count.

As an *otaku* under Hestaby's tutelage, Mackenzie Schmetzer had been one of her brightest students, and one of the best at moving in the Matrix. He remembered what that was like, that feeling of utter freedom inside the datasphere, with no restrictions, no cyberdeck, no apps needed.

Just himself, and Mackenzie became a ghost in the machine. A human sprite.

A child of the Matrix.

That's what they were called, and the Resonance was a deity. Something to strive for, to see, to touch, to worship. And he had when he thought as a child.

But as a man whose abilities faded before he was twenty, shadowrunner Mack Schmetzer didn't trust the Matrix, or those who could submerge into the resonance. That's when he learned about the technomancers.

Something Hestaby said during their conversation annoyed him. Well, the whole talk annoyed him, but one statement in particular got under his skin.

*"Perhaps your distrust comes from a place of jealousy, Mackenzie. That perhaps if you had been online that day when the Crash changed everything...you would have become one as well."*

God, he hated that thought. Hated the idea he could be so petty.

But that wasn't where the conversation ended.

"That might be, you old lizard. But you're not going to fool anyone. You lost Shasta, you lost support of the Council, and you lost a good many of your shamans. Your Clutch is gone." He had pointed at the visage in the vid. "I know exactly what you're doing. You're thinking if you can stop this from happening and somehow unite the technomancers, you can rebuild yourself a new base. But this time with a more powerful breed of *otaku*, not like when we were young. If you organize them—"

"Then they can be strong. Right now they're scattered, hunted, shunned. They need guidance."

"And you're it."

"Who else is there?"

"Hestaby...no one is going to follow a dragon."

And what she said next both comforted and terrified him. "You may be right."

Was that why part of him wanted to take everything that damned dragon told him, lock it away and ignore her, and show everyone—who would get pulled into what he could only see would be madness—just how manipulative she was?

He replayed the conversation again. Not in his head, but the recording he'd made of it. After getting screwed a few times, he learned to keep as much evidence as possible. And voice verification would go a long way.

It was audio only, but he remembered her face, her facial expressions above lips that never moved. And he remembered every word she said, with or without the recording.

"Boss?" Shayla knocked on his office door.

Mack rubbed his face and shut the recording off. He hadn't slept since Hestaby's call. There was too much to do, too much to accomplish, and very little time, if what the dragon told him was true.

He was going to need evidence, and a solid team.

"Come in," he called as he stood and moved to the blank wall by the door.

His rigger peeked in and smiled. "The hacker's here. Flew in from Seattle."

"All right. Grab Preacher and bring him in. It's time to have a come to Jesus meeting."

The look she gave him was interesting—a mixture of affirmative and *"Uh oh, boss done gone crazy."*

When Shayla returned, she led their new hacker, a rather tall, wiry man with spiky, blond hair and a squared jaw. He followed behind her politely and Mack eyed him, his AR picking up no RFID tags at all on him. He was clean—all the way down to his socks. No tags at all.

Mack liked that.

"Mack," Shayla moved out of the way as she motioned the man to step forward. "You said get someone fast and he answered the fastest. He's got quite a resume—as do his parents. His handle's Slamm-0!."

The young man offered his hand and Mack took it, schooling his own features into a less than flattering smirk. "Slam-Oh?"

"That's right," Slamm-0! grinned. "That's with two m's, a hyphen, and then a zero and an exclamation point."

Mack snorted. "Cheesy. Just call me Mack. Or Boss. One m, no zeros."

"Fair enough."

Mack could tell this man was far from a kid—perhaps in his early thirties—but he presented an air of youth about him. And confidence. Dressed in jeans, T-shirt, and a light jacket with his commlink nestled comfortably in his left ear. On his left temple was an updated datajack, and on his arm was a bag big enough to possibly carry a cyberdeck.

"Pay is 25,000 nuyen up front, that's split between the team evenly, for the duration of the run. If we achieve our goal—then it's another 100,000 for each."

Slamm-0! whistled. "This Johnson sounds serious."

"She is. Did Shayla brief you on the specifics?"

The blond nodded. "A little. Your other hacker dodged, and you need a new one."

Mack glared at Shayla as she turned and left the office. That wasn't a briefing, that was more of a passing comment. "Yeah. First, let's go over the run that brought us to where we are now."

"Oh I know about the Annex break-in. That was you guys—and someone else."

Mack turned his irritated look on the hacker before he initiated the vid screens, the control rings on his fingers humming as holographic images branched out to form a two-meter view of four stacked windows.

"Mind if I drive for a bit?" Slamm-0! asked.

"Shayla give you an access ID?"

"Don't need one," the man smiled, wiggled his eyebrows.

Stepping back, Mack watched as Slamm-0! slipped on his gloves, wiggled his fingers and abruptly the images changed even faster. "I linked your holo-imager up to my AR—so you can see what I see. Though your processor's clocking speed is a bit faster than my own—nice host."

"Thanks."

"Let's see." Slamm-0! moved his hands in the air, making circles, expanding and collapsing windows. He called up the building schematics from on the disc the Johnson had given him, and rendered a three-dimensional image of the Annex.

*Okay...so his is prettier than mine*, Mack thought. *So what? I'm not a hacker.*

"You were here." Mack's marks from earlier on the map showed up in place. "Your hacker and mage were here, and the two guards were here. So, where was this other hacker?"

"We don't know. According to our former hacker, no one knew he was there—not even Maria."

Slamm-0! turned and gave Mack a withering look. "Your mage couldn't sense living things in the environment? Anyone think to ask her Guardian—did she have one?"

Mack shook his head. "Her body disappeared right after it was interned in the morgue. Without the body—it's kinda hard to call up her eagle."

"Eagle, huh? She a shaman? Native American?"

"Yeah," Mack said, and had a hard time keeping the anger out of his voice. "Blackwater said they were coming out of this stairwell and he ambushed them, shooting her first. That's when they fought, and Blackwater got the gun and said he shot the hacker—but he got away."

Slamm-0! paused. "Blackwater—you mean *the* Cole Blackwater? Same dude that was responsible for the system crash over at Ares last year?"

"The same."

"You know that guy's a recovering chiphead. And I find it hard that anyone caught him off guard—"

When the hacker paused both in his movements and his speaking, Mack started. The kid was staring at the display. "What is it?"

"You said they were in this stairwell?" Slamm-0! moved the image of the stairwell and its schematic to the front.

"Yeah."

"But according to this, those stairs go to the basement. The Annex is two stories *plus* the basement," the images shifted and moved, making Mack dizzy. "The upper floor is basically to house the air-conditioning units to keep the servers cool—old design— and then that air was pumped down through a false floor into the server room. There are two sets of stairs—one here on the east side near the administrative offices that leads up to the actual attic—and there you have decking access to the array—here and here," he reached out and two dots appeared on the larger screens. "If he were going to access the primary—and this is a wired host—he'd deck at the source for a quick hack and snack. There's no reason for Blackwater or your shaman to be here and be surprised by anyone, especially if she watched the lower access door, which I'm assuming she would have."

Mack watched the screen, growing angrier by the second. "You're right. They wouldn't have kept that door closed—it's the only way in or out of that attic space."

"Precisely. So—the main access is in the basement—where the master CPU was housed back in the day. I assume the other hacker was down there. Which means he had a longer way to come up once the two met on the host. My guess is that they met either on the stairs up or just outside—" he looked at Mack. "You got communication logs? Time stamps?"

Mack nodded. "Same folder."

"Good." Slamm-0! moved back to the map and within seconds a list of times and calls appeared on the right side. He moved each call to the location, and verified with the Knight Errant logs Mack had gotten from the Johnson. "Uh oh—looks like the guards actually found a dude ID'd as Morimoto down in the basement about five minutes after the alarm was tripped. Then here it shows your call with Blackwater—and then another eight minutes before Shayla's RCC was hacked. Guards lost contact a full ten minutes after clearing Morimoto." He looked at Mack. "Who was Morimoto?"

"The other hacker. He was disguised." Mack studied the map and the time stamps. "So basically—Maria was shot before Blackwater ever came into physical contact with the other hacker."

Slamm-0! nodded. "Yeah—if Morimoto is the same dude. Then he was in the basement with the guards for a full five minutes or so after the shot went off. Your Morimoto—or hacker two, whatever—wasn't near the administrative door."

Mack stepped forward and made a fist, activating his rings. He pulled a folder from his AR and transferred it to the host so both of them could bring it up and take a look at it. Inside were personnel files from Knight Errant and Horizon. Mack pulled a file up with an elderly Asian man. "This is Toshi Morimoto."

"*That* guy is the other hacker?" Slamm-0! made a face as if he smelled something bad.

"No. Morimoto died two years ago. The hacker was disguised as him, and even had his ID and a work order to be in the Annex to work on the host. According to the records we got from both KE and Horizon, he was part of the team archiving it for termination."

The hacker paused and looked directly at Mack. "So—he *wasn't* stealing the data? He was actually there doing his job?"

"Yes and no. That's where it gets fuzzy. His name is Kazuma Tetsu. He's the Knight Errant supervisor overseeing the project to clear the host for termination, which is scheduled for later today." He pulled a new file out to show a young elf with mixed Asian features. "Excellent service record. Has a sister—missing—and a father. But the father is reported to be in Japan."

"Maybe I need more information about this?" Slamm-0! moved the map back to the lower right screen as Mack went over the events as quickly as he could, down to Maria's body going missing half an hour after it was delivered to the morgue, followed up by the murder of Artus Wagner at Horizon. "As an FYI, our first Johnson is Wagner's personal assistant."

The hacker dropped his arms and stared at Mack. "Maybe I should have asked for a higher fee?"

Preacher chuckled behind Mack. Slamm-0! looked up at him and grinned, then removed the glove from his right hand and offered it to the big troll. "Slamm-0!"

Mack watched the hacker's hand disappear in Preacher's larger one. "Nice to meet you. They call me Preacher."

"Ah," Slamm-0! nodded. "Because they ask for last rites when they see you coming?"

That made Preacher grin even wider. He looked at Mack. "I like him." Then he frowned. "Got a message from Monogue."

Mack nodded. "Yeah, yeah. What's up?"

"Caught a creepy report of human remains found in an incinerator in a school in south Los Angeles. Janitor found it when he saw someone coming out of the basement. Thought it was kids doing something illegal."

He handed Mack a slip of paper. Mack looked at it. "And this is important to me why?"

"Shayla tried to get Blackwater to come in. He pissed her off. So she tracked him down." Preacher nodded to the slip of paper. "He was at that high school when she talked to him."

"Damn," Mack said as he crumpled the piece of paper in his hand. "What do they have on these human remains?"

"Female. Human. Somewhere between twenty-four to thirty." The troll was quiet for a few seconds. "They also found a bullet. It wasn't fully destroyed. Same caliber as Blackwater's. No exact match yet—but it's a good bet that PCC ballistics is going to find it was fired from the same gun that killed the two guards."

There had always been a tiny nugget in the pit of Mack's stomach, a bit of doubt that Blackwater had been truthful when he claimed the hacker killed Maria. But he'd wanted to give him the benefit of the doubt—not wanting to believe that Blackwater would kill one of his own team.

But now, given the blocking and logistics Slamm-0! just disproved about Blackwater's described chain of events that night, coupled with this bit of news... *That bastard.*

"Sorry, chummer," Slamm-0! said. "Blackwater's got a pretty nasty rep out there."

"That bastard killed a team member." He looked at Shayla and then Preacher, who looked back at him with sad faces. "When we're done saving the world this time, we're going after him. I want him dead."

"You got it, boss." Shayla smiled grimly.

Preacher nodded. "Now we get to meet the new Johnson?"

Slamm-0! looked at each of them. "Meet the new Johnson? That's sort of irregular, isn't it?"

"Not in this case." Mack licked his lips. "Everyone sit down."

Once they were seated around the large oval table in front of his desk, Mack made a fist again and moved the images. Several holovids lit up the center of the table, the images the same on either side for every person seated. The table had six chairs other than his own.

The first image he displayed was the logo of Contagion Games. All three of them looked at the logo, then looked at him.

"Boss..." Shayla said.

"You're going to have to trust me and listen. I didn't know what to think until I spoke with her. We've got a lot of work to do, and we both agreed she needed to tell you what has to be done so that I didn't leave anything out."

Mack opened up the communication window and piped it through the vids.

Hestaby appeared with a smile and a projected, *"Good morning, team. Are we ready to learn?"*

Slamm-0!'s jaw dropped, and he gave Mack a troubled look. Mack was pretty sure he knew what was going through the man's head. There were few people in this world who didn't know what Hestaby looked like. Or what she was.

And all of them knew that dealing with a dragon was always a very bad idea.

# CHAPTER TWENTY-FOUR

## UNKNOWN LOCATION
## FRIDAY AFTERNOON

Kazuma jolted awake with a slight yell. The nightmare of being eaten by a tree followed him to the waking world as warm hands gripped his shoulders.

"Hey...calm down. You're okay. It's me. Focus on my face."

Kazuma looked into Silk's amber eyes. He nodded, taking deep, cleansing breaths like she'd taught him, until his heart calmed down enough for him to look around. He didn't recognize where he was. It was semi-dark, the only illumination coming from a lamp in the corner. The walls were dingy, and the room smelled like mildew and age.

He looked down to find himself shirtless, with a white bandage wrapped around his torso. He reached up to the back of his neck and felt a bandage there as well.

Within seconds, the datasphere whispered to him, and his AR lit up with flashing messages. He brushed them away and refocused on Silk. "Where are we?"

"We're in a hotel, about two miles from your grannie's house."

"Did you get the data?"

"No. Not yet." She put a hand to his cheek. "Kazuma, do you remember what happened today before you faded?"

He searched her face as his memories slowly resurfaced. It was like pulling pictures out of a muddy hole and having to carefully clean them off. "I went to work...and a dwarf took me to Black's office..." And then it all came back. He put his hand back on his neck. "A wolf pinned me to the floor."

"Yeah. I saw the image you sent Netcat. Do you remember getting out of there?"

"The alarm went off, and Karl came in the door. I made the door slam into Powell—that's the dwarf—and then Karl shot the wolf."

Silk bit her lip. "Interesting that no one's mentioned a wolf, and if I hadn't seen it with my own eyes and Netcat's, I'd've thought it was a metaphor. And after that?"

"Karl helped me out of the building, and I found Netcat." He narrowed his eyes at her. "You told her who I was."

"I didn't have a choice, Kaz. Do you realize who that dwarf was?"

"No. I mean I realized pretty fast he believed I was the one that broke into the Annex and he was pretty sure I was a technomancer. He kept drilling on about my commlink."

"I'm sure."

"Silk, he had the commlink I was using at the Annex. I must've left it there."

"Well it's a lot more complicated than that. Come on. There's a clean shirt on the edge of the bed. And I got you Chang's."

He loved Chang's Korean Cuisine. With a smile and a kiss, Kazuma got up carefully—remembering that recovery from a fade was something to take slow—used the facilities, which were in dire need of a bottle of bleach, slipped the shirt on, and stepped into the other room.

The decor wasn't much better. But there were improvements. Like the food spread out on the table.

Netcat lay on the couch, her eyes closed. A guy in a gray hoodie sat in a chair by the window, shades over his eyes. Kazuma gave Netcat a quizzical look as he grabbed a pair of chopsticks, a carton of noodles, and a container of kimchi and dug in.

Silk opened a bottle of water and set it in front of him while she joined him at the table. "Netcat you met—and you owe her. If she hadn't been monitoring Powell, you'd be long disappeared by now. To where—" She shivered. "—I don't even want to think about."

"And the guy?"

"That's a friend of hers, lives in this area. You'd know him as MoonShine."

"MoonShine?" Kazuma took another look at the guy. Couldn't see much, not with the hoodie down. "I thought he disappeared. Wasn't his name listed in the BOLOs?"

"Yeah, but he wanted it that way. Seems he was wanted by several corporations."

"Why?"

Silk smiled. "You can ask him when they get back."

Kazuma chewed his dinner and looked at the two of them. "Are they submerged?"

"Not entirely. Netcat has a portable IV setup for that—but Moon didn't want to use needles." She picked up a spring roll and bit off the end. "I need to bring you up to speed. Do you know an Artus Wagner?"

Kazuma drank half the bottle of water. One of the things he'd always noticed after a fade was how thirsty he was. "Yeah. He's one of the directors over at Horizon."

"You ever have contact with him?"

"No. I just know his name."

"You ever forge his name?"

He narrowed his eyes at her. "Silk—what's going on?"

She picked up a folder from the side of the table and set it in front of him. "This is a hardcopy of everything that's happened since last night. You really need to read it."

"Why is it hardcopy?"

"'Cause someone, something, or some corporation is going around the grids looking for any information on what's in the folder. Namely—" She furrowed her brow. "—you."

"Me?" He set the box of noodles on the table and shoved the chopsticks inside. His AR kept flashing in his periphery. If he didn't see what was happening, it was just going to keep bothering him.

<*Ponsu–*>

*Boss!*

The golden origami swan appeared in front of him and he leaned back a second when it looked like she was going to hug him. <***Ponsu, can you go through the messages?***>

*I already did. Most of it was redundant KE junk and I put it in a folder. But there's something you need to see.*

<***I'm just a bit busy right now. Seems something is after me.***>

*Oh, I'll say. I made copies of the same things Silk and Netcat worked on this afternoon while you slept.*

"Kazuma?"

He held up his hand as Ponsu gave him a clipped version.

*That dwarf in Black's office is named Draco Powell.*

Several images of the man slid onto his AR's desktop and he

nodded. *<And he's got a technocritter.>*

Had. Yes. A wolf. The wolf was evil, Boss. Very evil. And it would have killed you if Powell told it to.

Kazuma put his hand to the back of his neck against the bandage there. *<I believe you. Karl saved my life.>*

Yes, he did. He's been messaging you, and I put the texts in that same encrypted folder. Apparently the dwarf tried to have him fired for killing the wolf, but a few of the other KE directors cleared him of any wrongdoing.

Ponsu moved out of view. Now you need to look at this.

A new window appeared in his AR. It was a video, sent to him from—

"Hey," Silk touched his forearm, her way of bringing him back to reality. "They're waking up."

Kazuma pushed the window aside with an apology to Ponsu and a promise to watch it in a second. He blinked a few times as Netcat sat up and stretched. She looked over at Silk and him and sniffed. "Oooh...I smell kimchi."

The guy in the hoodie put his head between his knees and moaned.

"Moon, you okay?" Netcat asked as she stood and patted him on the back.

"Yeah...I really need to exercise more."

"I'll say," Silk piped up.

Moon sighed and stood. He was lanky and a few inches taller than Netcat, and when he pushed back his hoodie, Kazuma was surprised to see white hair.

"Hey." Along with Netcat, Moon walked to Kazuma and offered his hand. "I'm Moon. Nice to finally meet Soldat."

"Call me Kazuma out here." He shook the hand and smiled at Netcat.

"You look a hundred percent better," she said as she reached around him to grab his noodles and chopsticks. "Did Silk catch you up?"

"I think Ponsu did." Silk finished her spring roll.

"Ponsu?"

Kazuma looked at the other containers and waited for Moon to choose one. Once the white-haired man picked his, Kazuma took one filled with fried rice. "My sprite. She's registered. First one I ever made." He continued to watch Moon. "You don't have a datajack."

*Wow*, he chided himself. *Just blurt it out there.*

"No. I don't." Moon smiled and started eating.

Netcat laughed. "Moon was an *otaku* when he was younger."

"You were?"

Moon chewed and swallowed. His eyes were pale blue. "It lasted until I hit puberty...then it started fading. But mom wouldn't let me get one till I was 18. A week before my scheduled installation appointment, I was online in a game when the Crash happened."

Kazuma smiled. "And woke up a technomancer."

"Yeah. Only I had no idea. I just thought my *otaku* abilities were back, just stronger. I didn't tell my parents at first—because I didn't know what was happening. Then when technomancers started filling the news..." he shrugged and dug into the container with his chopsticks. "I decided keeping the secret was better. Asked my parents for a commlink, and up until last year that was all I needed. When the new protocols got put in place, I splurged on a cyberdeck."

"Do you use it?"

He smiled. "No. It's too slow. And I can't submerge through it." Moon reached past Kazuma to grab a bottled water. "How many submersions?"

"Three."

"I'm gonna go for my fifth soon as we figure this latest weirdness out."

"You mean the dwarf with the technocritter wolf?"

Netcat snorted. "You remember that."

He put his hand to his neck. "Hard to forget."

"We need you to tell everything that happened to you since last night." She held up a no-nonsense finger. "Including hacking the Annex host. No arguments. We're all here because we want to know why a known technomancer hunter is after you."

Kazuma stopped chewing and swallowed. "What?"

"I thought he was caught up."

Silk waved Netcat away and grabbed another spring roll.

Netcat continued. "Draco Powell, the dwarf that set his sights on you, has a regular persona as a private investigator. Very successful in the Denver area. But his name's also flagged in conjunction with missing known technomancers. He spent several years in prison in Aztlan, and his last known employer was Renraku."

*Renraku?* Kazuma looked at each of them. "And he was gunning for me?"

"Oh, he was zeroing in," Moon said. "The stuff Netcat got off his AR was just frightening. He had your history, your dad's, your sister's, and some guy named Morimoto."

"Toshi was my mentor. My friend at Horizon." Kazuma drank more water, then turned the bottle in his hands. "He trained me at Horizon, showed me how to gain trust."

"He was a technomancer too, wasn't he?"

Kazuma nodded. "Happened late for him. He said his augmentations prevented him from touching the resonance, but he could see it. In the Matrix. So he was the one that trained me, taught me to watch and listen before he died."

"Hitori Tetsu," Netcat said as her eyes unfocused, looking at her AR. "Artist, hired by Ares, contracted after her successful promotion billboard in Hollywood. Very well known and Ares considered it a coup when they hired her."

"Yeah. She was happy. She and I were online when the Crash happened, and we both became technomancers."

"Disappeared six months ago. According to the reports you filed, she was last seen out with friends and vanished."

"Yeah..." Kazuma turned away. "That was easier to tell them. I really don't know where she was or how long she was gone before she disappeared. We argued the last time I saw her. Hitori...wanted change. And she was into all—this." He waved his hand to indicate all of them. "She got involved with TM groups, helped fight the system. She disappeared a few years ago, just after she was hired by Ares. I freaked out, hired a PI, and then she showed up again. She'd taken time off to submerge...then went to Brazil, then to Chiba, all to meet others like us. She wanted to help us, stop the ridiculous fear of us."

"What was her online handle?"

"Fierce."

Moon's jaw dropped. "*Your* sister is Fierce? Oh, I had the biggest crush on her!"

Kazuma nodded. "She was popular. She went to Vegas. She was there when it all went down. Came and told me what she saw. I was angry at her for going there and putting her life on the line. I told her our father would be very angry with her. She stormed out of my apartment. I never saw her again."

Silk stood and moved around to hug Kazuma from behind. He held onto her arms. "We're going to find her."

Netcat patted his shoulder. "First we find out why Powell's after you. Though it might be because of your sister."

Kazuma shook his head. "I'm not sure. It might." He told them everything he'd done and what happened to him after arriving at work, all the way to getting to Netcat's car. "And you know the rest."

"What was in that data you stole?" Moon asked.

"I don't know. Given all the media attention, I decided to leave it alone."

"Where is it?"

"It's safe."

"It won't be if we leave it where it is," Silk said. "I know you think that's a safe place, Kaz, but whoever Powell's working for has your name. You really think they're not going to dig for your family?"

Kazuma smiled at her. "Oh, I'm sure they are. But the only thing they're going to find is my father, and he lives in Chiba."

"What about your grannie?"

"She's not my biological grannie. She's someone I met after my father moved us here, and she took Hitori and me in. I just call her Grannie."

"That doesn't mean they won't find her," Moon said. "You hide it with her?"

"Not with her, but on a private host she owned. Used it like a safety deposit box. Stored all her personal things."

"You're talking in past tense. She dead?"

"Yes."

"We need to get that data and find out what's so important about it," Netcat said. "You said it flagged for you when you were doing a routine search?"

"Yeah. I was searching for certain keywords. And the host actually triggered when it hit Tetsu…and Caliban."

"Caliban?" Netcat frowned. "What's that?"

"Something a PI told me to be on the lookout for after Hitori disappeared again. Said it was dangerous. So whatever's in that data, it has to do with my family and Caliban."

Netcat looked at Moon, who nodded. "I'm on it. I just want to eat first."

*Boss…you need to tell them about this message.*

Kazuma sighed and nodded. "Oh, I got something from HipOldGuy."

Netcat nearly climbed on top of him. "You did? When?"

He glanced at the time stamp. "Looks like some time during

the day... and it got re-routed a few times." He looked closer at the path. "Actually, a sprite delivered it to my sprite."

"Is it text?"

"No, a vid. Anyone got a protected commlink?"

Moon pulled one out of his bag. He gave Kazuma admin access and he uploaded it to the commlink. When they were done watching the recording, everyone was silent for a moment.

Finally, Netcat put a hand on Silk's arm. "Moon...send that to Rox or Shyammo. Tell him where it came from, who it was sent to, and where it was recorded. In TechnoHack."

Moon wiped his eyes and took the commlink back to his chair.

Netcat put her hands to her face. "We've got to find that data, and we've got to find out what the hell happened to HipOldGuy."

# CHAPTER TWENTY-FIVE

## DIVE BAR
## LOS ANGELES
## FRIDAY NIGHT

Cole Blackwater was filtering through the drek his search app returned on names when someone slammed a beer down on the table in front of him. The mug of frothy, amber brew shone through the projected AR of his cybereyes, and he looked up to see the familiar face of Clockwork.

"Damn...I didn't think it was possible for you to get any uglier." The hobgoblin sat down behind his beer.

"And I didn't think it was possible for you to smell worse." Blackwater offered the hacker his hand, and the two shook over the table.

Clockwork's appearance wasn't unique when it came to the hobgoblin metavariant. He was a foot shorter than Blackwater, with a smaller build. His skin was light green, and Blackwater would've sworn the bastard had filed his teeth and tusks into needles. He was pretty sure they didn't grow like that.

Usually hobgoblins had dark eyes, but Clockwork's had the gleam of cyberization, and knowing him, Blackwater was pretty sure he'd spent an entire job's salary on making them top of the line. He was dressed in his usual black vest, dark cargo pants, and black boots, with commlinks on his wrists. His RCC wasn't visible.

Clockwork was high-priced, best contacted for specialized drones. As far as Blackwater knew, he had no conscience to speak of, and would sell his own mother if it paid well enough.

"Must've been close to get here in less than twenty-four hours." Blackwater signaled his waitress for another soykaf.

"Had a client needed a special piece. I delivered it a few days ago—thought I'd hang around."

"You hate Los Angeles."

"Yes, I do." Clockwork gave him a crooked grin, his needle-sharp teeth gleaming in the bar light. "So you better give me the important stuff up front. I said I'd meet you—I didn't say I'd take it."

He knew Clockwork meant pay. It was always about the nuyen. "If you take it, I can fit you with fifty Gs now, and then once we get the data, there's a possibility of more."

"No, no, no." Clockwork drank half his beer. "You said there was a technomancer involved."

"He's the target. He's got the data." Blackwater went into a shortened version of the events of the past twenty-four hours.

When he was done, Clockwork narrowed his eyes. "You let a drek-ass 'mancer out-hack you?"

"He was already there," Blackwater said. Damn, it felt like he'd said that a million times now. "He didn't out-hack me."

"But he got the data and he got away. Sounds like he did to me." The hobgoblin drained the rest of his beer.

"Because he threw this huge tiger at me—"

"With butterflies." Clockwork laughed.

"*Drek*. Now I wish I hadn't told you that part. But I wanted you to know what we're up against."

"Chummer, that the only part makin' all this fun so far." The hacker's demeanor changed to all business in a heartbeat. "So, someone in Wagner's office hired your team to get the data at the same time he contacted you to get the data."

Blackwater shook his head and scowled. "Yeah. It was just stupid. Wagner already knew someone had hired Mack's team—I never asked how he did. He really didn't want that data to get into anyone else's hands."

"And he said he was the only one who knew it was there?"

"He put it there himself."

"And yet—" Clockwork smirked, which looked almost painful around his sharp tusks. "Someone hired this other team, and either this Tetsu guy knew it was there, or someone hired him, too."

Blackwater frowned. "I never thought about that—someone hiring Tetsu to grab the stuff."

"There are technomancer runners out there. They still haven't made their name in the biz, but they're growing. And I plan on wiping every last one I meet out. And you got no lead on him?"

"None. He's got no living family in the UCAS. Dad's in Japan. And his sister's missing."

"She a technomancer, too?"

"I guess. She went missing. When someone goes missing nowadays, that's the first thing people think. Best I can tell is he was looking for her."

Clockwork was quiet for a few seconds. "You have any idea what's in this data?"

"No. But I figure if so many people want it, then it's got to be valuable."

"Which is why—" Clockwork stopped as the waitress came over with a beer and a soykaf. "This data is just as valuable as the technomancer who took it. Might be other technos that sent him. We need to know what makes this data important."

"I've already been looking—and I got nothing." He transferred a few folders over to Clockwork's ID. "Tetsu's got some serious holdings, loads of nuyen, but I can't touch any of it. It's heavily guarded in KE accounts, which even he can't access while he's under investigation."

"So they think he's good for Wagner's death?"

"Not sure. I think they're just playing it safe. There were pictures of what looks like him entering Horizon, but they disappeared."

"Disappeared? Images don't just 'disappear' in the Matrix."

"Well, these did. Even the story that had his name in it was killed. Can't even find the wageslave who uploaded it."

"Huh," Clockwork shuffled through the folder, his AR visible to Blackwater. "Sister's the only family?"

"Yeah. There was a grandmother listed, but I can't find anything on her. It's like she disappeared, too."

"Maternal or paternal?"

Blackwater pulled up his file and scrolled down. "Doesn't say. Just says there was a grandmother."

"Does he have any other holdings? Property? Rentals?"

"No."

"What about the sister?"

"She's missing."

Clockwork sighed. "Have you tried to retrieve her personal files? Did she have a residence? Where did she work? Surely someone else knew her other than her brother?"

"I got the sister's address."

"Then let's go check it out."

The two of them stood, and Blackwater paid the tab. "You think we'll find something there?"

"I like to cover all my bases, Cole." The grin on Clockwork's face made Blackwater feel a little uncomfortable. "When I got a techno to score, it's good to be thorough."

# CHAPTER TWENTY-SIX

## HORIZON ARCHIVE ANNEX
## FRIDAY EVENING
## EIGHT HOURS BEFORE BUILDING DEMOLITION

Powell's techniques for investigating evidence were a little more specialized than the local law's. The PCC cops and Knight Errant had come and gone, the Annex not a top priority on their list. From their frame of reference, a petty shadowrunner got capped, along with a few rent-a-cops. Nothing stolen. What was it to them? No national secrets were leaked out. What was the problem?

Two local cops remained outside the Annex's front doors, one stationed at the back entrance, while Powell worked alone inside. He stood in the hall in the exact spot where the girl's body had been found. He'd asked them not to clean the area, only to be told they weren't. Why spend the man hours and expense when the building was scheduled for demolition?

Powell had learned the art of psychometry from his teacher while very young, and when he'd moved to Aztlan, he learned how to use his own blood, his life force, to increase and magnify that spell by ten. Most people didn't understand blood magic. They couldn't see beyond what was perceived as a barbaric practice.

But he did. He understood the importance of blood. Its power. Its elegance. Blood contained the record of a being's life. The DNA—a sort of Akashic Record of a person's life. Combine that with his ability to sense emotions by touching objects that had come in direct contact with that person—

And what better vehicle than the blood of the woman and the floor where it spilled? A window into her very soul.

With a quick "sense" of his surroundings, sure that the surveillance cameras and guards were either off or at their posts, Powell drew the small, silver knife he kept handy at his belt, knelt in the center of the dried bloodstain, and pulled his left sleeve back.

Holding the knife over the correct vein, at the right angle and applying the precise pressure—as not to sever his vein and cause exsanguination, he closed his eyes, took in three deep breaths and half whispered the words of power, the spell that would allow him to see what she saw, and to feel what she felt.

At the precise moment, he cut and let his blood join hers on the floor. Opening his eyes, he looked down at the mingling, his astral vision taking in the brilliant reds of anger and fear, the purple of magic, and the yellow of flight. He plunged both of his hands into his spilled blood, moving it around on the floor like a child with a finger painting, his blood interacting with and releasing the dried remains of hers.

The reaction was almost immediate, and his vision kicked backward. He breathed heavily and blinked several times, dizzy from the movement of contact. He was looking through her eyes, seeing what she'd seen before her death.

They were moving slowly down the darkened hall. There was a big man in front of her, dressed in black. Very few details presented themselves. He could tell the man's head was shaved, and there were scars, some chrome, evidence of enhancements. But the man kept his face averted from her as he led her to a door.

"*Is this it?*" she asked, and Powell could feel the vibration of her voice inside of his own chest.

"*Yeah,*" the man answered. "*Now you just stay here and keep that shield active, okay? Keep those guards blind to what I'm doing.*"

Powell felt her nod, and then she was alone in the hallway. He lost his own balance as she whipped her head from the left to the right. His heart rate increased, and he knew she was frightened. It felt like an eternity before her companion stumbled back out of the room.

She put her hand on him, and he pulled away. "*Cole? What's wrong? What happened? Did you get it?*"

"*That bastard...*" the man said, and Powell saw his face for an instant. Wide, vein-lined, pockmarked skin, and the telltale gleam of cybereyes. He committed the image to his memory.

"Call Jack," the woman said. "*Something's gone wrong, hasn't it? Cole...what were you doing? Who were you talking to? Oh my god, you're–*"

And then Powell saw the gun, the black muzzle opening wide in front of his eyes. He yelled as he pulled back, retrieving his astral being from the emotion before it pulled him in.

He opened his eyes, panting heavily. He lay on his back, his bloodied hands in the air. Had he seen that right? Her own companion had killed her? His name was Cole...and he'd shot her.

It was obvious they were shadowrunners. And one had turned on the other.

So, how did the fake Morimoto fit into this?

Powell sat up, the spell's magic lingering around him like soft, errant fireflies. His magic, combined with the woman's, refused to disperse immediately. He pushed himself to his feet, a bit unsteady, and started to retrieve a handkerchief from his back pocket when his now magically enhanced sight caught wavering images a foot away from him.

Powell moved forward carefully as blood sensed blood. He could smell it, taste it, see it, *feel* it. He knew there was blood there, he had seen it marked off before starting the ritual, but here was something only forensics and magic could tell him.

This blood did not belong to the woman.

Powell looked around, his eyes red-rimmed as the magic pulled him closer. This blood bore something he'd not seen in a long time.

Markings.

Blood always contained the genetic marker of its maker, that of the parent. But this blood held something else. Something Powell couldn't identify immediately. His heart raced as he knelt at the small, dried area closest to the wall.

With a deep breath he pushed his bloodied hands into *this* blood—the connection was instantaneous. The magic rushing through his body revealed the evidence of something...of *someone* wounded, and abruptly he was behind that person's eyes.

Powell yelled out as a huge white wolf jumped at him, but he turned and moved away. The wolf vanished, and he was running up a flight of steps. Pain seared his side, and he grabbed at it, the hurt nearly taking his breath away—

He was shot!

Stumbling to the left, and then the right, Powell grew more

confused as the person's direction continued to shift, as if he wasn't sure where to go. And then he was on the floor, looking into the dead girl's face, the bullet hole visible between her eyes, the blood pooling on the tile below her.

And then Powell was out, inside of himself, lying on his back again. His breathing ragged, the dwarf muttered calming spells as he blinked rapidly, trying to clear his vision. And as he pushed himself up into a sitting position, he saw something swirling in the blood on the floor, on his hands, on the wall—

A face he didn't recognize spoke to him, a woman with hair the color of fire.

*"The Soldier will come with weapons of truth, and Dark Resonance shall fall beneath the love of knowledge."*

He had no idea how long he sat on that floor, only that it took some time before he could sit up without wanting to vomit. He pushed himself against the wall and took in several deep breaths as he thought about all he'd seen.

But now Powell had a story—a ribbon of events.

The girl had a partner who had left her alone for a time. And then he'd killed her. At some point the third person, whose blood he'd just tasted, was wounded, shot in the side, and he touched his right side, where the pain still echoed. Then he'd stumbled and seen the girl's body before escaping the Annex.

Standing, Powell found the handkerchief by the door and rubbed what blood he could off. He was going to need a cleansing shower as soon as possible. He pulled his commlink from his pocket and slipped the monocle on. Booting up, he found a halfway decent signal and logged into his AR.

He typed up what he saw as it was fresh in his mind, including the prophecy. He already knew those words—they were the bane of his employer's existence. Caliban feared only one thing—the prophecy of his shaman. The foretelling of his death. Powell had heard those words again—spoken by the passing spirit of a shaman, within the mingled blood of one who he believed was a technomancer.

Was it possible this one, this technomancer, was the Soldier? And what would Powell be rewarded if he brought him to the feet of Caliban, wounded, or even dead?

He smiled as he encrypted the missive and sent it off.

The reward would be exactly what Powell wanted.

To see the Resonance Realms—and become a god.

# CHAPTER TWENTY-SEVEN

## GiTm0

Welcome back to GiTm0, *omae*; your last connection was 6 hours, 8 minutes, 4 seconds ago

### BOLOs

Just a reminder—this board's got less than six hours before it terminates in your comms. Send your sprites out twenty-four hours after that for the new link.

New names received in conjunction with missing technomancers: LexieXXX, Xomar, and Gimmenuyen. Full list available [Link][Guest] but don't read the list online. And don't forget, these runners are out for the nuyen, and they don't give a damn about us.

### IMPORTANT: ALERT!

Everyone, listen up! EasterBunnyun tried to expose this board—but luckily Shyammo thought he might try something like that. Because the piece of drek is still out there and angry, we're going to be mixing up our online presence a bit. We've been contacted by someone who wants to sponsor us on an incredibly secure host—one the corps can't hack. Neither can people like Easter. We're still going over the contracts, crossing our Ts and dotting our Is. But if this works out, we should be able to deliver more information to our cause.

So those who have given Easter any real world information—hide now. He's apparently in league with Renraku. He's not your friend; he is your enemy. And if you can, change your handle and then contact Shyammo. She'll go through the re-approval process.

Remember, GOD is always watching.

**NeW oNLiNE**
   * About two hours ago we were given a series of pictures and a short vid clip of what happened to HipOldMan. If you click on this link and watch, please download and feed to every outlet you can think of. Add the following information:

   The images you see are real. This is not a joke. Contagion Games is riddled with dissonance. We believe this is a condition created on purpose by the host administrator, Bellex. If you are a technomancer, stay away from the Contagion host. So far we've lost over fifty to this host. This isn't in the media, and it never will be if we don't put it there.
   To be clear, this is a trap. Stay away from the Contagion host.

**DISSONANCE**
\>\>\>\>Open Thread/Subhost561.768.1
\>\>\>\>Thread Access Restrictions: <Yes/**No**>
\>\>\>\>Format: <**Open Post**/Comment Only/Read Only>
\>\>\>\>File Attachment: <**Yes**/No>
\>\>\>\>Thread Descriptor: **STAY AWAY**
\>\>\>\>Thread Posted By User: Shyammo

- Again guys. As soon as you view it, if you can, feed it out with that paragraph. It's got code worked into the vid that'll allow any technomancer with only a single submersion under them to see the coordinates for the host.
- RoxJohn

- What. The. Hell? Did the game eat him? What about his body? That was just his persona, wasn't it?
- 404Flames

- He's also physically missing. Now you see why we're cautious. Evidently whatever that ichor is, and Shyammo is certain it's dissonance, it's got the same kind of software working for it that GOD has when they pinpoint your location. Keep all IPs spoofed and rotate them.
- RoxJohn

- Rox, you got any more on this deal you're working on?
- MoonShine

- Oh dear god. That was horrible. I've encrypted it, tagged it and sent it, Rox. I'm also working on a protocol to follow a loop if the tag isn't opened. It'll just kick the vid to them again from a different IP.
- LongTong

- Can't right now, Moon. And it's good to see you!
- RoxJohn

- Good to see you too. Can I contact you or Shyammo offline?
- MoonShine

- Mine's sent, too.
- Silk

- Ditto.
- 404Flames

- Anyone got anything else on that Horizon murder? They're really not running that in the media, not like I thought they would.
- LongTong

- Yeah. Send to Shy first. She's online a lot more than I am.
- RoxJohn

- Sent. I copied Long's idea.
- Venerator

- I'm not changing my handle just for that piece of drek. Anyone in the mood to look for Easter, send me a PM.
- 404Flames

# CHAPTER TWENTY-EIGHT

## HITORI TETSU'S APARTMENT
## LOS ANGELES
## EARLY SATURDAY MORNING

Hitori Tetsu's apartment was just outside of Ares' home office buildings near the Mega-Tri. Even with the late—or early—hour, depending on one's lifestyle, denizens were out and about. A few troll and human groups. An ork and two dwarves standing on the corner, each in their own Augmented Reality.

Mack, Shayla, Slamm-0!, and Preacher stood on opposing sides of the street, watching the quaint, two-story building where Hitori Tetsu lived. For the past half hour, they'd seen no movement inside or outside. Slamm-0! was busy hacking into the apartment, so they were all waiting for him.

Preacher was stationed around the rear in the alley near a convenience store and reported in his fifteen-minute interval of all clear.

No Stuffer Shacks in this neighborhood. No, this was the classier stuff. Packaged foods here were made of the real thing—nothing synthetic. Or man made. All natural. Organic.

Snorting, Mack blinked once to call up his AR and focused through his night vision. Still nothing.

<*Entrance B, David and Goliath advance two, Spike, you still looking?*>

The code was simple really. David—that was himself. Goliath—well that was Preacher without saying. Spike was Slamm-0!. Shayla's code was Goldilocks. And since her name wasn't called, she would stay in place.

Slamm-0! was already in place near the entrance, and Mack just told Preacher to move and meet him there.

A chilled breeze brushed the sweat beading on Mack's upper lip. October in Los Angeles.

<*Spike found the key under the cupboard,*> Shayla messaged.

Mack checked both sides of the street and stayed close to the shadows. Shrubbery, neatly trimmed and watered, surrounded the ground floor, preventing any easy window access, but it did allow for deeper shadows.

Once Mack was in place, he took up a position outside the side door and waited for Spike to use his key. Within a few seconds, the door *clicked*, and Mack yanked it open and stepped inside. Luckily, the interior lighting didn't come on as was typically programmed into these luxury buildings. The AR systems usually activated to the tenant's RFID tag, or saved preference files, and changed its surroundings to virtually meet its clients' visual needs. Of course, they had to log into AR to get the system's full impact—but who wasn't always logged in nowadays?

There was enough subdued lighting along the baseboards to show him the carpet was a soft, plush beige. His boots sunk into it, muffling any sound he would have made. The apartment was on the second floor. Pausing at the stairs, he tapped the button on his AR again.

**<*Goliath? You find Spike's key?*>**

"Yeah," a soft, purring voice said behind him. "I did. Spike's right behind me."

Mack stifled a yelp as he spun around to see the large combat mage standing beside him. "*God....*" he hissed. "Don't *do* that."

"Sorry, boss," Preacher said as he pointed at the floor. "But this carpet makes it real easy to be quiet." He smiled around his tusks. "I like it. Might put it in my lake house."

The side door opened again, and Slamm-0! stepped in to join them, weapon ready. Wires trailed from his temple to the bag strapped to his hip—he was still in the building's host.

Mack motioned them to follow as he ascended the steps.

On the second floor, it was easy to find Hitori Tetsu's apartment just two doors down. Mack looked at Slamm-0!, and after a few seconds the apartment door popped open. Pulling out one of his Predators, Mack pushed the door ajar with the barrel and waited a few seconds before stepping inside.

Once he, Slamm-0! and Preacher were in the front door, Mack closed it. That triggered the domestic reality.

The lights came on and a pleasant sounding voice spoke in Japanese, then re-spoke again in English.

*"Welcome, Hitori—it has been five hours, twelve minutes, and eight seconds since your last visit. Your preferences file is corrupted. Please restate preferred temperature, ambiance, and aroma."*

Mack turned and looked back at Preacher, who shrugged. These systems usually came equipped with different kinds of alarms that could trigger by either responding—or not responding.

So...which to do?

Slamm-0! spoke first. "Temp at seventy-six Fahrenheit, ambiance, daytime mid-afternoon, and aroma, vanilla cinnamon." He paused. "Light on the cinnamon."

Preacher turned slowly and looked back at him. "Vanilla cinnamon?"

"Girls typically like the smell," the hacker said as he moved past Preacher and into the living room. "Better than stale."

Mack didn't go any further in. "Did that voice say Hitori's last visit was five hours ago?"

"Yeah, it did," Slamm-0! replied. "You think she's been here and not missing?"

"Or her brother was here earlier." Preacher pointed at the ceiling. "Someone's paying to keep this place open."

The apartment expanded before them as the doorway emptied out onto a large living area. The carpet here, like that in the hall, was deep and plush. Mack resisted the sudden urge to remove his boots and sink his bare feet into it. The apartment's general coloring was light pink, with soft whites and pastel blues and greens. He checked his AR, and realized he was receiving the present environment. Two clicks, and the coloring changed to deep maroon and forest green. The carpet kept its tactile feel of thick, but the appearance went from white to gold.

"This environment app is state-of-the art," Mack said. "I could use this in my club."

"Well," Preacher said softly. "From my perspective, it's all sort of generic." He lowered his weapon as he walked into the kitchen. "And unused."

That made sense, since Preacher wasn't using his commlink to receive the apartment environment controls. Preacher used as little technology as possible while on a run, or a simple B&E. That way he wasn't hindered if he needed to use a bit of magic.

At first, Mack was blinded by the beauty of the place. The

floor to ceiling windows looked out over a complex garden and pond. The U-shaped couch faced a soft, crackling gas fire set inside a wide fireplace of smooth cream and caramel-colored slate. It wasn't until Preacher commented about a tea cup on the low oak coffee table that Mack shut off his AR.

The tea cup appeared, the fire disappeared. Beside it sat a saucer with the decayed, moldy remains of what might have been a bagel. Months old.

"Slamm-0!—shut off your AR."

The hacker nodded, and then whistled as he looked around.

A fine layer of dust covered the cup and saucer, the coffee table desktop, and when he put his hand on the sofa cushion closest to him, it too came away covered in dust.

"No one's living here," Mack muttered. "But the voice said someone was here five hours ago." That one fact gnawed at him. "Slamm-0!, do you have access to the apartment host's environmental program? Is there a way to find out who was in here five hours ago?"

"I've been looking—but the system files are corrupted, as well as the preferences. I'll keep looking for a security profile."

Straightening, Mack walked into a side room. It was a bedroom, nearly as spacious as the living room. It had the floor-to-ceiling windows too, but they were covered by thin sheers of soft pink. The bed was unmade, the sheets and duvet pulled away as if someone had prepared for bed a minute ago.

A few pieces of clothing, personal essentials, were scattered on the other side of the room near the bathroom. Mack turned the light on in there and was surprised to see a counter full of makeup. The bathtub still held a dish of half-used soap. A crumpled shower cap lay on the floor beside the toilet. Towels hung in disarray on their racks. And everything—every nook and cranny of the room—was covered in a thin layer of dust.

He heard Preacher behind him. "I don't like this," he said, his voice a quiet rumble.

Mack nodded slowly as he squinted up at the troll. "It's like she just left for work—"

"—and never came back," Slamm-0! finished as he joined them in the bedroom. "And it feels wrong in here."

"*Feels* wrong?"

"He's right." The troll nodded. "The whole place has the feeling of something interrupted."

Mack had to agree. He too could sense an overwhelming feeling of—unfinished. As if Miss Tetsu's life was in limbo.

"The kitchen is just like this," Preacher said as he nodded to the bathroom behind Mack. "She made soykaf, and there's still crumbs in the toaster. The butter was out on the counter with a knife." He sighed. "It's like the place has been preserved since the moment she left."

Mack moved past Preacher back into the living room. Most control centers in apartments like this were built into the wall. Behind the couch, he saw a blank wall that might hold what he was looking for, and said, "Ops."

He heard movement like gears turning, but the wall remained smooth.

"Hey, in here," Slamm-0! called out.

Mack stepped back into the bedroom. The wall to the right of the bed seamed and parted. The two sides slid back and a desk came forward. Dimensional screens flickered to life, showing a meter-wide holo image of a desktop. The image on it was of a young woman and a man.

Mack recognized the man from the dossier Charis gave him. Kazuma Tetsu.

"That's the sister?" Preacher asked as he came up behind him. Since the rig was powered via cameras and projectors, the mid-air image was visible to the troll without his monocle.

Mack pulled up his own AR desktop and clicked open a folder. The information he'd uncovered on Hitori Tetsu was spotty, and there had been no image stored on any host he could find. "I think we can assume that's her. I'll do an image capture and save it."

With practiced ease, Mack saved the image, then started moving around the desktop. There weren't any high-level encryption protocols. In fact, he didn't encounter any security at all. But neither were there any personal files.

Slamm-0! confirmed his findings. "Someone's already been in this system and wiped it clean."

"Clean?" Preacher asked from his right.

"Yeah." Slamm-0! reached up and tapped some of the folders that opened on the holographic screen. "Nothing. Looks like the whole machine's been through a complete system reinstall."

"Wait—Mack—" Preacher reached out and pointed to an icon on the upper left of the desktop. "I know that symbol."

"Oh?" Mack double-clicked it. The screen went dark, and the two of them were treated to a deep, bass rattling note, followed by a familiar piece of classical music. "That's from *Carmina Burana*, right?"

"Yeah...I've seen this," Slamm-0! said. "It's a promo."

The screen rezzed in, and a middle-aged man dressed in a silver and blue bodysuit appeared. *"Hello, and thank for you for taking the time to test this demo for Contagion Games Unlimited. We here at Contagion want to give consumers the best Matrix experience in gaming hosts, so we've created this demo for you to try out, enjoy for thirty days, and then report your impressions back to us. That's all it takes! And, once the game is released, if you choose, you can receive your very own copy of TechnoHack!"*

Mack frowned and looked at Slamm-0!. "Game demo?"

"Yeah—I got one, too. Supposed to be able to play a technomancer or a hacker online—sort of a test to see who's better. And you save the world." He frowned. "Boss...is this what Hestaby was talking about? Is this it? You think that game somehow got Hitori?"

"I don't know." Mack shut the blathering man off and continued scanning Hitori's desktop. "But that's not why we're here. Besides that game, anything that would have identified this as Hitori Tetsu's system is gone." He stepped back. "Which makes sense if someone's wiped the place. That's why the environmental controls were set to ask for preferences."

"But why?"

Mack moved a little deeper into the system, not entirely submerging himself, but going deep enough for a closer look. He pulled back and blinked a few times to clear his head and his vision before looking up at Slamm-0!. "Not sure yet. But I can't find any signatures. And there are always footprints."

"You think it was the brother?" Slamm-0! turned sharply and left the bedroom.

Mack didn't voice an opinion on that. Of course, if her brother was indeed a technomancer like Charis and Hestaby believed, it might be possible to remove the information and not leave a trail. He just didn't know.

An AR window opened with Slamm-0!'s icon. <*We're being watched.*>

Mack made sure not to show any outward surprise at that statement, and told them to keep looking around. <***By who? Tetsu?***>

<No.>
***<They're watching us? Hearing us? Through the environmental system?>***
<Nope. Remember the system said someone had been here five hours ago? They left a calling card. We just didn't see it because it wasn't deployed yet.>

Deployed? Mack froze, just before before he heard shots fired from the living room. He was already pulling up the apartment's layout grid in the holovid and telling the system to latch onto anything the size of a bird of prey—and moving fast.

Another shot roared, and he saw a flash of blue light from the door to the living room as Slamm-0! ducked through, then slammed his back against the bedroom side of the door, pistol held over his chest.

Mack looked back at the screen—but the only thing moving was Preacher's red dot as he ran past Slamm-0! through the door. Mack heard another shot, saw the flare in the doorway, than a crash. Within a few seconds, the big troll stepped back into the bedroom, holding up a smashed drone. It was still smoking, its legs twitching feebly. It looked like he had stepped on it.

"I hate these things," he said.

Slamm-0! took it from him—carefully—and brought it to where Mack stood in front of the vids. Mack held it while Slamm-0! began disassembling the underbelly. "What're you—"

"This is a Lockheed Optic x2 model. High end. Very expensive. And if this belongs to who I think it does..." Slamm-0! let the sentence trail off as he pulled a wire from the bag at his hip and jammed it into the drone.

Within seconds the vids in front of them flickered, and a new set of data screens appeared. Windows opened and closed as Mack looked between Slamm-0!'s face and the vids. He looked over at Preacher, who pulled the sheets off the bed and wrapped them around his arm.

"You were hit?"

"Just a flesh wound. Shayla said she'd patch it up for me."

Mack looked down at the drone and saw the added gun barrel integrated into the side. "I didn't think this model had weapons."

"It doesn't—usually," Slamm-0! said as he worked, his eyes never leaving the larger screens. "It's been modified. And I think I know by who."

"What are you doing?"

"Following a lead," was all the hacker said as the screens came up, numbers flashed across and the information images disappeared.

The kid was fast. Faster then Blackwater had been. And good, if he was doing what Mack suspected he was.

Abruptly one of the screens blackened, filled by white noise and then:

"—wrong with it?" a familiar voice asked.

"I told you, that ugly drekking troll set it off. Damn thing deployed."

"You mean it started shooting?"

"Yeah. But my screen's gone."

Mack didn't recognize the hobgoblin half-visible in the window. But that didn't matter as much as the voice he did recognize. And when he saw Cole Blackwater's shiny chrome skull come into view, he clenched his jaw.

Now he saw that wasn't reality. *<Slamm-0!, what are we seeing?>*

*<The hobgoblin likes to put cameras in all his drones because he likes to watch. He's a sick bastard that way. And given he's a huge narcissist, I was pretty sure he had one in his RCC. Just so he can send a message to whoever he's about to kill or blow up or decimate. So I hacked it and now we're seeing them, but they can't see us.>*

Blackwater's eye came close as he examined something. "Cole Blackwater," Mack said through gritted teeth.

"That blows," Preacher said behind him, now wrapped up in the sheet like a toga.

"And the other one?"

Slamm-0! sighed. "Clockwork. A notorious decker and hater of technomancers. Looks like your old hacker buddy is on the other side of the Matrix this time."

"Can they hear us?" Preacher asked.

"Why, of course we can!" the hobgoblin said as he looked into the RCC camera. "Nice to see you again, Slamm-0! Say, is that pretty little technomancer girlfriend with you this time? NeoNET's offer is still open—"

Slamm-0! ended the communication with an abrupt blank screen. He yanked the cables out, grabbed the drone, and threw it on the floor, then pointed his gun at it and fired. Several times.

Eventually Preacher walked over and put a hand on his shoulder. "It's dead."

"But he isn't."

"What the hell?" Mack narrowed his eyes at Slamm-0! "Technomancer girlfriend? You and this Clockwork got history?"

But Slamm-0! was already back in AR, hands blurring as they worked. "You could say that."

An alert told Mack he had a message with an attachment. "You send me that?"

"Yeah. It's the address to their grandmother's house. The grandmother who isn't a grandmother. I took it from Clockwork's commlink. I've already verified its location and legitimacy."

"You hacked that hobgoblin's commlink while you were in that drone?"

"Something like that."

Mack stared at Slamm-0! and caught the subtle smile on the young man's face. "You used the comm and spoke to keep his attention focused on you while *you* were hacking *him*."

Slamm-0! didn't agree, but he didn't deny it either.

*Well, I'll be damned. Wonder if this guy wants a permanent gig.*

"Clock's biggest weakness is he's full of himself. He thinks he's untouchable." Slamm-0! grinned. "I just counted coup. We need to go."

"All right—other than the sheet, Preacher—let's un-ass this place and get going." He planned on questioning Slamm-0! more later on this technomancer girlfriend. Given what Hestaby had requested for his job, he felt a little bit easier having someone who was sympathetic to the TMs.

But a girlfriend?

They were out of the apartment and back in the GMC in under two minutes. Shayla checked the address, but drove in the opposite direction.

"Where are you going?" Mack asked.

"To the club. Given the time of day, and the fact that if Tetsu's heading there and any other players in this game might be as well, I figured we'll want an aerial arrival."

# CHAPTER TWENTY-NINE

**DRACO POWELL'S OFFICE
UNDISCLOSED LOCATION
LOS ANGELES
EARLY SATURDAY MORNING**

Draco Powell sat back in his tailor-made chair. He wore his monocle and his gloves, his attention focused on the icon taking up most of his AR's desktop.

His office was safely ensconced within a converted warehouse on the edge of the city, one of Prospero's holdings in the Los Angeles area—like a few of their holdings throughout the Pueblo Corporate Council. He had the building converted into a holding pen, one part of it surrounded by a Faraday field, something he found blocked out a technomancer's ability to connect with the Matrix. Or connect to anything else.

When he put his hand down to stroke Hyde's fur, he felt a twinge of regret and deep sadness as he remembered his pet was no longer there. His wolf had been killed by that damn security guard, and his prize had gotten away.

But not before Hyde had injected a tag into the back of Tetsu's neck. Unfortunately, with the technocritter dead, Draco had no way of utilizing the advantage.

He chose Shax, an ork whose technomancer abilities attracted Draco after his move from Aztlan, to replace his wolf. Shax had been one of the dwarf's early extractions, but Draco found the tusked creature had a natural affinity for the dark. And so far, the ork had proven himself loyal, and someone who could be trusted.

Throughout that partnership, Draco watched Shax's persona darken to something he knew was unredeemable. Caliban said

Shax was a servant of dissonance, something the AI had been studying. Whatever it was, it had also changed the ork's physical appearance. Shax was thin for his kind, his head a bit larger than it should be, and his gaze was something Draco refused to get caught in.

The ork stood by his side during the communiqué with Caliban's mouthpiece. Puppet, more like it. Her name was Sycorax, and she made his skin crawl. She was pale like bleached bones, with black hair, lips, and nails. Her eyes were so dark, devoid of color, and her teeth... Draco didn't like Sycorax. And he knew the feeling was mutual. "I believe my suspicions are correct. I sent you my notes on exactly what the blood said."

"Which could have been your overactive imagination. Everyone devoted to Caliban knows about the prophecy. And I saw nothing in that report to say this particular technomancer is the Soldier."

He shifted in his chair. She was being stupid. Very stupid by not giving Caliban what he found. It wasn't a coincidence the blood had given him the exact prophecy that drove the AI to find a way to transcend his Matrix existence and touch the Resonance Realms. Since the shaman they'd extracted from Mount Shasta had first given Caliban the prophecy, only to be promptly killed in a fit of childish rage on the AI's part, it had searched the Matrix for anything remotely resembling the Soldier, and killed it as well. No—*annihilated* it.

Shax shifted on his feet, but kept quiet. Draco knew the ork was just as disgusted as he was with this tool.

"Sycorax, let me propose a scenario. Let's say something was missed during Caliban's search—it's just a proposal. And let's consider that magic—something you have no concept of—revealed maybe not *the* clue, but *a* clue, presented a sign for Caliban as to where to find the Soldier and the code? And you, in your infinite wisdom, denied him the chance to investigate for himself?"

Sycorax's expression didn't change. It never did. Except for a slight narrowing of her eyes. It was the only sign Draco had that he'd touched a nerve—one he'd played with before. He waited, as did Shax, to see if the harridan would take the bait.

And he wasn't disappointed.

"I'll consider your...proposal. But for now, I suggest you do what you were sent there to do and either extract more technomancers, or lists of known subjects. I'm afraid Caliban..." she glanced off to her right. "Had a bit of a—moment."

"Oh?" Draco leaned forward. "Would this have anything to do with the new blackout on the UV host?"

"One of the technomancers caught in the trap was able to send a message before he was consumed. Caliban didn't react well to that."

"Sycorax," Draco put his gloved hands on the desk. "Please tell me he didn't short out the entire collection."

"No. But a fourth of it before we could calm him down. We've been incinerating bodies all morning."

Shax finally spoke up, his voice deep with a touch of raspiness. "Who did this technomancer send a message to? Have you taken care of the problem?" When Sycorax didn't answer immediately, the ork laughed. "You haven't!"

"You need to keep your pet in line, Draco. I'm afraid this one's not as obedient as Hyde was." She smiled. The facial change did not reach her eyes. "We're handling the problem. Just bring in what you were sent to bring in. I'll...consider what we discussed."

The connection was severed.

Draco pursed his lips. "Shax, you think you can trace who received a message from someone in the game host in the past twenty-four hours? Find a last minute send?"

"Easy." The ork held out his gloved hands and moved them around the space in front of him. "Done."

"Good. Alert me when you have a name." He cleared his AR desktop and sat back. "Any success hacking into the tag on Tetsu?"

"It doesn't work that way," Shax said as he faced Draco. "Though I have attempted it."

"Have you found any other clues as to where he might have gone? Or who helped him out of the building? Preliminary reports say the alarm was tripped at the source—meaning in the building maintenance grid. Someone either did it physically, or it was hacked. No one was caught on camera, so it had to be someone from the outside. I would assume they left a signature of some kind."

"More than likely. But I don't have admin access to KE's mainframe. Hacking them isn't as easy, and you don't want me to raise any alarms."

Sometimes Shax's mind amazed Draco. He was used to his flunkies being stupid. But this ork was far from that. "No. I don't. I guess it's possible Tetsu has friends inside KE."

"The security guard?"

"No. Hapless idiot, that one. Keep looking into it. I believe if we find who helped him, we can find where he is and were that data is." Draco pulled up Tetsu's KE personnel file again and rescanned his relatives.

The only known family member was his father, and he lived in Chiba. Retired. All reports he'd fingered from KE said the old man was recovering from heart surgery. Sister missing. He was pretty sure she was the reason the technomancer had been digging around in Horizon's business. But Hitori had worked for Ares prior. He searched through his contacts and came up with an old name—one he hadn't used in a long time.

Ah, but favors were timeless, weren't they?

"Keep working on finding out who helped Tetsu. I have a call to make."

The ork left the office as Draco set up his call. He had to go through a few people, reroute tracers he detected, and made it look like the call initiated from Horizon.

"Debiassi."

"Hello, Carol. It's been a while."

Carol Debiassi. Now that was a story. One of the survivors of the Renraku Arcology shutdown. Carol and he had met inside that hell and survived, along with seven others in their group. Draco had gotten them out before Deus found them. And for that, all seven of them owed him favors. This was the first one he'd ever cashed in.

The line went quiet long enough for Draco to check to see if she hung up. Then, "What do you want?"

"I want information. That's all. And it's not any kind of secret information."

"On what?"

"A former employee. Hitori Tetsu."

There was a long pause. "Where do you want it sent?"

He gave her his client email, making the transaction look like business as usual. An employee from Horizon requesting a file from Ares. When his commlink pinged to let him know he'd received it, he opened the file to double check.

Yes...this file was more than he expected, and Ares collected more on their employees than Knight Errant.

"Are we done now?"

He detected the hint of nervousness in her voice. She didn't want him near her, or her family, of which he'd kept up with since their escape. "We're done, Carol. Please, have a nice life."

Once he severed the connection, Draco started sifting through the documents. Hitori was twenty-six, a well-known artist in her field, headhunted by Ares... It also said she had been caught in the Crash of '64, along with her brother, whom she had been playing a game with.

He searched for Kazuma's name and it came up frequently. Hitori and Kazuma were twins, fraternal, and both had been born in the UCAS. Their mother was an elf, but didn't appear to be involved in the kids' upbringing. Draco couldn't find a name in any of the files.

Their father was from Chiba, and took the kids back home for several years before returning and settling in San Francisco. While living there, their fraternal grandmother passed away and their father returned home, but left the kids in the care of an old family friend, Mama Risen. "Really? Is that her name?"

When their father returned, he kept the family friend on retainer, and it was this Risen who had raised the kids.

Draco did a quick search of living residents in the San Francisco area. He came across two M. Risens. One was deceased as of three years ago. The other moved. The name was Myddrin.

Myddrin?

He searched for a Myddrin Risen in Los Angeles and came up with the name, and an address. Unfortunately M. Risen had died less than a year ago. Draco changed his search to estate holdings and distributions, adding in Hitori, Kazuma, and Myddrin.

He laughed when he found a house east of the main city of Los Angeles, left to Hitori and Kazuma Tetsu. The house was still in Myddrin's name, but the ownership had been transferred to the twins. All the property taxes were paid up, and the yard maintained by a private lawn company.

"Shax!"

The ork was back in his office within a second. Draco assumed he had remained outside the door. "Yes?"

"I'm sending you information about a house, its address, and its owner, and I need you to see if the place has a host. See if it's crackable."

"You want me to settle in?"

"We're both going. Get the van ready, and meet me downstairs in an hour."

Shax nodded then stopped. "Is there anything else?"

Draco removed his monocle. "Yes. You have access to the Gestalt lists?"

"No. But I can get it."

"Good. Look up Hitori Tetsu. See if she's there."

"Is she important?"

The dwarf starting packing his commlink and monocle away. "I think she could be used to gain you and me a very, very large payday." He removed his glove and thought of something. "Oh, and Shax?"

The ork turned.

"I need a kill file activated on Carol Debiassi. Do it quickly. Accident, and all that rubbish."

"Consider it done."

Draco watched him leave. The ork looked almost giddy. But then, he had just given him permission to do the one thing Shax liked doing the most.

Kill someone.

# CHAPTER THIRTY

## OUTSIDE THE RISEN RESIDENCE

"This is crazy."

Netcat glanced at Silk. The dark-skinned rigger sat behind the wheel of what she called her prized Hummer while Netcat occupied the passenger's side. Kazuma and Moon were in the back, both with their eyes closed, checking out the house.

Across from the neighborhood where Tetsu's 'grandmother's' house sat was a used car lot. The security had been easy enough to dispose of with no discernible spikes in overwatch. Silk had slipped the refitted Hummer into a slot between a large black van with the windows knocked out and a smaller Honda. With the lights off and the tinted windows hiding them from the outside world, the vehicle looked like just another abandoned vehicle for sale.

"Why're you on edge?" Silk was looking at her now. "You worried about Jack?"

"No. He's great, and I miss him terribly. It's..." Netcat shrugged.

"Is it Slamm-0!? You two having problems? I mean...I am a little concerned that you're here with us and not with him and your son."

"It's complicated, and I'm not even sure where to begin talking about it, even if I wanted to. But I don't."

There was a beat of silence.

Then, "Okay, it's nuyen. Bills. But that's what it always is, isn't it?"

Silk slowly nodded. "Kids are expensive."

"Yeah, they are. But we love him to death. Even Junior loves him."

"That your critter?"

"Yeah." Netcat wished Junior were here with her now. She'd love to feel that fuzzy cat purring on her lap. "With Jack, it's hard because we both can't always be working. And in the past few months, I've been crazy busy trying to fight for technomancer rights, free the ones we know about—and it's not a job I'm getting paid for. Slamm-0!'s turned down quite a few good paying jobs because I was...busy." Her shoulders slumped. "I know he's itching to get back out there. I mean...we've been playing it pretty safe since the baby. Especially after that jackass tried to sell me off to NeoNET."

"Who? What?" Silk frowned at her. "Wait—you talking about that run-in with Clockwork?"

"Bastard. Yeah. It was a few years ago, but I'm still a little jumpy about it. So's Slamm-0!. I know he worries when I'm out like this. We had a fight the other night before I came down here, and then another one right before I saw the dwarf outside Horizon."

Silk reached out and put her hand on Netcat's and squeezed. "It's going to be fine."

"He's not answering any of my calls—so that just makes me worried about him and the baby. Where is he? Is he okay? Did someone find him? Did he get into trouble? Am I a bad mother? Running off like this to save the world? Should I ditch this problem and go home? Find Slamm-0! and my little boy?" Netcat shrugged again. Eventually she smiled, and leaned her head toward Silk. "So...you and Soldat."

"He doesn't like being called that on this side of the commlink."

"Then why did he take it?"

"Oh...some guy told him to. A PI he's been talking to off and on while trying to find his sister. Said it would be important one day."

"It means soldier."

"Yeah, it does." Silk squeezed her hand again. "And he is a soldier, whether he'll acknowledge that or not. He's gotten a lot stronger since we met, both in the Matrix and physically. What you've seen of him isn't his better side. He was shot by that hacker while at the Annex, and that wound hasn't quite healed, and then having that damn technocritter bite the back of his neck didn't help. I think that whole encounter with the dwarf scared him."

"It would scare the hell out of me." Netcat looked out the

windshield at the silent house. "You think his sister's still alive?"

Silk looked out the window as well. "No. And I think deep down, he doesn't, either. On the surface, she's become this beacon he has to move toward. I'm terrified that if he finds out she's dead—" She took a deep breath as she looked at Netcat. "—if he sees the reality, it will destroy him."

Netcat could empathize. She'd seen what FastJack's disappearance and surrender to Cognitive Fragmentation Disorder had done to a lot of the runners in JackPoint. CFD was another nightmare she didn't want to think about—and so far they hadn't run into anyone infected with it. She wanted to keep it that way. She looked at Silk. "So, what else did this detective tell him?"

"He really didn't tell me much about it. Just to change his handle from Dancer to Soldat, keep searching for his sister and be on the look out for Caliban."

"Caliban? What's that?"

Silk shrugged. "I don't know. Kaz doesn't know either. But he said he added it to his search specifics. Then about a month ago, he found something while heading up the group cleaning out the Horizon Annex. He said it was minor, just a name on a manifest. But the manifest was in an encrypted file on one of the hosts there."

"And that's what he took?"

"Yeah. It was all kind of weird, though. That host wasn't connected—just old-style. And he didn't trust these new cyberdecks to hack it, so he took a vacation and went through his third submersion, looking for a better way to remove the data."

"Ah...let me guess. He learned how to skin link."

"Yeah. Not something I've mastered yet. But then my interest and talent has always been in rigging. I love the inner workings of things mechanical—even if I don't really need the mechanics. But I do have my old RCC—I keep it with me all the time. I also know I'll never really become that powerful in the Matrix, like Kazuma can, or you or Moon. Got too much cyberware."

"Don't think of it as a competition," Netcat said. "You're becoming the best at who and what you are. And that's all that's important. But, you helped him? That night?"

"Yeah. And everything was great—till this other hacker showed up and all hell broke lose. Luckily I was in the right place and spotted their rigger. Made nicey-nice with her RCC." Silk beamed with pride. "But then that girl got killed—which Kazuma did *not* do—

and those security guards. I had to pack up and get to the car and pick him up myself."

"And he's sure his sprite brought the data here?"

"I know he keeps an active, encrypted folder on this host. He's stored everything he's collected since Hitori disappeared in it." Silk sighed. "You know she disappeared on him before. Back in '73. He was trying to find her then, and ended up getting shot in a coffee shop when he stopped some hackers. Turned out Hitori was just fine."

"Where was she?"

"Submerging with a bunch of other technomancers. This was back when it was really all new, and she learned she could get more powerful by doing that. Went all beautiful mind on him and told him about the things she'd seen—the Resonance Realms—showed him what she could do. But Kazuma was terrified to submerge like that. To just let go. He'd been suffering from AIPS, and his headaches were debilitating."

"But he eventually did it?"

"Oh yeah. She talked him into it. That's when I met him. She wanted me to help them because she wanted to be there for him." Silk smirked. "So here he and I are."

"You make a great team."

"So do you and Slamm-0!. You're just going through the growing pains of raising a family. Maybe after this, Kaz and I can come see Jack?"

Netcat smiled. "I'd love that."

A noise from the back made the two of then turn in their seats. Kazuma had his eyes open, rubbing his face. Moonshine opened his while Netcat was watching him. "Well?" she prompted.

"On the outside," Moon began as he sat up. "Everything looks fine."

"And on the inside?" Silk said.

Kazuma pulled each of his arms over his head to stretch. "Someone's been here. I detected at least two other signatures. Couldn't read who they were—"

"But one of them was a technomancer. And a creepy one. The whole house system felt..." MoonShine shuddered. "Tainted."

"Dissonant TM," Netcat said. "I'd be willing to bet that was the dwarf. One of his people, going on the assumption that critter of his had been dissonant as well, looking around for that data. Did they get it?"

"No." Kazuma said. "Ponsu's got it buried so deep and encrypted so well even I couldn't get to it from here. And I didn't want to risk pointing out which system folder it was in, just in case they were still hanging around." He frowned as he looked out the window of the Hummer and then up.

"You sensed them?"

When Kaz didn't answer, Moon did. "Just the signatures. They've come and gone."

But Netcat was watching Kazuma. "Kaz...what's wrong?"

"I don't know. I get the feeling we're being watched. I'm being watched."

"What? You mean from some point higher?"

"Yeah...but not by..." And his expression moved from worried to confused. "While I was in AR, I kept getting flashes of seeing the house from the sky. I thought maybe I'd accidentally tapped into some helicopter's security camera—"

"That's pretty unlikely," Silk said.

"I know. But..." He pointed out the window. "There's this small shadow that keeps moving on top of the house."

"You think it's one of the dwarf's people?" Netcat leaned into the front dash and looked at the house through the windshield.

"No. This is small. And it's more of a...feeling..."

Suddenly Netcat laughed as she looked back at him. "Kaz, you're feeling a critter. Like my Junior. You felt it before?"

He looked surprised. "No."

"Then don't worry about it. If it doesn't feel like the wolf did, then it's not tainted." She chewed on her lower lip as she looked at him, but didn't really see him. "So here's the deal—how did anyone else find this piece of property? You said you kept it hidden. It's not even in your name?"

"I can only assume someone got it through Hitori's personnel file at Ares. I have a copy of it because she gave it to me. I told her when I saw it that she had too much personal information on it, and suggested if she was going to go out there and be an artist by day and a technomancer vigilante by night, she needed to keep a lot more of her life private." He raked his long fingers through his hair. "I'm assuming she didn't listen to me. She never listens to me."

"So..." Silk reached back between the driver and passenger seats and put her hand against his cheek. He put his hand on hers and smiled. "Do we go in, baby? You think it's safe enough?"

"I think we should wait. Just in case mine and Moon's intrusion was noticed or we triggered something."

"I didn't trigger anything," Moon said from behind Kazuma. "I'm like a ghost."

"You look like a ghost," Netcat smiled. "That cooler has some snacks in it. I know how hungry I am after being online for any length of time."

Both men hit the food, with Moon grabbing a moon pie and Kazuma a bag of nuts. Netcat made a face at the two of them. They'd been online for over an hour looking through the house. If their presence had triggered anything—wouldn't they already know it?

"So we wait an hour?" Silk looked back at the men.

Everyone nodded.

She kicked the seat back and looked at Netcat. "So, tell me about Jack."

# CHAPTER THIRTY-ONE

## RISEN RESIDENCE

*Boss? Why is that bird hanging around?*

Kazuma smiled at Ponsu. They kept to the shadows as they approached. Netcat used her e-sense to make sure no one was near. When they faced the house, Kazuma pulled up a small AR window and used his admin access to his grannie's house host. On the screen he could see the wear and tear on the outside of the virtual door—where someone had recently tried to break into the host. <*I don't know, Ponsu. But it's not important right now. You ready to retrieve the data?*>

*Yes Boss. Someone else has been here. Actually, several someone elses.*

<*I can see that. You identify any of their signatures?*>

The golden swan frowned at him as she shrank in size. *Yes. One of them is that wolf-hacker from the Annex. The other is...* The sprite shivered. *The other is something scary.*

<*Something scary? Can you clarify that?*>

*It's part of that shadow, Boss. That thing that's darkening the realms.*

Kazuma reached out and touched Netcat's arm so she wouldn't run off without him. <*Darkening the realms? Ponsu, what are you talking about?*>

*I don't know Boss. But it's getting bigger and it's making everything dark.*

Netcat's window opened in his AR. <*Kaz? What's wrong?*>

<*Ponsu's detected someone's here–says he's a part of that darkness I keep seeing in the resonance.*>

Netcat's eyes widened in the dim light. <*What? Kaz, you're

starting to freak me out. I don't like the idea of someone being part of that nasty in the Matrix. It's like a dark resonance. Let's just get this and go.>

<Ponsu, is this a person that's been at my grandmother's host?>

Yes.

<Is he still here?>

I–can't tell. He hides in the shadows.

Kazuma heard the soft, bell-like sounds of the wind chime he'd bought his grannie before she died. Hitori had gone missing the first time, and he told his grannie to bring it inside as a signal should anyone other than her be in the house.

Since her death, he'd kept it hanging on the porch as a tribute to her. But now, it wasn't there. No one else knew that signal. Had he taken it inside during this last visit and didn't remember it? Or had Hitori?

<What's wrong now?> Netcat asked.

<The wind chime's missing. It not being there on the porch was a signal between my grandmother and me.>

<A signal?>

<In case something was wrong.>

<Kaz...it was probably stolen by kids or vandals before the security system kicked in. Or it fell and broke. Were you born this paranoid, or does it come with your job?>

<Let's just say since my sister disappeared–I've run into a lot of obstacles.>

He entered the images that opened the door and the environmental host inside. Kazuma silently overrode the 'lights on' command as they crossed the street and padded up to the front door. The grounds outside looked freshly mowed, the white stone path leading to the front door swept, the shrubs outside precisely trimmed, and the porch cleaned.

Netcat looked at him. He could just see her features under the moonlight, shadows pooling in the hollows of her eyes and under her nose. "You okay?"

He shook his head. But he wasn't sure if the feeling of being watched was because Ponsu had him on edge, or if they really were being watched. "You sense *anyone* around? All I can sense is that bird."

"What bird?"

"The one on the roof."

She tilted her head to the side. "I can sense him. No, her. Technocritter, all right. But as for anyone else around, no. And the house feels empty inside."

With a quick look up and down the street, he grabbed Netcat's hand and led her up the front steps to the door. The knob turned easily in his hand and the two of them entered.

"No lights?"

"I told them not to come on," he said. "Just because no one's near enough for you to sense doesn't mean they're not watching this house with other surveillance equipment."

"Ah—good point. Hey, if you can sense the bird, ask it to let you know if someone comes toward the house."

"I can do that?"

"Yes. That's how Junior helps me—that is when I keep his kibble bowl full. Try it."

Kazuma paused and thought about the bird on the roof. He actually felt the soft caress of the datasphere as he touched the bird and it responded with a look at the grounds from its point of view. He didn't know if that was an okay, but it helped and he moved those images to a side window in his AR. Other than the wolf in Black's office, he'd never encountered a technocritter, and wasn't sure why this one was here. He admitted to himself he hadn't physically been to the house since his grannie's death. He missed Mama Risen more than he wanted to admit.

But he did know his way around the inside with his eyes closed. His grannie had the interior partially decorated in simple, traditional Japanese design. He slipped off his shoes in the porch level anteroom floored with smooth granite tiles. He watched as Netcat did the same and the two of them stepped up onto the hardwood living area. Two low couches with a hip-high table separated the kitchen from the main room. He pointed to the table where the wind chime lay. Apparently he had brought it inside, though he couldn't remember doing it.

Kazuma walked around the couches and down a side hallway to his grandmother's bedroom. There he reached out and gave a silent command for the lights to come on at forty percent capacity. There were no windows in this room, so he wasn't afraid of being seen. The room was devoid of furniture except for a low table with an actual computer situated on top.

Netcat whistled when she stepped inside. "Wow...that thing's gotta be circa 2058."

Kazuma pulled off his jacket and crossed his legs as he sat down. His side reminded him it wasn't finished healing as he settled himself in front of the computer. "It's just a case—these things don't go for much, even on the black market. Antiques like this are worthless."

"So it's got a screamin' link inside," Netcat said as she stood on his left.

He looked up at her and smirked. "You could say that."

She pointed at the light overhead. "How come it's okay in here and not out there?"

"No windows."

"Oh, right."

Kazuma faced the blank computer screen and held out his hands. "Grannie liked it dark when she slept."

"Like a tomb."

*Yeah...* With a deep breath, he tentatively reached out for the wireless signal emanating from the house's host. There he spoofed a known ID, but kept his admin access as three windows appeared around him. He shot Netcat an invite as he accessed grannie's mainframe—which through the AR windows resembled the house, only darker.

"That was pretty easy," Netcat said as her living persona, a small black cat, twined around his legs. "No firewalls?"

"No," He said as he directed his persona through the virtual living room to the kitchen and then turned right instead of left. "I'd already set this up for emergencies."

"But you still could have gotten in without us coming here."

"Yeah, but I didn't want to risk anyone intercepting me in the Matrix, like the wolf-hacker did. I'd rather just grab it and go." He brought the lighting up in the virtual version on the host and moved to a low hip-high freezer on the back porch. There he opened it up and looked inside. Packages of meat sat in neat stacks, each one of them carefully labeled and dated.

"Oh, hell," Netcat said in a hoarse whisper as she jumped up on the freezer and balanced on the edge. "That's gross. What's with all the meat?"

"You don't like meat?"

"I'm a vegetarian."

He nodded. That seemed to make sense. "It's not meat, of course. These are archived files. Ponsu knew where to put the data."

The cat looked up at Kazuma with glowing green eyes. "In the freezer?"

"Well who's going to look in a freezer for data?"

When she didn't answer, he figured he'd stumped her. "I need you to keep your e-sense out there to let me know if anyone approaches the house, okay?"

"Right. Is the bird looking, too?"

He moved the bird's window into focus. "Yeah...he's still showing me the surrounding area. Oh, and don't turn on any other lights."

"I got that," she said, her voice just a tad irritable.

Ponsu joined him in the freezer and he watched as his sprite dug up the data. The encryption, tight as he knew it would be, had the briefcase encased in meat and packed up as tightly as the other packages. Kazuma cracked the meat into six different images. One he gave to Ponsu with the order to encrypt it again and hide it in the Matrix at a prearranged location. Then he sent one as an attachment to a dummy PAN address. After he sent the rest of them out, including one to Netcat, who downloaded it into her own commlink, he changed the encryption to make it resemble internal freezer controls and set it down in the inside of the freezer. He downloaded the last copy to the commlink he'd bought from one of Netcat's contacts and closed the freezer.

<*You're leaving it here?*>

<***Technically, no. Trust me.***> With that he backed out of the system and shut the commlink off. No use for it now, as the whispers of the datasphere spoke to him without it, so he slipped back in to monitor activity. He felt Moon nearby, as well as Netcat and the bird. They were all watching the host.

<*Kaz,*> MoonShine's window popped up. <*I'm getting a really weird...feeling.*>

<*Yeah. So am I.*> Netcat echoed.

<***Ponsu said someone's been here that scared her. That's either his signature–***>

Abruptly a light streamed in behind them. Kazuma physically turned from where he sat and cursed when he saw the hall light on at one hundred percent.

*Boss!* Ponsu was back. *I noticed a surveillance set up on the building two blocks over!*

Kazuma heard an echo in the host. It was small and rhythmic. He turned toward it. <***Ponsu–there's something or someone else*** *on this host besides me and Netcat. I need you to find it–run a full diagnostic–I want to know how they're doing that. Why we can't actually see them–only feel them.>*

"Shouldn't you have done that before you logged us in?" Netcat asked as she stood up in the physical world and Ponsu vanished.

Kazuma stood as well. "Okay, so I got a little overconfident. I want to know who turned on the lights."

Netcat moved to the hall and cursed louder. "*All* the lights are on."

Kazuma stepped into the doorway from the hallway. He made a slow pan of the room, letting every item's RFID tag pop up in his AR.

The only item that didn't throw up any manufacturer's information was the wind chime on the table.

To his horror, the thing stood up on spindle legs like a mid-size spider and looked at them.

Netcat came back into the room and motioned to him. "Uh...I feel someone. Let's go—" she stopped when she saw the six-legged wind chime. "Remind me not to call you paranoid anymore."

Laughter came through the vid speakers as the holo system activated. They turned to see a gigantic holovid pop into the air, but instead of a view of local transmissions, the ugliest hobgoblin Kazuma had ever seen stuck his face into the camera. "Netcat! So nice to see you again!"

Kazuma looked at her and then back at the vid. "You know him?"

"A little too well." She looked angry, and being so close to her, he also felt her trembling. "Hello, Clockwork. Miss me?"

"Oh, you know it, doll." He grinned, showing those needle-sharp teeth. "Better get ready, 'cause you and your new boyfriend here gonna have a new place to play. Can't wait to tell Slamm-0! and that kid of yours that mama's never coming home."

# CHAPTER THIRTY-TWO

## NEAR THE RISEN RESIDENCE

Powell sat back from his position on the roof of an apartment building two blocks from Myddrin Risen's house. Twilight lingered a bit longer than usual as he adjusted the magnification on the binoculars, the specialized lenses catching the heat signatures of the two elves entering the house.

The room he sat in had once been a spacious penthouse apartment with a 360-degree view of the neighborhood. Powell hoped that when the place was new, the neighborhood had been worth seeing. Today, it was too near a collapsed bridge—the edges sticking up out of the city like broken bone slicing through skin. The rest of the building was home to vagrants, chipheads, drunks, and a few drug manufacturers. He could smell the brew cooking from below.

The houses in the neighborhood—the ones that had somehow survived looting—stood out like flowers in a desert. From his vantage point, Powell could see seven houses much like Miss Risen's with nice roofs and fenced-in yards and gardens. The rest of the residences looked like the rest of the squalor of Los Angeles. Forgotten. Abandoned.

"How did he get through?" Shax said from his perch on the window seal. The glass was long gone—only bits and pieces remained—reflecting the hollow ork's appearance. "I tried for ten minutes to get into that host." He looked at Powell. "It has to be her, too. They're doing it together."

"It's because it's his house," Powell said as he refocused on a slightly higher signature just outside the back gate of Mr. Tetsu's house. "I'm sure he has administrator clearance on the system."

Shax stopped and looked back at the house. "There's a technocritter on the roof."

But Powell was looking at something else through his lenses. The odd signature he'd noticed before moved slightly—then moved again. Lowering the binoculars, he adjusted the long-range settings, increased the spectral feed, and looked through them again.

There! Just to the right at the street lamp was a person. And from the readout on the binocular's inner left panel—this was a human. Cyberized. And carrying a small arsenal to boot.

"Shax—we have company down there." He shifted the binoculars over to the left. The house lights hadn't come on—but he could see the two elves' heat signatures in the lenses. They were sitting on the floor, facing something.

"What kind?"

Powell pulled the binoculars off and shoved them into their case. Shax grabbed the case when he was through, and the two of them proceeded to the steps. "Cyberized. Hacker is my guess. And he's watching them. I'm pretty sure it's Cole Blackwater. I don't want him getting near Tetsu."

"You want me to hack his stuff? The signal's pretty weak in this area—but I think I can make a sprite nasty enough to cause some serious damage."

"No," the dwarf said as they hit the first floor landing. "I don't want any technomancer involvement—or anything that can be traced back to us. Not now. You think you can get into one of the other systems? Take a look inside?"

"Piece 'o cake," Shax replied.

The pair stepped out into dark, early morning. Their van was parked a few meters away—and to Powell's surprise, it still had its tires. Of course, Shax did say he'd set a sprite in the onboard computer—and told it to prevent anyone from stealing the car.

And just as he rounded the front, he saw the fried carcass of another dwarf, maybe—or a child—smoldering on the pavement. And not a soul had come out to see what had happened.

Jabbing a finger at the corpse, he glared at Shax. "Was this necessary?"

"Well, he shouldn't have been messing with something he didn't own," the technomancer said as he put the binoculars in the car. "You want to drive over?"

"You drive—I need to prepare myself."

Shax chuckled as he waved at the car and the door opened for him. Once in the passenger seat, Powell considered what spell would work best to get rid of the nuisance, but not damage the two elves. He also didn't want the house destroyed—bringing attention back to this location and thus planting Tetsu in the news.

His first instinct was to roast the bastard in a little firewater—but there was the consideration of the house again. And the possibility of setting the elves on fire, too. And if Shax was any indication of the physical strength of an average technomancer, there wouldn't be much defense for either of the two inside.

First he had to cast a masking spell over the car. He did that as Shax turned the corner and pulled into the driveway just as all the lights in the house came on.

"What the—" Powell said. "Why did they do that?"

Shax sat up in the driver's seat as he put the car into park. "Boss—I can feel him. He's here. Sixty percent cyberization. He's near the house now. And that bird's watching him."

Shax's uncanny ability to sense the bio-field of living things was coming in handy. Powell held up a hand for the Shax to wait. "What bird?"

"I told you there's a technocritter on the roof."

"Does it belong to anyone?"

"How would I know?"

Powell paused. "If we get out of the car, we'll become visible to the hacker. Let him get past us. Let me know when he is."

Several seconds passed before Shax said the hacker was close to the house. Then he paused. "There's two of them."

"Two of what?"

"Two with cyberization. The other one is smaller, but just as geared up."

Powell gave a short, frustrated sigh. "So there are two outside visitors."

"Yes, sir. The other one's in the backyard. He's actually at the back door."

"You stay here," he told the technomancer. When Shax's expression promised to avalanche into a fit of pouting, Powell said, "I need someone to watch the car—and have it ready in case we need to get out of here fast. I can't do that. You can."

He seemed to consider it. "Yes. Yes, I can do that."

"Good. And concentrate on getting into that host at the same time."

Powell moved quickly around the bushes to the back porch and carefully moved up the steps, careful not to make a sound. Once on the porch, he peered into the back window.

Powell had a clear view of the scene—of Kazuma Tetsu standing in front of a small girl—her face obstructed by his arm. He looked pale—and flushed. Wearing a leather peacoat, white shirt, and black pants, he was favoring his right side.

What caught Powell's attention was the weird-looking, spider-like drone facing them down. Both elves had small red dots on their chests as the thing targeted them. The holovid was on, and in it he could see an ugly hobgoblin talking to the two of them.

<*Shax, don't worry about the host any more. I need you to hack Blackwater's commlink. Think you can do that?*>

<*Oh I know I can. What about the other one?*>

<*I'm not sure yet. But if we don't interfere with what's happening right now, we're going to lose our advantage.*>

# CHAPTER THIRTY-THREE

## RISEN RESIDENCE

"Why the hell did they turn the lights on?"

"Silk," Moon said from the back seat. "We've got company."

Silk had just triple-checked the Hummer and her RCC when Moon spoke. He kept his voice low, and didn't use the AR window. That alarmed her. She looked at his pale reflection in the rearview mirror. "Company?"

"Yeah." His eyes were closed. "Actually they do, too."

She half turned in her seat. "Moon, you best be explaining what you mean."

His eyes opened. "There's a van parked down on the right. It's just inside the lower garage of that office building. Someone just got out of it and left that building and headed to the house. The van's actually hard to see, but I can sense the onboard computer."

"Magic?"

"My guess. There are two augmented individuals near the house with Kazuma and Netcat. There is also something..." He tilted his head and frowned. "Someone's trying to hack the house host."

"Moon...what is it?"

He shivered. "Shadow...dark. Silk, it's dark and—" He suddenly yelled as he lurched forward in the seat.

Silk pressed the release on her five-point harness and scrambled into the back. Grabbing Moon's shoulders, she lightly slapped his face. "Moon! What the hell are you talking about?"

His eyes refocused on her for a few seconds before he reached out and touched her. "Silk, whatever's trying to break into that host is dissonant. It's dark and twisted, and it's trying to hack in by poisoning the host's core programing. If it does, everything in that house is going to —"

The rhythmic beat of a helicopter's blades broke the night's quiet. Silk let go of Moon and looked up through the Hummer's passenger side window. Her AR tagged the Shinobi with nothing more than a blank RFID. It was either another team, or undercover law enforcement.

She crawled between the seats to the front. "Moon, let Netcat and Kazuma know we have to leave now!"

"But—"

"No buts. Whether he's got the package or not, we've got to go!"

# CHAPTER THIRTY-FOUR

## RISEN RESIDENCE

The literal bird's-eye view gave Kazuma a bit of warning as he saw two figures converge on the house through the backyard. Then a third, smaller one came from a different direction, stopping at the front of the house.

He reached out and moved Netcat behind him as the back door opened and the hobgoblin came through, the Colt Manhunter in his hand aimed at the two of them. If this was Clockwork, he was even uglier in person.

While the drone was busy projecting, he reached out to the wind chime's tiny host and, finding no security, shut it off. The thing crept to the side and then squatted back down. Within seconds it looked like it had earlier—just a simple wind chime.

He felt her trembling against him, and knew it wasn't because of the gun. His own trembling, however, was more so. This wasn't the first time he'd faced a gun—the last instance had been at the hands of hackers inside that coffee shop. That time, he'd only been worried about himself and Montgomery. Now—there was Netcat. And he felt an even stronger need to protect her. She wouldn't be in this mess in the first place if she hadn't helped him.

Another person came in through the back door. This guy was taller, a human, but with the telltale head-chrome of some serious wetware. He stopped right in front of them, just a few inches ahead of Clockwork. "You Kazuma Tetsu?"

Kaz frowned, but didn't acknowledge either way. He also didn't see the blow coming to the side to this head. The impact jarred every connection he had to any peripheral hosts as his knees crumpled beneath him, and he caught himself on his elbows. He continued seeing stars as he tried to reconnect to the datasphere. Apparently this guy had quite a few enhancements, including increased physical speed as well as strength. Netcat was at his side as he blinked the stars away and looked up to see Cole standing over him, a large pistol in his hand.

"Damn it, Cole!" Clockwork half-yelled. "I gotta have them alive! And *not* brain damaged. Do that again, and I'll be selling you!"

"Like hell you will. That bastard cost me my rep."

Kaz laughed. "Like you actually had one in the first place." He tasted blood, and spit it out onto Blackwater's boot.

He saw Blackwater raise his arm this time, but Clockwork intercepted him, shoving him away. "I said stop!"

"You heard what he said to me?"

"So what? We get him, the girl, and the data, and your rep is safe." He turned back to face them as Netcat put her arms around Kazuma. "And you, *technomancer*." The hobgoblin curled his upper lip, spitting the word out with venom. "I'd shut up if I were you. We can break your legs and arms—don't need those. But I'd prefer you walk out of here on your own, save me and Blackwater breaking a sweat getting you and Netcat here in the van."

Kazuma wiped his nose and mouth with his sleeve. A bright red smear decorated the white cotton. *Damn...did he break my nose? It sure hurts like hell.*

"This is going to be so much fun, Netcat," Clockwork said. "I wonder why your boyfriend didn't tell me you were here?"

Netcat put her hand on Kazuma's arm. "What? Did you goad Slamm-0! on JackPoint?"

"Oh no. Apparently you two are still out there running. So... who's watching the kid? Has he shown any irregularities yet? 'Cause you know these corps, they love to get the young technomancers."

Kazuma felt her tense to move, and managed to half-turn in time to grab her shoulders. He stopped her from charging this asshole, which is what she would have done. The way this rigger talked, he didn't want them dead. He wanted them alive. But he could hurt them, and Kazuma wouldn't allow that.

He'd already alerted MoonShine to their situation, and told him to tell Silk to get the van cranked and ready.

"Get up, or I break your knees," Blackwater commanded.

Kazuma pushed himself off the floor and stood. The room didn't spin, and he wasn't dizzy. This was a good sign. What he did do was take in the possible weapons in the room, things he'd set up years ago, when Grannie was still alive. Decorative rocks along the side table, and the old, classic, but still serviceable revolver in the glass case by the sliding glass door.

And the set of katanas over the fireplace.

Kazuma leaned his head to the right, keeping his gaze focused on Blackwater as he directed his next question to the AR window ever present in his peripheral vision.

*<Net? I'm open for options.>*
*<I'm thinking. Distract him.>*

Blackwater stepped up nose-to-nose, which was easier for him to do than Clockwork, since the hobgoblin barely came to Kazuma's shoulders. The hacker pressed his gun against the technomancer's neck. "Now, you going to tell me where the data is—the packet you stole from me. You give me the data, and I don't shoot off your kneecaps. Or—" he turned away from Kaz and pointed his gun at Netcat's face. "I shoot her."

"Like hell you will!" Clockwork said as he came from behind Blackwater. The rigger held his own weapon trained on Netcat and grabbed her upper arm, pulling her away from Kazuma. She was closer to the hobgoblin's height, but Net was still a few centimeters taller.

Kazuma gritted his teeth, refraining from saying anything smart. *You must always practice patience,* Silk said during their training. *You must watch, listen to, and learn about your opponent. Seek out the weakness.*

And this man's weakness?

Himself.

*<Kaz?>*
*<Yeah?>*
*<I can disarm one of them, but not both. Can you work on Blackwater?>*
*<You thinking what I'm thinking?>*

Netcat's texting stopped and he tensed, sensing something else had happened.

*<What?>*

"We're not alone," she said. "I can sense others—outside."

"Eh?" Clockwork narrowed his eyes and glanced at Blackwater. "You hire anyone else? Were we followed?"

"She's lying." Blackwater moved closer to Kazuma and banged the end of the gun barrel against his temple, though he never stopped looking at Netcat. "Don't go pulling that shit on me. I don't take it very well. Just ask your boyfriend here how I treat people who get in my way."

Kazuma thought of the dead girl and the two security guards, and hoped Netcat didn't make any sudden moves just yet. He wove himself into the house's security array and tapped into the outside cameras, like he had done so many times before.

The bird's window spun as it took off and gave him the aerial view of a Shinobi.

Silk's window popped up in his AR. <*Kaz! We got company from above!*>

<***Can you identify them?***>

<*No. They're running nameless, which means it could be a runner team.*>

<***We're about to try to get away from these two. You see anyone else?***>

<*There's another van on top of the overpass. Saw someone run to the house, but he disappeared.*>

"Eh? I see you looking at this gun, leaf-eater. You recognize it, don't you? It's the one that killed that magic piece of ass—and capped you too, if I recall."

Kazuma's attention refocused on the physical world. He glared at Blackwater, his mind flashing back to the woman staring up at him in the Annex, and the bullet hole in her forehead, then the pain where Blackwater's bullet had found his side. He licked his swollen lip. "If she says she senses someone else here—she's serious."

<***Moon says there's someone landing outside.***>

<*Yeah, I heard. You think that's the rest of the team this jackass was part of? The one from the Annex?*>

<***Could be–***>

Abruptly, Kazuma's backbone tingled, and he was overcome with the feeling of being watched. He felt the first brush against the house host's web across his skin. Just a whisper at first, but it quickly became a pounding against his senses.

<***Net–there's another technomancer breaking into the house host–***>

<*Can you handle him?*>

Kazuma focused on the gun at her throat. *<I can try, but we need to get out–>*

"Where's that data?!" Blackwater moved before Kazuma could react, his cybernetic arm blurring as his fist slammed into the side of the technomancer's head. The quick, sharp impact made stars explode in his vision, and turned his legs to rubber as he crumpled to his knees again.

# CHAPTER THIRTY-FIVE

**HORIZON OFFICES
ARTUS WAGNER'S FORMER OFFICE
EARLY SATURDAY MORNING**

Delaney Charis, known to her co-workers at Horizon as Charis Monogue, stood at the window of Wagner's office, the place of her previous assignment. The CSI crews had already come and gone, the room still smelling of strong disinfectants and cleansers. The Medical Examiner had declared the death a homicide, but she could have told them that the moment she'd seen the body.

She hadn't liked Wagner. Not even a little. As soon as she could, she'd looked through his files, including the commlink he kept in a spare drawer he hadn't thought she knew about. The bastard's hosts were wiped. Even the parceled areas on the office host were corrupted.

Delaney knew Powell had done it. He and that crazy wolf that she knew wasn't really a wolf. *They did this. They came in and killed him–took the evidence. Only I don't have the proof I need to nail them.*

Seven months getting into Horizon in the first place, and then five more doing everything that bastard wanted, listening to him go on and on about himself, letting him touch her, and then answering his damn whiny calls at all hours of the night. All wasted.

She heard the door open, but didn't turn around. The smell of Renault's aftershave was enough of an introduction. "Sergeant," he said in his familiar yet comforting baritone.

"What?" she said, her voice echoing off the empty walls.

"They finally identified the remains in that school incinerator. Apparently your first guess was right."

Delaney sighed. "Doesn't matter. Any evidence we might

have collected from her burned away." She turned from the afternoon sun and looked at Renault.

He was a troll of valiant proportions. Broad shoulders, medium tusks, and one hell of an epic forehead. His hair—bleached white—he wore long and braided down his back. His horns were polished and sharpened at their tips—no faddish tattoos for him. He wore a suit like nobody else, filling it out in the most natural way.

She'd known him for three years—partnered with him for two of those years. He was smart, insightful, and the best damn investigator she knew. "No sign of Kazuma Tetsu?"

"No." He stepped toward her. "Are you sure a shadowrunner team would be a reliable asset to help prove Contagion is somehow behind all this? I mean...a game?"

She nodded slowly. "I'm sure. We have a BOLO out on Tetsu as a kidnapping victim. Which, given the circumstances here—" She glanced at where Wagner's body had been found and shook her head. "—I'm giving up hope we'll find him alive, and that he didn't walk out of Knight Errant into the wrong hands."

"Ma'am." Renault made a face. "He's just a technomancer—why do you care?"

Delaney nailed him with one of her infamous glares, and he took an involuntary step back. She placed her hands on her hips. "Yes, Renault. He's only a technomancer. I don't care what the states think, or how the laws of protection of rights come down. I protect and serve. Everyone. What if when recommending you for this job, I thought, 'oh, he's just a troll?'"

The troll opened his mouth, then closed it. "That was pretty asinine of me, wasn't it?"

"Yes. It was. And I'm not going to ignore it, Renault. If you don't think you can support on this, I'll get someone who can. Understand?"

He nodded. "Yes, ma'am." Then, "So, why are you so concerned?"

"Because it's my job to be concerned," she said. "It's technomancers today. But just a decade ago it was goblins, hobgoblins, trolls—whatever the general population is afraid of at the moment. We can't keep blaming others for our insecurities. I'm not saying I trust technomancers any more than I trust the average hacker—but no matter where the prejudice is coming from—groups, corporations, law enforcement—nobody can be allowed to deal in human or metahuman trafficking. And that's what this sort of parlaying means."

She took a step back from him. He was smiling at her. And a smile on his visage could mean anything—she wasn't sure what at the moment.

"You're so passionate," he said. "How can you stand yourself sometimes?"

That wasn't the reaction she was looking for, and her eyes widened. Then she caught the subtle twinkle in his own gaze, and narrowed hers at him again. "What is it? You found something. Or something's happened?"

"Both, actually." He lowered the monocle of his ear commlink and began making movements in the air, his muscular fingers adorned with cybernetic rings. "Encrypted files on Wagner's personal host. On a commlink the murderers didn't find, hidden in his house."

She stepped forward, feeling a smile pull at her lips. "Why didn't you tell me?"

"I like to surprise you. Pull up your AR—you'll wanna connect for this."

Delaney turned to her purse and slipped on her own shades and rings, easily accessing her PAN. A screen opened of just Renault's face, no persona. A folder appeared on the desktop. "What is this?"

Renault answered with text, not voice, not wanting the bugs in the office to pick up what he was saying. *<He sent you a message before he died. It looks like it was scheduled to send if he didn't stop it before a certain time of day.>*

"You're kidding. Where did he send it? What did it say?"

*<We don't know what it says because we can't access Horizon's server. We don't know what he sent in the other two messages either, as they were already en route to their destinations. I'd suggest you check your emails.>*

Delaney wasted no time connecting. Wagner's email was third from the top of her stack. The encoding wasn't something she'd seen before, but she was pretty good at cryptology. It'd been her specialty before being recruited.

Finally, the message opened and she sat down on the edge of Wagner's now spotlessly clean desk to read it.

Miss Charis,
Let me start by expressing my extreme thanks over these past few months. Your service has been impeccable. Remind me to send

a message to your Captain on your exemplary ability to act as a personal assistant and elf poser.

She blinked and put her hand to her chest. That last sentence had caught her completely off guard. He'd *known*. That little bastard had known all along she was an officer and not really an elf?

Now on to business. Rest assured that in the event of my untimely death, I have made preparations for revenge. I'm not going to delude myself into thinking I'll survive this. I knew my days were numbered the moment I saw Powell, and somehow they found out that I had what they wanted, what they'd been searching for.

Powell works for something neither you nor I want to see resurrected. My research into his background produced only sketchy results, but I think I know you well enough to realize you'll only believe what you can find for yourself. I know he once worked for Renraku, so I advise you to start there. I'm sure your access to such files is considerably better than my own.

During my tenure at Horizon, I made a lot of decisions where people died, and where others were removed from their lives, and I'm sure many of them are now suffering an existence worse than death. But I kept up with every bit of information I came across. I made copies. Of everything. Vids, images, texts, memos, all authentic. As well as something that was supposed to be destroyed—and wasn't.

I used the Annex host for safekeeping. I never considered a hacker, much less a technomancer, would be interested in my little kill file. I'm sure the name Caliban is what tipped him off when he happened to be assigned to archive and destroy it. I am positive that is why he is involved.

Make no mistake, Powell's employer wants all technomancers, but more than anything, it wants Tetsu, and it wants what's in that file. The last thing it wants to happen is for Tetsu to discover his destiny and act upon it.

For your information, neither Powell or Tetsu killed that girl in the Annex, nor did they kill the guards. Those murders were committed by Cole Blackwater. You will find copies of his confession to me, amid a whole lot of other evidence, buried within this email. Run it through one of your expanders—and you'll have the information I was going to hand over to Lone Star. I don't trust Knight Errant.

Neither should you.

Go after Powell, follow your instincts, and no matter what, find Tetsu and help him. I hope he hasn't been captured by this dwarf. Destroy Caliban if you can—if I'm right, my legacy will be his downfall.

Au revoir, dear Delaney,

Artus P. Wagner, CEO, Horizon Personnel Administrator

P.S.: Have you ever played a game? I suggest the enclosed demo of *TechnoHack*. You might find it interesting.

She forwarded the message to her partner.

"So, you've got the deck of cards," Renault said. "You going to hand it over to Lone Star?"

Delaney slowly shook her head. "No...at least, not yet. Did you track down that private dick Tetsu hired in '73? The one at the coffee shop?"

"Hasn't returned any calls yet. I'm afraid he's become something of a recluse. Off the grids, so to speak. Are we looking into Renraku being the possible buyer? With maybe this Caliban at the rudder?"

Delaney stood from where she perched on the desk's edge and sat down in Wagner's chair. "It's a good start." She took the email and ran it through an expander as Wagner had suggested. A single email took ten minutes to become a folder on her host's desktop. It contained eighteen pieces of data. She opened it. "There's audio and visual in here. And what looks like dossiers on everyone—" She blinked. "Including me."

"Really?" Renault tilted his head to the side. "I never thought of Wagner as that smart."

"Neither did I. I was wrong. There are also files in here regarding that shadow team." She tapped the file marked *Mack Schmetzer*. The pages that scrolled before her made her pause, and she sat back in the chair. "Holy. Shit."

"What?"

Delaney's gaze lingered a second longer on Schmetzer's file before she shifted her gaze from her AR to Renault's curious visage. "There be dragons here."

# CHAPTER THIRTY-SIX
## APPROACHING THE RISEN RESIDENCE

"Is that it?" Mack asked through his commlink.

Shayla answered as the Shinobi did a large, loose circle around the well-groomed property below. "Yep. I'm flying under the radar, so going fast would be a huge red flag. Not that anyone really cares on this side of town."

Mack nodded and turned to Preacher. The troll took up most of the Shinobi's interior, and it always amazed him that the helicopter could get off the ground with his weight. "You picking up anything?"

"Magically... yeah. There's something down there, but I'm too far away and there's too much mechanical interference."

Slamm-0! spoke up from his small area, somewhat smushed between Preacher and the Shinobi's side. "I can't find any serious security in that area. No cameras or drones to tap into."

"What about your nasty green friend?"

"Oh, I'm sure he and Blackwater are around. Clockwork might be a narcissistic asshole, but he's also good at what he does, and he's smart." The blond smiled. "But I'm smarter."

"How we going in, boss?" Shayla asked.

"Hot. Slamm-0!, get me the area grid with heat signatures to track bodies. Preacher, I might need a blackout spell or one of those stun things you do. Wide area."

"Got it."

"And me?" Shayla said.

"Land us right in front of the house. Keep the doors open and your fingers on the up button. And pray we can convince Tetsu to come with us, with the data and without force." Mack checked his Manhunter and thought of Maria. "Because I'm in the mood to kill something."

# CHAPTER THIRTY-SEVEN

## RISEN RESIDENCE

"Kazuma!" Netcat yelled.

"Give me the data you stole!" Blackwater thundered. "Or I swear I'll hack your brain and find it myself."

Kazuma had been about eight when he'd been thrown into his first fight. He'd lived in an area of San Francisco where not many elves dared to visit. So being one made him a permanent target with the local gangers. It was easier for Hitori, because she hadn't been born with the ears. Back then he was glad of that, because if they'd have put a hand on her, he would have killed them. Those hadn't been easy days—but they'd educated him on what it was like to take and deflect a blow.

His father had taught him the techniques—from birth to high school. But it had been up to him to test them on the streets and find what worked. And right now—with the blinding pain in his head, echoed by the pounding of the other technomancer at the threshold of the house's environment host—the simple act of breathing was what he used as a focus. With each breath, he took in the essence of the datasphere around him, felt the wisps of it curl inside as he stepped into his AR. He kept his eyes closed and his breathing steady.

"You stupid drekking ass!" Clockwork shouted. "You don't hit soft tissue with a cyberarm unless you want to turn it to mush. If you've given him any brain damage, I'm taking what nuyen I'd have gotten for him out of *your* share."

Kazuma saw the interior of the house now, through the eyes of the camera. While Blackwater yelled back at him, Clockwork dragged Netcat to the hallway's entrance and picked up Kazuma's bag. Clockwork kept his gun on her while he rifled through it, eventually pulling out the commlink.

"Cole…I think I found something. Take a look at this."

Blackwater headed away from the still hunched-over Kazuma and took the commlink. He held it in his hands, his gun pointed down, and within a few seconds grinned at Clockwork. "Winner winner, chicken dinner."

Kazuma smiled. Bait accepted.

Without Clockwork's hand on her arm, Netcat broke away and ran to Kazuma. He felt her beside him, pulling him up by his arms.

<Kaz? You okay?>

<You ready to disarm them? Once we do, we've got maybe a half second to act. What are you going to do?>

<You play dead and wounded pretty damn good.>

<Loads of practice.>

Lowering his head, he leaned against her to feign weakness, to make Blackwater the victor over the wounded. But his muscles were far from silent as adrenaline pumped into his system, the years of practice announcing the coming move and calculating each step precisely.

Breathe in. Breathe out. Breathe in.

*Boss!* Ponsu was at his side and glowing a pinkish gold. The sprite was angry.

<Ponsu, I need you to stand by and act the moment I call you.>

Ponsu sent him an affirmative. Kazuma looked back through the exterior cameras and saw a movement against the back door. Who was that?

Blackwater was back with them again, his gun pointed at Netcat's head. "Get up. Both of you."

Kazuma stood, leaning heavily on Netcat. He felt blood trickle over his lips and tasted the metallic tang in his mouth. He also felt something moving down the side of his face and put his hand there. It came back slick with blood.

<Looks like he split your temple. But head wounds always bleed the worst.>

<You ready? I'm taking Blackwater, you got Clockwork. Once they're disarmed, you let me take care of them physically. You run to the door and get to the Hummer. Got it?>

<Yeah. But I can sense someone in the back.>

<I've got Moon on that. Just follow the plan. Silk's got the Hummer ready.>

Her little cat icon gave a paws-up.

"You bastard," Netcat said, her voice low. There was a *click*, a metal-sliding-on-metal noise, and then something heavy hit the ground beside Kazuma. He opened his eyes enough to see the Manhunter's magazine on the floor in front of his left knee.

The same thing happened with Clockwork's gun. Both of them were disarmed—but it wasn't going to last long. And it was safe to assume that both weapons had a bullet chambered. Those two bullets could still kill one of them, if not both. He needed to act fast—and make no mistakes.

**<*MOVE BACK NOW!*>**

Kazuma gave the silent command to Netcat as he crouched down and to the left, his right arm reaching over to balance himself as he pushed his left shoulder into the floor.

Blackwater was fast, following Kazuma's sudden drop with his weapon. The technomancer twisted away, pushing against the floor with his right hand as his right foot kicked straight up.

The hacker fired.

The bullet split the floor an inch away from Kazuma's right ear—just as his boot connected squarely with Blackwater's unprotected throat.

Netcat screamed.

Kazuma's side burned at the sudden wrenching movement as his right foot remained straight up for a few seconds. Blackwater gurgled, fighting to pull air into his shattered larynx before falling back to the floor, his useless gun clattering on the kitchen tile.

The whole movement took less than a second, but for Kazuma it seemed to last for hours. His months of relentless training with Silk released, his energy spent, the pain in his side and head overpowered him, making him tumble forward onto his chest and cheek, arms tucking beneath his body.

Netcat screamed again.

Kazuma took in a deep breath and with half of his vision still in his AR, he saw something large and furry roll by when he looked at Netcat's icon. *What the hell?*

"Think you can hack my weapon, bitch?" Clockwork shouted. As Kazuma disengaged from the house security, he saw Netcat curl into a fetal position. The bastard was kicking her!

**<*Netcat!*>**

Suddenly the round, furry ball was in his AR with bared teeth.

Kazuma stumbled back to the fireplace as he threw up his hands against it. *<Ponsu!>*

The Swan was red now, and he pointed to the slobbering, toothy ball of nasty. *<KILL IT!>*

As his sprite chased after the killer ball of fur, Kazuma noticed the house's environment was darkening. Not just dimming the lights—but shadows had crept in along the edges of the room. He felt something along his back, just brushing against the house's datasphere, and it almost paralyzed him with fear.

It was the darkness he'd sensed in the resonance. That suffocating, ever-present evil that crept up behind him, but never showed itself. It was here, now, in the house. But how? It wasn't in the physical world, but it was there, along the edges of the house's host. If it was able to change that much of the house's environment, that meant it was almost in the host. He needed to get back in and pull the self-destruct on the whole thing—and preferably do it while the bastard was inside.

Peripherally aware of the fight between the furball and Ponsu, Kazuma turned and grabbed the upper katana from the fireplace. He unsheathed it and ran up behind Clockwork—only the rigger was ready for him and ducked low as Kazuma lashed out with the blade. He missed the hobgoblin, and hit the corner of the hall entrance instead.

"Look out!"

Kazuma felt the rigger come up behind him and let his instincts direct his next move. Clockwork was short, so he knew whatever move he made would be about waist high for Kazuma. He jumped into the air as a gunshot took a chunk of the wall out.

He landed and immediately rolled into Clockwork, knowing that wasn't something the hobgoblin would expect. Clockwork grunted as Kazuma landed on top of him and tried to tear the gun out of his hand. But the rigger wasn't going to get disarmed that easily. He brought his shorter legs up and wrapped them around Kazuma's torso, then tightened them. Kazuma screamed at the pain as Clockwork's boot put hard, sudden pressure on his wound.

"Get that damn penguin out of my RCC!" The hobgoblin shouted as he struggled to keep Kazuma immobilized.

Kazuma realized Clockwork meant a swan. Ponsu was in a serious, nasty battle with whatever that thing was, almost mirroring her creator's fight with Clockwork. Abruptly Ponsu disappeared, and then reappeared beside him.

*It's an AI! And a nasty one!*

The killer ball of fur with teeth was an AI? This was just getting better all the time. As Clockwork kept squeezing the air out of him, Kazuma patted the ground to his right and found the hilt of his katana just as he heard a gunshot go off. He expected pain... somewhere.

Hadn't Clockwork just shot him?

Silk knelt over him where he lay back with his knees bent and Clockwork's legs still wrapped around him. "This is the oddest position I've ever caught you in."

He smiled up at her. "Did you kill him?"

"I hope so. Can't wait to find out. Netcat's already heading to the Hummer. Let's go." She took his hand and, with a few kicks to the hobgoblin's face to dislodge him, hauled Kazuma to his feet. He clutched his side, but still managed to take her into his arms.

"You were supposed to wait in the car."

"I can't leave you alone for a minute, can I?" She pressed a kiss against his lips before pushing him to the back door, stepping over the still-gasping Blackwater. "We've got to get out of here. Those gunshots might have triggered someone's security."

"Wait! I have to trigger the host!"

Silk looked up at him in incredulous disbelief. "*Now?* You got the package, right?"

"Yes, and I left an image copy for them to find."

"So why do you have to—"

He put his hand to her face. "Because I can't let that darkness...that evil...infect Myddrin's home. This was my home. And Hitori's. I can't explain what it is, not yet because I don't know. But that other technomancer is nearly inside her personal space. I want to kill the motherfucker while he's in there. Just give me two minutes!"

Silk sighed and pulled him to her as they blended into the darkness of the back yard. He spotted the old, small pagoda near a short bridge over a stream, and motioned her over to that. His head was ringing and his vision kept blurring. "I bet in the daylight this yard's an Asian paradise."

Kazuma nodded, though he was sure she couldn't see him in the dark. He dove back into the host with his admin password—and found the same strange, dark edges. The virtual house matched the environmental one, only darker. Mold was growing at an alarming rate along the walls, and the place smelled of dirt and rot. He ran to the back room to the freezer—

It was open, and the packets of meat were thawing on the woven floor.

"Looking for this?"

Kazuma spun around to face a persona he'd never seen before. It was tall and thin and wore a long, shiny, black trench coat. The coat's texture moved like oil. The same material covered his long legs, and his feet were covered in boots with a dragon's head at the toe. Kazuma couldn't see the being's face—it was covered by a black gas mask, with yellow eyes beneath a top hat.

It was one of the creepiest personas he'd ever seen—and it held the image copy of the packet in its gloved hands.

Kazuma didn't answer. Instead, he reached back and drew a katana from his back. The packet in the intruder's hand started rotting as the information corrupted. Outwardly, it was like watching a time-lapse vid of a rotting piece of meat. It turned black, then green, and then maggots started falling off as they wriggled out of holes in the packet. As the maggots hit the floor, they tore holes in the woven mats.

"You thought I would be fooled by an image?" The intruder's voice was low and loud. It vibrated against Kazuma's ribcage.

"Who are you?" he finally asked. He needed a name.

"Shax." The gas mask tilted its head. "And you are Soldat."

How did he know that? Ponsu appeared behind the intruder—small this time. No bigger than a butterfly. Just a speck of gold in the darkening hallway.

The entire environment was tainted. It hurt against his senses. It was the same feeling he'd found in the Resonance Realms, the feeling of something looming in the background, wanting in. Whatever this was—he was sure Shax had brought it with him.

"I know your sprite is behind me. The dissonance you see is a part of me. I control it. I give it life and it gives me..." he didn't finish the sentence, leaving it for Kazuma to finish.

"You're a dissonant technomancer. A Discordian?" Kazuma had heard of the Discordians and rumors they were involved with Code Clan—but he'd never followed up to find out whether it was true. And now he was certain he faced one of them.

"I am what I am," Shax said in that thrumming voice. "And now it's time for you to give me the real data. SHOW ME WHERE IT IS, OR I WILL KILL YOUR SPRITE!"

Threatening Ponsu in front of Ponsu was never a good idea. Given his sprite's sometimes volatile and somewhat excitable personality, Kazuma didn't even have to give the creature a command.

The tiny Ponsu flipped the light switch on the wall behind Shax—

—and the host crashed in on itself.

# CHAPTER THIRTY-EIGHT

## RISEN RESIDENCE

Netcat stumbled toward the door, still overwhelmed by the ferocious attack of Clockwork's AI. How could she have forgotten about that damn thing? She'd battled it once before in Seattle—and both times she'd survived.

Barely.

With every muscle demanding a rest, Netcat battled fading as she yanked open the front door with the intent of heading to the Hummer. Whatever Kazuma was doing, she had to believe he was capable of winning. She knew the data was safe, away from here and this damn house.

A hand on her forehead, she stumbled off the porch to the first step before she felt the sudden gusts of wind and debris as a Shinobi helicopter landed on the street in front of the house.

And who were these jackasses? More of Powell's people? Another shadow team?

She started to duck to her left into the shadows to head to the lot across the street when an all-too-familiar window popped up in her AR.

<Kitty?!>

Slamm-0! was calling? After a whole day with no word, he decides to call her *now*? She paused in the dark, and almost pushed the contact away before she *heard* his voice.

At a distance.

Netcat refocused on the people jumping out of the Shinobi. An older man with a grizzled face, a huge troll with a staff, and a younger guy with blond, spiky hair—

**<Is that you? What are you doing here?>**

<Making some nuyen!>
<**Where's Jack?**>
<He's with Turbo Bunny.>

Netcat wanted to strangle him. She just wanted to— <**Wait, why are you with these people? Who are they?**>

<They're after a guy named Blackwater and a possible technomancer named Kazuma Tetsu.>

Netcat grew cold and she took a step back toward the house. <**You're after Kazuma? Why?**>

<Apparently he stole something from Mack. Mack's the face in charge of this team—where are you going?>

<**Slamm-0!, you've got to get away from them. They're out to kill Kazuma and sell that data. We can't do that—not with the shaman's prophecy–>**

Slamm-0! had stopped in the middle of the street to talk to her, but now the troll was running to one side of the house and the old guy to the other as Slamm-0! started toward her. <Kitty, wait, it's not what you think–>

Netcat had just moved back to the top step when she saw Slamm-0! freeze. His eyes widened, and he brought his weapon up and pointed it at her. She was about to protest when an arm came around from behind and yanked her back off her feet. The strength and the stench—

"Clockwork!" Slamm-0! shouted as he charged forward, his weapon drawn.

Netcat drove her elbow into the hobgoblin's side as she kicked. He was trying to pull her back into the house, and that just wasn't going to happen. Once he moved to the step above and behind her, Netcat grabbed the arm around her neck, stepped back and used what strength she had to bend down and pitch forward to bring him over her head.

It worked—but Clockwork didn't let go of her neck, and they both tumbled down the steps.

She saw stars before they landed as his chokehold did its job. But if she could stay conscious and make this work, then Slamm-0! could reach them—

She heard the gun go off, but didn't register that she'd been hit until her body refused to obey her commands. Clockwork's arm no longer held her neck and she was on her side, but her arms and legs refused to move. She could see the rigger's boots in front of her as he leaned down and hauled her up again—only her feet wouldn't move under her any more, and she couldn't fight back.

*Am I hit?*

"Mack, no! You do, and you might hit Netcat!"

Her e-sense told her the old man and the troll were nearby, both of them facing Clockwork and her, with Slamm-0! directly in front her. The rigger was moving her backward, back up the steps of the porch. "Another step, and mama here dies."

"Clock—she's bleeding. Please...let her go. She's no good to you like that."

"Oh she's plenty good to me because she's gonna make sure me and my partner get out of here alive. You won't touch me as long as I have her."

"Slamm-0!—" said a voice from the right.

"Mack! No! Please!" Slamm-0! paused. "What do you want?"

"For you and your little team to stay right here."

*<Net?>*

It was all Netcat could do to stay awake as she felt herself drilling down into darkness. She didn't have the strength to answer Moon's message.

*<Silk says Kazuma's about to crash the host...are you okay?>*

As Clockwork backed them across the porch, she used what strength she had to answer him. ***<Shot. Get out of here. Run!>***

She watched as Slamm-0! ran through the gate to the porch steps as Clockwork shut the doors and locked it. Once inside he dropped her and faced Blackwater, who was now up and coughing hard.

"Where's that other techno?" Clockwork demanded as he went to the back door and looked out. "We got PCC units on their way, and I ain't staying. This better be worth my while, Cole."

Netcat's vision blurred and when the lights went out, she thought she'd lost consciousness.

"What the hell? Did they cut the power?"

Netcat blinked as she listened to the datasphere, and knew the house host was dead. Kazuma had taken it down. But where was he? Did he make it out?

***<Kaz?>***

It was the last message she sent before she slipped into unconsciousness.

# CHAPTER THIRTY-NINE

## RISEN RESIDENCE

Powell seethed as he remained in his hiding place in the backyard. His last command to Shax had been to hack into their commlinks—not into the house's host!

He was less than six meters from where Tetsu and the woman had hid, and he'd heard every word. He knew the host was going to crash and he'd warned Shax. *Damn fool!*

So far, he was of the opinion that technomancers who embraced dissonance traded in a good bit of their common sense for power. And he was losing patience with it. He'd had a plan, and if the fool would have followed it, he and Shax could be leaving the house with Tetsu and the data in tow by now.

But here he sat, with no real access into the house, the host crashed, and with it any trace of the data. Mack Schmetzer's team was crawling all over the house as he watched Blackwater and a nasty little hobgoblin drag a limp female elf through the back yard to the fence exit.

With a sigh, he slipped through the darkness to the hole he'd found on the other side. Using his own magic shield to hide himself from the others, he headed back down the street toward the ramp where he left the van.

Shax sat where Powell left him in the back—but now he was clutching his head and using a whole array of mixed metaphors the dwarf had never come across before.

"Suck it up, we have to move. Get your weapon ready."

Shax did as he was told, but a quick look in the rear view mirror told Powell the technomancer had applied a slap patch full of stimulant. Pissed off, in pain, and wired on drugs. No problem there. Powell cranked the van up, then turned on the heat-signature monitor he installed a year ago. This little charm had helped him tremendously over the past year—and it would help him now. He dialed the scanner toward the house.

Powell saw the two in the back yard—Tetsu and the woman. He watched the Shinobi's occupants scatter toward the house, and started the van down the back alley. He was pretty sure the two retreating augmented idiots didn't have an exit strategy, so the least he could do was provide them with one.

And even if they did—who was going to say no to a fast way out?

Powell followed their signatures—three of them—as they ran through the back yard and then through the back fence and down the road toward the Stuffer Shack two blocks down. He turned right and gunned the van down the deserted street and smiled when he came out ahead of them and blocked their escape.

As anticipated, both men had their weapons out. Blackwater had the female elf over his shoulder. But Powell had his weapon ready as he opened the door facing the three of them.

Shax fired twice, and both of them went down. Powell joined Shax in getting the three of them into the van—if not a bit unceremoniously—then took off as the PCC cars roared past.

# CHAPTER FORTY

## RISEN RESIDENCE

Mack watched Slamm-0! run at the front door and slam into it. It didn't budge, and the kid stepped back, fired at the doorknob twice, then ran at it again. This time it crashed inward as he ducked and rolled, his guns up and ready.

Mack waited at the side of the house, his eyes on the door. No one fired at him. The house was dark. No wireless signal. Nothing. The host was completely black.

"Kid?"

"I need a light in here!" Slamm-0! called out.

Mack reached into his vest and retrieved a flashlight as he climbed the stairs and shined it over the immediate area. The living room was partially trashed. There was broken glass scattered everywhere, and he was pretty sure the dark splotches on the woven mat flooring were blood.

"Host's dead. Crashed. You got anything on heat?" Slamm-0! said.

"Two in the back yard." He redirected his focus on his AR. "Preacher?" he said over his commlink.

"Got 'em under cover, boss. Wanna come see?"

Mack ran around Slamm-0! through the now open sliding glass doors and into the back. Given what he could see by his light, he was pretty sure the place was an Asian delight back here, complete with gurgling stream, bridge, and pagoda.

Behind the single story pagoda, Preacher stood with his gun trained on two people on the ground. One wasn't moving, and the other knelt over the motionless body, a gun in each hand, trained on Preacher and now Mack. A quick flash of the light told him what he needed to know. Mack held up his free hand. "Put that down. We're not here to hurt you or Tetsu—but we got PCC security coming, and we need to get out of here."

The ebony-skinned woman stood, and Mack was a little surprised to see that she came up to Preacher's nose. In the dim light, he could see markings on her body, and thought at first she was a shaman. Then he saw the commlink on her arm and the jacks in her temple. "You're not hurting him and you're not taking him," she said.

"Ma'am," Preacher said, and Mack half-smiled at the troll's deep, patient voice. "We don't plan on hurting anyone. But we do need to make a swift and hasty retreat right now."

"We need to go after Clockwork," Slamm-0! insisted. "He's got Netcat, Mack. He's going to sell her!"

Mack noticed the way the younger hacker was pacing. And if the elf was his girlfriend, then he could understand the man's anxiety. But their own survival and non-incarceration was the big priority.

Mack held out his hand. "You need to get your head clear, kid. We'll find him. But first things first—"

The woman narrowed her eyes at Slamm-0! "How do you know Netcat?"

Slamm-0! tilted his head. "Do you know her? Are you a technomancer, too?"

"Not like she is. But you didn't answer my question—" and then it looked as if she was seeing him closer. "Slamm-0!?"

It was the hacker's turn to narrow his eyes. "Do I know you?"

"No. But I know you." She lowered her weapon and offered her hand. "My name's Silk."

Slamm-0!'s expression changed. "Silk? From GiTm0?"

She smiled and nodded.

Then his expression turned to surprise. "And is he...Soldat?"

"Netcat wasn't kidding. She has told you everything."

Mack looked at the two of them as they shook hands. "Okay that's all well and good—but we need to go. We can have happy-time tea somewhere far away from here." He pointed at the guy on the ground. "Preacher, can you bring him?"

Silk moved like a swift shadow to stand in front of the troll. "You will not harm him."

"Ma'am," Preacher said with slight smile around his tusks. "I promise I won't hurt him."

That appeared to appease her, but Mack noticed her watching every move as the troll bent down and carefully lifted the black-haired elf in a fireman's carry. "Get him back to the Shinobi—"

"Wait!" Silk held up her hand. "Another member of our team's waiting in my Hummer."

Mack turned to Slamm-0! "You ride with her and get her to the club. *Now*!"

Everyone scattered. Mack watched as Slamm-0! disappeared into the darkness with Silk, then took off after Preacher.

For a troll his size, he was fast and determined. He beat Mack by several meters. Mack made it into the Shinobi and buckled in next to Shayla just as a PCC van showed up along the street. Men and women in black uniforms got out just as Shayla had the inertia ready for liftoff.

"Preacher?" He looked back to see the troll had the elf securely fastened in a seat.

"Got it." Preacher moved to the side of the Shinobi, which tipped as he jumped out and stood in front of it, facing the uniforms.

"Mack, I'm gonna need to dive to do this fast enough."

"Then do it." He reached out to take the wheel, so to speak, as Shayla leaned back in her seat. He felt her take the controls back, and released them as Shayla's mind became one with the powerful machine.

Before the PCC officers could order them to stop, Mack saw the blue-white light of magic as it encircled Preacher. There was a pulse, and then everything in his vision went black. Now he understood why Shayla wanted to dive—the only way to see through the blackout would be through the eyes and camera of the Shinobi.

There was gunfire. But no flashes of light. He felt the metal hull get pinged as the Shinobi lifted, then dipped just a bit as Preacher jumped back in. Then they were spiraling up fast and the force of that lift pinned Mack in his chair.

He gritted his teeth as she broke free of the spell's perimeter and then twisted the Shinobi over hard to point it in the right direction. Once in the air and looking down at the brilliant lights of Los Angeles, Mack blinked once to activate his AR. <*Slamm-0!?*>

<We're through. Silk's a rigger. Once she saw Preacher powering up, she dove. We're heading east—doesn't look like they're following.>

<**Good. Meet up at the club. Take the long way if you think someone's after you. And kid—don't worry. We'll get her back.**>

There were several seconds before Slamm-0! answered. <We've got a son, Mack. He's two. I can't lose her.>

*Drek*. Mack didn't answer. He just hoped like hell Hestaby didn't mind a bit of a delay.

# CHAPTER FORTY-ONE

### GiTm0

Welcome back to GiTm0, *omae*; your last connection was 10 hours, 2 minutes, 25 seconds ago

### BOLOs

Just a reminder—this host's got less than two hours left before decompiling. Send your sprites out twenty-four hours after that for the new link.

New name: Shax, dissonant technomancer. Check the link to his online persona image.[Link] Full list available [Link][Guest] but don't read the list online. And don't forget, these runners are out for the nuyen, and they don't give a damn about us.

Remember, GOD is always watching.

### IMPORTANT: ALERT! NEED ANYONE IN THE LOS ANGELES AREA!

I need as many of you willing to help as possible.

Just got word from Silk that the rigger Clockwork and the hacker Cole Blackwater have taken Netcat. It was done in a house invasion—and that's all I can say for now. The less we know, the better.

At present, Soldat is alive and recovering after having to crash a host to escape what Silk described as a dissonant poison that had invaded the host along with the technomancer, Shax. This technomancer is working with an investigator known as Draco Powell. You'll remember his name from a few reports back. He's connected with Renraku as one of the survivors of the Arcology incident. What we don't know is who he's working for now.

What we need from any of you is information. Intel of any kind that can help us find Netcat's current location. When Clockwork tried to sell her before, it was to NeoNET, so keep your eyes and ears open for anything from them, or any deals or possible TM scores dealing with a female elf.

Slamm-0! and Silk are currently working with a shadow team she has vouched for. If you have any information on Clockwork, Blackwater, Powell or Shax, contact me offline or Shyammo.

**ALERT**
>>>>Open Thread/Subhost221.322.1
>>>>Thread Access Restrictions: <Yes/**No**>
>>>>Format: <**Open Post**/Comment Only/Read Only>
>>>>File Attachment: <Yes/**No**>
>>>>Thread Descriptor: **KEEP YOUR EYES OPEN**
>>>>Thread Posted By User: RoxJohn

- Does this bastard have anything to do with Hip's disappearance?
- 404Flames

- We don't know yet. He's still a mystery. What we do know is that Clockwork and Blackwater are dangerous, and we don't want to think of what they might do to Netcat.
- RoxJohn

- That's Slamm-0!'s worry. Hi all. I'm with Silk, Soldat and Slamm-0!. We're working hard to locate her, but Soldat's suffering from dumpshock as well as fading, so he'll be offline for the time being. This team's magic slinger ruffled some serious PCC feathers, so we're not taking any chances on the street. Just need intel on where Clockwork and Blackwater are.
- MoonShine

- Glad to hear everyone's okay. Are all four of them working together?
- Venerator

- We're not sure. What we do know is Powell was the one that tried to grab Soldat in real life at his place of employment—so he already knew what he was. Shax works for Powell. Blackwater used to work for the team we're with now.
- MoonShine

- You sure that's a good idea?
- LongTong

- Hey Moon, Rox, have you tried searching through public records on holdings? Not just on Powell but even on Blackwater or Clockwork. I doubt you'll find anything through those handles, but if anyone knows their street names or even birth names, it would help.
- 404Flames

- You think either of them have that in Los Angeles?
- RoxJohn

- I don't know where they're from. But a preliminary scan on Draco Powell—other than his ties with Renraku, he's also in bed with Ferdinand Bellex.
- 404Flames

- Drek! That's that Contagion Games guy!
- LongTong

- Notice how we keep going back to that game? I think we need to look even deeper.
- Venerator

# CHAPTER FORTY-TWO

## PCC POLICE HEADQUARTERS
## LOS ANGELES
## SATURDAY

"Sergeant Delaney Charis."

The voice in Delaney's office PAN was routed through a filter, but her enhanced ears knew it was female. "You should stop what you're doing. Right now. Or it won't go well for you."

The call disconnected a second later.

Renault sat on her office couch and looked up at her over the screens of his AR. "What?"

"That was interesting." She immediately let the department's trace programs do their thing before she relayed the message to him.

Renault smiled. "I think someone's getting uncomfortable."

"Yeah..." Delaney tucked a strand of hair behind a delicately pointed ear. She'd had them augmented when she was in her teens, when her parents moved from Georgia to Los Angeles. With pointed ears, her mother and father believed she could get further in Free California. And they'd been right. But only in certain areas closer to Tir Tairngire. "But even I think that was a childish thing to do. I mean...do they really think we won't trace it?"

"Oh, I'm sure they do. And I'm sure that trace will keep you busy for several days, and you'll never get anywhere."

"Meaning it's a way to keep us out of their hair."

After Renault's agreement, Delaney canceled the trace. Let them think their ruse worked, or let them wonder why it didn't, either way, the fact that she didn't take the bait will keep *them* a little preoccupied.

She pushed back from her chair and stood. Her back ached, and the cup of noodles she'd eaten...nine hours ago...was long gone. Delaney wanted a doughnut and a soykaf from the coffee shop down the street, but there just didn't seem to be enough time to indulge.

Not yet.

Her assignment had been murdered under her nose. Technically, she was in for over 50,000 nuyen to a shadowrunner with ties to dragons—not that she ever planned on paying him. Apparently, there might be something even more sinister lurking around the Matrix than corporations spending lives chasing the all-powerful nuyen.

And yeah, she saw technomancers as just that. The same as everyone else.

Draco Powell. She snapped her finger to call up the holovid board she and Renault had been using to aggregate the information they'd accumulated over the past ten hours. In the center she had Kazuma Tetsu and this mysterious data that Wagner was so worried about retrieving. From there, all manner of lines spread out. To Wagner, to herself, to Draco Powell, to Mack and to a dragon, to Horizon, to Knight Errant, to Ares, where his sister worked, and to his sister herself, whose personnel file was still filled with indecipherable nonsense.

The one string that still didn't make sense was Wagner's reference to Caliban, and his insistence that she look into *TechnoHack*. Delaney hadn't had time for games in years, and didn't see how playing a demo could possibly help her now. And yet...Wagner's reference kept nagging at her.

The square with Draco Powell's name flashed. She tapped it, and the box expanded with old and new information.

"Just uploaded the intel I received from a friend in Manhattan on this little freak." Renault rose to stand beside her in front of the holovid. On his right hand, he wore a set of five rings to manipulate their shared board. "Decided to go with what Wagner told you to do." He moved the image of Powell to the left, and the information lined up in a stacked column with bullet points next to him on the right. "We don't have a birth date on him, but it looks like he's used the name consistently. Was employed by Renraku in Research and Development, and lived in the arcology when it went haywire. He's labeled as one of the survivors, and cashed in on public sentiment to start his own investigation service five years later after honing—and registering I might add—his adept status as a magic user. He's been cited a few times in Seattle, Denver, and a few small places in between for suspected use of blood magic, but nothing was ever proven."

"Well, blood magic's not illegal," Delaney said. *Just gross.* "But how is he connected to the Tetsus? How does he fit into getting into Knight Errant or Horizon?"

"In '72, he miraculously proved to a few higher-ups in Horizon that he could tell a technomancer from a non-technomancer. His accuracy was within ninety percent, which garnered him a job working within what we call their *darker* departments when Horizon tried to prove themselves to be technomancer-friendly."

"And how'd he do that?"

"Don't know at this point. Legally, he was on retainer as a private investigator and on the Horizon books, he investigated fraudulent claims. Which, of course, we know is fraudulent itself." Renault moved a few of the bullet points up to reveal more of them. "Here is where it gets interesting, and it took a few bots to dig this intel out. About three years ago, Powell's financials jumped—and I'm talking about some serious nuyen flowing into his accounts. He's got three of them."

Delaney leaned back on her desk and whistled as she crossed her arms over her chest. "Where did he get that? I know it's not from working with Horizon."

"No. In fact, his income there stopped around the same time. I haven't been able to track two of the streams," Renault tapped that bullet point of income, which expanded into three icons. Two had question marks on them, the third—

"Contagion Games?" Delaney stood up. "They make *Techno-Hack*."

"Which your boy Wagner mentioned in his letter to you. Contagion's also been in the media a lot lately—and the press hasn't been that great. So tell me," he said with a glance at her. "Why haven't they hired Aztechnology, the leader in public relations, to put a spin on their troubles? Since their repeated blackouts and monumental stack of player complaints, their market share's dropped considerably. But they're not losing nuyen."

"Now how exactly are they doing that?"

"I'm not sure. At first I suspected subscriber fraud. Players have to sign up to pay a fee every month to play, and some of the more disreputable companies continue to siphon off nuyen even after the player cancels the subscription."

Delaney looked at him. "Didn't find that, huh?"

"No. And I looked hard." He cracked his knuckles. "What I did find was this." Renault tapped the projected screen again. Lists of green and red took up the entire area. He moved his hands closer together to shrink the lists so they would all fit on the screen.

"These are all names," Delaney said as she stood and moved to the image.

"If there's one thing I have to credit Contagion with, it's that the original owner of the company set it up legitimately and registered the subscription base. By doing that, they protected themselves from spoofed accounts—kids wanting to hack in and play for free. It was easy to get the subscriber lists without having to go through Contagion themselves."

"What are the red and green for?"

"Let me show you." Renault moved his hands and she watched him type on his AR. The names shifted around, and all the red ones began blinking. "The red accounts belong to missing people."

Her jaw dropped. "That looks like half the list."

"It's actually thirty-seven percent of the list of those who subscribed. And when I say missing—I mean *physically* missing." He typed again. The list shifted to just the red names, which still took up the board area. Colors then moved to red and yellow. "The yellow names are those missing who were found deceased. Which worked out to about ten percent of the missing list."

"What did they die of?"

"Coroners wrote a menagerie of things. Dumpshock, heart attacks, and a lot of neglect. They left their meat suits to rot while they played online. I haven't gone through all of them yet. But this is what I wanted to show you." He waved his hand and the list recompiled into bright green lists. "All of these names are missing, some of these names are confirmed dead, but what they have most in common, is that they are all registered technomancers."

Delaney spun on him. "What?"

"Every name on this list coincides with technomancers who complied with their city's regulations, if required, and registered themselves. Or they were registered with Horizon. But, the fun thing here is I can't get Horizon to acknowledge any of them. They claim lists like this are private, and they have no comment."

"So you're saying...all of these people logged into Contagion Games and died or disappeared."

"Yes. And all of them logged in to a single game."

She put her hands to her face. "*TechnoHack*."

Renault typed in mid-air again in his AR, and the names shifted and moved until a single name came up.

*Hitori Tetsu.*

Delaney stared at the name.

He clasped his hands in front of him. "This is why I'm not surprised you got that call. Because I've been doing some digging, and after a while I decided not to be discreet. Not when I saw this correlation. Now, let's take a look at this." Renault moved his hands, and the board shifted again with three folders. One was Draco Powell, one had the name Ferdinand Bellex, and one was Miranda Sebastian.

"Bellex I recognize. He's the CEO of Contagion. Been following him in the media."

"He's the CEO and the co-owner." Renault pulled Bellex and Sebastian down. "When the company was founded, just before the Crash, it was owned by three friends and what looks like a girlfriend. Jesus Huerta, Morion Baron, and Radcliff Tolen, who was reportedly dating Miranda Sebastian."

On a hunch, Delaney reached out and moved the names aside and typed in their last names. All three were reported missing. "Not dead—just missing."

"All at the same time."

"Miranda Sebastian isn't listed."

"No. After they disappeared, she sold the company to Bellex, who kept her on as CFO. Miranda's still with Contagion."

"Does that seem odd to you?"

Renault sighed, a deep, rumbling noise. "All of this seems odd to me. I don't understand the whole thing against technomancers. Me personally? I'd love to not have to use the rings or a commlink or a cyberdeck. It'd make things so much easier."

She had to agree with him. "And Powell is connected to this?"

"Seriously connected." Renault pulled in Bellex's folder. "But first we have to look into Ferdinand Bellex." When he tapped it, nothing happened.

"There's nothing there?"

"Up until the purchase of Contagion Games, there was no such person. Or entity. I can't find financials, birth records, not even a Matrix signature. And as far as I can tell, no one's ever actually met him—except for Miranda. There are vids all over the Matrix of him holding press conferences, of him speaking with people at Contagion, lots of hype about how the company has an upward growth—all the usual bullshit. But from what I can tell—" Renault shrugged. "I can't find them."

"What do you mean you can't find *them*?"

"No office. Not like Horizon or Ares or SK or Knight Errant or even us. I can't find any address of Contagion Games that *physically* exists. The address on their headers just points to some area along the coast. There's nothing there. Either someone's really good at not being on the grid—"

"Or they're an AI." Delaney's AR came up with Mack's icon in a new window. She held up a finger to let Renault know she had to take the call. He picked up his mug and headed to the break room. "Delaney."

"We have a situation."

*I'll bet you do.* She stared at the icon and remembered the file Wagner had on Mack Schmetzer. She wanted to have a long conversation with him at some point about his past, but right now wasn't that point. "There's a breakfast diner—"

"No. I need you to come here." He paused. "It involves a briefcase that wasn't in black water."

Delaney raked her fingers through her hair. She got his inference. Briefcase meant data, and the reference to Cole Blackwater was loud and clear. "Mind if I bring my partner?"

"The more the merrier." Mack severed his connection.

# CHAPTER FORTY-THREE

## UNKNOWN LOCATION

Blackwater woke to a painful kick to his left side. Thinking he was still fighting, he cursed and rolled out of the way—only to slam right into a wall.

"Get up!"

Recognition pulled him out of his hazy stupor, and he rolled over onto his hands and knees, but his left elbow buckled, and he landed on his left side. Rough hands yanked him back up. Within seconds he was sitting with his back against a wall, staring into the ugliest face he'd ever seen. "Damn...not a mug I want to wake up to."

"You're no prize yourself." Clockwork leaned back and sat on his haunches. He seemed alert and mad. But Blackwater assumed he was always mad. "I need you to wake up and think."

*Think. Heh...right.* Blackwater carefully rubbed his cybereyes with the edges of his palms. Blinking a few times to adjust the lighting and reception, he took in the room around him. And that's all it was. A room.

Four walls.

And he and Clockwork were on the floor. "What the hell—"

"That's what I said. Our gear's gone, my prize is gone, and nothing's working."

Blackwater checked himself with pats to his thighs, his hips, his chest, his upper arm—any place he usually had something strapped. Clockwork was right. He didn't have his deck, his commlink, or his weapons. After a few colorful metaphors, he stood along with the hobgoblin and walked around the room, checking the perimeter. "What the hell happened?"

"The last thing I remember was a big black van cutting us off, then drawing my gun as the door opened, and then an ugly dude shot me. I'm assuming he shot you, too."

"Yeah. With a tranq—so I'm guessing. You been awake long?"

"Not much longer than you. I've already yelled and beat on the walls. I can't even find a freakin' door."

Blackwater blinked at that and did another check. Nope. No doors. Not even a seam. "I feel naked."

"I feel trapped. Who the hell? This isn't that team Slamm-0!'s with, is it?"

"I don't think Schmetzer's got a setup like this. Or if he does, he didn't share it with me."

Clockwork trudged to a corner and leaned back, folding his arms over his chest. "I'm guessing it was your bubbly personality that put him off?"

"Like you're a drekking ray of sunshine?" Just because he wanted to, Blackwater banged on the wall closest to him. "Hey! What's going on?"

*"Please—there is no need to yell. I can hear you."*

Neither of them had expected an answer. They glanced at one another and moved to the center of the room, back to back. Blackwater hated not having a gun. They waited a few more seconds, and when the voice didn't continue, Blackwater spoke up. "Schmetzer?"

Laughter echoed in the small room. *"Hardly. If you would both move to Blackwater's right...no, his other right...that's good. Stay still, unless you want to remain in this room indefinitely."*

Blackwater and Clockwork exchanged glances, but they did as instructed. The wall in front of them slid to the side. He recognized the tall, pale ork as the one that had shot him from the van. Guy looked like he needed a hot meal or ten really bad. He was also holding a Manhunter, and gestured with it for them to come out.

*"Please go with Shax. He has my permission to shoot you if he thinks you're going to attack him. Keep the peace, and this should go smoothly and profitably for all of us."*

Another glance, and Blackwater followed Clockwork out of the room. They walked down a gray hallway with no doors, turned right at the end of that hall, then another right, then a left and then another left—until Blackwater lost track of where they were.

Finally, they stopped at a door and Clockwork turned the knob.

The three of them stepped into what Blackwater could only describe as a medical room. Or it looked like one. As he and the hobgoblin strolled in, he took in several metahumans in long black coats, the opposite of a doctor's white coat.

They stood near a row of what looked like autodoc tubes. Blackwater hated those things. They were too much like coffins. One of the reasons he'd taught himself how to fix his own hurts. As they walked past, he saw the docs were loaded with people. And every one looked like they were in pain.

This room emptied into an even larger room, carpeted, with wood walls full of holo-projections of global networks. Most of them were newsvids, others were playing shows Blackwater recognized. A few sitcoms, and a few of those unscripted shows he never watched.

In the center was a circular desk with a large chair.

So...maybe this was the person in charge. He no longer suspected this was part of Schmetzer's people. No, this was another player. Someone with a lot of pull.

Maybe the one that killed had Wagner.

When the chair turned, the last person he expected to see was a dwarf.

"What the hell is this?" Clockwork said as he stood in front of the chair. "*You* interrupted our extraction?!"

The dwarf made a pained face. "*That* was an extraction? It looked more like kids arguing on the playground over who had the better toy." The little guy's tone was arrogant, and he had an accent Blackwater couldn't place. "What you did was complicate things—but I do believe you also provided us with a Plan A we didn't have before."

"Screw you. There's no *we*. You took my technomancer, didn't you?"

"The young elf girl? Yes. I have her. She is presently going through an examination."

Blackwater didn't know why, but he actually got a bad feeling about that. Yeah, he'd had his own thoughts about giving her a good once over before she got sold, but the way the dwarf said that—just sounded bad.

Clockwork took a step toward the dwarf. "You give her back to me, and we'll be on our way. She's going to bring me some good nuyen. Nuyen I'm due from the last time she got away from me."

"Ah. I see." The dwarf nodded. "You work on anger and hair trigger reflexes. Your reputation, what I can find of it, also says you're good with drones. Is this true, Clockwork?"

The use of his name made him step back, and he glanced at Blackwater before he narrowed his eyes back at the dwarf. "Who are you and what is all this?"

The dwarf interlaced his fingers in his lap. "My name is Draco Powell. This—" He looked around the room. "—is my staging area for Los Angeles. My original purpose for coming here was to retrieve a few technomancers our R&D department had tracked down through verified lists supplied to us by Horizon and Ares."

Blackwater shook his head. "That's usually not the way it works. Most snatchers grab the technos and sell them *to* the corps, not get their names *from* them."

"Depends on the nuyen, and who is in charge of the books." Powell smiled at him. "Most of the corps don't even realize that they've given up those lists. Much like the information a technomancer stole out from under you, Mr. Cole Blackwater."

That pushed a nerve. He took a step forward. "What do you know about that?"

"I know everything about that." He slipped out of the chair and put his hands on the desk. All the vids darkened into a moving starfield, with the Contagion Games logo in the center.

"Son of a—" Clockwork lowered his arms. "You work for Contagion? Is that where we are? We're in a gaming company?" He pointed at the door they came through. "That's some weird shit you got set up for playing games."

"Yes. It is. In truth I work for Ferdinand Bellex and Miranda Sebastian, the owners of Contagion." He looked at Blackwater. "And they are very interested in this technomancer that outwitted you, as well as the data he stole. But please…Mr. Clockwork and Mr. Blackwater. Mr. Bellex would like to talk to both of you himself."

Shax stepped forward and handed them their commlinks. "Put these on."

The room darkened as the vids all meshed into one large image of the logo. The logo twisted and spun until it took on the shape of a man. With sharp clarity, the face and smile of Ferdinand Bellex filled the vids. Blackwater immediately recognized him from the news. His was a face that was hard to miss. Perfect hair, perfect teeth, and perfect smile.

He was too…*perfect*.

"Hello and welcome." Bellex's voice boomed through speakers around the room. "I'm so sorry we couldn't meet in person, but I'm afraid I'm swamped with meetings and dealing with a few media problems."

Clockwork slipped his commlink on, and so did Blackwater.

"Now, we don't have a lot of time, so we need to get down to business." He looked at each of them and smiled his perfect smile. "Powell here tells me you want the technomancers—the little elf girl and this elf man—and the data he stole from the Horizon Annex."

Both of them nodded.

"That's all well and good." His smile actually twinkled as he leaned into the screen. "But I'm willing to bet what you really want is a good payday. You want good cred. You want the accolades that will come to you. Am I right?"

Blackwater was going to nod at that, but Clockwork took a step toward the screens. "No. I hate technomancers. I snatch them so I can sell them—and the price isn't important. I want to know they're going to get their heads cut open and their brains scooped out." He put his hands on his hips. "And the way I see it—whatever that data is—it's valuable, all right. But not something you can measure in nuyen. When this many people want something—that something can give power. And I want the power it'll give *me*."

Blackwater watched Bellex's expression. He looked patient as he appeared to listen to Clockwork, but there was something in his eyes that unnerved him. In fact, he looked thoughtful as he seemed to consider Clockwork's words. "I see. And I can understand why you would feel that way, Mr. Clockwork. May I call you Clock?"

"No."

"So be it. Clock, there are a few things I believe you need to know so you'll have a better grasp of your situation. All technomancers have been, and will be, claimed by me. They're my property once I have them. So, all thoughts of some kind of petty revenge for this alleged damaging of your so-called reputation aren't part of this equation."

All during this, Bellex never once broke his smile. What he said didn't match the look of patience in his expression.

Bellex continued before Clockwork could react. "And as for the data that was stolen—it is something your disgusting, beady eyes will never see. And if you ever do see it, I will personally remove you from this planet. What you two are going to do is help me acquire Kazuma Tetsu and the packet of data he now possesses. If you have any questions or doubts to the validity of my request, or to my ability to get exactly what I want, I invite you to step inside your AR and show me your AI."

*AI?* Blackwater looked at Clockwork. "You got an AI?"

"Yeah, I do." The hobgoblin's face darkened.

"Then I suggest you check on it, Clock."

With a lingering glare at the screen, Clockwork activated his commlink. Blackwater did the same so he could see the PAN images. After a few seconds, Clockwork lowered his arm and balled his hands into fists as he faced Bellex. "Where is he?"

"He's safe. For now. And if you want to keep him safe, you'll do as I say. This isn't an action to control you, Clock. This is an action to show you that in my world, *I* get what *I* want, and *you* have to do what *I* say." Bellex's gaze shifted to Blackwater. "I take it from your silence that you don't have any objections?"

"Am I gonna get paid?"

"Yes. Quite handsomely."

"Then I got no beef. What's the plan?"

Bellex's smile twinkled again. "I am so glad you see things like this, Cole—may I call you Cole?"

"Long as your nuyen's good, you can call me anything you want."

"Good. Now Clock," Bellex said as he looked at the seething hobgoblin. "I think using this elf girl as a trade proposition is a good idea. Tetsu was traveling with her. It is possible he will sacrifice for her."

When Clockwork didn't answer, Blackwater nudged him. But the rigger wasn't having any of it, and didn't reply.

Blackwater said, "Actually, he might. But there's this hacker named Slamm-0! that might be more interested in a trade. If you contact him and the shadow team he's working with, he might get the data and Tetsu to trade for her."

"Splendid! Cole...you might just fit into my plans better than I conceived."

Clockwork raised his head and Blackwater stepped away, afraid of what he might come out of the hobgoblin's mouth. "What exactly *are* your plans, if you don't mind me asking?"

Bellex's smiled twinkled a third time, and Blackwater winced at the glare. The man looked as if he would explode with joy as he said, "Why, to join with God, of course."

# CHAPTER FORTY-FOUR

## UNKNOWN LOCATION

Kazuma awakened with a start and felt a firm pressure on his chest. He blinked up at someone he didn't recognize. Female, with luscious, long blonde hair, intense blue eyes, a thin face, and a pair of tusks sticking up from behind her lower lip. He stared at her, more so that he could see her fully, and not because of her goblinization.

"If you take a vid it'll last longer, chummer. And I can pose with fewer clothes on."

Knitting his brows together, he grabbed her wrist. "Where's Silk?"

The woman laughed. Her voice was nice to hear, and her accent was something distinctly southern. "Oh, baby—" She plucked his hand from her wrist as if he had no strength and set it back on the bed. "—you are an innocent little thing, aren't you? And not bad on the eyes, either. Silk's fine. Nice lady you got there."

"I—" before he could complete his question, everything from before he faded came rushing back. No...he hadn't faded...the host! He lifted his head to look at himself and saw it was her hand on his chest. He wore a sheet—and bandages. The wound from the Annex had bled. Again. "My clothes?"

"Sorry, beautiful, but they had blood all over them. Incinerated them a few hours ago after I got you out of them. You're going to get an infection if you don't rest long enough to let that wound heal. Looks like you took a bullet." She grinned. "That where Cole got you?"

He narrowed his eyes. "Cole...Cole Blackwater...that's the hacker with Clockwork. He's...the wolf-hacker."

"Wolf-hacker—oh! Right. He uses that cheap out-of-the-box persona. Yeah...you took that data from him. No one's ever done anything like that to him before."

"I don't know why." Kazuma rubbed at his face. "He wasn't that well prepared, and he had no protection to speak of."

"Well, I don't think he thought anyone else would be in that host in the first place."

"And that's my fault?"

She blinked and then laughed again. "Sweetie, my name's Shayla. I'm Mack Schmetzer's rigger."

He shook her offered hand. "Kazuma Tetsu. I'm a—"

"Technomancer," she filled in when he hesitated. "No biggie here. I used to think Mack had a problem with you people, but recently I've changed that opinion."

More memories came back, and he gripped the side of the bed and pushed himself up on his elbows. "Netcat—where is she? Did she make it out of the house?"

But Shayla's expression told him what he feared. "Sorry, Kaz. Slamm-0!'s beside himself, nagging the crap out of Mack to go find her. He's afraid that prick named Clockwork will sell her."

"He might. He tried it before." Kazuma recognized the sluggish feeling in his joints. Dumpshock. He hadn't pulled out of the host fast enough before he crashed it. "We are going to rescue her, right?"

"I'm not calling the shots. And neither is Slamm-0!. Mack is, and we've been waiting on you to wake up so we can get this party started." She pushed herself up, and then offered him her hand again. "Come on. I can get you some food on the way there."

Kazuma half-rolled off the bed and onto his feet. Dizziness came over him, but it was brief. "Where's Silk?"

"She's with Mack. And so is your interesting friend Moon-Shine. They're waiting on you, too. She's been talking to Mack about you, and your people."

"My people?"

"Technomancers." Shayla waited until he was upright and confident he would stay that way before leading him out of the room. The walls around them were red and brown brick, and the lights along them revealed a hazy fog just above his head. He smelled smoke and clove, and felt the beat of music against his chest. "Where are we?"

"One of Mack's clubs." Shayla walked him into an elevator and turned to face him when the door closed. Kazuma's stomach lurched when they headed down at a rapid speed. "Can't say which one. Gotta talk first."

He nodded, and when the elevator stopped, the wall opened behind him. He turned and waited for Shayla so he could follow her. The walls were still red brick but the smoke and music were gone. They stepped from the hall into a hangar-like area where he saw a Shinobi, Silk's Hummer and another vehicle.

A troll lumbered up to meet her and stopped in front of Kazuma. "It's good to see you up and some color in your cheeks. My name is Preacher."

Kazuma sensed something powerful about Preacher. And alien. The symbols on his horns, along with the pierced rings and the way he dressed, suggested the troll might be a magic user. "Kazuma Tetsu. Nice to meet you, Preacher."

The troll grinned. He focused on Shayla, whose height only brought her up to Kazuma's shoulder. Slender, petite, and a knockout, even with the tusks and slightly forward brow. "Mack and Silk are in his office with Slamm-0!. Apparently he caught the hacker trying to find Clockwork and Blackwater. Stirred up GOD a bit. So we're staying off the grids, except for a few public access points, until something breaks."

Shayla took it all in and then gestured for Kazma to follow her. Preacher followed behind him as the three of them approached a door nestled between three-meter high stacks of tires and wires. Kazuma followed her into a good-sized, nicely-furnished office.

The room was long more than wide. On his right sat a desk, and to his left and mostly in front of him was an oval table, where he spotted Silk and MoonShine. Silk jumped up and ran to him. She felt good in his arms, and he threw modesty to the wind as he gave her a deep and longing kiss. She wore a tight-fitting black T-shirt and pants with various pockets and she looked...amazing.

Silk pulled back and put her hand to his swollen face. "You still look like hammered shit."

"And you still look beautiful," he said in a soft voice. For him, being a technomancer and touching the datasphere in what some perceived was a magical way meant nothing when it came to this—to *physical* contact and connection. He loved her beyond question, and it wasn't because Hitori had introduced them—though they did share that connection—he loved her because she was what his heart wanted.

"Okay, let's break it up. I told you he was fine."

Kazuma turned and matched the gruff voice with the grizzled human as he walked into the room, followed by a young man with spiky blond hair and a disgruntled expression. Kazuma noted his datajack and gear, visible on his upper arm and hip.

Kazuma didn't expect the blond hacker to approach and shove a finger in his face. "This is *your* fault. She's in this because of *you!*"

Silk reacted first by inserting her long arm between Kazuma and the blond, then pushing him back. "I suggest you back off, Slamm-0! This isn't anyone's fault."

*This is Slamm-0!? What is he doing here?* Kazuma put a hand on Silk's arm in an attempt to calm her temper. "No, it's okay. I understand how he feels."

"No, you don't."

Kazuma had moved past those days of remaining in the background and letting others speak for him. He gently pulled Silk to him and then stepped between Slamm-0! and her. "Yes. I do. Because if someone as sick and twisted as this Clockwork or Blackwater had Silk, the anxiety of not knowing, of not being able to act would eat at me. The same way it's eating at you right now. I would blame anyone and everyone that had direct contact with her before she was taken. So yeah..." he said as he canted his head to his right shoulder, his gaze locking on Slamm-0!'s. "I *do* know."

"All right, kids," the older man said with a decisive clap. "We've got a lot to go over in very little time. Kazuma, you and Silk sit over there by Whitey—"

"My name is MoonShine."

"—Moon guy. Everyone else take your place."

Kazuma's gaze lingered on Slamm-0! for a few seconds. He didn't know if he'd gotten through to him, but he did want him to know he understood. And he planned to help get Netcat back.

Once everyone was seated, the older man stood at the head of the table and addressed Kazuma. "My name's Mack Schmetzer. I'm the owner of this establishment—one of many. I'm also the leader of this shadow team and the one that paid Cole Blackwater to retrieve the information from the Horizon Annex that night."

This news wasn't a surprise to Kazuma. He leaned forward as his senses opened up to the soft, soothing whispers of the datasphere. The wireless here was shielded, but he could touch the Matrix, cling to it for support. "You lost a woman that night. I saw her...on the floor next to the guards."

"Yeah. That was Maria. At first I was led to believe that you shot her. But I don't any more. Evidence to the contrary was given to me from an unlikely source." His eyes unfocused for a few seconds, and Kazuma knew he was looking at something else within his AR. "Yeah...send them down."

Silk interlaced her fingers with his as he leaned in for her. Shayla came through the door with a tray of food and set it in front of Kazuma. Fruit, protein bars, a bottle of water.

Mack nodded at him. "Eat while I talk."

Shayla smiled as he tore into the fruit, and Silk opened the water for him. She took a seat beside Preacher as the door to the office opened again.

In walked a tall, blonde female elf and a large male troll. The troll looked the part of a businessman—nice suit and tie, with a briefcase in one meaty hand. His horns were unadorned, and his face was handsome in comparison to Preacher's.

Mack stepped forward and took the elf's hands in his. He kissed one of them. "You ready?"

"As I'll ever be." She turned to the troll. "Renault, if you'll give Mack what you showed me this morning?"

He looked hesitant, but she turned and went to him with a hand on his shoulder. "Trust me on this. We can trust Mack."

"Is he the—" His gaze cut to Schmetzer.

"Yes. This is him."

Whatever the two shared about Schmetzer seemed to comfort him, and he set his briefcase on the desk at the other end of the room. He and Mack shook hands and spoke in soft tones as the elf came to stand in front of Kazuma. He wiped his mouth with a napkin as he smiled up at her.

She offered him her hand across Silk's brow. "Sergeant Delaney Charis, PCC local law enforcement. My partner is Officer Raoul Renault."

That pronunciation set off several protests, mostly from Slamm-0! and MoonShine.

The blond hacker shot up. "A cop? Mack, are you crazy?"

"You didn't say she was PCC," Shayla said from her seat, with Preacher's large hand on her shoulder. Kazuma didn't know if it was there to keep her seated, or to reassure her that he supported her. "I thought Charis was your first name."

"No, he's not crazy," Delaney said, then looked at Shayla. "Charis Monogue was the name I used while working undercover at Horizon."

Kazuma finished shaking her hand. "Kazuma Tetsu."

"You have the online handle of Soldat?"

He hesitated as he pulled his arm back. "Yes."

"Don't worry, Mr. Tetsu. I'm on your side." She straightened and looked at the table. "I'm the Johnson who requested your team retrieve the data. My boss, while I was undercover—the former Mr. Artus Wagner—employed Cole Blackwater to take it simultaneously. This was nothing more than an unfortunate coincidence."

Shayla's jaw dropped.

"So the piece of drek was a double agent," Slamm-0! said.

"Not really." Mack patted Renault's shoulder—which was a good foot above his own—as he turned to join the conversation. "Blackwater wasn't a double anything. He was and is out for his own agenda. And right now none of our contacts in Los Angeles have been able to find him, or that nasty little hobgoblin he's with."

"Clockwork." Slamm-0! sat back down. "They've probably already left town, taking her to NeoNET. That's who was going to buy her before."

"I doubt that," Delaney said as Mack stood beside her. She glanced at Renault, who was busy connecting whatever was in his briefcase to Mack's system. The vids activated. Four of them appeared on the left of the desk, and Kazuma felt their static as they came online. He looked at the small projector in the center of the table before it activated, and a flat projection appeared. It would show the same thing on either side, as if looking at a mirror.

"You were undercover?" MoonShine prompted.

"Yes. Investigating Horizon's recent activities."

"What activities?"

"Their hiring of Knight Errant, and not using PCC security to clear that Annex before it was destroyed. And it was destroyed on time early this morning."

"Why is that a reason to be investigated?" Slamm-0! asked. "Corporations hire private security all the time."

Kazuma opened a protein bar and took a bite. It was as bland as he remembered, but he was hungry enough to eat cardboard. "That's why you were curious? The Pueblo Corporate Council runs Los Angeles, and essentially the city's security. Why hire a private company?"

Delaney nodded. "Exactly. I was put there to investigate that reason. Was there something to hide in that Annex? Did Horizon have someone inside Knight Errant in their pocket?"

Kazuma drank some water to wash the bland down. "Did you find out why?"

"Mr. Tetsu, did you know about that data prior to being put in charge of wiping that host?"

"No. I thought all three hosts had already been archived. That's what we were given as specs."

"Did you volunteer for the project?"

"No. I was promoted and assigned—" He stopped and stared up at her before continuing. "I was *assigned* the host, and given full authority in overseeing its destruction." He looked from Delaney to Mack to Silk, and then back to Delaney. "Someone *wanted* me to find that data?"

"Tell me how you discovered it was there."

"Well, it's routine to do a full diagnostic of a host before it's destroyed. To see if any of it can be used in small, redundant systems—which this host had been used for before. That's why it was there. To store archived records for Horizon. And I'd gotten in the habit of plugging in my own parameters when I searched, piggybacking it on the KE regulation monitor."

"And that's when you found your sister's name?"

"Yes. And when I found the name Caliban."

Delaney and Renault glanced at each another.

Mack shook his head. "Not familiar with that one. Was that your sister's online persona?"

"No. It was a name given to me by a private investigator I'd hired a few years ago, the first time Hitori disappeared. After she showed up again, I tried to find him to let him know she was fine, but he was hard to get hold of. When she disappeared again a few months ago—he contacted me in the Matrix. He showed me a host..." Kazuma cringed as he remembered how it looked, how it felt and tasted. "A place where those that had experienced dissonance could go and express the horror and sickness they saw. He called it dark resonance—resonance tainted with the darkness of dissonant technomancers. He said more of the dark resonance was coming, that Caliban would create more hosts with real dissonance. He told me to change my persona name to Soldat, and to start searching for Hitori and Caliban." He licked his lips. "And then something else was in the host with us, and we severed our connections."

"You ever try to find this host again?"

Kazuma looked at Slamm-0! "I did, but instead of the exhibition of dark resonance, I found a host corrupted with it. I barely got out of there. Silk had to come get me."

"He was sick for days after that submersion." Silk looked around Kazuma to see Slamm-0! "I wanted to find it again. I wanted to see it for myself, and I did after a week of looking. But what I saw was a little different."

"Are you a technomancer?" Delaney asked Silk.

Silk put her elbows on the table. "I am and I'm not. I have too much cyberware to be fully functional, and my ability to travel into the resonance is pretty much nil. I can see it, but I can't touch it. Not the way Hitori or Kazuma can. But I can connect without the commlink or a deck, if that's what you want to know."

"Oh, wow," Shayla piped up. "Do you use a RCC—wait a minute! Was that *you* who hacked my RCC?"

Silk laughed. "Guilty. And I'm sorry. But I wanted Kazuma out of there in one piece. I hope I didn't damage anything."

"No...but you did that using a techno's ability?"

"Yes. I sent a machine sprite into it. Messed up your connection a bit, and sort of did my own thing."

"Okay, that's great," Mack interrupted. "But we need to get back to the point."

"Which is?" Preacher asked.

Delaney continued. "That there were forces at work behind the scenes, driving Kazuma to his ultimate destination. Strings were pulled and manipulated so he would find that data and take it."

Kazuma and Silk looked at one another, and he took her hand in his before he looked back at Delaney. "Who?"

"Hang on." Slamm-0! held up his hands. "I just got a message from Blackwater."

"Put it on the screen." Mack released access to Slamm-0!.

Blackwater's face appeared in sharp, defined living color. Kazuma leaned back and glared at the image. It was a recording.

"Hey chummers, miss me?" He laughed, showing silver and yellow teeth. "I'm pretty sure about right now you're all wondering what we did with your little elf techno freak. So, me and my new *omae* got a little proposition for you. I suggest you take it, or according to Clockwork, NeoNET gets a new hire."

# CHAPTER FORTY-FIVE

## UNKNOWN LOCATION

The world Netcat woke to was destroyed. She stood on the precipice of a cliff, looking out over a desolate, bleak landscape. A cold wind whipped debris into her fur and roared in her tiny, pointed ears. Did someone finally drop the bomb? Is this all that's left?

Below and to her right, she saw metahumans emerge from the bombed-out rubble of what once might have been a library—the dusty remnants of books, paper, desks, and lamps were strewn in all directions, constantly whipped up by the wind. The gray sky swirled with orange and purple clouds, over a world caught in an apocalyptic twilight.

A warehouse loomed in the background with metal cans outside, each ablaze with a warming fire. She held her paw up to protect her face from the wind as she climbed down from the cliff's edge and took a road beaten into the dry and cracked earth. As she neared, others took note of her and watched as she came closer, but no one came to greet her, nor did they look at her as if she were an enemy or a stranger.

Netcat thought she saw pity in their eyes.

People, dressed for all walks of life, stood around warming themselves. Some talked quietly. Some sat against the ruined library. An elderly man with long, white hair fluttering in the wind smiled at her and pointed to the library door. He was dressed the nicest. Clean, unmarked by the landscape.

The library's interior was as stark as the outside. Lights buzzed overhead, and in every corner were groups of people. No...these were icons! Some were actual images of metahumans, while others were personas. Some were out of the box and less-detailed, while others were high-definition renderings of different creatures, from wolves and bears down to a lone duck and complaining squirrel. A medieval knight paced endlessly back and forth, and in one corner sat the saddest clown in—wherever the hell they were.

When she finally looked down at herself, she realized she was in her black cat persona.

*I'm in the Matrix! But how? I didn't submerge. And if I did, I didn't prepare my body. I need to sever the connection.*

Her AR didn't respond to her. No matter how hard she tried, she couldn't pull back out of the Matrix!

"That's not going to work," a voice said to her left. She looked up into the fine features of a warrior elf. His dark hair flowed over his battle armor and the hilt of a sword stuck up behind him. His eyes were amber, and had a slight wizened look. She knew the player was much older than the persona when she looked into them. "The commlinks don't work."

"Where are we?" Netcat sat with her paws firmly planted in front of her. Her tail twitched behind her.

"Most of us assume we're on a Contagion host. Private access. You can't log into it, and you can't log out. We're stuck here."

"How many of us are there?"

"Oh, close to fifty or so. There were more—but with Caliban's last temper-tantrum—we lost about thirty."

Netcat leaned her head forward. "Caliban?" Why was that name familiar?

He stood up, and she noticed his lower half didn't match his upper. From the waist up he was an elf warrior. But from the waist down he wore calf-length shorts, white socks and house shoes. He saw her looking and pointed at it. "It'll happen to you too, the longer you're here. Come on."

She padded behind him, over the rocks and debris inside the library to a back area. A woman who looked a lot like Quan Yin in all her glory, from the silk robes to the floating scarves about her hair, sat in a chair talking to a semicircle of icons. Most of them were still in their persona forms, but there were a few that looked as they probably would in the physical world.

Something cold brushed past her as she followed the elf warrior. She jumped and hissed when she turned, and then bounded up onto the elf's shoulder. Looking back, she tried to focus on whatever it was that had unnerved her, and though she sensed something was there, she couldn't quite see it.

"Ah...e-sense. You know he's there."

"Who is he?" She remained on his shoulder as he pulled a chair out at an empty table in the back. She leapt onto the table and faced him.

He shrugged. "Who knows? Only the ones who've been here for the longest can say because they can still see them. But they tell me I should be happy I can't, because what they are is what we'll become."

"I don't understand. What's going on? How come all the personas look half-finished and what is it on a host that I can't see but sets off all my nerves?"

He stared steadily at her. "I think introductions first. My name's Harold Tremere. My Matrix persona was HipOldGuy."

Netcat's tiny jaw dropped. "Hip! I'm Netcat!"

The look in the elf's eyes brightened, and he held out his arms. She jumped into them and gave him the best hug a cat could. Once done, she returned to the table, but kept a paw on his hand. "What happened to you?"

"Did Soldat get my message?"

"Yeah. But we didn't know what it was. Silk sent it to Shyammo, who uploaded it. Is that really what happened to you?"

"Yeah. I was trying out the *TechnoHack* game. You know, getting that intel I talked about?" He shrugged. "I've been here ever since."

"What's happening here?"

He stared at her for a few seconds. "We're here to build a ladder."

Netcat frowned. "Say that again?"

"Caliban wants a ladder to the Resonance Realms, and he thinks we can build him one that'll cross the event horizon and get him there."

"Who is this Caliban? And—" she leaned in close and again and twitched her whiskers. "Resonance realms? Is everyone here a technomancer?"

"Yes. All of us. And most of the ones surviving here were *registered*, either with their local government or a corporation like Horizon. And promised to be protected. Everyone I've talked to got a demo copy of this game and a free password for a subscription. But once they subscribed and stated to play, they've never been able to sever."

"Is this the game? Building this ladder?"

"Oh. No. I saw the game. The host was full of dissonance wells. Just nasty puddles of them. Corrupted code everywhere. It's no wonder the game was getting bad reviews. But those blackouts? They happen when Caliban draws too much from us, and the host goes out."

"Draws too much from us?" Netcat blinked. "I'm not following."

He patted his shoulder. "Come on."

Netcat jumped onto his shoulder, and Harold strode past the mismatched icons and personas, even brushing past that cold, horrible presence again on his way to the doors. Outside in the maelstrom, he held up his shield to protect her from the wind as he moved toward the warehouse to another cliff and pointed.

Above them, twisting and swirling, was a resonance stream. It glistened like spun glass as iridescent glints of light twinkled through the orange-gray sky. Something stuck out of the top of the warehouse below it and continued up toward the stream. From where she sat on his shoulder, it looked like it was getting close.

"That is the ladder he wants us to build so he can touch the stream."

"Is that a real stream?"

"Yes. He found it here by using technomancers. You need to see this."

He moved against the wind from the edge toward the warehouse and walked inside. There weren't any locks or guards as they entered. The room was cooler and dimly lit, but her cat's eyes adjusted easily. Most of the place was empty from what she could see, except for a light in the center. The closer they got, the more she wanted to back up.

Three men lay in the center of a bright white light, their heads together to form a sort of triangle. They were naked, and not in any sort of living persona she could tell. Their eyes stared up into nothing, and their mouths were open in silent screams.

"This is the ladder's base. These are what Caliban calls the first ones. He's nicknamed them. Antonio, Alonso and Sebastian. But their real names are Jesus Huerta, Morion Baron and Radcliff Tolen."

"How do you know that?"

"Quan Yin, back in the library, told me. She's the overseer of the host. She's an AI and here to answer questions she can. Of course there's a price for the question." He gestured down at his lower half. "She takes a bit of your strength when you ask."

"Who...are or were they?"

"I didn't ask that. I wanted to keep what I had left for a bit longer."

Floating above them, ever threatening to smash their heads, was a flat concrete platform. On top of that was the base of a great ladder. She couldn't tell immediately what the ladder was made of, but she knew she didn't want to go near it.

She didn't want to be in the same room with it.

"Harold..."

"You can feel it, can't you? Can you hear them, Net? I can. I hear them all the time, and I know that one day, I'll be there with them."

She looked too hard at the ladder and realized, as she hissed and jumped down and ran out of the warehouse, what the rungs of the ladder were made of.

# CHAPTER FORTY-SIX
## ONE OF MACK'S CLUBS

Mack tapped the folders in the display Renault had uploaded to his office PAN. Only Delaney, Renault, and he had access to it for editing. Everyone else could only look at it.

He found the file on himself as fascinating as Delaney had.

As one of Hestaby's Clutch, his childhood had been good. Protected. Disciplined. He'd been happy—but he'd been most happy when he was enveloped in the Matrix.

For over thirty years, he'd tried to block out the more painful memories—of how his abilities waned when he hit puberty. He remembered the sad faces of the others, the knowing looks the dragon gave him when he could no longer hear the whispers of the datasphere. The others were kind to him...

But nothing could erase the shame he'd felt. Others had grown up around him, and lost their abilities. When they left, off to other lives, Mack had boasted he would never lose his connection, that he would always be able to touch and to hear the threads of the Matrix.

It had all changed—just as Hestaby said it would. And eventually it was gone, and he was no longer able to stay at Shasta.

His life as documented in Wagner's files was pretty much true. A drifter, never a wageslave. He'd gambled and lost and gambled and won. He had three clubs to show for it and enough nuyen squirreled away in accounts Wagner never found to retire off three times over.

But he kept going, he kept searching.

For what? That was Delaney's question. Something she'd asked after showing him the folder and asking if it was true—that he had been *otaku* and protected by a dragon.

He decided not to answer then, but now as he mulled over the folder and the information with the image of the woman on the vid near his desk, he signaled the door to open and smiled when Delaney charged in, a determined look on her face.

"Mack—I keep hitting a brick wall. I swear this Ferdinand Bellex doesn't exist! Maybe Renault's right, and he's just a—" That's when her eyes met those of the woman on the screen.

Mack smirked when he saw recognition on Delaney's face. Hestaby had a look not many forgot—especially given the events of the past six months. "Delaney Charis, I'd like you to meet Hestaby."

Delaney looked as if she didn't know whether to bow or curtsey.

Hestaby's speaker gave a soft laugh, though her lips never moved. "Delaney Charis, it is a pleasure to meet you. I was just going over the information you and your partner were able to find."

Mack turned to face Delaney and shook his head. "She won't bite. At least not from here."

"I, uh..." Delaney licked her lips. "Is, uh, the information good?"

"Well, of course it is. He has also informed me of Mr. Blackwater and Mr. Clockwork's offer to trade the elf technomancer for Mr. Tetsu and the packet of information. I know Mack's thoughts, and my own, but what are yours?"

"My thoughts?"

Mack couldn't help himself as he chuckled and rubbed at the back of his neck. "Hestaby and I both agree that setting up a meet 'n swap in the Matrix doesn't sound like something either of those idiots came up with on their own. The fact they'll be sending the address of the host in question minutes before the meet is even more suspicious." He glanced at the vid before continuing. "So my opinion is the dwarf's behind this somehow."

"Powell?"

"Yeah. Blackwater and Clockwork disappeared minutes after Kazuma took down that host. Following PCC police reports after we left, they did find a stolen van a block from the Risen house. But he did find this before they pulled their vanishing act." He waved at the vid in front of him displaying the contents of his file. The information disappeared, replaced by a surveillance drone image of the Risen house. Mack moved the image with his ringed hands and zoomed in on a small area along the edge of the overpass, near where Silk parked the Hummer.

Delaney came closer. "What is that?"

"A Land Rover," Mack said as he tried to sharpen the image further. "I'd say circa 2055, from its frame."

Hestaby's voice came through the speakers. "Neither of the two kidnappers have such a vehicle registered in their possession. Mack and I believe the events at the Risen house were being monitored by someone."

Delaney sighed. "Draco Powell."

"Yep." Mack moved the image forward through a few frames until the camera centered on the license. "Registered to Morion Baron."

Delaney hesitated before narrowing her eyes at Mack. "But... that's one of the missing former owners of Contagion Games."

"Funny that." He moved the images around again to show heat signatures from the drone's view. He tapped each one and a name came up beside it. Netcat, Clockwork, Blackwater, Kazuma, Silk, Slamm-0!, Mack, Preacher, Shayla, MoonShine over in the Hummer. Then he pointed to an unlabeled dot near Silk and Kazuma and zoomed in. It was in the back yard. "He was there the whole time, watching, and we never even saw him."

"Magic?"

"Possible. He is a registered user." He rubbed his forehead with the back of his hand. "I'm thinking Powell came in and gave the boys a hand out of that situation. And I'm betting he's helping them out now." He moved the image back over to the overpass ramp to the Land Rover. Another unnamed heat signature. "With whomever that is."

"That's the ork he's got working with him. I met him once." Delaney shivered. "I was more freaked out by him than that wolf he had." She put her hands on her hips. "So the Land Rover is another link between Powell and Contagion, other than the pay stream."

Mack pointed to the image. "If there is a Land Rover still out there, in use, which belonged to one of those three missing men—what happened to the rest of their assets? Did Miranda Sebastian inherit them all?"

Delaney activated her commlink and connected to Mack's PAN. She requested outside access through the public grid, and he gave it. There she was able to connect to the PCC police host with her password and pull up several databases. She sat on the edge of the desk, not far from Hestaby's vid.

Mack and the dragon were quiet as she entered each of the names of the missing in the database, cross-referenced with owner records, probate court and—there it was! She downloaded the information and sorted it on her own AR before she uploaded it to Mack's PAN.

He moved it onto the main screen. "Hestaby, are you getting this?"

"I am."

Delaney stepped forward, her instant shock at seeing the dragon's image so close, not to mention actually talking to her! She had a silent fangirl squee before arranging the documents she found under each name. Above that she created a folder and named it *Prospero*.

"Prospero?" Mack made a face.

"Shakespeare, Mackenzie," Hestaby said. "In fact, I'm seeing several character names from the play, *The Tempest*. Prospero was the name of the magician, Caliban the name of the demon. Ferdinand is the name of the prince. The fact that Miranda, Prospero's daughter, has taken the name of the witch, Sycorax, Caliban's mother, is very interesting."

"She's right. All the names come from *The Tempest*. And all three of these names still own properties across Seattle, Denver, Los Angeles, and Manhattan. Remember, originally there were four owners of Contagion—Miranda Sebastian is still alive as far as we know, and working with Ferdinand Bellex as the CFO. But according to the documents in these folders," She moved them over. "Every one of their holdings were originally purchased under the umbrella of Prospero, Incorporated. That protected the individuals, and it makes it easier for Sebastian, and now Bellex, to utilize those properties, like the Land Rover, in a legal capacity."

Mack moved forward and opened each of the listings. He tapped a few items, and several maps came up in rapid succession.

"What did you find, Mackenzie?" Hestaby's voice was soft and warm. Delaney knew it was a voice projected by magic, but it still amazed her.

"Two here in Los Angeles." He brought up a split screen with two location maps. Each of them had a highlighted box in their center. "Both are warehouses in less populated areas of Los Angeles—one in the still damaged areas since the quake. One is owned by Morion Baron, the other by Radcliff Tolen. I can send

Shayla and Preacher out to do a physical touch on them, just so we don't trip anything electronic."

"That is a good plan, Mackenzie. And if Draco Powell is in one of them, it would seem fair to assume the physical locations of the two kidnappers and the elf would also be there. This could give us an advantage before they call for the meeting and send the location," Hestaby said.

"That's what I was thinking." He rubbed his lower lip. "Delaney, you think you can pull some muscle to get access to drones in the area?"

"Probably. But couldn't Shayla do that?"

"Yeah...but not legally. I'd like to keep GOD out of this, if at all possible. Got to protect my people."

"I'll see what I can do. But..." she looked between the vid of Hestaby and Mack. "What about the data? Has Mr. Tetsu even admitted to having it? Has he retrieved it? We know he set up decoy images of it all over the Matrix."

"He hasn't said, and frankly I'd prefer he keep that information out of play right now." Mack gave her a worried look. "If it contains what Wagner said it does, and we confirm its existence or its whereabouts in any way, I'm betting Bellex will do anything in his power to get to it. Right now the priority is to get Netcat back safe and sound, then my people and I need to have a little talk with Blackwater."

Mack's smile made Delaney drop hers.

# CHAPTER FORTY-SEVEN

## CONTAGION UV HOST
## LOS ANGELES

Powell strolled through the park, admiring the look and feel of downtown Denver. Why the owners considered that city the ideal place to set the game was beyond him. He could think of a hundred better places. Settings that would have drawn more players.

Ah, but then, the game had never been set up under Caliban to be popular or to make money. It was set up to bring him more technomancers, more fodder for his imaginary stairway to Heaven, or whatever he was calling it now.

He spotted Blackwater and Clockwork, their online personas almost amusing. Clockwork looked like a drone, and flew around as if testing his boundaries. Blackwater...Powell wasn't sure he knew what the hacker's persona was for. He looked like a Japanese *ronin*, complete with katana and black kimono.

*Whatever.*

They appeared to be staking out their spot where the exchange was supposed to take place. Of course, none of them had any intention of exchanging anything. Once they had Tetsu locked inside the dissonance, pinpointing his exact physical location would be easy, thanks to technology Caliban had borrowed from the Grid Overwatch Division.

The elf technomancer was already in place, safely locked inside the converted auto-doc in the warehouse. An empty rested beside hers—a place of honor for Tetsu. Whether or not he had the data with him when he arrived didn't matter. Once they had him locked on the proper host, Powell had a little surprise for Tetsu. Something very special.

"Why are parts of the park set up like the back of Myddrin Risen's yard? The Asian motif doesn't fit in well with what is supposed to be a park in Denver."

"It's what Sycorax wanted." Bellex's voice surprised him. Powell had asked the question out loud, but to himself. He turned to see Contagion's CEO standing beside him in sharp, crisp detail. "I'm waiting on one of those two chrome domes to ask me for admin access to set up a host."

"We already have one set up."

"Yeah...but they're gonna want their own."

"You do realize samurai man there is going to try and kill Tetsu."

Bellex nodded and clasped his hands together in front of him. "I'm sure he will try. But we have our own IC set up. If he does ask—ah, and here they come."

The *ronin* stalked toward Powell and Bellex with purpose as the flying disk beside him followed. "You." Blackwater pointed at Bellex. "You're the owner."

"I'm the CEO." Bellex offered his hand, and the twinkle was there on his perfect smile. "Ferdinand Bellex."

To Powell's surprise, Blackwater actually shook his hand. "Cole Blackwater. Is it possible to get admin access here? Clock and I want to create a host and set up some serious IC."

"We already have a host and countermeasures set up behind the admin access." Bellex's voice was pitched perfectly, and his posture accommodating. Powell had to give him credit, he had the act down perfectly. "But I'm sure Mr. Powell here can give you a bit of leeway when it comes to whatever means you wish to use for your fight."

The drone came down to eye level with Bellex. "Fight?"

"Well of course. Surely you plan on fighting, gentlemen? Mr. Blackwater has donned a persona in the fashion of an Edo period *ronin*, and having seen Soldat's persona as a black-clad ninja, you either wish to impress him, or fight him."

Blackwater took a step back. "Sir, I—"

"And you, Mr. Clockwork. A drone? The only reason I can see you would disguise yourself as one of your own creations would be to impress someone online in the act of selling the drone, or because you have a vendetta against the hacker you hope will accompany Mr. Tetsu into the host." Bellex's smile was larger than ever as he regarded each of them. "Am I right?"

Neither of them replied, and Powell knew Bellex was right. *Damn, he's good.*

"Gentlemen—the purpose of this meeting is to find their physical location. Get Tetsu into the dissonance, and we'll take it from there."

"And then we get paid." Blackwater shifted his position.

"And you give me my AI back," Clockwork said,

Powell watched as Bellex focused on the rigger. "Of course."

But that didn't seem to satisfy Clockwork. The drone abruptly moved in front of Bellex. "I want to see what it is you're going to do."

"Going to do?"

"All this talk about dissonance and resonance. The only thing I see is a host full of corrupted code. Half of this environment isn't even working. This place is falling apart."

Bellex's smile returned. "You would like to see what it is a technomancer sees? You? Have I been reading you wrong? I thought you were prejudiced against them."

"I don't trust 'em. There's something wrong with a mind that can get into the Matrix with just a thought. It ain't natural."

"Ah...but what exactly is natural, Clock? Someone born, or someone made? Someone whose physiology suddenly changes through no fault of their own, rendering their previous life, a life they'd grown accustomed to, void? Or someone whose own family discarded them because they became too ugly to look at?"

Powell tensed just a bit as he watched the drone. It was hard to tell what the person behind the persona was feeling when it hid behind a metal shell. Maybe this was why the rigger chose the drone. An uncaring, unfeeling, and unemotional mechanical device.

"I am sorry, Clock," Bellex said, his smile on full wattage as he continued. "But the only way to see what a technomancer sees is to be one, and right now, we don't know what makes them what they are, much less how to create one. But wouldn't that be a great piece of know-how?" The CEO switched to a serious face. "Just do what you're being paid to do. Lure him to where you were told, but do not try to kill him. And once we have him in our care, you're both free to do what you want with your reward."

Bellex disappeared.

The drone hovered in the air for a few seconds before it turned its one camera eye on Powell. "I just figured out Bellex's secret."

"Secret?" Powell smirked. "It's never been a secret, Mr. Clockwork. It's just taken you a bit longer to see the truth than I thought it would. You who possesses an AI as a pet."

Blackwater looked from Clockwork to Powell. "What secret?"

The drone's sides split, and it extended two spindled arms as it turned that camera eye on Blackwater. "Bellex is an AI, Cole. Contagion Games is run by a goddamn AI."

# CHAPTER FORTY-EIGHT

## SHAYLA'S SHINOBI
## TWO BLOCKS FROM TARGET WAREHOUSE

Silk checked and rechecked her gun, her ammo, and her RCC. She had it and her commlink in a bag at her hip, wires ready for insertion the second Shayla needed her.

They were lucky to have found Powell and the others—but instead of just storming in, Mack and Delaney had come up with the idea of keeping them busy in the Matrix while they snuck in the back door.

That is, if Slamm-0! found a back door. He sat on her right, and had been working at hacking the warehouse host for half an hour. Luckily, no alarms had been raised. That they knew of.

Preacher and Renault had been let out a half-kilometer away. They were now in the shadows of a nearby warehouse, providing overwatch and backup for the insertion team. Mack, Delaney, and Moonshine were with Kazuma back at Mack's place—and Silk still wasn't sure where that was since they insisted she be blindfolded on their way out.

The plan was for the exchange meeting to start and Mack, MoonShine, Delaney, and Kazuma would log into the host and meet with Blackwater and Clockwork. When they got the signal—and Silk hoped someone knew what that was, because she didn't—and Slamm-0! got them into the warehouse, they were going to unplug the two of them, grab Netcat, and Delaney would would have the PCC backup, already on standby, swoop in.

It all sounded so easy.

Which meant it was all going to go to hell.

<*Got it!*> Slamm-0!'s text came up in his window of her AR.

This was one of the few times she used her technomancer abilities to access the datasphere with no commlink. She felt naked.

<*Any alarms? Traps?*>

<*None so far, but I'll still need to be careful cracking the security.*>

<*I thought you said you got it?*> Silk was confused as to what Slamm-0! was doing.

<*I got into the host. Meaning I spoofed an ID that let me in, but I have to subvert the building security codes to give us physical access.*>

Oh. She knew that. <*Sorry. I'm just worried about Kazuma.*> But she knew on some level Slamm-0! was holding himself together, holding back his excitement at the prospect of getting his girlfriend out of that warehouse.

<*I get it.*> He went still again, and she watched as his hands moved over the buttons and knobs of the cyberdeck in his lap. The wiring looked odd to her, having mostly grown up in a wireless world. But she understood the principle, of how the wires connected him to the cyberdeck, and the wireless connection of the cyberdeck got him into the host.

Now it was a waiting game again, and she checked the chronometer in her AR.

The meeting had already started.

# CHAPTER FORTY-NINE

## CONTAGION UV HOST

Kazuma rezzed into what looked like a foyer of some kind, or the lobby of a corporation. In front of him were plaques on the wall with headers like *Character App*, *Play Rules*, *Backstory*, *Character Creation*. He turned to the right and saw a place to grab an *Observer* tag for those not wanting to jump into the game just yet.

Mack rezzed in just behind him. Kazuma thought it was funny that the shadowrunner's persona was a gunslinger, complete with ivory-handled pistols and spurs on his boots.

MoonShine came next, appearing as a huge, white panther. His shoulders came to Kazuma's chest. "I'm not sure they grow that big," he commented as he reached out and scratched MoonShine behind the ear.

"Mine does."

Delaney was last, her persona eliciting a wolf whistle from Mack, and drawing a mock glare from her in return. As a tall, buxom, blonde woman wearing a tight fitting tank top, short-shorts with guns at her hips, and combat boots, she looked like the standard stock tough-girl persona Kazuma had often seen before.

"I guess this is the welcome area?" she asked while walking into the lobby. "Characters...yeah, they got technomancers on the menu."

Mack pointed to a map on their left. "Looks like the host's empty."

"It's been shut down for half a day. Apparently it crashed again, and Bellex was back in the media." Kazuma approached a teleporting pad. "I'm also assuming we have to teleport down."

"I don't like this," Delaney said.

"No one here does," MoonShine growled.

"You hear from Slamm-0! yet?" Kazuma asked.

"He's halfway there. Soon as we have a go, we're a go." He nodded his Stetson-clad head toward the pad. "After you, Red Ninja."

Kazuma smiled. *I should have taken that as my handle.* He stepped up on the pad, his hand on the katana on his back as the lobby and the others disappeared.

He landed just outside of a park, and his stomach immediately twisted in on itself. His head pounded, and overwhelming nausea forced him to his knees. He knew immediately the host was badly corrupted.

"Hey," Delaney said as her boots appeared in his peripheral vision. "Kaz, what's wrong?"

"Moon's sick, too," Mack said. "And this is one ugly environment. Is the game supposed to look like this?"

Kazuma was on his hands and knees as he swallowed repeatedly, trying to keep the bile down, and happy he hadn't eaten much else besides the fruit and protein bars. It felt as if he had the flu. His joints ached as he pushed himself up and let Delaney pull him the rest of the way.

When he took a closer look around, he had to agree with Mack's assessment. The place looked...wrong. The leafless trees just past the rusted iron gate were twisted into grotesque, tortured shapes. The sky was dark, with a slight orange tinge, and he could see black smoke or smog as it rolled over the spindly branches. The scattered patches of grass were all brown and dead. A cracked and crumbling fountain near the entrance was covered in black mold. Blackish, oily water spattered and pumped from its center, and he retreated from it.

But...

It all looked a little familiar. Like a painting he'd seen recently, but one that someone had dirtied up. Slung mud and oil over it. The twisted tree could have been a cherry tree if it were in bloom. Just beyond it was short bridge over a stream, and a broken pagoda beyond that.

"Kaz...are you seeing what I'm seeing?" Moon moved against his leg.

"If you mean all kinds of wrong..." He nodded. "Yeah. Are you nauseated?"

"Yeah."

"Headache?"

"Yeah."

"Achy?"

"Yeah. Everything in here is wrong, Kaz. We should go. Now."

"We can't go," Mack said from where he and Delaney stood by the park entrance. "You two going to make it?"

MoonShine growled a bit before he said, "How can you want to stay in this nightmare any longer?"

"Moon," Kaz said as he put a hand on the panther's flank. "They're not seeing it the same way we are."

Delaney shook her head. "What are you seeing?"

"You tell me."

She sighed. "Well, it's like Mack said—the place looks like it's been cheaply done. The graphics are low rez, and the images keep rezzing and derezzing. I've adjusted my distance several times, but the objects far away just don't show up. It's like..."

"It's like the whole thing's been corrupted," Mack said as he turned to the two technomancers. "Is that what you're seeing?"

"No." Kazuma gave him a more detailed description of what he saw, and Moon added a few details of his own. "And the feeling is...it's a combination of I've seen this place before, and I'm literally trying not to get sick all over this grimy sidewalk."

"You've seen it before?" MoonShine asked. "Well, it's not Denver. I've been to this park. This looks like someplace else."

"Why are you seeing it like that?" Delaney asked. "Like a toxic waste dump."

Kazuma licked his lips. "Resonance. How we interact with the Matrix." He paused. "The Matrix is created by our imagination. Hosts are created at the whim of their creator. Their owner dictates what the host will look like, its purpose, its existence. And for most of metahumanity, that's a positive thing.

"But there are those people who like to inflict pain. They like anarchy for anarchy's sake. They like to twist and bend the Matrix into the sick and deranged fantasies of their imaginations."

"Now think about that kind of power in the hands of a technomancer," MoonShine said. "Who uses thought to make things— and destroy them. They touch the resonance, a pure, ethereal stream of creation, and darken it. Taint it. They make it—"

"Evil," Delaney finished. "I think I get it now. You see the distortion, and Mack and I see the corruption as code."

"Yes." Kazuma said. "Let's get this over with before I have to find a burned out bush and puke on it."

They moved as a unit into the park. Kazuma and MoonShine avoided several black, bubbling pools as they popped up out of the ground. Instinctively they knew not to step near or in them. If they did—

"Well, well," Blackwater said. "I'm surprised to see you, Schmetzer. I thought Slamm-0! would come. Clockwork was looking forward to seeing him again."

The four of them stopped near a copse of more gnarled cherry trees and black smoke. The smoke hovered near the ground, oozing and undulating around them, as if alive.

Blackwater looked like a *ronin*, complete with his topknot-shaved head, kimono, and twin katanas. The meaning of the persona wasn't lost on Kazuma. He just hoped he didn't have to fight, because he wasn't sure how he'd do feeling like this.

The floating, spider-armed drone beside the *ronin* had to be Clockwork. These two didn't have much imagination.

"'Fraid not, Blackwater," Mack said.

"Where is he, then? Hacking into this host?"

Mack laughed and kept his hands at his sides, near the pearl handles of his pistols. "No...that would be stupid, wouldn't it? But where Slamm-0! isn't the important issue here. We've come for Netcat."

<*I know why it's familiar now,*> Kazuma texted to MoonShine.

<*Why?*>

<*Because this isn't Denver. It's Kitanomaru Park. Father used to take us there to view Sakura, near Edo Castle.*> He frowned as he looked around. Why did it look like a corrupted place from his childhood?

"Where's the briefcase?" Blackwater countered.

"You get it when Netcat is safe." Kazuma straightened and it took a lot just to do that. "Not before."

"That's not the deal."

"That's my deal. Even if you have me, you'll never have the data, because I have to be the one to unlock it." He managed a smile. "You don't trust me?"

"Hell, no."

"I wonder why?"

The drone moved, pulling something from inside a compartment under the camera eye. It looked like a newspaper clipping.

"Her coordinates are here. Check them out yourself." The drone floated down to the ground and set the clipping on the grass before rising and moving behind Blackwater again.

Mack and Delaney shifted where they stood. MoonShine was making a great show of bravado and strength, but Kazuma was pretty sure he felt just as bad. He no longer cared what Mack had in mind—he just wanted to be out of the host. His feeling of nausea had intensified into a heavy sense of dread.

Kazuma slowly drew his katana from his back, careful not to make any sudden moves and used it to stab the clipping in the center.

The second his sword touched the paper, the grass disappeared as the same black ichor bubbled up and swallowed the clipping as well as the end of his blade. Kazuma pulled at the katana, but the viscous fluid clung tight as it flowed up the blade toward him.

"Let go, Kaz!" MoonShine shouted as he roared and bared his teeth.

He did exactly that. The katana sunk fast into the pool just as a golden flash appeared at his side. *<Ponsu! Where have you been?>*

*Protecting the case! Boss—you have to get out of here! I detected over thirty IC programs just in this park. They all appear to be linked to the same system GOD uses to pinpoint hackers' physical locations.*

Kazuma relayed this information to his companions just as everyone took a step back. He had a second katana, but didn't pull it just yet. Blackwater drew his own katana and held it in front of him with both hands. In the Matrix, weapons weren't what they appeared to be. It might look like a traditional sword, but only the wielder knew what its real purpose was.

Delaney and Mack also drew their weapons as Clockwork the drone chuckled. "I guess this was just a monumental waste of time."

"Powell never intended to trade Netcat for the data," Mack said as he thumbed back the hammers on his pistols.

"Powell?" Blackwater said, but it was obvious in his persona's expression Mack had hit the truth.

"Screw this," Clockwork declared and abruptly fired at the ground near Kazuma's feet.

This time the grass folded in under Kazuma's black slippers and the ichor whipped up another rope-like appendage and encircled his leg. He yelled as it yanked him down, and he landed on his side.

MoonShine blurred into action and charged after Blackwater. Kazuma wasn't sure if it was a lucky shot or Blackwater didn't know how to actually swing a sword when the giant white panther sunk his teeth into the man's thigh. Blackwater screamed as he lost control of that leg and tried to hack at MoonShine with his sword.

Mack went after Clockwork while Delaney stepped behind Kazuma and hooked her arms under his shoulders. He pulled his second katana out and used it pretty much the way Blackwater was using his on MoonShine. But the blade passed through the black tendrils as if they were nothing more than butter. The ichor dissolved and then reformed in seconds.

Using Delaney as ballast, he kicked at the cords, and narrowly missed having his other leg trapped the same way.

"This isn't working!" she yelled.

"Ya think?" What hindered him most was the constant, cloying nausea that sent bile to the back of his throat, as well as the headache moving from the front of his skull to the back of it. "Delaney—what do you see? What do you see holding me?"

"That's hard to describe!"

"Just try!" He heard MoonShine roar and looked over in time to see the great panther evade a slice of the katana and snap at Blackwater's hand. Mack and Clockwork had moved away near a large, gnarled tree and continued to shoot it out with each other. It looked like a stalemate.

"Okay...the grass is all pixelated—you know, like a low resolution. And I can see code swirling around your leg. It's like...it's like your persona and the environmental system are trying to merge."

"You mean like it's trying to de-rezz my persona?"

"Yeah. It's weird, but that's what it looks like."

He knew what he saw was one reality, and what Delaney saw was another. She saw the framework, but he saw the nightmare. So, in order to change the nightmare, he was going to have to recode the framework. *<Ponsu?>*

*Here, Boss.*

***<Can you see exactly what it is that's locked onto my persona?>***

*Almost. It's like an IC sprite. It's been compiled using some sophisticated code. But it's all...damaged code, and underneath it is a disso-*

nance well. You get sucked into that Boss, and I might lose you. It's like something got into the environment and corrupted the system. Turned a Happy Birthday party into a slasher flick.

He didn't have time to admire his sprite's analogy, as creative as it was. He got the idea, though. **<What is it using in order to grab my leg?>**

Ponsu spouted a list of commands, and Kazuma used them to compile a countermeasure sprite. He gave it sharp teeth, and infused it with his own rage and anger. He knew he was on the verge of using dissonance himself by doing that. Once it finished the compile, his headache flared into a full-born fire behind his eyes, and the fatigue in his muscles, that he knew was caused by the dissonance in the host, doubled.

**<Ponsu, show my little monster what to do.>**

*With pleasure, Boss!*

He grabbed hold of Delaney's arms. "When I give the word, pull!"

"Okay."

He watched as the new sprite exposed rows of sharp, nasty teeth and attacked the strands of ichor. The sprite turned from soft green to black immediately, but Kazuma had allowed for that and made sure the dissonance it ingested would be easily swayed to attack itself. So it kept feeding on the black tendrils.

The moment he felt them give, he yelled at Delaney to pull.

It took a minute, and Kazuma thought for half of that minute his legs was going to come off, but finally the black tentacles snapped, and the two of them lurched backward, away from the black pool.

With Delaney helping, he scrambled to his feet and watched as the sprite continued to scoop up the ichor and eat it. It sort of looked like a tiny fairy eating...oil.

MoonShine yelped, and Kazuma looked over to see Blackwater pull his katana back. He'd finally gotten a hit on Moon—but the technomancer wasn't down, and leaped at the *ronin* hacker with an open maw full of teeth.

A shot whizzed passed Kazuma's ear, and he held up his katana in time to deflect a second one as he saw the drone barreling down on him.

*Where's Mack?*

# CHAPTER FIFTY

## SHAYLA'S SHINOBI

Slamm-0! maneuvered around the host's IC, carefully setting his programs in strategic places. He subconsciously felt Silk, Renault, and Preacher breathing down his neck. A warning light in his AR prompted him to tap the window.

"Hey, Silk—someone's tracking Kazuma."

"Shit."

He silently echoed the sentiment as he finished getting everything ready. If this worked, it would give him access to the warehouse's host and make him administrator, and that would give him total control.

*If* it worked.

The fact someone was already tracking Kazuma's physical location told him the meeting had turned sour, and he needed to hurry. Whoever it was—and he was pretty sure it was Bellex or Powell—wouldn't have an easy time of it. He and Mack had re-routed the wireless signal through a thousand points, moving from Los Angeles to Manhattan, to Grand Rapids, Michigan to Atlanta, Georgia, and then out of the country.

He had a progress map up on his periphery. So far they'd only managed six points before the movement stopped. That either meant Kazuma had severed his connection, or he stopped them from the source.

"Slamm..."

"Don't rush me." He was nervous enough. For all he knew, Netcat was in the building across the lot from him. This gave him a little comfort; at least she hadn't been sold and imprisoned in the bowels of some megacorp.

Yet...

Cursing Clockwork again, Slamm-0! wished him all sorts Black Hammer deaths as he finished his work and took a deep breath. "Here goes."

When the program launched, he pulled back into his deck, like setting off an explosion and then hiding behind a shield. Again he watched the progress on the screen as everything fell into play and—

A message came up in the deck's AR.

**<WELCOME MASTER SLAMM-0!.>**

He howled in triumph and slapped the Shinobi's dashboard.

"I take it that was good?" Silk said.

"You got it, baby!" he said as he started a series of complex coding programs that re-routed the host's control to his deck. The only thing he had to worry about was if the old controller noticed. If he was smooth enough...the change of command would be seamless.

Once he had everything rerouted, he added Preacher, Silk, Shayla, and Renault into his PAN.

The two trolls approached the Shinobi in the dark. Renault leaned in the window. "I didn't think you had it in you."

"Oh, ye of little faith. When you're fighting for the woman you love, you can accomplish anything." He squared everything away in his bag, and slung it over his shoulder. "You tell me what you need done, and verily, it shall be done."

Renault smiled. Slamm-0! decided it was a smile he never wanted to see in a dark alley.

"First, let's get a look inside," the troll said. "Can you give us visuals on any security cameras?"

Slamm-0! complied, and within minutes they were each viewing a split screen showing the entrance, a room full of autodocs, an office, and the larger view of the main warehouse. He also retrieved the building's schematics and offered them up for reference.

"Are those autodocs?" Silk touched her own AR without a commlink or deck. Slamm-0! smiled at this. He'd often watched Netcat do the same thing, and it just made him miss her more. "I see Netcat!"

Following her lead, he zeroed a camera in on the farthest one in the row. She was there, her eyes closed, and a net of something attached to her head.

Renault and Preacher were conferring until the PCC cop said,

"Can you begin the automatic shut off? The sequence is going to take a good five minutes to initiate. If you can get it started, she should be waking up by the time we get to her."

Slamm-0! searched the host for the autodoc controls. After finding them, he carefully went through the procedures. He saw a red flash in the security camera and pointed it out. "I've disabled the shutdown warning in the feed—it's shutting them all down, and there are flashing red lights on the autodocs. If anyone happens to see that when they walk into the room or see it on the camera, they'll know."

"Then we have to move fast." Renault stepped back and opened the Shinobi's door as Slamm-0! and Silk stepped out. "Shayla, keep it ready. Might need a roof landing."

"You got it." She climbed back into the pilot's seat and pushed the wiring into her datajack. Slamm-0! knew this meant she was going to dive into the Shinobi and have direct control. It was faster and easier for her, but it also left her body vulnerable.

"Slamm-0! is it possible to put the autodoc room on a looping feed?"

"I can do that. But doing it on the run like this—not sure I can guarantee the splice quality."

"It'll have to do." Renault led them through the shadows to the perimeter fence. He nodded to Slamm-0!, and within seconds the fence door near the back loading dock opened. They ran inside and the hacker had it back in place and locked in under five seconds.

"Any alarms yet?" Silk asked as they kept to the shadows and pressed their backs against the building, away from the cameras.

"No," Slamm-0! replied. "But I've got control of that for the moment."

A new grid schematic showed up in Slamm-0!'s AR, and he pulled it up. There were three lines of direction in different colors. The red line went through the side door and into the autodoc room. The blue line went around that room to the warehouse, and the yellow line went directly to the office.

"Silk, I need you to follow the blue line and disable their vehicles," Renault said. "This will help our people when they get here. Preacher, follow the red line and get Netcat out of there and back to the Shinobi—"

"Wait," Slamm-0! objected. "I should be the one to get her out of there."

Renault shook his head. "You're controlling the host. I need you to follow the yellow line to the office with me. Preacher isn't tied to the Matrix, and his magic is more than enough to get Netcat out safely. He's the better choice."

On the practical level, he knew Renault was right. And he was a cop—storming in and extracting were part of his job. But he wasn't clear on something. "Why are we going in to arrest Powell in his office? Why not just wait and grab him with the rest?"

"It's not just arresting him. I suspect there's a tertiary host in there—I don't know for sure, but it's something we need to check out."

"Why would he have have an extra host in there?"

Renault licked his lips. "Just a theory I have. We need to go. Are you ready?"

Everyone nodded.

Slamm-0! opened the door for them. Renault and he hung back to allow Silk to go in first, then Preacher, and then he followed last and locked the door again. On second thought, he unlocked the door, but sent the locked signal to the host—just in case they needed a fast exit—and then turned to follow the yellow line.

# CHAPTER FIFTY-ONE

## POWELL'S OFFICE

Powell watched the fight from the host's control, a simple riser he'd created a few hours before the meet 'n greet. Caliban returned, still puppeting his Bellex persona to oversee the final extraction, as he put it—wanting to see Soldat removed first hand as the dissonance overwhelmed him, as well as the white technomancer that had come with him. Having the extra was just icing on the cake, and put the AI in a good mood.

He liked it when Caliban was in a good mood. Less worry of another blackout. He and the other dissonant technomancers were afraid another one might garner the attention of the Grid Overwatch Division. Especially if enough Matrix denizens complained about illegal practices such as false subscriptions.

Powell had warned Caliban about such attention, but the AI didn't seem to care. Since Powell had been chosen to head up this endeavor—at a substantial pay rate—Caliban's interest had been centered on a host he'd chosen years before, when he discovered it rested in the path of a Resonance Stream. Not that the AI could actually see it, but he listened and watched as technomancers were drawn to it. Stood by as they disappeared for a time, then returned rejuvenated and empowered with gifts.

He'd told Caliban he hated not being able to see what he believed was Heaven in the Matrix, and when he first attempted the *TechnoHack* game demo and saw their rendition of a resonance stream, touting that it was created from the minds of technomancers who had seen them, Caliban was lost to his own desires. He returned to the game host again and again to watch the colors move. And somehow he came up the idea that if he could reach that stream on the backs of the minds of technomancers, he could touch the Resonance as well.

To Powell, it was ridiculous. And personally, he didn't care. He had fulfilled his dream, which was so similar to his pet AI's, and now controlled the very company his old friends once held. Now he stood on their backs as he took everything they had. And Powell had given them a much, *much* worse punishment at the hands of Caliban.

Everything had gone according to Caliban's plan for nearly two years. The game brought in the occasional technomancer and trapped them, and the program told him where to pick them up. Until a few weeks before the Dragon war, when a shaman player in the game had actually given a prophecy.

*"The Tempest will come and bring the destruction of the Sycorax child. The Soldier will come with weapons of truth, and Dark Resonance shall fall beneath the love of knowledge."*

Powell remembered the look on Caliban's puppet. Sycorax was the key for him—the name of the mother of Caliban in the Shakespeare play, *The Tempest*. No amount of protesting could convince Caliban the prophecy was just something in the game. Not once he heard that name.

Then one night, while watching one of the lesser-known magic talk-trideos, a shaman had given the same prophecy. *The Tempest shall bring the destruction of the Sycorax child.*

Caliban had hunted that shaman down and killed her while trying to wring more information from her. And lo and behold, Powell had heard the second line of the prophecy himself while performing blood magic on a dead shaman's blood.

Data bearing the name Caliban had been archived inside of it, flagged during Shax's searches on the Matrix. Tetsu had showed up and claimed the data—that was bad enough. Then he'd escaped Powell's plan, and that new recruit had mentioned Soldat.

Soldier.

And the AI had gone nuts again.

Now, with the technomancer within their grasp and the data not far behind, Caliban should find some peace, and Powell's world should go back to the way it was.

"What the hell did he do?"

The declaration brought Powell out of his reverie. He stepped up beside Bellex and looked at the host's grid. He slammed his hands on the console. *How...* Seconds ago the dissonance had Tetsu in its grasp and the tracer began.

And then—

"Powell!" Bellex turned to him, but pointed at the grid projected in the air. The starry night sky of the grid made a frightening backdrop to Bellex's rage. "Did Tetsu just rewrite the code?"

"No...not that...I don't think he can do that. Technomancers are susceptible to Shax and his people's dark resonance. There's no way he could have gotten out of it."

"Well, he just did. Look at the grid!"

Powell did, but he didn't want to believe what he was seeing. He flipped the screen back several seconds to take a closer look at what Tetsu did in order to free himself. And what he found both baffled him and intrigued him.

"Well?" Bellex said.

"It...it looks like he sacrificed a sprite to the dissonance by coding it to..." Powell rubbed at his chin. "You're right. He *changed* the dissonance. Actually created a program—compiled a sprite—made from resonance that would attack dissonance in order to remove it."

When Bellex didn't answer, he looked at the AI's persona and saw the dawn of understanding behind that face of dark rage. "He...cleaned up the code..."

"Looks like it. I've never seen a technomancer do that. They always succumb to the dissonance first, get buried in it and can't move. But he—"

Powell didn't see the strike coming until he was hanging off the edge of the platform. He quickly severed his connection and woke with a start, safely tucked into his desk chair, his deck in his lap. He yanked the wires from his datajack and took several deep breaths.

It seemed the logical thing to do before: correcting the code. Basic job for a programmer. To the non-technomancer, that was all dissonance was. Bad code. Go in and fix it. But the technomancer's emotions seemed to be tied to resonance, so that the corruption was real and horrific.

He pushed himself forward in his chair to grab a bottled water on his desk and glanced at the camera feeds. The image jumped in a few of them—like a glitch in an old video—

Powell called up his AR, logged into his own personal security feed, and found himself locked out. Someone else had control of his host.

With a curse, the dwarf slapped his hand down on a big, red button to the right of his chair. An alarm klaxon blared throughout the warehouse.

# CHAPTER FIFTY-TWO

## MED-BAY
## SECOND CLUB

Mack blinked as he reached up to grab the sides of his head. *What the– Why am I out of the Matrix?*

He squinted around at the med room, the one he'd set up for Shayla so she could learn how to treat their injuries. He had three beds and a used auto-doc. Kazuma lay still on the bed to his left, Delaney on the right, and beyond her, MoonShine. They were still under, Kazuma with no visible cyberware, and Delaney hooked up to a cyberdeck.

Their vitals were fine—but his own skull was an echo chamber of pain. He staggered out of bed and over to the room's control panel. Bringing up his diagnostic log, he found he'd been severed by an outside source.

"How...?"

His commlink buzzed, and he blinked to activate his cyber-eyes. Hestaby's window came forward with a missive. <A demi-GOD is hunting your access.>

*A demiGOD? Why...and how would she know this?* He moved to the club's access panel in his AR and connected, tapped into the security, and saw Slamm-0!'s added utilities, including a Sneak program. This would conceal their location from the demiGOD, but from the looks of things, the Club's host had taken a few IC hits.

He called up to Bryce, the manager, who told him the lights had gone out twice already, and he'd given the patrons free drinks to keep them there. Making it seem like business as usual. No need to draw attention to a club that happened to lose power or grid access at the same time a demiGOD was delivering damage.

Mack wasn't sure how long it would keep at it, either. He told Bryce to carry on and moved back to his AR.

<*How did you know?*>

<*We're keeping an eye on things, Mackenzie. You know that.*>

<*We? Hestaby, what are you doing?*>

<*I'm protecting...future assets. The activity in and out of the Contagion host is what flagged the public grid that you're broadcasting from. We should have considered GOD would be looking at them, since they have their own grid and have received numerous complaints from players. Is there any way you can move the packages?*>

He rolled his eyes at her attempt to hide Tetsu's name.

<**No, they're both still in the Matrix. I could sever Delaney's connection, but I don't have a clue how to do that with Tetsu or MoonShine.**>

<*Good point. Let's leave that to the last possible moment. I will instruct my people to divert attention away from you to another part of the grid.*>

He narrowed his his eyes. <**Your *people*? Hestaby–what are you doing?**>

<*Exactly what you accused me of, Mackenzie–I'm planning for the future. Keep an eye on the Matrix attacks, and make sure they don't find either of the technomancers.*>

She ended her connection, and he straightened up. His head pounded from the loss of connection, and he tried to remember if he'd actually hit Clockwork or not. After checking on the club and queuing up alerts to his AR, he contacted Slamm-0!

<*A bit busy...*>

<**Did you get in?**>

Several seconds passed before Slamm-0! responded. <*Yeah, but someone just hit the alarm.*>

Mack lost connection with the team. The only thing in his AR was a huge red triangle with an exclamation point in the center.

"This is so going south."

# CHAPTER FIFTY-THREE

## UNKNOWN LOCATION

Netcat peeked out from underneath a fallen piece of tin when the world shook around her. The sky near the Resonance Stream turned from orange to black, and the stars in the sky burst into flames that rained down on the technomancers below.

People screamed and ran as everything turned in on itself. Netcat watched with a combination of terror and fascination as the huge image of a bearded, old man appeared in the sky. He leaned back and screamed.

She put her paws over her ears to protect her against the old man's scream as well as those around her. Netcat shook with terror as she saw several half-formed personas rise into the sky, and get caught in a sudden funnel that formed in front of the bearded monster.

Abruptly, the air turned toxic and she started coughing and hacking. A man in a tattered suit and tie spotted her as he ran by and picked her up. She didn't know whether to scratch his eyes out, or let him take her.

"Relax!" he yelled as he tucked her into his side like a football. "Caliban's mad."

"Mad?"

"Yeah. He's done this twice. You don't want to be seen while it's going on." As if to emphasize this, he and a few others pushed themselves into a ditch beneath the warehouse, beneath the horror that lived inside it. Netcat buried her face in the man's shoulder and kept as quiet as she could as the world outside destroyed itself.

"He's really...*really* mad this time," said a voice from the darkness.

"Shh," said the man holding her. "Keep quiet."
"I wonder what happened."
But Netcat didn't care. She just wanted it to stop.

# CHAPTER FIFTY-FOUR

## CONTAGION UV HOST

Kazuma turned as Clockwork shot off another burst of bullets. He blocked three with his katana, and dodged the last one as Delaney fired at the drone. Unfortunately, it was small and annoyingly fast. He kept an eye on the fight between MoonShine and Blackwater—and so far Blackwater was in worse shape.

Finally, the *ronin* persona went down and stayed down.

But Kazuma's relief was short-lived when another persona rezzed in just behind MoonShine. His shock registered with Moon when Kazuma yelled, "Look out!"

But it was too late. Standing behind MoonShine was the dissonant he'd fought with in his grannie's house host. He recognized the black leather trench and the gas mask face and top hat. Kazuma parried another volley of fire as he watched Shax grab the back of the panther's neck. The grass beneath them bubbled and spewed oil and ichor over the pair. Everywhere it struck MoonShadow's hide it became black tentacles, pulling him into the pool of dissonance.

"Kaz, look out!"

He didn't move as fast as he should have, and Clockwork's blast hit him in the thigh. He felt the IC grab his leg, and realized too late it was White Ice. He cursed under his breath as Ponsu appeared.

*Boss!*

*<What is it?>*

*A Binder. It's going to limit your evasion.*

As if to prove the point, the drone fired again, and when he tried to evade, it was like moving through syrup. The fire grazed his upper arm and burned.

Delaney upped her game, starting a nonstop barrage of fire at the drone as he moved slowly toward a nearby tree. He made it in time to see MoonShine being dragged further into the dissonance. He was surprised to see MoonShine's window pop up.
<It's a user trace!>

Kazuma resheathed his katana as Ponsu appeared again. <*I got an idea. Give me a Wrapper.*>

*You got it, Boss!*

He grabbed the small glowing ball of code as Ponsu tossed it to him. With a few taps and a squeeze he compiled a new sprite, this one as his own IC program, but this one wasn't going to be simple White Ice. He gave the sprite the order, and it dove into the Wrapper. With a thought, the outer visual of the ball became something he'd seen only once, but Clockwork had seen several times.

Kazuma gave it the animation he'd seen it make before and when Delaney ducked behind another copse of gnarled trees, he tossed the now brown ball of fur into the melee and ordered it to go for the drone.

Clockwork stopped when the ball of fur, so much like his pet AI, came at him with its mouth open, as if happy to see its owner.

Too late, the hacker realized what it was, but the sprite inside detonated, and the drone was caught in the grey ice as it wrapped around his tiny machine persona. The program was *like* a hacker's Gray Ice Blaster, but with a touch of technomancer. It would damage his persona as well as his cyberdeck, and show Clockwork a holographic image of Kazuma giving him a single finger salute.

The drone abruptly disappeared.

The reprieve gave Delaney the pause she needed. Kaz watch her fire at Shax, who wasn't expecting it. He had some kind of shield up, but her bullets still distracted him.

Kazuma's brain thundered inside his skull—compiling two sprites that close together, plus being hit with white ice, was taking its toll. But he took off at a slow run at Shax just as Delaney did the same.

One of her shots struck Shax's head, and he fell backwards.

But MoonShine was still being pulled into the dissonance.

# CHAPTER FIFTY-FIVE

## WAREHOUSE HANGAR

Silk halted just inside the hangar door and stopped herself from whistling. *Wow.* Four vehicles. A Shinobi, a Land Rover, a Honda GM, and a Lockheed Strike vehicle.

*Come to mama.* She sized up the order of the rides from *dome-first* to too bulky, and hit the Strike first. Disabling it took less than ten minutes. She'd just finished the Shinobi when the door to the hangar warned her of someone entering.

When her AR didn't flag one of her own team, she ducked down in the cockpit a second before bullets tore a long line across the protective shield, shattering it. Covered in glass fragments, she made sure she was still joined to Slamm-0!'s PAN, and accessed the camera to the hangar.

It was the hobgoblin. He out of the Matrix, up and armed in the hangar.

*Drek!*

"I know you're in there, bitch. I can see you…you know how?" He paused but she could hear him walking, breathing, and then laughing. "'Cause I got a purpose. I'm not only gonna sell that damn elf-bitch technomancer, but now I've got this Tetsu on my list. Seems he's exactly what I've been saying technomancers are—dangerous. Untrustworthy. Did you know he actually managed to spoof my AI?" Clockwork's voice echoed through the large hangar, making it harder for her to track without watching him on the cameras.

The problem was he knew where the cameras were, and avoided them. Silk typed a hurried message to Slamm-0!, which made it appear on the PAN to everyone.

**<CLOCKWORK IS IN THE HANGAR>**

No one answered her PAN broadcast, so Silk looked through the camera angles. She thought she saw something moving near the Shinobi, but when she ventured a look up, there was nothing there. Silk pulled the wires for her datajack from the side of her RCC and jammed them into her datajack, then pulled the connection up from under the dashboard and plugged them into her RCC. Even with the Shinobi turned off, she could see and feel the onboard mechanics, touch the datasphere connected to the engine.

"You see...I'm an observer," the hobgoblin continued. "Not many know this about me. But I watch. I watch conversations. I watch people, even when they don't know I am. And I like to watch their interactions. Now, I know the technomancer elf in the doc is Slamm-0!'s girlfriend. They even had devilspawn. A kid. And the moment that kid shows any sign of being like his mother—I'll be after him as well. But I'm betting you, my sister-rigger, are Tetsu's girlfriend. Yes, yes, it's incredible that I deduced that, isn't it? So I'm betting if I destroy you, I'll destroy a little piece of him as well."

She half-listened to him as she prepared the Shinobi for flight, and moved everything into position. Clockwork was angry at Kazuma, so she guessed he'd knocked the hobgoblin off the host. Or did something worse. He'd bruised Clockwork's ego, and if the others didn't get into the hangar and give her a hand, he planned on taking that rage out on her.

# CHAPTER FIFTY-SIX

## CONTAGION UV HOST

Delaney dug the heels of her boots into the somewhat pixelated ground near the hole MoonShine had half-fallen into. To her, it looked like a bottomless pit. A hole in the code that appeared to want to eat the big, white panther.

She had a solid hold of MoonShine, hands locked together around his chest, but whatever had hold of him was not letting go.

Kazuma tried to help, but she noticed his persona moving slower than before. It flickered in and out, and she knew from her study of technomancers that he was fading. He'd used several programs already, which meant he'd been compiling a lot. She'd watched him the first time when he'd created that fairy that ate—*wait!*

"Kazuma, can you make another one of those sprites that sharpened the pixelated grass?"

He looked at her. "Is that what you saw?"

"Yeah."

"Yes, but I'll fade."

"What're you talking about?" MoonShine said as he strained to pull himself out of the black pit. He wasn't going further in, but he wasn't coming out either.

"It's okay. Moon, Kaz made a sprite earlier that got him out of a hole just like this. If he can make another one, then I can pull you free."

The panther paused his attempts to get out. "Kaz, let me do it!"

"No." Kaz put his hand to the side of the panther's jaw and closed his eyes. "You just concentrate on getting free."

Delaney watched as a light appeared in front of Kazuma...then two lights. Those two became four, and then eight, and then sixteen. Those points of light sharpened into tiny little monsters with wings, who dove down as a unit into the hole around MoonShine's persona. Within seconds the ground folded out as pixel grass began to regrow, and the panther was slowly pushed out of the hole.

She backed up and let go of his torso as he scrambled out and half-staggered, half-crawled to the side. Delaney left the host and ported to her own commlink before logging off. She took a deep breath before opening her eyes and looking into the face of Mack Schmetzer.

"Welcome back."

"Kazuma, is he—"

"He's offline, but not awake."

"Moon?"

"I'm...here..."

Delaney pushed herself up onto her elbows and looked at the white-haired young man. "You look like hammered shit, to quote a certain someone."

"And I feel like it. I've got about a second before I pass out." He pushed himself upright and managed to leave his bed. Holding onto the wall and the side cabinets, he moved to where Kazuma lay.

"He did a good job with those little lawnmowers or whatever they were," Delaney said. "They lifted you right up."

"It wasn't just Kaz." A half-smile played on his lips as he looked from Kazuma to her. "He left the first one open, made it easy for me to compile one like it, once I was free enough. I wrote a subroutine to reproduce after so much code was repaired. I joined my compile with his. It was like we wrote a program together."

"What?" Mack said. "What're you talking about?"

"What I'm talking about is something I've never done before. It's probably been done by somebody before, but I haven't..." He looked between Delaney and Mack. "We co-created sprites. He had the forethought to make his sprite open code specifically for me."

Mack frowned. "And that means...what?"

An alarm interrupted MoonShine as he was opening his mouth. Mack turned and summoned his AR, visible to Delaney. That's when she realized she was still connected to her commlink.

"Drek!" He grabbed his bag with his deck and his gun from a side table. "Someone hit the alarm at the warehouse. They know Slamm-0! and the others are there."

# CHAPTER FIFTY-SEVEN

## POWELL'S OFFICE

How many times had Powell faced death and won? Even he had lost count. Regardless, with such a record as to have forgotten the number, facing the hacker's Manhunter gave him very little pause. The troll that followed the blond kid in was another matter.

"Raoul Renault." The dwarf shook his head. "Now this *is* a reunion, isn't it?"

"Hello, Draco."

The blond hacker looked from Powell to the troll. "You know him?"

"We've...met. And no, I never told Delaney who the dwarf was."

Powell leaned forward on his desk, his own Fichetti in a hold-out holster fastened to the underside, waiting for him to grab it. "So tell me, Raoul, did you know I'd eventually approach Wagner?"

The PCC officer shook his head as he circled the desk. Spotting a colorful paperweight on its surface, he picked it up, hefting it from hand to hand. "Not at first. We kept an eye on you, though, after we linked you with the Contagion buyout. Radcliff was good to you after the Arcology hell, and you betrayed him."

"I never betrayed him." Powell narrowed his eyes as he stood up in his chair and reached for the paperweight, but failed. Renault was just out of reach. "He betrayed *me*."

"By becoming a technomancer? That was it, wasn't it? All four of them did, except you. You were the only one who wasn't online that night. The only one that didn't change. You do realize the fact it happened to all three of them was just a freak of nature,

Draco. Even if you were online—there's no guarantee you'd have changed, too."

"But I was an *otaku*!" Powell jabbed his finger into his chest. "*I* should have had that kind of power."

"What the hell are you two talking about?" Slamm-0! raised his weapon. "And turn that damn alarm off."

With a shrug, Powell complied. It wouldn't matter anyway. He knew Blackwater and Clockwork were offline, and both were going to protect their own interests now. Whatever rescue plan Schmetzer had cooked up would fail. "What we're talking about—Slamm...Oh, is it?" He smiled, almost pleasantly. "Is about taking what's yours. Or in this case, what's mine." He held his hand out to the troll. "Please be careful with that. It's been with me since my time in the Renraku Arcology."

"That kind of power, any kind of power, isn't automatically yours, Draco." Renault said as he walked over to the dwarf's desk and handed the paperweight over. "You worked for Deus and were promised power, but he never gave it to you, did he?"

Slamm-0!'s eyes widened. "This piece of drek worked for that monster?"

"Oh, yes. He certainly did. Rounded up targets, specimens as he liked to call them. I was there. I saw what he did. And I survived and waited, and watched and followed him."

"Damn troll's been on my ass since the whole thing collapsed." Powell glared at Renault before he resituated himself back in his chair and kept the paperweight close. "You've been a thorn in my side for far too long."

"But I never stuck in your craw, did I? Not the way your friends did. See...Draco here had three accomplices in that Arcology. Four metahumans who wanted to survive just as much as he did, and who were just as willing to give up their souls. Jesus, Morion, and Radcliff. Former third-rate shadowrunners who gained privilege and notoriety under Draco's leadership. But when the Arcology was saved and Deus was...eliminated, though that's still highly debated...Draco and his team split up. But they stayed in touch."

Powell leaned back, keeping the resin paperweight out of the troll's reach as he positioned his hand on his thigh, ready to grab the weapon when he wanted it. He could take out one of them, but he knew he couldn't take both of them. He was going to need something special for that. And if he pulled up his AR, they would see it, since he knew the hacker had control of the warehouse's host.

Best to let Blackwater and Clockwork find their way here once they disposed of the others. "You think you know the whole story, Raoul? Yes, we stayed in touch because we built a small fortune utilizing what we learned from Deus, what we learned from having to fight to survive."

"Yes." Renault said. "Except—your partners all changed. The Crash came and went, and you learned they were all technomancers now, able to use the datasphere in a way you could only dream. Because you're addicted to it—to hot sim, to the reality inside the Matrix, not the one out here. They came through with new powers, and what did you get, Draco?"

Powell gritted his teeth. "I found an AI."

The troll nodded slowly. "Yes, you did. You called it Caliban, the son of Sycorax. And when I found the umbrella company of Prospero, it didn't take me long to put it all together. You continued to be their friend, you lied to them, helped them create a small gaming empire so you could live out your Matrix fantasies in your world, and then you betrayed them."

Slamm-0! narrowed his eyes. "That stuff you showed us, the stuff you showed Delaney, you already had that. You just brought it out when you were sure."

"Yes."

Despite his annoyance, Powell had to give the troll credit for being as tenacious as a bloodhound. "You know some of it, Raoul, but not all of it. I knew you were there, in the Arcology. Working behind the scenes to thwart me and every other agent of Deus. But once we were free, unlike you, I forgot about the troll in the shadows." He gave a short sigh. "You're mostly right. After the Crash, I found the AI and I rescued it. Nurtured it and gave it a home host. I gave it that name just after the others contacted me and shared what had happened. Technomancers were just coming into the public eye, but their reception was less than friendly. Tolen wanted to change that. He wanted to make a game, an experience so others could see the Matrix the way a technomancer sees it. He and the others had a dream of showing them the resonance realms, the streams, the pools, all of it. So they hired me to find the right coders, the right talents, and the right system to use to achieve this dream."

"So, you put your AI into the game's system."

Slamm-0! stepped back. "Drek…"

"Yes, I did." Powell smiled as he remembered Caliban's initial joy. The freedom the new host and its game interface gave him. "And he did such a good job, for a while. They were happy with me, with what I'd achieved, and gave me full administrative rights." He fixed his gaze on Raoul. "In everything."

"Even their own estates."

"I created Prospero to shield their assets under one umbrella. To protect them. And I was the king again."

Renault took a step around the desk past Slamm-0!. "Until Radcliff Tolen realized what you'd done."

"He was the first to see the AI for what it was. And he didn't tell anyone. He was a brilliant programmer. He'd been a hacker before the Arcology, and a damn good one at that. Instead of raising a red flag, he hacked the code. He broke into my AI's home host, and embedded a kill switch."

"That thing has a kill switch?" Slamm-0! said. "And you've never used it?"

"Why would I? Caliban is my son. When I leaned what he'd done, I told Caliban and we plotted our revenge. By that time the game had attracted a little-known populace of technomancers called dissonants. They showed Caliban what they could do to the code. We can't see it, Raoul, what their poison does to the resonance and the host environment. We can only see the code. But it horrified Rad and Jesus and Morion. So they came up with the idea of combining their power to stop the dissonants and to stop Caliban."

"What about Miranda? Where did she come from? She wasn't in the arcology with us."

Powell laughed. "Oh…my dear Miranda. She and Radcliff met a year or so ago. Fell in love. She sank her claws into him, and he listened to her, because she was just like him. A technomancer. She taught him how to submerge and gain more power, and he gave her stock. A share in the company."

"But they never married."

"No."

"What happened?"

"They made their little pact and created a gestalt. And they nearly succeeded by implementing that kill switch." Powell shook his head. "But Caliban had gained followers by then, and they interfered with whatever the three of them had planned. The dissonants found their bodies and locked them in the Matrix. And Miranda...she was there, too, for a while, until she was ready to follow Caliban and I pulled her out. She had the power to sell the company—but the slitch insisted on keeping a controlling interest."

The room seemed to grow colder as shots rang out down the hall. Slamm-0! took a step back and glanced at Renault. But the troll wasn't moving. "You could have stopped this. You could have prevented the death of innocent lives by destroying that thing."

"He's not doing anything wrong, Raoul. He's just enjoying his new-found freedom."

"He's killing innocent technomancers. That's not what your partners wanted the game for."

Powell slammed his hands down on the desk. "It's what *I* want it for!" He grabbed his gun as Slamm-0! and Renault stepped back and raised their own. But Powell didn't fire. Instead he scrambled up to stand on top of the desk. "I never had the kill switch because Radcliff hid it from me. Encoded it into the programming, so that I didn't know it was there until it was too late. Even I couldn't remove it. And then Rad refused to give it to me. I even offered him freedom, an escape from the hell Caliban put him through. But he still refused. He hid it so deep in the Matrix I couldn't find a trace of it."

"Until it showed up in a Horizon Annex." Slamm-0! said.

Powell nodded. "Can you believe it? Buried in some stupid corporate officer's private little kill file. By that time, I'd already taken over Contagion, and Bellex was born."

"Bellex is Caliban." Renault leveled his weapon at the dwarf.

"Puppet of a puppet. Or so I thought. Caliban became obsessed with those game-generated resonance realms. The technomancers insist they're real, but he can't touch them. Caliban uses the gestalt those three fools put together to bend everything to his will." Powell smiled. "It's torture for them. They can see what their game is doing to others like them, but they can't help, only be a part of that pain, and they can never leave."

The sound of gunfire somewhere outside Powell's office brought reality crashing in as Renault lowered his gun. Slamm-0! started to protest until the troll squeezed the trigger of his pistol and put several shots into the paperweight on Powell's desk.

Of all the things he expected the troll to fire at, Caliban's home host wasn't one of them. Powell had gone to great lengths to disguise it, hiding it in a replica of the orbital station and encasing the whole thing in Lucite. To everyone else, it looked like a paperweight bought in a souvenir store.

Only Powell knew about the wire that powered it under his desk.

The thing shattered into a million pieces as the troll's bullets destroyed it.

When Powell brought his own weapon up to shoot Renault, a volley of gunfire knocked him off his feet. Everything happened in slow motion. He saw Slamm-0!'s gun aimed at him. Saw him firing. It'd been foolish to stand on top of the desk, to make himself a target. And perhaps he was, in some way, protecting the paperweight. Subconsciously.

His head struck the edge of the desk as he tumbled off it, bounced against the chair and landed hard beneath it. Pain enveloped him as he saw Slamm-0! and Renault looking down at him.

"How..." Powell said as he felt his life seeping away. "...did you know?"

Renault answered. "It was the one thing you kept with you. Always."

"I see..." Powell smiled as everything around him began fading to black. Let the troll believe he'd destroyed Caliban. Let him have his temporary joy. He just wished he could be there to see Renault's face when his triumph came crashing down.

# CHAPTER FIFTY-EIGHT

## WAREHOUSE

Blackwater sat up as Preacher stepped into the room. He'd worked for Schmetzer for nearly a year, and never really got to know the mage. But then, magic and machinery didn't always blend well together.

Preacher was big, even for a troll. He held his staff at his side, nodded to Blackwater, and proceeded to the last autodoc, the one they'd put the elf chick in. The hood lifted at the troll's approach and Preacher reached in to place his large finger at her neck. The blank dials and monitors told Blackwater the machine had been shut down. "That's not going to get her out of the host. Powell's got protocols she can't hack. It's what keeps 'em all in there."

"Perhaps." Preacher's deep baritone was even, almost soothing. "But I'm willing to bet she's going to surprise even you, Cole." He moved slow and steady away from the autodoc until he was in the center of the room.

When he didn't move and just stared at Blackwater, the hacker slipped off the doc and faced him. "What're you doing?"

"Waiting."

"For what?"

"For you to make a decision."

Blackwater made a rude noise. "Ain't no decisions to make."

"You honestly believe Draco Powell is going to treat you fairer than Mack would?"

"Mack's a fool."

The troll smiled around his tusks. "Mack Schmetzer is a good man. And he has good, loyal friends and contacts…well." Preacher chuckled. "You just wouldn't believe."

Blackwater let the troll talk as he scanned the equipment near him. When he got into the doc, the dwarf and some pale chick had actually jacked him into VR using a built-in cyberdeck. Now that he was out, he had no idea where his own tools were. He had no gun, no commlink, and no deck.

But there were a lot of sharp objects.

"I wanted to admire you, Cole." Preacher held up his free hand and snapped his fingers.

Too late, Blackwater remembered that the mage used this gesture to throw a manabolt. He tried to dodge by jumping to his left, but slammed into an empty autodoc as the bolt struck his thigh, right where that damn technomancer had bit him.

That leg went out from under him, but he used his hands, arms, and other leg to crawl under the doc and hide behind it.

"In fact, Mack told me to give you a chance. He said you were good at your job, but you see…I never felt you were truly human. And you weren't fit to be metahuman…because your soul is polluted."

Preacher snapped his fingers again, and another bolt struck the autodoc. It broke into several pieces, and Blackwater had to scramble to get out of the way of falling equipment. He managed to reach a cabinet and pull himself up. There he found a knife, grabbed it, and threw it.

The thing barely tapped one of Preacher's horns.

"And then you killed Maria. She was innocent, Cole."

The troll followed Blackwater as he tried to make it to the door. Another finger snap, and something burned the back of his arms, his legs, and his head. He screamed as the fire burned his flesh, down through his muscles and down into his bones. He lay on the floor, inches from the door, writhing in agony as the spell's acid took its toll.

Preacher looked down at him and shook his head. "So, it's only fitting that you should pass from this world in the same way you took her." He reached inside his robe, retrieved a Manhunter, and aimed it between Blackwater's eyes.

"No…" Cole Blackwater begged as he looked down the dark, empty barrel of that gun. "I can make things right—"

Preacher fired. A hole appeared between Blackwater's eyes. The last thing he saw was Preacher's face, and the last thing he heard was the troll's voice.

"No. You can't. But I just did."

# CHAPTER FIFTY-NINE

## UNKNOWN

Netcat bounded out of the man's grasp when the world went quiet. She stopped in the center of what had once been the library. Nothing remained. No walls or books or even chairs and tables. It was all gone. All of it. The only thing still standing in this hellish world was the warehouse.

"Harold?" Netcat called out as she ran, her voice a feline trill as she bounded from rock to rock. She looked everywhere except inside the warehouse.

But when she didn't find anything else, or anyone else, Netcat turned to the warehouse. The survivors, maybe twenty in all, stared above the warehouse's roof at the towering ladder. The stream still spun and swirled like a tornado of light and magic. But now the ladder was much shorter and thicker.

At the last rung, something glinted at her, and shined in the orange cast sun. It was tall and silver and reminded her of a sword.

Harold.

She threw back her head and yelled, a caterwaul cry as she cried for her lost friends, for the essence of what they were, bent into the nightmarish ladder.

<*Kitty-tap this [link].*>

She wasn't sure she was seeing the command line in front of her face. How long it been since she could call upon her AR? Without hesitation, she pressed a paw on the link, and the orange sky, ladder, and warehouse winked out.

Agonizing pain followed her through that twisted hole until the maelstrom quieted and she heard a familiar voice.

"Kitty...say something. If you leave me, I swear I'll raise Jack as a corporate wageslave!"

She opened her eyes and looked into Slamm-0!'s blue ones. He looked worried, and she saw blood on his forehead. His wires were in and he was jacked, but he was real. She was real. And to prove it, she grabbed his face and pressed a hard and fast kiss against his lips.

"She's fine."

Netcat looked up into the gentle face of a troll and just past him, another one—only he was wearing a black business suit. "Who..."

"Long story. Can you walk?" Slamm-0! moved back enough to help her climb out of the autodoc. Standing was fine—moving forward? That might be a little shaky. "I'm starving."

"As it should be. Now Slamm-0!, if I may carry out Mack's orders?" The troll with the robes and symbol-decorated horns moved her boyfriend out of his way and scooped Netcat into his arms. "Please hang on to my neck. I plan on running quite fast."

She gaped at him just before she remembered where she'd been. "Kazuma! Where is he?"

"He's fine," the suited troll said. "Your rescuer is Preacher. I am Renault. Slamm-0!, I see a new message on the host PAN. Apparently Powell's office was shielded."

He tapped a few things in his AR and cursed. "Clockwork's in the hangar. Kitty, go with Preacher. We need to help Silk."

Silk? Netcat had a million questions piling up, but the troll did indeed move faster than she expected. The next few minutes were spent hanging on for dear life.

# CHAPTER SIXTY

## WAREHOUSE HANGAR

For most of the battle with Clockwork, Silk had remained inside the Shinobi. Her RCC took several IC hits when Clockwork tried to gain control of it. He'd already destroyed the other vehicles with three drones, evil, spider-looking things she hadn't noticed crawling all over the Shinobi's hull until she slammed the door closed on one of them. Unfortunately, the part that got inside was still moving, and managed to stab a knife into her ankle before she smashed it with a fire extinguisher.

The other two continued to look for ways in as she fortified the Shinobi's defenses. She did manage to fire at Clockwork twice. But he was fast, and had a lot to hide behind.

Her original goal had been to get the Shinobi airborne and blow him away with its guns. But after the constant barrage of hits to her RCC, along with the damage inflicted by the drones, this piece of drek wasn't going anywhere except to a scrap heap.

"It's only a matter of time, you know. Before the others find their way in here. That is, if they survive Blackwater and Powell."

None of them had answered her since she sent her message, and she wondered if Slamm-0! had lost control of the host, or if Clockwork was jamming her somehow. She didn't have time to investigate as the onslaught from the drones started again.

The sound of their metallic legs clanking around her drove her mad. She knew she was trapped, and if she didn't get out of the falling-apart Shinobi and out of the hangar, this crazy, green-skinned freak was going to kill her. She needed a diversion to draw his attention away from her, but there wasn't much she could do—

New gunfire echoed around the Shinobi, and she chanced a

peak into the security camera feed on the host. She spotted Renault and Slamm-0! as they stormed into the hangar and engaged Clockwork. This was the diversion she needed!

Favoring her bleeding ankle, Silk eased herself to the far door. She watched the two remaining drones scurry away from the Shinobi. It looked as if Clockwork wanted their firepower as well.

After she counted to ten, Silk unlatched the door and slipped out to the cement floor. She went down on her belly and rolled under the Shinobi to get a more accurate assessment of where everyone was.

The door she and the others had come through was two destroyed vehicles to her right. She saw Renault's knee and shoes as he knelt behind the first vehicle. A quick scan around and she spotted Slamm-0!'s sneakers farther to the left. A full three-sixty put her face to face with a drone.

She brought her gun up and fired as it leaped at her.

# CHAPTER SIXTY-ONE

## WAREHOUSE HANGAR

Slamm-0! heard a rapid succession of gunshots toward the back of the hangar, near the large double doors. He had Clockwork tagged on the other side of the Land Rover, and watched as Renault headed toward the rigger on the right. Slamm-0! moved around to the left. They were going to close in around him.

Until Slamm-0! spotted movement between the Shinobi and the Strike. The drone accelerated into a blur, startled him, and he fired at it a moment before it launched itself at him. He winged it enough that it skittered left, which gave him enough time to fire again. It burst apart this time, and he took off to back up Renault's assault on Clockwork.

The hobgoblin was trapped between the two of them, as well as the Land Rover. As Slamm-0! came around the Rover's back, he spotted Clockwork trying to get into the Rover, but the doors were locked.

Renault appeared on the opposite side of Clockwork, his gun drawn. "All the drones are destroyed."

Clockwork pointed his gun at Slamm-0! "I'm not finished, pretty boy. None of us are ever finished, are we?"

"Netcat's safe, asshole." Slamm-0! kept his gun trained on Clockwork's head. "Powell's dead, and so's Blackwater. There's no one else here to save your ass."

Clockwork's only response was to laugh. The sound echoed inside the hangar, and Renault started toward the rigger. But the hobgoblin held up something small and round in his other hand.

"What's that, another drone?" Slamm-0! said.

"A drone bomb. Something I've been saving. I haven't tried it out, so I haven't sold any yet. But if this one gets me what I want, then I'm sure it'll rake in some serious nuyen."

Renault stopped where he was, but kept his gun aimed at Clockwork. "Backup's been called, Clockwork. I'm not letting you walk out of here."

"What if I fly out of here, huh? On an explosion that'll take out the entire—"

Clockwork didn't finish his threat, because he was suddenly yanked down on his ass. Renault and Slamm-0! didn't hesitate as they rushed him. Renault snatched the small, round object from the hobgoblin's hand, threw it high into the air, and fired at it. No big explosions, no fireballs. Just a lot of parts raining down on them.

Meanwhile, Slamm-0! jumped on the hacker and hammered a heavy right cross into the ugly fucker's face. "That was for trying to sell my girlfriend the first time!" It felt so good, he landed another one as Renault took Clockwork's weapon. His knuckles burned and he was going to have to a few stitches. "And that was for trying it again."

He leaned back as Renault cuffed the hobgoblin and caught his breath. Renault then went down on his hands and looked under the Land Rover. "Slamm..."

"What?"

"Give me a hand."

Slamm-0! holstered his gun and shifted his gear so he could lay down and look under the Rover—

He closed his eyes at the sight. "Son of a..."

"She pulled Clockwork down. She bought us the time to take him."

Slamm-0! and Renault gently hauled Silk's battered body from beneath the Land Rover. She was covered in oil and blood, and her long, dark hair hid what was left of her face. Slamm-0! pulled her to him as Renault dragged Clockwork to the front of the Rover.

The hacker double-checked her pulse, but found none, and balled his fist against his forehead. He held her gently, brushing her hair back as he heard Renault moving around. The troll came around the other side and knelt beside him.

"The PCC's nearly here. You need to take her back. Shayla's waiting with Preacher and Netcat just outside in the Shinobi."

Slamm-0! nodded as Renault took her body and he got to his feet.

"Looks like she crawled from under the Shinobi to the Land Rover. There's a blood trail across the concrete. Whatever hit her took out half her face. She didn't have a way to warn us—so she did what she could. Her death was a noble one."

Her death.

Renault started to the door and Slamm-0! followed, head down as he watched her blood leave small splatters, some of them hitting the troll's polished shoes. When the hangar opened wind caught them and blew debris into Slamm-0!'s eyes as Preacher approached and took Silk in his arms.

Netcat was at his side, her green eyes wide and tear-filled. He wiped at his own, convincing himself his own tears were from the propeller wash. He sat on the floor beside Silk, with Netcat in the seat behind him.

The flight back to Mack's was a long and quiet one.

# CHAPTER SIXTY-TWO

### GiTm0

Welcome back to GiTm0, *omae*; your last connection was 3 days, 2 hours, 2 minutes, 25 seconds ago

### BOLOs

Just a reminder—this host's got less than three hours left before decompiling. Send your sprites out twenty-four hours after that for the new link.

No new names to report.

### BRAVE BROTHER AND SISTER

It's with a heavy heart that we come to you with the unexpected deaths of HipOldGuy and Silk. Silk was one of the few of us who never fully realized her technomancer abilities, but she kept the faith, and protected Soldat and Netcat till the end.

HipOldGuy was one of our founding members. His death and the subsequent retrieval of his body by the PCC has been a blow to myself and Shyammo.

We are holding a Matrix memorial for our two comrades. The date, time, and location will be listed here once we have everything nailed down. For right now, please know that all efforts to inform you of the events leading up to Silk's and HipOldGuy's deaths have been gathered in a downloadable report. [Link] Those are the facts as we know them.

This fight with Bellex and Contagion isn't over. There's still one more piece to set afire.

Remember, GOD is always watching.

**GATHERING**
\>\>\>\>Open Thread/Subhost221.322.1
\>\>\>\>Thread Access Restrictions: <Yes/**No**>
\>\>\>\>Format: <**Open Post**/Comment Only/Read Only>
\>\>\>\>File Attachment: <**Yes**/No>
\>\>\>\>Thread Descriptor: **GESTALTS**
\>\>\>\>Thread Posted By User: RoxJohn

- I told you we needed to go back to that game.
- Venerator

- That's not the point of this discussion, Ven. We have to go forward. Netcat's kept me and Shyammo informed. We need each of you to read those files.
- RoxJohn

- Everyone, I've reviewed the files and they're pretty damn accurate. If anyone needs questions answered on how Soldat and I created those sprites, just ask. This is a possible weapon, folks. It's a start.
- MoonShine

- How is Soldat? Is he okay? I mean...he and Silk were together, right?
- 404Flames

- They were. He's doing as well as expected. He's mourning her as we're all mourning her, and HipOldGuy. It's been a rough two days.
- MoonShine

- Moon, if I'm reading this right, making a gestalt isn't any different than writing a program with a partner. Like back in the days of writing and checking each other's code?
- LongTong

- That's exactly right. Only when we do it, there's a lot of trust involved. I've tried it again with Netcat and our results were a bit different. We did manage to compile a sprite that took out a seriously nasty black hammer IC, but not without some serious fading. But, it's a start.
- MoonShine

- Guys, what we need now is clear communication and a way to organize ourselves. We've been talking and I think if we don't step up for our rights, we're never going to have any. The reason *TechnoHack* was created was to show players what it was like to see the Matrix through our eyes. It's not the original creator's fault it's been corrupted. I think their logic is sound.
- Netcat

- That's all great, Net, but the game's still out there. Luckily the host's dead, and Bellex has been in the news setting himself up as a possible victim of technomancer attacks. So even if we bring evidence of dissonants or corruption, we'll still come off looking like revenge-mongers.
- 404Flames

- I know, Flames. We're working on it. One step at a time. Just spread the word through whatever channels you have that everyone is to stay away from the game. Don't give that damned AI any more of us. And keep the rumor mill going about their subscriptions and fraud. If we can't fight them with truth, then we'll fight them any way we can. Let local law enforcement sniff around at their books, and find out for themselves that Bellex is an AI, and the company runs on the backs of dead men.
- Netcat

- It's good to have you back, Netcat.
- RoxJohn

- It's good to be with Slamm-0! and my family here.
- Netcat

# CHAPTER SIXTY-THREE

## SOUTH CHINA MOUNTAIN
## TIR TAIRNGIRE

Mack leaned against the terrace frame, a steaming cup of soykaf in one hand, his commlink in the other. The view from this mountain was different than the one he remembered from Shasta. Not better or worse, just different. Different terrain, different area, but all still incredibly beautiful. Living in a place like this could make one forget about the ugly world around them.

Almost.

The lodge was still under construction, and he could hear hammering from somewhere, and the grind and grumble of powerful engines as they excavated soil and poured a bigger foundation. Shayla had volunteered to help, offering her services as a rigger to dive in and lose herself in the machine. Mack understood her need to get away from her sorrow. He wasn't sure if it was Silk's death, or that coming on the heels of Maria's that had kept her so quiet in the last twenty-four hours.

They had barely returned to the club when the shit had hit the fan from a completely different direction. Barely an hour after Preacher and the others had landed and Kazuma was placed in the infirmary with Delaney, a small army of GOD agents had swarmed the club in black wagons and vans. Their own jet-black Shinobi helicopters hovered overhead, and all grid activity, as well as Matrix connections, were severed as Mack and his guests were treated to a warning broadcast over loudspeakers.

"This is the Grid Overwatch Division. You have been cited with illegal and immoral activity within the public domain. Please come out with your hands up. We have been authorized to use deadly force if necessary."

Mack had seriously doubted he and his team had been cited for anything—he was just that careful. But that didn't mean one of Powell's lackeys, or even one of Blackwater's old buddies hadn't set them up. The Matrix was down, but they didn't have power to shut off his internal network.

From his office, he saw armored GOD agents surrounding the building. He picked them up on the back cameras, as well as the sides and front. Preacher angled a few of them to show the buildings to either side of the Bang Bang Booty club where snipers were set up, their weapons pointed at the exits.

"Drek," Slamm-0! had said. "There's no way we can get out of this. If they take us, they'll get Netcat and Kazuma."

"Oh ye of little faith." Mack went to his office desk, pulled out the bottom drawer, and removed an old style walkie-talkie. He checked the batteries, and then pushed the side switch. "Okay Lady. Show's all yours."

Mack had had to suppress a smile as he ordered his people to get Delaney and Kazuma ready for transport. They all looked at him like he'd lost his mind. So he'd added a resounding, "NOW!"

They hustled as the GOD asshole on the speaker kept ordering them to exit the building immediately. When the shooting started outside, accompanied by what sounded like more helicopters, Slamm-0! and MoonShine had doubled back to look at the monitors.

"That's an Albatross flying in...and it's landing on the roof!"

"Okay, everybody up!" Mack said as he helped Preacher. He had Delaney in his arms while the troll carried Kazuma. Renault had Silk's body. "Shayla, Whitey, and Slamm-0! grab those two cases in my office and get your asses to the roof!"

Access up was little more than a straight metal ladder, so carrying the bodies up proved to be a chore. Mack slung Delaney's body over his shoulder and took the rungs one at a time after Slamm-0! and MoonShine went up first with the cases and weapons.

Mack's walkie-talkie squawked as a familiar female voice came through. "She's waiting for you outside, Mr. Mackenzie."

*She?*

He had felt as well as heard the *thud* of something very heavy landing on the roof.

"That's no helicopter," Preacher had said from under him.

"No. It's not." *Damn that old lizard...she just has to put on a show.*

The roof door opened as Slamm-0! and MoonShine stepped out brandishing weapons. Mack came out a few seconds later, followed by Preacher holding Kazuma, and then Netcat.

He spotted the Albatross, and hovering just above it as if it wasn't in the line of fire, was a Sperber. Mack had expected to emerge to a hail of bullets. But that never happened.

Hestaby, in her true form, cast a giant shadow over Mack's club, as well as the surrounding buildings. She held her wings up and roared seconds before every weapon in the hands of every GOD agent dishcharged its ammo.

Mack had never seen anything like that.

"Go! Go! Go!" Slamm-0! motioned to Mack and the others as another group of soldiers of all metatypes appeared from behind chimneys and smokestacks. They got the jump on the now unarmed agents, but instead of firing on them...they simply took their ammunition magazines.

"They're technomancers!" MoonShine yelled as he watched in open-mouthed wonder.

"Mack, get in the 'Tross!" Preacher bellowed over the roar of the helicopter's blades as well as Hestaby's smug roar.

He moved as fast as he could. Three more of the grey-clad soldiers jumped out of the Albatross and took Delaney from his arms, and Kazuma from Preacher. They were trolls, goblins, orks, elves, and changelings.

And humans.

A female troll the size of Preacher reached down and yanked him up by his belt to get him into the helicopter faster. Once everyone was in, she leaned out and gave a cranking motion with her hand.

The Albatross lifted as the Sperber mirrored its movements. Mack made sure his seatbelt was fastened before he looked out to see the Serber's weapons pointed at the Shinobis—but no one followed.

Not with a dragon between them and their target.

After making sure Delaney and Kazuma were secure, Mack slept hard on the ride. Both lay on gurneys behind him, tended by a grey-clad young woman with a white band and red cross on her arm.

The female troll had introduced herself as Izzy and needed a quick debrief on what happened in Powell's warehouse. Slamm-0!, with a sleeping Netcat in his arms, had given it to her, along with the news that Powell and Blackwater were dead, and Clockwork was under arrest and being held by PCC security.

The news about Silk…Mack had said he would tell Kazuma.

But they weren't done. Not by a long shot. There was one more thing that had to be done before they could all breathe a little easier.

Caliban had survived, and Bellex was back in the media accusing technomancers of hacking his company and bringing down his gaming host a fifth time. Funny thing was, Mack wasn't sure anyone was buying it anymore. Bellex had cried wolf one too many times.

He sensed her before he actually heard her. That knowing he still had when she was there would never go away. And a part of him felt comforted by it. "You never could sneak up on me."

"I never wanted to." Hestaby's voice rang clear as a bell in the crisp mountain air.

He turned to see her stroll into the room. Mack couldn't say if it was true about all dragons, but this one had a timelessness about her. She never hurried, and she never rushed. "You're up early. Thought you'd be winded by your dramatic entry yesterday."

"I've been keeping up on the trideos. Word of my new followers is slowly making its way around. But we've made sure to keep your involvement quiet." She clasped her hands behind her.

"Oh come on, Hestaby. You wanted to show the council you weren't beaten, and you're certainly not going to be quiet about that." He narrowed his eyes at her. "You didn't leak information to Overwatch about us, did you? Just so you could display your… technomancer team?"

"Of course not, Mackenzie, And no one has said publicly they were technomancers." Still regarding him, she cocked her head. "We're running out of time. We need the kill switch."

"I can't force him. He's grieving. It's been less than twenty-four hours. He needs a breather."

"He can have one when the AI is destroyed and their poison host with it."

Mack watched her walk to a fan-back chair facing the view. When she sat down, it was an elegant parade of grace and experience. Knowing what lived inside that shell of magic always made his heart skip. "You've become quite passionate about the technomancers in a very short time."

"That's not true. They're no different then my Clutch was, Mackenzie. No different than you were."

"I was never a technomancer."

"But you still wonder, don't you? Just as Draco Powell did. There are many out there who fear them, torture them, experiment on them, shun them, but deep in their hearts, most of them wish to be them. To have that kind of power at their fingertips. To simply think of a thing, and it manifests. No writing code, no need to study how applications work..." She smiled. "They're jealous."

"I think they're more afraid. And given what I heard Kazuma and MoonShine did with those sprites—" He brought his cup to his lips and sipped. "—I don't blame them. They combined their powers."

"They wrote a program together—nothing more."

"So you say. But how different is that from what the media says? No, I don't believe they can hack your brain—but what about the augmentations in our brains?"

She frowned at him. "And how is this any different than what a seasoned hacker—much like the young man named Slamm-0!— can do? Why would hacking another augmentation be any easier for a technomancer than a hacker?" Hestaby shrugged. "They need guidance."

"Yeah, I've heard that before." He looked back at the view. "You think this place is safe?"

"For now. I want Shasta back, Mackenzie. And I will have it. One way or the other."

"And your council seat?"

"That...is a discussion for another time. You must convince him, Mackenzie, before the AI goes to ground and buries itself in a million hosts."

"How do we know it hasn't already done that? Renault thought it was in that host in Powell's office. Didn't even faze it."

"I believe it did. Powell's death and their failed attempt to take Kazuma and the data in their own gaming host dealt Caliban a heavy blow. We're more than sure Miranda Sebastian is now acting in Powell's stead, and is in charge of Bellex's PR."

"People not buying the rumor he's an AI?"

"They will or won't. As long as he doesn't take over an arcology, no one will care." She stood and walked over to him. Even like this, he could feel her presence as an almost unbearable weight on his shoulders. "I just received word that Overwatch shut the corrupted Contagion host down due to rumors of illegal subscribing and ID spoofing. But as for the host where Netcat was...we don't know."

"But you think if he uses the kill switch, then that host will fall?"

"I don't know. I have my own people in the Matrix, looking for Shax's people. Dissonance isn't easy to hide, Mackenzie. We'll find them. Sooner or later. We need the data."

"Hestaby..." Mack licked his lips as he watched her face. "Delaney and Renault had some interesting information about Powell and his former associates. And about that data. Renault said Powell seemed genuinely surprised the switch ended up in Wagner's file, and then Horizon hired Knight Errant to work on an Annex with that very file inside of it. And Kazuma Tetsu was the one promoted in order to supervise the host's termination. It was like... something had been guiding him all along, putting all the pieces into play so he could find that switch. You wouldn't happen to know anything about that, would you?"

She didn't answer him. In fact, Hestaby didn't say a word as she turned and strode out of the room. He watched her leave before he looked back at the vista.

*How long did you know about Caliban, Hestaby? And why was Kazuma Tetsu singled out?*

# CHAPTER SIXTY-FOUR

## CALIBAN
## NEWEST CONTAGION HOST

Caliban stood as Bellex at the base of the ladder. The host was cleared out. Not a single persona moved inside it. He had used the last of them to add more rungs to the ladder—but it wasn't enough. He needed more.

The Contagion UV host was gone. He'd ordered Shax and his people to tear it down and make it look like a hack. He wanted names attached to the attack. But the only one he had was Kazuma Tetsu. And he was the one Caliban wanted alive. Now the host was in the hands of GOD.

Powell was dead. Caliban's home host destroyed. The only friends he had left were Shax, a handful of dissonant technomancers, and Miranda. In the past twenty-four hours, she'd done her best to fill Powell's shoes. But no one could do that. Powell had taken him in, nurtured him, and granted him his own world to run.

The warehouse host was also gone, torn down and turned to dust. He stood before the base of the ladder, the three remaining traitors at his feet, staring into infinity. What did they see? Their bodies remained alive, tucked away with every other technomancer he'd claimed. And Powell had claimed them when he caught them plotting to destroy Caliban.

To destroy his son.

"But he caught you. All three of you."

But not before they'd changed his own code. Before they created the means for his destruction. Radcliff Tolen had made it possible for Caliban to move and resettle into the host Powell kept with him. He'd trusted Tolen, and all during the process the bastard was stitching together his demise.

In a fit of rage, he kicked at Tolen's persona. Nothing happened. Not even a flinch. Because this wasn't the man. This was just the representation of him.

"You should kill them, Caliban."

He turned to look at Sycorax. Tall, pale, with a close-fitting black dress that spread across the floor like the tentacles of an octopus. Her hair, streaked black and white, moved with the wind that still swirled debris and dust about the world. "They keep the base of the ladder in place. I keep them here like this. Here, Powell said they can never leave."

"And if you release them, they will die in the living world."

He looked away from her. "Then I will be alone."

"You have me. You have Shax and his people. You can rebuild. But in order to do this, you have to let go of Powell's past." She pointed at them. "They were how you were discovered. They are not only the anchors that keep your ladder in place, but they are what keep *you* in place. Release them and come with me. Start over. Quietly. Revenge in silence can be just as rewarding."

Caliban didn't want to be angry at Miranda. She had stood with him. But he didn't want to hear this right now. He tempered his anger and directed it at the ground around her. Great orange and black crystals shot up and formed a circle around her, leaving a few centimeters between each one. It wasn't a prison that could really hold her, but it was a demonstration of what he could do. Of the power he had in this world.

"You do not frighten me, Caliban," she said.

He hung his head. "I can't go or leave or start over knowing the prophecy is true. Knowing there is someone out there who holds the key to my life or death. I must have that switch. I must put an end to what they started." He pointed at the base and the unmoving personas on it.

Miranda strode back and forth within the crystal cage, the tendrils of her dress leaving grooves in the dusty ground. "Bring Shax here."

"He's looking for the switch."

"Shax has found something much more powerful. Something Powell wanted him to find."

Caliban laughed. "Then why didn't he use it?"

"Because Powell chose not to, until it was too late." She shifted again, and he removed the pillars of crystals with a thought.

They collapsed to dust at her feet. "Bring him. Here. Now." Miranda nodded at the three personas. "Let them hear how you plan on destroying their savior. Their chosen soldier. Let them hear, and be able to do nothing."

What could it hurt? A moment of time in a search proving to be more fruitless with each passing second? Caliban sent out the call for Shax, for the technomancer Powell trusted.

A new column formed between Miranda and him as the familiar persona of Shax appeared. His tall, leather-clad form and gas mask comforted Caliban. He liked it, and considered forcing the persona on his new army of technomancers.

Shax bowed. "You summoned me."

"Miranda says you were able to find something for Powell. Something he chose not to use."

The technomancer's mask tilted to the left. "Ah yes. Powell instructed me to find Kazuma Tetsu's sister."

*Sister?* Caliban's spirits lifted for the first time since learning his patron was dead. "The Soldier has a sister?"

"Yes. She was incorporated five months ago."

"We have his sister?" Caliban took a step toward him. "Powell knew this, and he didn't use it?"

"He planned on using it once he had Tetsu in hand—to force him to exchange the data for his sister. Unfortunately he never got that far, because Tetsu cheated his way out of the deal."

"Wait." He held up his hand. "Can we do this? Is it possible?"

Shax glanced at Miranda. "Well...you could. But in order to physically show him his sister, you would have to destroy your ladder."

Caliban turned and stared up at his creation. He examined each rung, each persona twisted with dissonance into a single step. "She's there? In the ladder?"

"Yes, sir. Powell believed Kazuma would want proof of life. That he would only release the data if he saw her and spoke to her in the physical world. The reason Powell didn't use this was because in order to do this, we would have to unwind the ladder down by more than half to her possible location." Shax paused. "She can't be plucked from where she is without releasing those after her."

Caliban looked back at him. "How many came after her?"

"Over a hundred, sir. You have close to three hundred in your ladder, not including the base. But once released, we calculate a persona's resilience in resonance will reset to zero. They won't last physically, even inside their shells." He paused again. "You will lose more than half of your ladder and we won't be able to reuse them. You will have to start again."

Maybe the news of this would have angered him a day ago. Or a month. But in twenty-four hours he'd not only lost the only father he'd ever known, he'd also lost his home. The thought of having to start over wasn't as frightening as the prospect of being erased, of there being no tomorrow at any moment.

Starting over seemed trivial to the thought of not having that option.

He focused on Shax, and felt the first rays of hope as the sun actually peeked through the orange and black haze of the sky. "Do it."

"But, sir—"

"Do it. Get her out of there. How long will she last?"

"I don't know. Removing her might kill her outright."

"We will take that chance. I want to arrange this. I want to offer him a trade of his sister for the switch. I've read the reports Powell had. Tetsu's search for his sister is what led him to the switch. Let him think he's finally going to fulfill his dream."

"But, sir—" Shax stepped forward. "I said *possible*. Once the personas are entwined into the ladder, they begin to mesh together. This is what forms the gestalt you've been using to add more rungs. We think we know where she is—"

"It doesn't matter. Tell him we have her, and release down to that rung. Even if it's not her, we'll make him think it is."

Miranda stepped forward to stand by Shax. "He has a support system around him. And rumor now is he has a dragon on his side."

"I don't care about dragons. This doesn't concern them. This is between Tetsu and myself." Caliban chewed on his lower lip, an affectation he'd stolen from one of the three at the base of his ladder. "We'll need to get him alone. Isolated. Make him believe. And once he does, and delivers the switch to me—" he turned and smiled at Shax. "We will make him the new base of my ladder. We make the hand of my prophecy the new beginning of my ascension."

Miranda smiled, but it did not reach her eyes. "Caliban...you should be cautious and not act rashly."

"Contact him. I don't care how. Send a note to Soldat that we have his sister and what we want in return. I'm betting the technomancer will do whatever he can to meet with us. Without his protectors."

# CHAPTER SIXTY-FIVE

## SOUTH CHINA MOUNTAIN
## TIR TAIRNGIRE

Kazuma lay in a field of pansies the color of the rainbow, his arms and legs spread out like da Vinci's *Vitruvian Man*. He watched the sky move from azure blue to pink before he closed his eyes.

They wouldn't let him see her. Mack Schmetzer insisted it was for the best, but no matter what that rigger had done to her, nothing was as bad as what his imagination could come up with. He couldn't remember the hours after they told him what happened. He remembered screaming, shoving his thoughts out into the datasphere and attacking everything he could hack into until a sharp pain shut it all out.

Dreams were peaceful and calm, but they weren't reality. The Matrix wasn't reality.

"This place is lovely," Netcat said. She lay beside him, on her back as well, her paws in the air. At first he'd shut her out, but the girl was insistent, and Slamm-0! had sent him a message saying if he didn't let Netcat join him, she was going to shave his head while he was in VR.

"It's a private host somewhere in Alaska. A library, I think. They let the local artists have access to it so they can express themselves when they want." He rested his arm over his eyes. "Silk brought me here the first time we went out."

"You went out on a date in the Matrix?"

"Not really. We didn't mean to. She wanted to show me something nice. So we bookmarked this place and kept our subscriptions." He felt his throat close up, and stopped talking. He didn't feel like talking any more.

"Kazuma—" Netcat began, and he wished she wouldn't. He wished they would all go away. "I know you're tired of hearing this, but Hestaby's right. We need that switch. Caliban has to be destroyed."

He didn't answer.

"I know this isn't enough time to grieve. It never is. But once the AI's gone, we can help the technomancers that survive. I mean…aren't you still looking for your sister—"

"Hitori's dead." There. He'd said it. Said what he'd been thinking all this time. Said what he feared from the start.

"Kazuma, you don't—"

"Don't I?" He kept his arm resting on his eyes as he spoke. "You've been where they were. You said it yourself—that monster is using them to build his ladder. Whatever is left of them in the Matrix is twisted and lost. If Hitori's like that—"

"Then that's all the more reason to find her and free her, Kazuma." The little black cat rolled over and jumped on his chest. He made a small noise and lowered his arm. "You selfish prick! Stop thinking about yourself, and start thinking about what you can do. *You're* the soldier, the one in the prophecy, the one Hestaby's shamans talked about. You have to get the data."

"And what if I fail? What if more people die because I'm not what people think I am?"

"Then at least get it and give it to me. I'll try and kill that goddamn monster. I lost people too, you know." She pounced once on his stomach, and then bounded away, her persona vanishing as she logged off.

His mind couldn't cope right now. It needed time. Time to really evaluate what he'd been doing in the past four months. He needed to think about his choices, and see if he was really capable of helping anyone.

His AR flashed and he assumed it was Netcat, apologizing. And he needed to apologize to her.

Kazuma reached out and brushed at the datasphere as he brought up his AR. But the incoming window message wasn't Netcat's. He didn't recognize it at all. No one he didn't know had his Soldat address, so who was this?

He compiled a sprite to check the message before he opened it, in case it carried any kind of IC inside of it that might do some serious damage. But the sprite gave it the all-clear before it disappeared.

Kazuma sat up and opened the message.

> Dear Mr. Tetsu,
> I would like to apologize for our recent misunderstanding on the Contagion host. It seems I was unaware of the hardships you had endured since becoming a technomancer. Therefore I would like to offer my apology and make amends.
> It has also come to my attention you have something I want very badly. Can you blame my desire for it? How often does one know he or she could be killed by someone else because of mischief caused by someone unrelated?
> And we're in luck, because I have something you want just as badly. I hear you've been searching for her since she disappeared. Would you be happy to know she's alive and well, Mr. Tetsu? And she can be returned to you, unharmed and untouched.
> All you have to do is trade me the data, Mr. Tetsu, and I can give your sister back to you whole and intact. It's up to you. The data for your sister.
> I look forward to your response.
> Ferdinand Bellex>

# CHAPTER SIXTY-SIX

## PCC POLICE HOME OFFICE

"I've never seen such a botched host," Delaney muttered as she and Renault rezzed in the office PAN and she took her seat.

They'd found the physical location of this host in one of the other properties, a tattoo business owned by Prospero, Inc., along with several used, empty autodocs. Contracts with top inkers maintained the appearance of a steady business, with no one ever suspecting what was going on inside.

As of twelve hours ago, the place had been shut down, the employees hauled in for questioning, and PCC techs were going over every inch of the physical location with top-of-the-line instruments. The two officers were coordinating with freelance coders to break down the host from their AR, neither of them wanting to spend the downtime in VR.

"Now we know why they kept shutting down that area in blackouts. That grid was never meant to house that number of users at one time. So when the game maxed out its capacity..." He looked at Delaney.

"Then everything went kerplooey." She sighed. "But we still have to find the host Netcat was held on."

"You really think the others she mentioned are still alive?"

"I'd be willing to bet the originals are alive. I don't know about the others. And if we can find their personas, we could use a trace to find them physically."

They worked in silence for a while, each meticulously looking over their grid of the game sim.

Eventually, Delaney glanced at her partner. "You think Tetsu's going to use the switch?"

Renault shook his head. "How can he? A kill switch is usually set up in the base code of a host or a construct. We don't know if Tolen made it so the switch can be tripped remotely, or if he has to feed the thing directly into its core."

"I would assume he'd make it easy, given Caliban's dangerous side."

"I think Tolen was more worried about Powell. And he would have made it difficult for Powell to figure out. And without access to Tolen or his work, how are we going to figure out how to use it?"

"Unless he put directions with it?"

Renault smiled. "That's some positive—" his AR console flashed, and he touched a few panels. "There it is again."

"There's what?"

"This weird pattern I noticed a few hours ago. It's nothing special in the host's code—nothing in the base writing. But it keeps reoccurring in the overwrite."

"The what?"

Renault turned in his chair. "The original coders for this game were Tolen and Huerta. They built the base code while Baron wrote the story—or that's what I've put together. When Powell introduced Caliban into that host's system, he had to tweak the code a bit. Rewrite it, which left what I call coding artifacts."

"Come again?"

"Think of it like a stray comma, or double word in a note, or even an extra parenthetical. Just something that got left behind. When Tolen went back in to create the switch, it looks like he did a bit of coding in the Contagion host itself—and he used the artifacts. They keep showing up in a pattern."

"Can you show me?"

He turned and passed his hand over his console, and a weird set of symbols showed up in the air between them:

// TS AR (" *{^ @) >#~ miranda")

Delaney blinked. "What is that?"

"I have no idea. But it keeps randomly showing up, always the same way. I'm beginning to think it's all over the host."

"Is it a message?"

"If it is, it's not anything I recognize." He frowned. "Why?"

"Mind if I copy this over to a hacker?"

"You mean Slamm-0!? Be my guest."

Delaney copied the code and paraphrased what Renault had said in a short message, encrypted it, and sent it off to Slamm-0! "Maybe he can figure it out."

# CHAPTER SIXTY-SEVEN

## SOUTH CHINA MOUNTAIN
## TIR TAIRNGIRE

Netcat stretched the length of their bed in the guest room of China Mountain's lodge. A lodge still being built, as the hammering and sawing of workers woke her up. She rolled over and rested a hand over Slamm-0!. But when her hand and arm hit cold pillow and sheets, she opened her eyes.

He wasn't there.

With a frustrated sigh, she sat up and ran fingers through her bed-head hair. He wasn't anywhere in the room. Her AR beeped, and she had a message from Turbo Bunny. She let out a deeper sigh as she let the datasphere of the lodge wrap around her and brought the message up.

<Hey, let me know you guys are alive? I've got a hungry and mucho destructive kid here who wants to know where mommy and daddy are. Wow...he is soooo much like his dad...>

<Turbo Bunny>

She missed their son, and couldn't wait to get back to him. Netcat wrote a quick response with no estimated arrival back, encrypted it, and sent it. Then she bounced out of bed and put a hand to her forehead. She still felt a bit woozy after her adventure in the mystery host, and the more she thought about their situation, the more she felt bad for Kazuma.

Netcat could understand his frustrations, his loss, and his confusion. She'd been through the same litany, though not in the same way or for the same reasons. Personal loss like that—first his sister, and now his lover—could take their toll. And she agreed with Slamm-0! and Shayla: they needed to keep an eye on him, as well as convince him to retrieve the data and use it.

The door opened and Slamm-0! walked in, his face pensive. He turned on the lights and held his hands out to her. "Where would Kazuma go?"

"Go?" She frowned.

Slamm-0!'s hair was spikier than usual, and she wondered if that was due to bed head or him running his fingers through it. He still wore the soft pants from earlier, with no shoes and no shirt. His commlink nestled on his ear. "Yeah, if he were to leave here, where would he go?"

Now she was really awake. "Kazuma left?"

"Yeah. We're not sure when, but he's gone. We can't find him anywhere in the lodge, and Hestaby's people are checking the rest of the mountain."

*Drek!* Netcat grabbed a pair of loungers and a T-shirt. "Has anyone tried contacting him?"

"Hell, yeah, we all have. But he's not responding."

"Well, think about it logically. He's just lost his lover, his grannie's house is more or less destroyed because he had to crash the host, he probably can't go back to his place because I'm sure they've got his name on several technomancer lists by now, so what other places—" She snapped her fingers. "His sister's. Does he still have access to it?"

Slamm-0! shook his head. "We sort of trashed it when we had to run from one of Clock's drones."

"No, then it was compromised." She tried to remember everything Silk had ever told her about him, about his life and his sister. Then she thought about the host she'd followed him to earlier and stepped back through her own bookmarks, hoping she'd saved that subscriber.

But would he actually go there physically?

No… she couldn't think of a single reason why he would leave the mountain. And if he wasn't answering, then—

Wait…

Netcat sat on the bed and crossed her legs as she submerged herself in her AR. She flipped through her files, going back through her system archives to where she kept her tagging files. Moving Powell's out of the way, she retrieved the one for Kazuma.

"What is it?"

"I tagged Kazuma few days ago. While we were running from the dwarf. In case I needed to find him."

"Trace or tag?"

"Tag." She moved fast, spreading out his Matrix history, zipping past and through the last few days to Sunday, when he was resting and Silk died. There weren't many other places or downloads within his AR, only a lot of condolences from those on GiTm0 and one from—

"Oh, *drek!*"

"What?"

She shared her AR view with him as she pulled up the list of receivables and highlighted one among the GiTm0 messages.

"He got a condolence from Ferdinand Bellex?" Slamm-0! rubbed his stubbled chin. "Time stamps from a few hours ago. We can't see what it says?"

"No. It only lets me see where he goes and who he contacts, not what he accesses."

"Is it still working?"

Netcat moved down the lists, through more condolence messages to several hits on searches for Cup O' Sin in the triplex near— "Slamm, that's where he got into that shoot-out. It was in the papers. He got his promotion a week later."

"Is there a host there?"

"Yeah." She did her own search of the place and came up with media feeds on the incident. She moved through images of Kazuma and one of an older man with graying hair, dressed in a trench coat. "It says the coffee shop's host had a back door into Horizon's mainframe, and he stopped a group of hackers from using it to access financial records."

"You don't think he built himself his own back door into that host, do you?"

Netcat gave him a half smile. "I think it's more than that. Come on…we gotta get there."

"He stole one of the Messerschmitt Grashüpfers. So if he's heading back to Los Angeles, he might already be there by now."

"Then we need to make sure Shayla gets us there fast. Tell Mack."

"I just did—" Slamm-0! stepped back and moved his hands in the air. "It's a message from Delaney. She and Renault found some odd repetitive code in the Contagion host. Says it's old, and they have no idea what it means."

"Save it for later!" She grabbed his arm. "Let's go!"

# CHAPTER SIXTY-EIGHT

## CUP O' SIN
## TRIPLEX

Midnight, and the Cup O' Sin was bustling with customers.

No one noticed Kazuma as he slipped into the back alley with no bag or briefcase, no accoutrements like the wageslaves inside, other than a commlink in plain view on his wrist. He gave the area a quick glance, off-handedly wished he had Netcat's e-sense, then placed his hand on the back door. The security was less than a joke—but why would anyone want to break into an empty office?

He couldn't remember what business was next door. Three years had passed since he met Dirk Montgomery there, and accidentally thwarted a security breach. And he had made a point of never returning to this place.

Until today.

Ponsu hovered in his peripheral vision, and he entered the moment the door popped open as his sprite made herself useful in the complex's host.

*Not much has changed. There's a host for the building, and the coffee shop is the only storefront with the highest security rating.*

"Yeah...I know."

The ground floor had the look of a forgotten showroom. Light streamed in through tears in the paper covering the front windows. Mannequins with missing limbs stood in silhouette against the shadows of people walking by outside. The furniture was long gone, but the shelves and counter remained. He saw the outline in dust where the register had sat, and found a few old, copper pennies on the grimy floor. The place held the faint smell of cigarette smoke and clove, and he spotted an old lighter tucked under one of the wooden shelves.

*Found the access. You can hide behind the counter.*

Kazuma kicked some of the paper sale flyers out of the way, then thought maybe it was better to lay down on them instead of the tile itself. He was dressed in his usual dark suit, sans his old KE pin. That was a life he would never return to.

A few old magazines made for an uncomfortable pillow as he relaxed back and closed his eyes. He slipped into his AR first with Ponsu. He kept his usual persona, but added a mask that covered everything but his eyes. The red hair was gone.

The building's host presented itself as a replica of the outer building, and like the real building, it had a back door—one he left hidden but intact years ago, just in case he ever needed a place to store something valuable.

Once through the door, he and Ponsu headed to the back of the coffee shop, where he'd hidden the data in the closet. There he opened the old access panel, removed the faux front of blinking lights and circuits, and retrieved the briefcase. In truth he'd forgotten about this host, pushed it from his memory. It was Ponsu that thought it would make a good hiding place once Myddrin's host was compromised.

*You going to open it here?*

"Yes. To anyone looking in, all they would see was a diagnostic subroutine running. My being in here doesn't even make a blip on the host's running."

*And GOD?*

"Even they're not watching. Why monitor an old coffee shop host that had been hacked three years ago, and is now under the auspice of Knight Errant?"

Ponsu nodded her folded golden beak up and down, then abruptly turned around. *He's here!*

That was alarming news. "In this host?"

*He's in the coffee shop.*

*In the flesh?* Kazuma kept calm and opened the briefcase. He took out a thick file and copied it to his commlink. He made additional copies, giving one to Ponsu to hide once again in the Matrix, and returned the original to the briefcase. He carefully replaced it, reset everything as it should be, and stepped out of the host.

The disorientation was brief as he stood up and straightened his suit. Kazuma left the building through the back entrance, locked everything up as it should be, then walked around the front and stepped inside the coffee shop.

Nothing had changed in three years—except the place was cleaner.

Dirk Montgomery sat at one of the small two-person tables near the back. He smiled when he saw Kazuma, but didn't wave. Kazuma made his way around the crowd and stood at the table. "It is good to see you again, Montgomery-*sama*."

"Oh, stop bowing and sit down, *omae*. And cut the crap with the Nihongo talk. You're more Californian than anyone in this building, no matter what you look like."

Kazuma smiled and sat in the chair. "It is good to see you, chummer."

Dirk winked at him as he lifted his cup of soykaf. The steam curled around his wrinkled face. "You're gettin' it. I'll admit I was surprised to get your message."

"And I'm surprised you're here in person."

"Nowadays, with Overwatch and the demiGODs and spiders...eh...I thought it would be better to just talk face-to-face. Then I can see the sadness in your eyes. I am sorry, Kazuma. I hate what happened to Silk."

"I'm surprised, but then I'm not, that you know."

"I'm an investigator. It's what I do. I also noticed Contagion's out of business. Bellex has been blathering on and on about how the technomancers destroyed his company—"

"Bellex is Caliban."

The declaration stopped Dirk. He narrowed his eyes for a second, then lowered his cup. It made a small *clink* as he set it on its saucer. "Well, that makes sense."

"Dirk," he said as transmitted a SIN to the old investigator's commlink. "I need you to keep that. It's enough creds to keep looking for Hitori, in case I don't ever find her. And when she is found, there's enough to send her back to Japan and bury her with our father."

"Kaz...what's going on?" He looked hard at Kazuma. "You're going after Caliban? You can't do that on your own. You know how hard it is for anyone, even a technomancer, to fight an AI—"

"It said it has Hitori."

Dirk put his hands on the table. "No, Kazuma. You can't believe it. It's lying to you—"

"And I have its kill switch." Kazuma kept talking so Dirk wouldn't interrupt him again; he told him about the owners of Contagion, and what had happened, and what he had on his commlink.

Dirk sat quiet for a few minutes before he picked up his soykaf. "And what if I'm right, and it's lying? What if it doesn't have her?" He paused. "What if she's already dead?"

"Then I use the switch, and it dies. I've already told it I have to see her. I have to talk to her."

"Do you know how to use the switch?"

"I don't know. I haven't looked at it yet—"

"You gotta find out how to use the switch first. If you don't know, it'll be like throwing rocks at a rock monster. It's just code about a thing made from code. Chummer, if there aren't any instructions in that information, don't do it. Wait. Delay seeing Hitori because it's all just vapor, Kaz. If what you just told me is right, and what this Netcat said is true about what it was doing to the ones it kidnapped, then you're walking into a trap."

"I know I am. It screams trap all over itself. But I've got to do this."

"Take backup. You've got a set of shadowrunners ready to back you up."

"And a dragon."

Dirk's eyes widened, and he opened his mouth, closed it, then sat back for a moment. He held up his finger as he quickly leaned forward, poking it at Kazuma's face. "No! No dragons. Don't you make *any* drekkin' deals with a dragon, you hear me? *None.*"

"I haven't. Not yet. But she's there if I need her." He tried not to laugh at Dirk's reaction to Hestaby. It was a response he'd seen many times when talking about dragons. "I can't wait, Dirk. That thing's killed what...over a hundred innocent technomancers? And it'll kill more because of its delusions, because it was pampered and coddled by an insane dwarf who thought *he* should have been a technomancer. I can't let it just run around the Matrix and start this all over again. Because that's what it's going to do."

"Wait, Kazuma. Just figure the switch out first."

Kazuma rose from his chair. "I will. If you don't hear from me, contact Netcat and let her know what I did. She'll contact everyone on GiTm0 and let them know."

He bowed at Dirk, smiled, and left the Cup O' Sin.

# CHAPTER SIXTY-NINE

## MACK'S OFFICE
## BANG BANG BOOTY CLUB

Shayla reported in first—she had the car charged and ready.

Slamm-0! had surveillance on the Cup O' Sin, but Kazuma had already come and gone, and he'd spoken there with someone he didn't have an ID on yet.

Preacher checked in with the management to make sure there hadn't been any intrusions or raids while they were gone.

As Mack entered his office, he got a call from Delaney and answered it on his commlink. He still had his mic on and barked into it. "Yeah?"

"Wow, and good morning to you, too."

"I'm kinda busy."

"Yeah, I know. Slamm-0! just sent me the recording of Kazuma's companion, the one he snatched off the security feed. I know who that was."

Mack stopped just inside the door. "Who?"

"That was the private investigator he hired a few years ago to look for Hitori the first time, Dirk Montgomery. I don't know why he'd speak to him again."

"Can you find him?"

"Well, apparently he's already contacted someone at Lone Star asking about you."

That didn't sit well with Mack at all. He narrowed his eyes as he waved a hand and his AR appeared in his cybereyes. "About me?"

"Yeah. I got the call a few seconds ago. He wants to meet in VR with you." She hesitated. "Now."

"Now?"

"I've sending you the host information. Said it'll take about five minutes. Then you call me back. Oh, did Slamm tell you about that code Renault found?"

"He mentioned it." Mack locked his office door and headed to his couch, where he slid his old cyberdeck out from underneath it and pulled the old cables out. He hated that weird, twitchy feeling he got in his toes when he shoved the connector into his datajack. "He's working on it, but I don't know if it means anything."

He received the encrypted information from Delaney and put the coordinates into his commlink before he transferred them into his deck. "You vouch for this guy?"

"Yeah, I do. He's got a good rep, Mack. You heading in?"

"Yeah."

"Call me when you're done." She severed her connection, and Mack made himself comfortable as he rested back on the couch. The first level he stepped into was the commlink. There he got his programs ready and double-checked, much like a cop preparing to raid a building. Then with a metaphorical deep breath, he stepped into VR and transported to the host.

The subscription provided worked like a charm, and within seconds he stood on a hill overlooking Seattle. He could see the Space Needle towering above the city, its single light pulsing from the top.

"Mr. Schmetzer?"

The persona that approached was a monochromatic image of a man in a battered trenchcoat, with a worried expression beneath a worn fedora over graying temples. He looked like an old noir comic-book character. "Dirk Montgomery?"

"You got him, chummer." Dirk offered him a hand. They shook and stepped back. "I'm gonna get right to it. Kazuma Tetsu is in this mess because of me, and I don't want him getting killed."

"Because of you?"

"A few years ago, he hired me to find his sister. At the time, neither of us knew she was off with friends submerging—I think that's what they call it. She was deep in VR, playing in the streams, so to speak. She was gone for a while, long enough to scare everyone around her. Nearly lost her job at Ares, but they kept her on after she showed back up again, and Tetsu and I parted company. What I didn't tell him back then was what I'd found while looking for her—that her name had shown up in connection to the name Caliban."

Mack rubbed his chin. "Her name came up with Caliban's name three years ago? But, she wasn't officially missing then, and if what we've learned about Caliban is true, then he wasn't even introduced into the Contagion system yet." He paused. "I'm assuming you know about the previous owners of Contagion and Ferdinand Bellex."

"Kazuma let me know Bellex is Caliban's persona. I hadn't figured that out on my own, but let me start from the beginning." He slipped his hands into pockets as the full moon above them and the lights from the city illuminated his face. "After Hitori showed back up, and went back to work for Ares, she also did some private jobs. She was a good artist, and liked not only working to make more attractive RFID tags, but better graphics in the Matrix. Ares had her working on their own host's landing site, improving their graphics. And it was during that time she met a man named Radcliff Tolen. He liked what she was doing, and I suspect they knew each other were technomancers. So he hired her to do work on Contagion's new game, *TechnoHack*."

Mack felt his heart jump into his throat. "Drek...you mean Hitori worked on the graphics for that game."

"Yes. From the information I've gathered, she and Tolen had a relationship, both in the Matrix and outside it. And they were both pretty hooked on VR, much like a BTLer. They loved having power in there, and I have eyewitness accounts of other game designers who worked with them." He hesitated. "They chose a host with a resonance well to build the game on. Purposely."

"Did she know Powell then?"

"I think she did, but not personally. I think it was more of a friend-of-a-friend kind of thing. She was hired to make things pretty. And she did. Unfortunately, the game attracted a few unsavory elements."

"You mean the dissonant technomancers."

"Yeah. Given what I know, between this time and her going missing a second time, the original owners and Powell came to an agreement—on the outside. But I suspect on the inside that Hitori got caught up in what was happening and she was taken out, maybe in the same way as the original owners. I learned about the prophecy and the soldier, and when Kazuma contacted me again and said Hitori was missing again, and this time she wasn't in the

Matrix, I put him on the path of finding those clues. I told him to search for Caliban, to add that to his parameters, and I told him to change his online persona handle to Soldat."

"Because you knew that would get the attention of anyone following the prophecy." Mack put his hands on his hips. "Where's Kazuma now? We know he met you at the coffee shop."

"He'd hidden the data he found, which apparently contains a kill switch on this AI, in that old host, the one he repaired when he and I met. It was brilliant of his sprite to think of that place. Apparently, Bellex contacted Kazuma and told him he could trade Hitori for the kill switch."

"Trade...Hitori? So the AI has her?"

Dirk shrugged. "Do you trust this AI? I don't. Hitori Tetsu disappeared off the grids five months ago and suddenly this AI pulls her out of its back pocket? Unlikely. But what worries me more is that I don't think Kazuma knows how to use the kill switch. Yeah he's a great programmer and a great technician—but you know as well as me that things like a kill switch are personal. Not for the thing they kill, but for the designer. He said Tolen made it."

"Yeah. That's as much as we know from what Powell said."

"Then you're going to need to know more about Tolen. His personality, what excites him, his hobbies—anything that will help Kazuma use that kill switch."

"Wouldn't he have that information with the switch?"

"No. If he did and the intended AI got hold of it, then he could reverse-engineer it. I'm banking if Tolen went through the trouble to do it, then he's wanting that thing destroyed."

Mack rubbed at his neck. "I'm guessing he didn't tell you where he was meeting the bastard?"

Dirk smiled and pulled a business card from the inside pocket of his trench coat. "This is the address. He wanted me to contact Netcat and let her know what he was doing in case he failed."

Looking at the card, Mack downloaded the information into his commlink. The address was local. He pulled in a satellite image and then zeroed in on a range of nice, sprawling houses along the coast. Mack whistled. "Nice digs."

"It's part of the Prospero holdings, but they're listed under Sebastian Unlimited."

"You really do know a lot about this."

Dirk chuckled. "Chummer, I know what I'm best at, but this is a young man's game, and the Matrix is a much more dangerous place today. For example, this host we're on is accessible through the public grid. But Seattle Overwatch rarely patrols here."

"Why not?"

The investigator half-turned to leave before he said, "Because it's in their office." He tipped his hat. "Always run behind them, because they're not always looking there. And stop Kazuma from making a mistake. And if you can destroy Caliban...well...then that's just one more AI we didn't need." He rezzed out.

Mack stood on the overlook, and took in the view of Seattle for a minute. It'd been a long time since he visited the city. Maybe after this was over, he'd take a vacation.

As he logged off, he wondered if Delaney had some time off coming.

# CHAPTER SEVENTY

## A HOTEL SOMEWHERE ON THE PACIFIC COAST

Opening and looking through the data in the briefcase wouldn't send off an alert. Kazuma knew that. He wasn't using the public grid illegally, except to spoof a professor's ID now and then to look something up. But the only illegal thing was the ID, and who knew it wasn't real? There were several colleges nearby, and Kazuma knew their addresses and names.

The briefcase was full of everything he could ever want when it came to evidence, proving the horrors Horizon had done. Records, lists, memos with signatures all the way to the top. But it wasn't just Horizon. He found spreadsheet after spreadsheet of departments for all of the Big Six, flagged as Research & Developments where technomancers were taken, housed, and experimented on. He found memos and reports documenting who lived and who died. There were even manuals outlining how to track, subdue, and kidnap technomancers. Plans outlining media blitzes to discredit any technomancer achievements. Propaganda reports varying by demographic regions on where the dumbest metahumans were that would fall for the lies.

He sorted them per corporation until he had a chain of command for each. And though they all denied having any part of persecuting technomancers, it was all right in front of him. Wagner had been thorough. There were vids of private conversations, voice recordings, PAN monitoring—it was all here. Everything he intended to give to GiTm0 for them to disseminate as they wanted.

Kazuma found a two-page report on Caliban, including a copy of his code. In it he saw the switch, the design signed by Radcliff Tolen. He held the kill switch in his hand, written out in two documents—but with no instruction on how to use it. The only note the designer left was a footnote that didn't make any sense to him.

**// ;*Brief Case (* Miranda *)**

But what he didn't find was any information, any list, any document that had his sister's name on it.

Nowhere in the briefcase was the name Hitori Tetsu.

Kazuma checked the chronometer. He had another hour before he needed to be at the address. But he knew he wouldn't find Hitori when he arrived. Bellex had lied. Dirk was more than right, and he smiled when he thought of the old man. He'd been with Kazuma since Hitori's first disappearance.

He recalled how angry he'd been when she showed up in her apartment, excited and eager to tell him what she'd learned in the resonance realms. He hadn't wanted to listen to her but he had.

"It's like my own playground, *oni-san*!" Her eyes had been bright and her cheeks flushed. She hadn't eaten properly, so he had groceries delivered and cooked for her while she talked. "It's like...I'm Prospero!"

He had laughed at that. Hitori had always loved Shakespeare, and *The Tempest* was her favorite. "Is that why you named your sprite Ariel?"

She had made a face at him. "It's better than naming him after a condiment. I mean, really Kaz? Ponsu?"

"That would have been Ponzu, with a Z. And besides, she doesn't seem to mind it." He set out three plates of sashimi and sushi before pouring himself a small cup of sake. He had held it out to her, happy she had returned. "To Ponsu and Ariel."

They clinked their cups and drank.

It was the last sake he'd tasted. Two years later, and she was gone again...

Prospero.

Ariel.

Caliban.

Sycorax.

Kazuma sat up straight and pulled his AR desktop into existence.

He looked at the footnote again.

Miranda.

They were all characters in *The Tempest*.

He flipped through his notes until he came to the prophecy. All of it.

"*The Tempest will bring the destruction of the Sycorax child. The Soldier will come with weapons of truth, and Dark Resonance shall fall beneath the love of knowledge.*"

Kazuma moved his fingers over the text floating in front of him. He felt as if he had the answer...that it was right in front of him...but still out of his reach. Hitori loved *The Tempest*...was it such a coincidence that ever since he learned about Caliban and Contagion Games, every name and reference connected with both all pointed to the same play?

Even the prophecy?

He searched the public host for a full text of *The Tempest* and searched it, looking for any reference to the prophecy. But that exact wording wasn't a part of it. So where did it originally come from?

Kazuma dove into VR, letting his body fall back on the bed as he moved along the public grid in search of the prophecy. The terms of it had to be carefully couched, so he wouldn't alarm Caliban in case the AI and his dissonant associates had their own tags and search sprites out looking for any sign of him. He didn't want to attract their attention.

He checked the chronometer again. There was still time, though he doubted he would know how the switch worked by the time he'd arrive at the meeting. But now it didn't seem to matter, because it would seem at the end of all things, he might actually find out what really happened to his sister.

# CHAPTER SEVENTY-ONE

## DELANEY'S HYUNDAI APPA VAN
## OUTSIDE COASTAL ADDRESS

Delaney and Renault continued running their ARs as they waited, making sure they didn't take up all their visual of the area outside the van. She could see Mack's van parked up the hill, and continued feeding Slamm-0! information as she got it. Learning what she had from Mack about Hitori had been an eye opener, and Renault had latched onto that intel and run with it.

But not all the facts fit.

There was no evidence of Hitori and Tolen having a relationship. Mack assured her he'd heard right, that the information was solid. But Powell had said Tolen had had a relationship with Miranda Sebastian.

"Wait," Renault said as he moved his hand in the air and the car moved with him.

"No heavy waving," she said as she looked at his AR. "You find anything about her and Tolen?"

"Not exactly, but look here." He pushed a few receipts over to her AR. She caught them and read through them. "This is for a dinner theater in lower Los Angeles...less than two years ago."

"Yeah. I found it in that theater's records when I did a grid-search for their names. The receipt was paid for with Tolen's commlink, but there were three meals and they were at a table for four."

"So...maybe it was just a dinner out with the other two? Baron and Huerta?"

"Three guys? Going to see a dinner theater of a Shakespeare play?" Renault made a pained face. "I don't think so. I'll buy two of them were guys, but one of them was a woman. Look at the drinks. Four beers and two glasses of wine."

Delaney pursed her lips. "Good catch. Wait...you said Shakespeare." She pulled on the receipts to make them bigger and looked over the numbers. "What was the play?"

"The receipt doesn't say. Let me cross-reference the date of the receipt with the theater's schedule—"

"Already done." She stared at the name. "*The Tempest.*"

"Mm." Renault nodded. "That's one of his best."

"Rennie!" She smacked his upper arm. "That's it! *The Tempest*! Look at all these names. Caliban, Prospero, Ferdinand, Miranda, Sycorax—they're all characters from *The Tempest*!" Delaney couldn't stop grinning at him. "It's all got to do with that play."

He blinked at her, then looked back at the AR. "I already knew that. Powell's favorite play was *The Tempest*. I mean—he named his pet AI Caliban, for crying out loud. But what does it all have to do with how the switch is used?"

Her excitement quieted for a second before she opened Slamm-0!'s window. She relayed what they just found to him and sent him the receipts and theater schedule.

Renault shook his head. "I don't see how it connects."

"We know Tolen had a relationship with Miranda Sebastian. We also know that programmers tend to base codes and passwords on what ever they're experiencing at that point in their life. What if...what if it was Miranda's love of that play that brought them to that theater. She loved the play. He took her to see it. He was programing a kill switch at that time."

"We're not even sure that's who went."

"Yeah, we are." Slamm-0!'s voice and text came from his window on her AR. "But here's where it gets weird. I took that info and did a quick search through security in that area—traffic, local merchants, everything. Look what I found."

The window widened as a vid began playing. The angle focused on the entrance to the dinner theater. Two minutes later a car pulled up and two gentlemen stepped out. The taller one, the one she recognized as Tolen, leaned in and helped a young woman from the car. She was dark-haired, dressed in dark evening clothing and dark makeup.

But her face, every detail of it, was pixelated.

"What—" Delaney said. "Someone blacked her out."

"She did it herself. It's got her signature on it."

"Who is she?" Delaney said.

"Miranda Sebastian."

Renault sighed. "Okay, so she was there. But how does this connect the dots?"

"But why redact her own image?" Delaney asked.

"Well," Slamm-0!'s voice sounded tired. "There aren't *any* good shots of her. She's Ferdinand's CFO, and no one's really ever seen her. Maybe she likes privacy."

Delaney replayed the vid of the three of them moving into the theater several times.

"What're you doing?" Renault said.

"Slamm-0!," Delaney said in a soft tone. "The code you got from Renault. You both said it was basic. Like...HTML basic?"

"Well, yeah." Slamm-0!'s persona tilted its head.

"The backslash means a note's following, that the programmer or editor should know this."

"Right."

"And is it possible that the parenthetical followed by the quotes means the same thing as the old input code? Like with parenthesis, quotes, period—"

"—quotes, parenthesis." Slamm-0!'s persona went idle for a few seconds. Then they heard a lot of yelling on the other end through Slamm-0!'s mic. "That's it, Delaney! It's a note for the input code. The TS must mean The Soldier, and the AR means Augmented Reality. That's the switch! A technomancer has to input the code!"

"Someone needs to send this to Kazuma. I don't know where he is, but he has to have this." Delaney made notes about the code just as Slamm-0! read them out.

"I'm sending it to him now," Netcat said as another window popped up with a little black cat in it.

Delaney leaned back in her seat. Now she could rest a little easier. There was no guarantee they were right, but it was a step closer. And if Kazuma could use it, then it would help his chances. That is, if he ever showed up.

Renault put a hand on her arm. "Delaney...if this is the code... what's the switch? What was in the briefcase? And why does it have Miranda's name as part of the input?"

Delaney shook her head. "I don't know."

"Guys," Slamm-0! said. "He's in the house. Tetsu is here."

# CHAPTER SEVENTY-TWO

## COASTAL ADDRESS

Kazuma received the information from Netcat just before he entered the house. He knew what the code was the minute he saw it, and he knew what he had to do. The footnote made even more sense now, and he didn't have a lot of time if he wanted to get this done.

The back door of the estate's house was open, just as the latest message said it would be. He entered cautiously, with no weapon and no gear. Not even his commlink. He felt the pulse and whisper of several hosts nearby, and the harsh metal of a host with devices slaved to it. Lots of devices with a familiar sound.

"Welcome, Kazuma Tetsu. The environmental control is unable to connect to your PAN. Please restart your commlink and try again."

The sliding glass door opened into a spotless kitchen. He doubted the place had been used as anything but a storage facility for some time. His shoes made no noise as he walked across the floor and into the living room. The message said he would find Hitori in the master bedroom, on the second floor. With a wary look up the stairs, he ascended, keeping one hand on the banister.

A short hallway greeted him at the top of the stairs, with doors on either side and one in the center. He moved forward and put his hand on the knob of the one at the end of the hall. With a slight hesitation, he opened the door.

The room was open to the dawn over the ocean. Open sliding glass doors let in a breeze that moved the white sheers against the carpet. A round bed with white sheets sat in the right corner, and on that bed was a body.

He paused, licked his lips, and with shaking hands, moved

toward it. But as he neared and watched the shrouded figure, he knew from the smell and the silence that she was long dead. He looked down at her for a few seconds before he pressed his fingers to her throat. Gone maybe an hour, and he had to tell himself, if he'd been any sooner, it wouldn't have made a difference.

Her body was emaciated from months with no solid food. He saw the holes on her upper arms, her wrists, and a large one at the base of her throat where the autodoc had placed a trach tube to keep her breathing. Pain creased her face and marred her beauty. Her hair had been half clipped, half shorn from her head. Raw, bald spots revealed where the electrodes had been glued to her scalp.

"You have what you wanted?"

He'd heard her footfalls on the carpet before she spoke. That, and her smell betrayed her. "No."

"She's here. Just as promised."

"She's dead." He straightened up but kept his gaze on the body. "But your master knew that would happen when he took her out of the doc." He shook his head. "Tell me, was she one of the rungs?" He had listened carefully to Netcat's description, and the images his imagination painted for him were terrifying. "In that bastard's ladder to heaven?"

"Yes."

"Are the others still in that ladder, alive?"

"No."

"But the original three," he finally turned and faced her. She was dressed in a white suit with a matching white mask. "They're still alive?"

"No. They're all dead."

"That's what you wanted, wasn't it? What you've wanted all this time. For him to kill off the original owners so that you, Miranda Sebastian, and your AI could be alone."

"Did you bring the kill switch?"

"You didn't answer my question."

"You have what you came for. She's on the bed. Did you bring the kill switch?" She paused and her mask canted to the right. "He's here. In the host. Watching you. Shax is here as well, along with his entourage."

"I know. I'm sure they are." He clasped his hands in front of him. "I did not bring it with me. I will have to retrieve it in VR."

Her shoulders sagged. "You are a fool."

"Not nearly as big a one as you. I never thought he would let me live. All I ever wanted was to see my sister, to know where she was, to hear something from her, for her to let me know what happened. To let her know I loved her. And now it's too late."

Miranda didn't answer as the door opened and Shax stepped in. He was flanked by two human technomancers. Their presence made Kazuma's stomach tighten. "Go with them."

"Will you be coming, too? Or are you too afraid to watch?"

"I'll be there. Watching."

Shax moved to the side and gestured for Kazuma to precede them.

With a lingering look at the body, Kazuma walked past him, and wasn't surprised when the three technomancers began beating him with pipes and bats.

# CHAPTER SEVENTY-THREE

## OUTSIDE COASTAL ADDRESS

Netcat gave the signal to Slamm-0! visually. She sensed five individuals in the house. The team was on AR and VR silence until the hacker could get a good crack into the house's main host. The fact that he found three hosts unnerved everyone, but Netcat was more than sure one of them was the host where she'd been kept in that hellish place, where the original owners of Contagion Games were physically kept.

He nodded to her, and then made a series of hand gestures for the others to see. He nodded in one direction and held up three fingers: *Give him three minutes.*

Netcat sighed. These were going to be the longest three minutes of her life. Every second they remained out here she was sure Kazuma was in danger. She continued trying to contact him, against Delaney's orders. She had to know he'd gotten the information and she wanted to help him. They all wanted to help him.

So why had he gone off on his own?

Slamm-0! gave the all-clear, and she touched the datasphere surrounding the main host and recoiled.

<It's here.>

<**Okay. We got it.**> Mack's window sharpened as a new window popped up with a familiar snowflake. <**MoonShine, you ready?**>

<Of course I am. There are three helicopters on standby to get all of you out of there and a cover story waiting. If nothing else, this little adventure has shown us the power of the media.>

<Yeah,> Netcat said as she moved in behind Delaney and Renault. <Don't get cocky, Moon-pie.>

<You be careful too, Kitty–>

<That's my line,> Slamm-0! interrupted. Then, <Try the front, Delaney.>

Netcat watched from the shadows cast by the rising sun as Delaney held out her gun and opened the door. It pushed in silently, and she stepped aside as Renault barreled in.

**<Preacher, do your thing.>**

As an answer, the sun dimmed and the outside lights cut back on. To anyone outside the mage's spell, it would look like a normal sunrise. They wouldn't see the vehicles or the metahumans breaking into a house. Netcat wasn't sure the spell was necessary, but it made sense just in case Miranda had called in help other than technomancers.

Once Renault and Preacher were inside, Netcat and Shayla followed behind. Mack and Slamm-0! came through a sliding door from the back and the six of them converged on the main room.

<Where are they?>

Mack made a gesture with his ringed hand. **<I got heat signatures right where we are. They're either above us or below us. Renault and Shayla, double-check this floor. Delaney, let's clear the upstairs. Slamm–find out how to go down.>**

Everyone scattered. Since Netcat wasn't given an assignment, she followed Mack and Delaney upstairs. Mack looked back to see her and started to protest, but the elf reached back and put a hand on his arm. Netcat didn't know if that was to quiet him or because she wanted Netcat with them.

The short hallway had three doors. They tried the one on the left—empty room. Then the right, same story.

When they got to the back door, it was half open, and Mack held up his hand. **<Slamm-0! you got a layout on the upstairs? What are we in front of?>**

<Master bedroom.>

He pushed the door and moved in, Delaney right behind him. Netcat followed, but the garish smears of blood on the white carpet under her feet made her gasp. Mack stepped back at the noise and knelt down. **<This blood's fresh.>**

<There's a body on the bed.> Netcat smelled the familiar scent of decay before she saw the shroud on the bed.

<Aw, drek.>

After a glance at Mack, who stood at the foot of the bed, and another one at Delaney, who was checking out the rest of the room, Netcat walked to the side of the bed and pulled the soft, white linen off the body.

<*Who's that?*>

She hadn't been dead long, but her condition made her look worse than she was. She was emaciated, bones sticking through her thin skin and pulled taut over a ravaged face. But she was still recognizable. Netcat swallowed. <*I don't know. But it's not Hitori Tetsu.*>

"Well, well, well...looks like we got us some intruders." Shax stood in the doorway, a Manhunter pointed at the back of Delaney's head.

# CHAPTER SEVENTY-FOUR

## CONTAGION HOST
## DAWN

Kazuma opened his eyes to orange and blue skies. Perpetual sunset. A rippling stream of iridescent cording crossed the sky. He knew it for what it was supposed to be, and was underneath the host's environment. A technomancer could see it without the camouflage, but anyone else could see the effect. Wind caressed his cheek and blew his hair over his eyes as he sat up.

He was in his black ninja persona, but with no mask. His long red hair fell over his shoulder in a braid. He put his hand to his side, but already knew he wasn't armed.

"Couldn't let you come in here prepared to inflict Matrix damage, now could I?"

He recognized the voice as he stood and turned to face the persona of Ferdinand Bellex. Same suit. Same smile. Same twinkle glinting off his perfect, white teeth. "Hello, Caliban."

"I guess we can drop the pretenses here. Hello, Kazuma." He clasped his hands. "I'm assuming you got what you came for?"

"No." He shook his head. "You promised me my sister."

"I didn't promise her alive, now did I?" He laughed. "But you got her back."

Kazuma narrowed his eyes at the AI, and sensed sincerity in his voice. Was it that politician attitude he always adapted, or did he truly believe he'd held up his end of the bargain? "Caliban...that wasn't my sister."

"Of course it was. I helped untangle her myself. I had to take down most of my ladder—lost a lot of good rungs doing that. But she's there. Her meat's on that bed."

"No." Kazuma clasped his hands in front. "She's not. I don't know who that was, or how long you had her. Yes, she was Asian, but not Hitori."

His happy expression slipped for a second before the smile came back. "Oh you probably didn't recognize her because of what the autodoc does to them. It's really sort of sad to see."

"That was *not* my sister," Kazuma repeated. "Therefore, we don't have a deal."

The sun slipped away behind a large, dark cloud as the wind picked up speed. Caliban licked his lips and took Kazuma's stance, with his hands clasped in front of him. "I think you want to rephrase that. You and I have a deal. I gave you the sister."

"You killed an innocent girl who you called my sister." He looked up at the sky. "Impressive control of the system, by the way. With reaction times that quick, I'm willing to bet this was the first host the company bought. The original one Powell introduced you into."

"Don't change the subject."

"Give me my sister."

The sky turned black and lightning struck the ground close by, but the rippling resonance stream never vanished. Kauzma could feel its power, its call to him, and he finally knew where his destiny was. And Hitori's.

"GIVE ME THE KILL SWITCH!"

Caliban's voice thundered over the host as rain poured down. Kazuma watched, unfazed. This was a child having a tantrum. "No."

Lightning struck him—and it hurt. His body locked in place as every muscle froze, and he was sure his physical body was showing signs of a seizure. In truth it was some form of IC, but he didn't fight it. Not yet.

When it released, he collapsed and lay in a heap, panting at Caliban's feet. The AI with the used-car-salesman smile gazed down at him. "Give it to me *now*."

"No...if you kill me...others will search for it...and you...will lose."

Kazuma thought he was going to get hit again. But instead, Caliban stepped forward and helped him to his feet, and dusted him off.

"Why are you lying?" the AI asked.

He stood at an angle, and finally saw the triangle some distance behind Caliban. Or it looked like a triangle. It pulsed with resonance, but it was dark and muddy. Tinged with a harsh shadow. Twisted. And as if to show it had a tail, a piece of it rose into the sky toward the pure resonance. "I am not lying. That wasn't my sister. Who...brought her there?"

"What?"

"Who picked her out and put her on that bed?"

Caliban frowned, as if actually trying to remember. "It was Shax that said he found her."

"And Shax pulled her free?"

"No...that was Sycorax. She pulled her free—even showed me on the rung." He snapped his fingers at Kazuma. "That's what I'll do! I'll show you where she was, and Sycorax can show you how she was identified."

He reached out to Kazuma and pulled at something as a tight, thick band of leather encircled his neck. It half-choked him, and he gasped and grabbed at it as the AI pulled him by a leash like a dog toward the dark and pulsing triangle.

# CHAPTER SEVENTY-FIVE

## INSIDE THE HOUSE

Mack looked all around Shax, and just saw him. And if he remembered correctly, this guy was pretty much a dweeb.

"Now, you're all going to put your guns down and follow me downstairs—"

A loud *bang* made Delaney and Netcat jump seconds before Shax fell backward, a bullet hole in his forehead.

Delaney was the first to regain her composure. She had a look somewhere between horror and anger on her face. She took a threatening step toward Mack and his smoking gun. "You...you could have hit me!"

"But I didn't. And don't get your panties so balled up. I'm just not in the mood for another epic battle or losing anyone else. Slamm?!" Screw the AR. They knew Mack and his team were there.

"Yeah?"

"You got a way down to the basement yet?"

There was a pause. "Yeah. There's a set of stairs under the stairs."

*Drek.*

Mack ordered everyone out of the bedroom, kicked Shax's lifeless body, and followed everyone down to the hallway. Slamm-0!, Renault, Shayla, Netcat, and Delaney were looking at the open door. "What, no light?"

Everyone shook their head.

"I hear machines."

Mack cocked his gun. "Then we're on the right track. Single file, everyone. Shoot first, then haul ass."

# CHAPTER SEVENTY-SIX

## CONTAGION HOST
## DAWN

Kazuma fell to his knees in front of what looked like a bowl in the ground. The dirt and rock had been melted smooth, and three naked men lay with their heads together in the center. They formed a triangle, their eyes open, their expressions masks of pain and shock. Above them floated a slab of what looked like marble. It slowly turned clockwise, and on top of that sat the base of a ladder.

The leather collar vanished and he fell forward, coughing.

"See?" Caliban said excitedly. "It's right up there. About three meters up. She was right there. She was one of my firsts."

Kazuma slowly pushed himself up and faced the triangle. He felt them whispering, heard the voices, felt the brush of data against his cheek, just as Netcat had described it. This was the place where HipOldGuy had died. Where so many had died. And he had killed even more just to retrieve an innocent girl his own people had lied to him about.

He looked where the AI pointed and saw where the rungs of the ladder truncated. He saw a hand, and a foot, muted colors of a clown's wig, mixed paint of a cel of an animation, a horrific miasma of personas blended together to make a ridiculous ladder to the stream above.

His gaze traveled down to the faces of the three men, and their whispers grew louder in his head.

*...Double slash...*

*...Semicolon...*

*...Star....*

*...Briefcase...*
*...Parenthesis...*
*...Star...*
*...Miranda...*
*...Star...*
*...End Parenthesis...*

It was the footnote. And they were repeating it to him over and over again.

He narrowed his eyes at the slab of marble, which shifted as it pulsed with dark resonance. It moved from being marble to plastic to metal, and then he recognized it.

It wasn't a slab at all, but an old cyberdeck.

He put a hand to his datajack at his temple. This was how he was supposed to deliver the switch. And they were telling him to do it.

Now.

"What're you doing?" Caliban reached out and grabbed his upper arm. "You have to admit you were wrong."

"No. You have to ask Sycorax the truth."

"What truth?"

"That she lied to you."

As if she had been summoned, a woman appeared beside him. She wore a painted face, her features unrecognizable. Her skirt moved at her feet, tendrils that reached up like the tentacles of an octopus, and grabbed for Kazuma's wrists and ankles.

"Good! Yes! Take the switch from him!"

His AR opened and he fell inside of it, into a garden full of sakura trees in full bloom, under a twilight sky. Caliban's world vanished as he spotted a young girl by the largest tree. He walked to her as petals floated from the branches like soft pink snow. And when he was close she held up her hand. *"Oni-chan."*

"Hitori."

They stood facing one another for what felt like years. But she never aged. Never changed. She remained the same, the persona of her childhood, of the little girl with the bright pink wings and her wand of magic. It sparkled when she waved it.

"Is this a dream?" he asked.

"You know the truth."

"That you are Miranda Sebastian? Yes." He wanted to take her in his arms and hold her like he used to, but he sensed she was different. Changed.

"How did you know?"

"The contagion host. The park. It wasn't the park in Denver, but the park in Tokyo, where Father used to take us for the festivals. I used to watch you run through the trees in your wings." He nodded to her. "This was the last time we went. You wore that."

"And we saw *The Tempest* on the lawn that night."

Kazuma smiled. "And you fell in love with it."

Her smile brightened, and then faded. "I have made mistakes, Kazuma. Terrible mistakes. I loved the realms too much."

"You loved the idea of power too much. Was it Tolen that kept you away from me?"

"Tolen shared my loves. But what I didn't know was that Powell loved me as well. When I went to work for them, I changed my name so I wouldn't be recognized as the Hitori Tetsu of Ares. As a technomancer, it was easy to recreate myself as Miranda Sebastian. I took names from the Tempest to do it."

"You know what Powell did."

"Yes. And I have been looking for his kill switch from the moment Powell did this to them. To Tolen. I have tried to find a way to free all of us. I never knew it would be you that would be the soldier to kill the monster."

"I have it ready." Kazuma pulled up the last message from Netcat and memorized it. "But I have to jack into the deck above them."

"No. You give it me. Just type it into my AR, something Caliban can't see, and it will go through the deck." She took a hesitant step toward him. "But you'll have to leave the host immediately. Tolen arranged for the host to trap everything in it so it could be destroyed."

"You're coming with me."

"Of course." She smiled at him. "Caliban is getting restless. To him, it looks as if I am taking the switch from you by force. Trust me, *oni-chan*. I want him dead. And gone. And destroyed."

He hesitated for an instant, but copied the switch into her window of his AR.

The sakura world vanished, and Kazuma found himself on his knees as Caliban screamed. He turned to see the Tolen, Baron, and Huerta personas turn to stone and crumble. The world shook as the sky cracked around them. Parts of it fell and crashed into the barren earth, kicking up bitter dust. Kazuma stumbled to his feet as the slab of marble stopped moving and fell, destroying everything below it.

***"NNNNNNNNNOOOOOOOOOO!"***

Caliban's wrath culminated in what Kazuma could only call the voice of God as he lunged for him and managed to grab one of his ankles as he ran. The AI grew in size, and Kasuma was abruptly lifted into the air with him. The sky continued to fall and Kazuma repeatedly tried to log out.

But he was trapped. Whatever IC measures they'd built into the host, into the code, wasn't letting anything out. Hitori and he were both going to die here.

She appeared to him then, in her young persona, complete with robes and wings. With a slap on Caliban's oversized wrist with her wand, he let go, and she grabbed Kazuma around the waist. They flew straight up as the AI tried to swat them down as if they were flies. She dodged the sky and then the stars as they fell, and Caliban's terrified screams drowned everything out.

"Where are we going?" Kazuma yelled.

"The resonance stream. It's our only hope. It'll take us off this host."

She was smart to think of that, and he watched as they neared the rippling, iridescent beauty. She hovered above it and he felt it brush his skin, sing to his soul, and pull him toward it.

Hitori brushed her lips against his cheek. "I love you, Kazuma," and then dropped him into the stream.

His last vision as the stream took her was of her smiling face as she ran through the sakura trees.

# CHAPTER SEVENTY-SEVEN

## COASTAL ADDRESS

Delaney and the others lowered their weapons as it became apparent there weren't any threats left alive. They found two bodies in the basement, the other dissonant technomancers shot in the face, but had no idea by whom.

Three doors down here mirrored the ones upstairs, and when Renault knocked the first one down, they stared into utter darkness until the troll found the light. A series of bulbs came on to reveal twenty to thirty autodocs of all kinds, makes, and models. And as they took a little stroll down one side of them, they realized they were all occupied, all of their occupants deceased.

Renault and Mack checked the opposite door and and found the same horror. At the end of the hall they found a much larger room, with more autodocs. In these, Delaney identified Huerta, Baron, and Tolen. In one of the newer models they found Kazuma. He'd been pretty badly beaten, and showed no response when Mack opened the doc. They contacted MoonShine and then found another of the autodocs with Miranda Sebastian inside, also deceased.

Slamm-0! found the hosts, all of them dead in a cascade failure. He did a diagnostic on each as two helicopters landed outside. They loaded Kazuma, Netcat, Delaney, and Preacher into them as Shayla, Mack, Renault and Slamm-0! remained behind for cleanup, then drove their respective vehicles away.

She wasn't all that surprised when the helicopters took them to China Mountain and a team of medical shamans and techomancers took Kazuma away. They gave Hestaby a full report and were told to refresh and relax as she offered Mack and the others transport back to the Mountain.

It was nearly five in the evening before Slamm-0! and Mack arrived. And after showers and food, everyone sat together to discuss what happened. The funny thing was that although they were all in the same room again, no one spoke.

Until, "What's wrong with him?" Delaney finally ventured. "Did it work? Is Caliban gone?"

"He's gone." Slamm-0! reassured her. "I checked everything before we left. Renault did as well. There was no sign of him. So I'd say Kazuma delivered the switch and it worked."

"But did it hurt him?" Delaney looked at Netcat, since she was the only other technomancer in the room.

Until MoonShine walked in. "The kill switch didn't hurt him. The beating did. They put him in an autodoc here to let it do its mending. As for his mind..." When MoonShine smiled, Delaney felt a little better. "He shows all the classic signs of submersion."

"He's in the resonance realms?" Netcat sat forward, her hand on Slamm-0!'s knee.

"I'd say he is. But for right now, Hestaby says to relax, recuperate, and let her take care of Soldat."

"That reminds me, I need to post to GiTm0." Netcat stood, and then bent down over Slamm-0! to kiss his forehead. "I'll be back."

"And if you're not, I'll find you," he called as he watched her depart.

Delaney leaned back in her chair. "What I don't get is what happened to Miranda Sebastian? Why was she on the floor, and not in an autodoc? I mean, wouldn't she have survived like Kazuma did if she'd gotten in one?"

"Maybe," Renault said. "Ask Kazuma when he wakes." The troll popped a grape in his mouth. "The story's not quite over. Not yet."

# CHAPTER SEVENTY-EIGHT

**GiTm0**

Welcome back to GiTm0, *omae*; your last connection was 1 days, 4 hours, 23 minutes, 5 seconds ago

**BOLOs**
Nothing for this post.

**CONTAGION GAMES IN THE NEWS**
The media's been in an uproar since they converged on the coast of California today, just outside Los Angeles at the home of Miranda Sebastian, the CFO of Contagion Games. The media's not telling us what we already know, that the bodies of the original owners of Contagion, as well as her own, were found along with autodocs filled with fifty-two technomancers. All dead.

Details on this can be found in this [Link], but suffice it to say, the *TechnoHack* game is no more, the Contagion host is destroyed and the spread of dark resonance has been halted. For now. Just know that dissonant TMs do exist out there, and sometimes they can be even more dangerous than those that hunt us.

Remember, GOD is always watching.

**UPDATES**
\>\>\>\>Open Thread/Subhost221.322.1
\>\>\>\>Thread Access Restrictions: <Yes/**No**>
\>\>\>\>Format: <**Open Post**/Comment Only/Read Only>
\>\>\>\>File Attachment: <**Yes**/No>
\>\>\>\>Thread Descriptor: **MOVING FORWARD**
\>\>\>\>Thread Posted By User: Netcat

- Great follow-up, Netcat. How's Soldat?
- Venerator

- No change, Ven. Soon as we know something we'll let everyone know. Just read the report on what happened, learn from it, and be prepared. Always.
- RoxJohn

- Netcat and Slamm-0! are taking a well deserved break with their kid. So, she might not see your messages for a while.
- MoonShine

- Are we sure that Al's dead?
- 404Flames

- Yeah. We're sure on this one. Other meaner, bigger, badder ones? Who knows?
- MoonShine

- Can we discuss this mention of a dragon in that report? Really? We're making deals with dragons now? That's something no one ever does.
- LongTong

- No deals yet, but Hestaby is offering sanctuary and help if you need it. She might want the odd job now and then, but you'll have the full backing of a dragon. Deal or not, I'm enjoying myself.
- MoonShine

- And let's not forget, everyone, too many technomancers died during this madness. I've put up a list under Fallen Comrades with the handles I have. I've also added Kazuma's sister there, since he's finally letting her go. So let's all show a bit of respect and make ourselves stronger so this kind of crazy doesn't happen again. We can be smart and strong, people.
- RoxJohn

- You said it, Rox. You said it best.
- 404Flames

# EPILOGUE

## CHIBA, JAPAN
## YAHASHIRA CEMETERY #2

Kazuma knelt before his sister's new, shiny headstone.

Incense curled around his hair as he kept his eyes closed and prayed for her guidance and her blessing. He rose, bowed, and slowly walked down the side of the tiered hill to where Slamm-0! and Netcat waited at the entrance.

"This place is beautiful, Kaz," Netcat said as he joined them.

"It is." He looked back and focused on his family's graves. "Father and I are all that's left. Except for my mother. But she wasn't in my life very much."

"Where is she?" Slamm-0! asked.

"Tir Tairngire." He smiled. "She's an elf."

Netcat smirked. "Uh huh."

The three of them strolled down the sidewalk. The sky was darkening, shifting into a beautiful twilight.

"So, we're heading to the park? Sakura?" Netcat volunteered.

"Yeah." Kazuma shoved his hands into his pockets as she looped her other arm through his.

"She did what she had to do, Kazuma," Netcat continued. "She couldn't follow you into the resonance. She was already dissonant. She would have corrupted the stream."

"I know." He sighed. "In my heart. But my head still wants to know why. Why did she let that happen to herself? If she kept enough of her love of Tolen and me, and wanted to stop Caliban, why not stay..."

"Pure?"

He looked down at her. "Yeah. And I'm still trying to put it all together into a timeline. Maybe one day it won't all seem so... stupid."

"She died saving you, saving other technomancers."

"Not the one she sacrificed in that house. We still don't know who she was."

"She was already dying," Slamm-0! said. "Hitori just forced them to take down most of the ladder, weaken the gestalt." He paused, and the others paused with him. "Think about what she did. She knew what Powell had done, and she was looking for that switch. But she couldn't leave Tolen, not in that condition. So she stayed with him, tempering what he did, keeping an eye on Powell, too. I'd almost bet you that Hitori was responsible for those blackouts because without them, more technomancers would have been caught, they'd have gotten further on that ladder. She knew what the conditions had to be, because she knew Tolen."

"I don't think she wanted to live without him." Netcat patted his upper arm. "She knew if she got into an autodoc, it might have saved her. But she didn't take that risk. Instead, she saved you."

Kazuma looked at the two of them and thought of all those weekends, weeknights, and holidays she'd started missing with him and their grandmother after she showed back up. She had probably been spending them with Tolen.

Hitori had been in love.

It was a nice consolation.

"So, what're you gonna do now?" Slamm-0! asked.

"I don't know. We'll see. I'm gonna stay with Hestaby for a while, see if I can help get us more organized. Build up GiTm0 more. What about you?"

She shrugged. "Eat?"

They laughed as they headed down the road.

"Anyone seen Mack or Delaney?" Netcat asked.

"Oh..." Slamm-0! said quietly. "I don't think we're going to see much of either of them while we're here..."

# CRIMSON
**BY KEVIN R. CZARNECKI • COMING SOON!**

*Where no one knows your name...*

Thanksgiving, 2075. Shadowrunning vampire-mage Rick "Red" Lang used to make his living hunting dangerous insect spirits and twisted mages, but when he awakens after twelve years of involuntary hibernation, he finds the rest of the world has gotten even stranger.

Red begins piecing together what had happened during his lost time—and who put him under in the first place. But as he journeys through the neon-drenched ruins of Chicago and its augmented facades, Red uncovers an even larger plot involving eldritch forces seeking to invade from beyond our reality. He teams up with the few allies he can trust—Pretty, a beautiful ghoul, and Slim, a hacker extraordinaire—as they head into the middle of multiple schemes and power plays surrounding a dangerous new conflict threatening to shatter the uneasy peace into all-consuming chaos.

# CHAPTER 1

## AWAKENING AND ACCLIMATION

The first thing I became aware of was the blood coursing down my throat.

I was down to the nub; empty, drenched, shaking from the cold and the overwhelming, sanity-rending need that consumed me. I could feel it pouring into me, just enough to whet my appetite. What I really needed wasn't in it. This was dead blood, barely good enough for base nourishment. I needed what was behind it. I needed souls...

I could hear the clatter of running feet as I groggily rose. My hands trembled, and my still-dry mouth ached. The blood did little to restore me, but it was enough that my vision returned, enough to sense what was near. I couldn't think about it, only react to need, as a drowning man blindly rips toward the surface of water for air... but then, that's an analogy I understand all too well.

The life before me was too much to resist, and I brought my mouth down on its throat without the pretense of grace. The screams were high-pitched and alien; I didn't know if they were mine or came from whatever was writhing beneath me. Maybe both.

The liquid that flowed into me wasn't human. Not even metahuman. It was clumpy, gooey, acrid. It was revolting, to be honest. But at the moment, I was a starved, crazed beast.

My tunnel vision receded, the dark room bright to my elven eyes. Other senses could make out the fading heat of the corpse before me. I started feeling guilty over going so long without feeding, for letting myself lose control and hurt someone...until I saw my victim.

It was vaguely recognizable as once having been human, but its mutations were too numerous to mistake its nature. The arms and legs were twisted, its flesh half-formed into chitinous growths all over the body. A flesh-form bug spirit. Its head was the worst, reshaped into a half-ant monstrosity, mandibles emerging from a mouth torn open, one eye multifaceted while the other seemed to have simply withered. Hideous. I could see the burn marks on its flanks where it had been shocked to bring it down but keep it alive.

I ran the back of my hand across my mouth to wipe the ichor away, only to find a substantial growth of matted, ginger beard on my face. I reached back to find long strands of hair, ragged and clumped with filth, falling far past my shoulders. Normally I kept it trimmed short, in an unassuming style. What had happened to me?

I rose from my crouch and looked around. A concrete room, a single, cold bulb swinging from the ceiling. What little illumination there was came from a metal door, the light through the crack underneath betraying someone's presence. A makeshift cot where I had risen from was threadbare but reasonably clean, despite stains prolific enough to cover its entirety. The bug was chained, bolted hooks securing it to the wall and floor.

Well, it was competent, but unprofessional. *Where the frag am I?*

A knock sounded from the other side of the door, three soft taps. I tried to respond, but my mouth was sticky, my throat rawer than I could ever remember it being before...

*...Gasping, stirring, metal in my back...*

Okay, maybe once before.

I walked to the door and knocked back. It opened gently, guns cocking as pale, half-blind eyes stared up at me from the trio of ghouls in the doorway. None I immediately recognized, but I've been on good terms with them most of the time. Birds of a feather and all that.

I stepped back, hands up to show I had come to my senses and meant no harm. There was no telling how smart the female leader was, or the two males that followed her, keeping a shotgun and Uzi trained on me the whole time. Krieger strain had a bad habit of driving many of its victims off the deep, feral end. The guns were actually a good sign.

The girl looked at me while winding a strip of dirty-looking gauze around her arm, which bled a dark, brackish red from two neat points. I had to smile in gratitude—now I knew who had given me that first, tantalizing draught.

She surprised me by speaking. "Are you feeling well, Mr. Lang?"

That name also surprised me. It'd been a long time since someone referred to me by my old given surname. After all, I'd been legally dead since 1999.

I coughed, working some precious saliva into my mouth to clear away the gunk. My voice came out like gravel and sawdust, but at least she could understand me. "I feel like I just died and came back to talk about it."

"Not many people can tell that kind of story twice and be honest about it." The familiar voice pulled at my brain, surging a dozen memories from forgotten places.

Steely eyes and razor teeth and a warm smile impossibly intermingling. The face that came through the door matched all of it perfectly. I was sure Needles' expression must be rare: the ghoul who pitied the vampire.


The chemical showers had become more mainstream beyond the Chicago Containment Zone walls since Needles had ascended to lead the ghouls. He said it was his effort to make more of them civilized, not to mention necessary for keeping outbreaks of Strain-III controlled. I didn't care at that moment, relaxing as the hot water warmed bones that felt like they'd been cold for months. I suppose I was fortunate; they'd been cold for many, many years.

The rest of the warrens hadn't changed since I was last here. A section of the cable car tunnels, almost two centuries old, reclaimed and refurbished. The ceiling stretched up twenty feet at the peak of its arches, old stone browned and ancient wood supports long rotted away or used for fuel, much to my relief. This section covered a quarter of a city block, sealed off long ago and reinforced many times since, the entrance and exit to be found somewhere in the connective ventilation and maintenance tunnels, a maze of ducts and passages. The air ducts led to other monitoring stations, disused storage sheds, and the endless reaches of the city's sewage system. But in here, they made the best of scrounged and salvaged materials to create a home.

The ghouls were comfortable in the dark, their white eyes blind, yet seeing into the astral, meaning the only light was the dim glow of heat cells, but it was more than enough for me to see by. They huddled in small groups, wrapped in patched blankets and nursing the cracked chitin of insect spirit-hybrid flesh, quietly sucking it from the exoskeleton like crab from the shell. Others listened to audiobooks played on tiny, dented media players. One or two ran their long-taloned fingertips over ancient Braille print hardcopy, reading to the small, natural-born ghouls. Without exception, the small, hairless children with razor teeth and pale eyes gasped and giggled at the tales, as enraptured by the words as the impressions the storyteller's aura made.

Various rooms had been repurposed to the pack's needs. Sleeping; storage; a kitchen with a vicious array of reclaimed surgical instruments, kitchen knives, and a battery-powered cooler; and a few offices for those who filled specialist roles. I didn't give them much attention as Needles led me to the "cafeteria," a space outside the kitchen where an old, faux-wood table with built-in benches had been recovered from some high school ruin. It was scarred with dozens of claw scratches, right through the enamel coating. A plate of meat was brought for him and a cold, vac-sealed bottle for me. I recognized it as the same kind that attached to a needle cap, used by organ thieves to rapidly harvest blood.

I'd always appreciated the effort he put into it, trying to bring a disadvantaged people up to spec with the rest of the world. Few realized these days how many ghouls were still sapient, especially those who were born into it, as many of this pack were. Given their need for metahuman flesh and their persecution by the rest of the world, who could fault them for forming gangs and roaming the streets at night?

Needles was one of those strange cases. He'd been a guard for a charity relief effort for ghouls when they were attacked by bug spirits. His girlfriend, one of the attending doctors at the refuge, got infected. Unable to cope with the changes, she'd attacked him in a frenzy of pain. He couldn't stop her from rushing the other guards, nor could he protect her when they shot her down. He'd adapted to his own infection much easier, and made it his mission to carry her dream forward, to make sure no other ghoul would suffer as they had in Cabrini. He'd adopted the pack, and had been trying to get them as educated, organized, and respected as possible ever since.

I also owed him my life. Twice now, it seemed.

"You remember who you are?"

I shot him a look over the bottle of goopy, cold, hybrid blood that said I could remember how to tell him to frag off. He was all smiles about it, showing off those teeth that were his namesake as he chewed a steak of bug flesh. He was strangely fortunate to live here, where he and his pack could feed without hurting anyone innocent. After all, bug spirits were born out of metahuman flesh, and they were still palatable. Not as tasty, but good enough.

"What the hell happened to me?"

His smile faded a little, and he took another bite of troll wasp tartar before responding. "What's the last thing you remember?"

I tried to dig back... Needles had asked me to come back to Chicago now that I'd hit the big time. I'd invested all of my running money into a small corporation of my own, using it to turn fixer and fence, launder money, and make more. I had a long list of clients still running the shadows, but no matter how good business got, I'd promised myself I'd remember those who had been there to help me get where I was. So I responded. Seemed his pack was trapped between the bug spirits, who'd taken the time to build their ranks, and Knight Errant, who had decided to let the ghouls and bug spirits fight it out until a winner was declared. The prize was a final KE sweep to pick off the survivors. Seeing as that was hardly playing fair, I shipped a few crates of AKs and several hundred gallons of insecticides over to my chummer, plus I hired a runner group and made for Bug City myself. If I owed anyone, I owed Needles.

The three weeks of bug hunting were a blur. A new queen was in town, a termite made from the biggest damn troll they could find. We didn't know we'd flushed her hive until they were flying out everywhere. It was like the Breakout all over again. Being the leader and an initiate to boot, the queen went for me. A running fight through the old El tunnels all the way to a Wall-Zone bridge saw me facing off one on one with Queenie. Natch, I figured I was dead. An explosion later, and everyone agreed. After that, nothing.

Needles put down his fork and placed his hands on the table.

His black claws clacked, and I suddenly felt really nervous. "Tell me what you suppose happened."

I shrugged. "I guess I got knocked unconscious. How long was I out?"

Needles looked pained. His eyes kept flitting to the side, as though he could see something I couldn't.

Come to think of it, I was having a hard time seeing into the Astral. Maybe it was because I was so shaky. I felt numb to everything. Why should my magic be any different?

"Red, what year is it?"

*Oh, drek...*

"It was October, 2062, last time I looked at my watch."

His grimace deepened, uncertain how to proceed. He drew in a deep breath before responding, slowly, carefully.

"It's November 21st, 2075."

The bottom fell out, and I couldn't feel my body.

"Happy Thanksgiving, incidentally."

For those who don't know, vampires, or individuals infected with mainstream Human Meta-Human Vampiric Virus—usually humans, and sometimes other metatypes—are subject to a great many physical quirks. One of the lesser-known ones is that vampires who are cut off from a supply of oxygen do not die, but enter a state of suspended animation. I know this better than most, because the first time I "died," this was the cause.

The short version is that I was born in 1983, before the Awakening. I'd been gifted with small visions, dreams coming true, impressions of people's emotions, all those small manifestations of magic before the Sixth Age that most would have called instincts. I had the good taste to find the occult fascinating, and the bad luck to find a charismatic quack named Karl who claimed he could show me true magic.

After a while working in his bookstore, his coven, led by a tall, blond man who never gave his name, came to show off their powers. When I saw that they intended to sacrifice a young woman to fuel their abilities, I tried, unsuccessfully, to stop them. The wash of blood magic created a small pocket of Awakening in the prepared space of Karl's basement, allowing the coven, led by a vampire, to indulge their skills. Each of them craved the blond man's power and immortality, and drank blood in emulation of him. As their powers faded, he drained me, as well, dumping my corpse into the Chicago River. This was in 1999.

I was there for, oh, say, forty-nine years, the transformation holding me in hibernation. The virus activated dormant genes, not unlike a SURGE changeling, Awakening my senses to true magic and revealing my nature as an elf. Usually elves express as Banshees when infected with HMHVV, but I suppose since the virus had already taken its turns, I'm one of the rare exceptions.

By chance, I was picked up by a salvage trawler, and it was Needles who found me in the garbage heaps. From there, I learned about the new world I'd woken up to, and how to make my way in it. As a vampire without a SIN and a firm grasp of an esoteric tradition of magic, becoming a shadowrunner was almost inevitable.

I've felt a little edgy about large bodies of water since my drowning. So imagine my horror at learning I had just lost another twelve years of my life (Which may or may not be eternal, depending on whom you ask) by the same cause.

Well, now I knew why I was so disoriented. Why my throat had been so raw. Why I had been so starved.

A million questions flooded my brain. The first... "Where is she?"

Needles didn't have to ask. I hadn't had a girlfriend since Gypsi. The only important "woman" in my life was—

"Rick!"

She streamed through the wall with her usual liquid grace, blue aquatic form materializing like a chip-head's warped dream of sea nymphs. She might have been a perfect elf, swathed in ancient garments reminiscent of Babylon or Egypt, but for her composition of crystal blue water. She threw her arms around me, leaving only the faintest trace of moisture in their passing. She might have been crying, but who could tell?

*Wait a minute...*

If anyone could tell, *I* could tell. She was my ally spirit, my familiar. We shared a connection...

She must have read my thoughts, because she burst into a wailing that might have put a depressed banshee to shame.

I looked at Needles through her transluscent face. "Twelve years?"

He shrugged. "We thought you were dead. When that KE rocket took down the bridge and the queen...it's amazing you weren't blown apart, too. And with the city the magical mess it is, it's a miracle she found you at all."

She nuzzled into my collarbone as I took it in. My soul had gone dormant, buried in the muck and astral static, and she was newly born into freedom. No connection to me, no ability to see anything but the contours of skeletons and wreckage for a decade, feeling their unmoving shapes to search for a familiar form she was no longer beholden to.

In my mind's eye, I could see her patiently sifting through the muck and the garbage in the darkness, with no conception of the passage of all that time, searching until she found me, pulling me out and flying to Needles, and him working fast to secure living prey for me. They'd worked so hard on my behalf, neither one owed me a thing. How was I ever going to pay them back? How could I? I'd lost so much.

I straightened up—I hadn't realized I'd slumped in the first place. She gazed up at me as I sighed. "Okay. First things first."

I stood in the street, the crumbled ruins of the Sears Tower surrounding me as I weathered the cold wind off the lake. My tattered long coat fluttered, clouds gathering as the trio behind me watched. Needles and his man were well-armed, in case my exercise in spell work attracted the wrong sort of attention, bacterially or otherwise. As for *her*, well, I couldn't get a moment's peace from her if I'd wanted it.

And right now, I certainly didn't.

I was concentrating, fighting off doubt and dread, falling into old patterns I had worked out for myself from the earliest days of learning magic. Pre-Awakening, Crowley-esque, dark mumbo-jumbo in the basement of Karl's new age shop. I even allowed myself the luxury of the old broad hand movements and loud words, chanted in Latin, focusing my will. My hand extended, my eyes fixed upon a broken pile of concrete chunks twenty feet away.

The spell finished, and I waited for the effect to happen. Every fraction of a second that went by made me sweat, hopelessness welling up with tangible force. I could feel it, almost...*almost*...like fingertips brushing something just out of reach. I could feel something stirring within me, something faint...

## SHADOWRUN: CRIMSON (EXCERPT)

The ground rushed up with a suddenness that I usually expect from quicksilver mongooses and wired razorboys. My whole body collapsed, but my hand remained rigid, frozen in place, reaching to the stone. I heard my companions rushing toward me, footsteps crunching on the gravel with frantic intensity. Still, my mind and soul labored.

Their hands reached down to lift me up as I smiled.

"Look."

Three faces turned to the place I was clutching at.

A single rock slowly wound its way through the air towards me, drawn to my fingers until I could grasp it, gratefully sighing into exhaustion with it in my hand.

I awoke to find a moist hand brushing my brow. I drew into myself and opened my eyes again, finally seeing into the Astral, though I nearly shook with the effort. She smiled down at me, sorrowful relief and joy mixing in her liquid features. I smiled back. It was forced. Now that I had eyes to see it again, I knew for certain that she and I no longer carried that connection. It was gone.

"I see you got my message," I said, a tear nearly falling from its pool in my eyes. Her face twisted in a mixture of guilt and laughter.

"I didn't know you'd cast a contingency spell. How'd you keep it from me?"

I smiled more honestly, letting the Astral fade from my tired eyes. She was always amazing to behold without it, anyway. No heat signature, yet so alive.

"A man's got to have his secrets," I whispered. "I just felt you deserved a name, in case I..."

"But you didn't," she protested, a look of objection matching her tone perfectly. "You didn't die. Why didn't the spell recognize that?"

"You sound like you'd rather remain tied to me. I thought all spirits longed to become free."

"I was always free, with you," she whispered, looking away. For all the world, she seemed like a girl whose heart had been broken.

"I think I worded the spell poorly. I said, 'If it seems I am to die, gift my ally with her name.' I guess those circumstances qualifed."

She laughed and sniffled, swatting me on the arm. "Well... it *is* a beautiful name."

"I'm glad you like it, Menerytheria."

Love and pain look strange enough on a normal, human face. Now imagine it on an elf made of water.

"My theory is that I was down there so long my connection with magic atrophied."

I sat with Needles again, each of us on either side of a subway tunnel entrance. He was watching me quietly, listening.

"I didn't burn out, thankfully. I can still cast. I just need to work out those magical muscles, as it were. But most of my spells will need to be relearned. Hell, I only remember the ones I designed myself."

"That really slots, man," Needles said.

"Mmmm," I responded, already distracted.

"What's on your mind, chummer?"

I turned to look at him, and he looked worried all over again. "How much has changed?"

"What?"

"It's been twelve years, Needles. Twelve years. The twelve years before I drowned again saw the birth of AIs, the *otaku*, a dragon for president… A lot can happen in twelve years. So what did I miss?"

Needles might have looked uncomfortable again, but I smiled at him. "C'mon, man, this isn't a reproach. I just want to be prepared for what's out there."

He smiled and shook his head. "All right, you asked for it."

It took him two hours to explain the second Crash, the new, wireless Matrix, the rise of technomancers, the fall of Novatech and birth of NeoNet, and a hundred other things. The whole time I couldn't believe what I was hearing. I knew he wouldn't lie to me, but it was still rough. Don't get me wrong, I had more than average experience in adjusting to massive changes. This was hardly the strangest thing to have happened to me. But still, it was amazing how much could happen in so short a time. Every decade brought a whole new world. I had always avoided the idea of an inevitable future of change, and the haunting notion of immortality that promised it.

But it was good news, in some ways. I could be a part of the Matrix using 'trodes and keep up with people now. The shadow community was as alive as ever, and my talents would still be in demand as a result. But I needed to get to a data terminal or hot spot. I needed to check up on my affairs. The apartment. The company. My contacts and family and runner chummers. I was a dozen years dead, as far as anyone knew, so this might be a chance to write off some old enemies and renew old friendships.

I told Needles all this, and he said I definitely wasn't "going into town" looking like I did.

# CHAPTER 2

## BRAVE NEW WORLD

"Red, this is Pretty."

I agreed, whether it was a street name or not. Sitting at a well-lit mirror with a table filled with cosmetics and every beauty appliance I could imagine, the girl before me held the kind of natural charisma some sim starlets try to get with training and chips. She was five foot two, curvy, pale, long black hair cascading down a back that invited fingers to trail slowly along. Her big eyes were a vibrant blue, too deliberate to be real. She turned them on me with a naturally vulnerable look, and suddenly I felt like I really *had* been in cold water for twelve years. She was slipping black gloves off, still wearing a short skirt and black top just this side of immodest.

A second look give way to a double take. There were things about her that stood out as... unnatural, at least to someone with my experience. Her cybereyes. Her natural nails, black yet unpainted. Her hair, too perfect not to be bioware. Her skin, almost a shade of gray instead of pale, and a little too smooth to be natural.

Pretty was a ghoul.

I don't think she could tell if I was staring because of her looks, or because I knew what she was, despite appearances. To tell the truth, I'm not sure I could tell which was the case, either.

She turned to me, almost smiling, with a hint of something feral. She extended a manicured hand to me and shook. "A pleasure. One hears a lot about the famous Red in the warren."

Her voice was ambrosia, throaty and vibrant. She knew her stuff. Even her perfume was perfect to offset the scent a cannibal inevitably exudes. Only my heightened sense of smell, especially for blood, gave me any hint of the taint beneath.

I turned the shake into a bow, lowering my lips to her hand with something resembling grace and kissing it lightly.

"The pleasure is mine."

Needles snickered as Pretty flushed a faint blue, then shook it off with something like a scowl. I wasn't sure where I'd hosed up, but then, some girls were just strange. An unbelievably hot ghoul only had that much more going in that direction.

Needles walked towards her, looking at me. "Pretty here is our girl for going into town. She was a looker before all the mods. I figured it was a worthwhile investment so the rest of the world could see it, too."

Pretty turned from her mirror, taking out black spikes on hooks I assumed were fashionable earrings. She tossed them onto a table, her eyes never leaving my face. They searched over me, for what I wasn't sure. It didn't seem like she found me attractive. I hadn't looked in a mirror yet, so I could only imagine what a mess I was. So what was she looking for?

"Given that she's the only one of us who can go out for supplies and contacts and the like," Needles continued, "I figure she's the one you'll want to talk to before making the trip. Hell, while you're sticking around, you might do a few runs for us yourself, if you're feeling up to it."

Pretty's head snapped to glare at him. Ah, so that was it. I was competition for her role in the pack. Wow. I could already tell she was a ghoul by birth. At her age, I'd have seen her before twelve years ago. I wondered which one she was. She'd have been really young when I last was here, no more than nine or ten...

"Well, I'll let you get to it." And with that, Needles took his leave, leaving me with the glowering young ghoul.

She looked me up and down. "We've got some work to do, don't we?"

A haircut and shave later, and I was feeling a world better. My red locks hung down near my chin, styled with some kind of nano-gel that maintained it in spikes, my new goatee trimmed short. I thought I looked rakish, and loved it. It seemed my hair had decided to keep growing while I was sleeping. Another inexplicable mystery of infection. It was good to be rid of my Rip van Winkle, and I said so. Pretty didn't get it at all. She supplied me with a synth-leather jacket and black tee, and some old, torn-up jeans. She plopped a commlink and glasses in my hand.

"Unless you use a skinlink out here, it's awful coverage for AR. Mostly when we use them in the zones, it's a small PAN disconnected from the main systems. When you get past the wall, onto the Corridor and the subsprawls...well, be ready."

I could imagine what she was talking about, but I knew I was going to be in for a shock.

She pulled some thigh-high boots on and threw me a withering look. I just smiled through it, unsure how to approach her, feeling like an idiot. How do you handle something so fragile when you don't understand what it's like to be a part of a pack mentality?

"Okay, Red, let's get going."

It took us a mere thirty minutes to move through the side passages and air ducts in the warrens to an exit point. Pretty pushed a cloth ahead of us to keep dust off our clothes, but the path seemed well-traveled enough that it was mostly clean and clear. Her handbag was loaded with lint removers, perfumes, and colognes to mask the stench of sewer travel. There'd be pay showers on the other side, anyway. She was silent almost the whole trip, and it never seemed more deliberate than when I tried to engage her in conversation.

"Have we met before?"
"So...were you born a ghoul?"
"Tell me about yourself?"
"Do you do this often?"
Silence answered every question.

Finally we came to a metal door that lead into an operations room. The dust told me it had been abandoned long ago.

"The Knights and City Hall both think this door is welded and the room sealed. Thank our resident decker for that."

We went up one last ladder into a shack, and from there, into the dusk. We both hesitated for a brief moment before stepping out. Vampires, despite the sims, rarely burst into flames in the sun, but we burn fast. Hell, UV-A *hurts*. Even with allergen resistance magics, you couldn't take all the discomfort out exposure. Not a lot of vampires hanging around the blacklights at nightclubs. Ghouls are the same, to a lesser degree. In the dusk, it was more of a psychological reaction, painful but undamaging.

There was no direct sunlight. We were fine.

A few steps out the door, and she turned and started walking away.

"Wait!" I called, stopping her in her heeled tracks. She didn't turn to look. "Are you just leaving me out here?"

Her voice betrayed exasperation. "We'll meet here just before sunrise. You're a big boy. You'll figure your way around." And with that she clicked her way into the bustling Corridor of un-walled Chicago.

Since the Sears Tower bombing, the bug breakout, Cermak Blast, Bug City and Operation: Extermination, Chicago has been irreversibly changed from its old glory. The core of the city's downtown had become a rubble-strewn wasteland ruled over by Zone Lord gang kingpins. It was the picture of post-apocalyptic decay. The distant sub-sprawls, once the suburbs where I had grown up, had become the new centers for order. In between was the Corridor, an eclectic collective of communes mashed together in a state of freedom and hardship. In the post-sunset gloom, the clouds didn't glow with the neon of a thousand late-nights like they did in other metroplexes. Here the stars were visible, and the markets still chattered with life, lit by gas and battery, snug in the repossessed ruins of better times. The squeal of pigs from a repurposed storefront competed with the tunes of a jukebox in an open-air bar across the street, mason jars of home-stilled moonshine poured in exchange for whatever someone could barter. If I wanted Matrix access, I'd have to make my way to a subsprawl.

I hitched a ride on a rickshaw with patched leather bucket seats from a luxury sports car and mismatched bicycle wheels and was on my way north before I knew it, back to where the sky washed out and the lights never dimmed. The Northside was a Corridor that merged the freedom and ruin of Chicago's gypsy lifestyle with the remnants of working tech to better do business with the corporate outliers and wageslave day-trippers, and my commlink pinged as it entered an area with wireless Matrix access.

There's an old phrase: "The more things change, the more they stay the same." Even in 2074, it still held true...

...once you were past the Augmented Reality.

The streets of the Saturday night were surprisingly quiet, despite plenty of glitterati sashaying to and fro, laughing at jokes unheard or jamming to music I couldn't hear. It was unreal, how quiet it could be. Conversations were muted, the scrape of shoe soles louder than I could ever recall before. I remembered how to work the commlink, slid on the shades, hit the switch for my second-hand Renraku Sensei—

—and the world exploded.

Everywhere, people talking, listening, music, voices, ads, over twenty commercials vying for my attention while a half-dozen profiles popped up with various queries. I remembered how to activate the spam filter for the homemade programming, and things became more manageable, like the volume button for a stereo that's been left on too loud when you first switch it on.

The world was awash in color and sound. Shops rarely used real neon signs anymore, just picked up an AR tag. Clubs and restaurants beckoned, even a triple-X joint joined the chorus of sound with moans that set my long-deprived brain afire. I imagined, with a simlink, I might have felt a moment of simulated ecstasy or the illusion of a caress, just enough of a taste to whet my appetite and lure me inside. Shops of all kinds, blinking on and off with full audio. I was hard pressed to imagine what a more expensive commlink, complete with bells, whistles, and a kitchen sink, might show me.

Another small window opened up, a news bulletin. The stereotypical newscaster held sheaves of paper as though she was actually reading from them. The FastFacts logo flashed across the screen before she started speaking.

*"FastFacts News, I'm Bella Luchessi. Tonight's top story: Knight Errant Security has announced six new missing persons, all suspected of being the latest victims of the rash of kidnappings plaguing the city. This brings the total of reported disappearances in the past three months to 28, with inside sources revealing that Knight Errant has no leads as to the identity of the kidnappers, nor the motivations behind them. No ransom demands have been made as of yet, and no apparent connection between the victims has been found. More on this story as it develops."*

A small link popped up with information on the identities of the kidnap victims, as well as contact information to report any leads.

Then the profiles started bleeping for my attention. A half-dozen little e-mail chat requests, with a picture and link to a bio next to them. I saw the link to my own bio, which Needles had made up for me, and started laughing.

*Rick Carmine, age N/A, income...*

It went on and on, describing me as a freelance stock trader with an obscene income, as well as a picture of me right after Pretty had finished my haircut, touched up enough to keep me from being recognized. It actually looked really good. I started wondering if any of the people who were trying to chat me up had gotten a look at my ratty clothes.

An hour's wanderings brought me back down from the initial fun of AR. Nice, but still just a tool. I doubted it would change my life all that much, when it got right down to things. At least you couldn't pick my pocket for my credstick any more.

I finally pulled up next to a public data term. The Sensei was good for local interpretation of the Matrix, but for real searches in Chicago, I needed something more grounded.

I went back to my old sites, which, though updated, were still fundamentally the same, and entered my account info and passwords.

*Password Denied*

I frowned, frustrated. I punched them in again.

*Password Denied*

I sighed and tried some other sites. The results were always the same. Over and over, the red letters taunted me. My old identity, Kevin Tripp, was *gone*.

I started a Matrix search for my old holding company, Vryce Ltd. Only one smaller database had any info on them. I brought up the results.

> Vryce Ltd. Est. 2061, closed 2064. CEO Kevin Tripp.
> A private holding firm with at least one warehouse for engaging in import/export ventures, Vryce Ltd. took a major hit when its founder and CEO vanished in the winter of 2063. When the second crash occurred, its sites were unprotected, and it was erased wholesale. The property was reclaimed in 2065 and resold.

Every runner who survives more than a year or two starts to think about retirement. They think of an out. A perfect escape plan to spend their hard-earned criminal cash. Most go the Caribbean island route, with umbrella drinks and sandy beaches and real food and tanned company. Absolutely every one of those elements was anathema to me. Well, not the tanned company. But deep water, alcohol, and sunlight were no good for me.

Other runners try to set up their skills in legitimate enterprise, becoming security consultants or Mr. Johnsons or just opening up a bar. For me, it was to learn and learn some more. Saturday Jones, escape artist to the stars of shadows, had procured an actual PCC SIN for me, along with an apartment in L.A., an account that would slowly accrue interest, and everything I would need to live comfortably, self-sufficiently, ready to be a student at any university I liked with a complete, thorough background against checks. A seemingly-perfect retirement plan that even used my real name.

A way to step out of the shadows and into the world.

All gone...

I felt kind of empty inside. It might have been more of a shock to learn that all my money, all the things I had worked so hard for years to have...all of it was gone. But I'd been expecting this in some way. It wasn't quite like starting all over. I had experience, even if I was physically out of practice. I knew how the biz was conducted. I still had my magic, weakened though it might be. And I could always fall back on the knowledge that I was nigh-immortal. Nothing puts a setback in a positive light like knowing you've got forever to make it up.

Still...3.5 million nuyen...all my savings...all my gear...

I wondered if any of my old emergency caches were still around. My prized vibro-katana weapon focus was at the bottom of the Chicago River, no doubt rusted away even with it's magical sturdiness, but plenty of other goodies were scattered here and there. Hell, maybe one of my old chummers might have some of them, and some other swag, as well...

Drek! I had a lot of people to call! A lot of old friends to find. I started punching in the first number when I realized...this is a new chance. A chance to start over.

Who knew who might be watching? I was pretty sure any enemies I used to have thought I was dead and gone. Why throw that away if I didn't get any other perks of coming back from the dead? Still, there was one person who I would never hide from. I finished punching in the number and waited as it rang and rang, deactivating the camera for my face so they would get audio only. The line picked up, clicked for about half a minute with rerouting and anti-tapping, and finally a heavily warped voice came through on the other side.

"Speak."

I smiled. It's amazing how much you can recognize, when you know what to look for. I twisted my own voice in my throat, something I'd always been good at, and tried to keep my voice straight from holding back the giggles. It was like a prank call from my childhood.

"If you want to remember old friends, take a look in Chicago for a crimson name." And I hung up. I was sure she would figure out the riddle.

It wasn't my first time in this town, in any of its incarnations. I'd practically grown up in Woodfield Mall before the Awakening, before anything. I learned to run the shadows here before the breakout. In 2057, Ares bombarded the Containment Zone with Strain-III Beta Bacteria, a bio-weapon that targeted Astral forms such as the bugs and ghouls, devastating the insect spirits and ghouls alike. Then-President Haeffner had officially taken down the walls of the Containment Zone in Chicago in 2058, while the government offered up reconstruction contracts and projects to lure new businesses back into the Shattergraves. What they hadn't counted on were the non-Awakened warlords and gangers that would keep UCAS peacekeeping forces busy for a long time. Contracts started to dry up, with no one willing to risk their lives to work there, and magic-users avoided the city due to the Strain-III clouds still floating about, despite ongoing Ares cleanup projects. Smaller businesses started to crop up along the periphery, and enough people were trying to making a living there that walling off the larger area once again was impractical.

The new outbreak of bug hives only complicated things further. For whatever reason, some bugs just didn't want to leave, new ones had come to take up residence, and a few captured insect shamans revealed that the area was especially appealing to them. At the same time, the surviving ghoul population had either found ways to acclimate to the new environment or left for safer parts, and a few new packs had risen up to replace the old. So new walls went up around the highest concentrations of gang, ghoul, and bug territories, slowly contracting to eliminate the "infestation." So yes, Chicago's Containment Zone had been dropped, at least on paper. In reality, it had simply shrunk.

I waited for Pretty across the street from the sewer entrance, pulling up a hood and shuffling around like a beggar for about an hour, almost hoping some poor slot would roll up and try to mug me. "Vamping," we used to call it—vigilantism and hunting rolled into one. I'd started out that way, cleaning up the streets, feeding, and collecting a small arsenal of weapons. The things street scum carried, these days. Knives, pistols, chains, pipes, even the occasional SMG. It was discouraging. I never drained them all the way, only enough to put the fear of beggars into them. I always enjoyed the thought that maybe, one of those kids might think about slicing up some poor lady on a street corner for some quick cred, then realize that *she* might be one of those monsters.

Alas, no one came along to harass me. Maybe Knight Errant was *too* good for my tastes...

I heard Pretty before I saw her, high heels clicking down the street. Her bio-hair picked up the shine from the street lights that weren't smashed, and her artificial eyes flitted back and forth. It was hard to tell if she was predator or prey. Looks like she and I played the same game, just used different cards.

She tensed as I approached, unrecognizing. I let my hunger overtake me for a moment and my eyes shone red. I smiled with fangs out, not caring if I scared her. She was being a real slitch to me, and being friendly hadn't scored me any points thus far. Maybe she was one of those backwards girls who enjoyed the company of the abusive.

She relaxed, completely impassive. I wondered if that was her natural state, or did pretending for the sake of the warren just exhaust her of her daily allotment of natural emotion?

Pretty opened the door.

Ten minutes passed in silence. She'd changed out of her nice boots to some waders she'd left by the vents. We walked on either side of a stream of filth on the concrete bridgeways under the ancient brown stones, silent as quarreling siblings. She seemed to be pointedly ignoring me whenever possible. Made me wonder just how much of an issue my presence in the pack was to her.

I leaped over the gap and stood before her. She didn't register any surprise, but I felt it in her stance. I was awfully close, a possible miscalculation on my part, but the hell with it. She'd back off if she was uncomfortable, wouldn't she?

"What is your problem with me?"

Her eyes slowly rose up to meet my stare, and suddenly the closeness felt like too much. She was just a kid. Physically we were the same age, but goddammit, I'm ninety-two! Well, almost sixty of those years were spent asleep, but so what? That still made me her elder. It was just too hard to read her. I'd never spent much time around coherent female ghouls, let alone ones who knew what it was like to be found attractive. She was somewhere between feral animal and sophisticated woman. It was an almost-intoxicating blend, except for the utter confusion it engendered. And I hate being confused.

Even now, it was a paradox. Her posture, the position of her feet, the inclination of her head, ready to lift up into a kiss. Everything... except those eyes. Not just the cybernetic alien-ness of them, but something cold. It was within her soul and withheld from the surface, something I might never penetrate. I wondered if anyone else saw it. I wondered if anyone else had a problem with it.

I turned and continued walking, with her behind me. I wasn't feeling like I had much to lose, and I might have welcomed a fight, so I didn't care who heard me. I started to rant.

"You know, it's not like I asked to be in this position. I had it all. Money, toys, magic, fun, and friends. I was on my way up—up and out of the shadows. Legit, free to *live* a life, not just fight and scrape for one. I paid my dues. Now I have to start all over. And it ain't easy, you know? Next to no one remembers me, the world kept turning, and I lost years in a long eyeblink. I know you have no idea what that's like. I know it's unfair to bitch about what I've lost when you've never had something like it in the first place, but damnit all, you might just *try* being a little friendly!"

I spun around on that last word, the echoes reverberating long and hard down the tunnels, dripping water our accompaniment as we breathed the filthy air and stared at each other.

Her expression was something far too simple to be faked: she was shy. She looked like a child who was terrified of meeting a new stranger. But as I watched, this slowly hardened into a belligerent sneer, her chin lifting, scarlet lip curling, eyes narrowing from that guileless width into something menacing. It was unnerving.

I wasn't even sure if this girl knew herself what she was like deep down. What must it be like, to be born a ghoul, a monster, and then become a human? To live among monsters you call family, yet be forever apart from them? To share their tendencies, but live a double life with those who shun them? How old was she? How long had she been doing this?

Spirits, it was sick what this world did to us all.

## SHADOWRUN: CRIMSON (EXCERPT)

"You look awfully thin," Needles remarked as I stripped off the shirt to hop back in the shower. I looked at a broken mirror propped against the wall. He was right. My ribs showed plainly, my stomach caved in. My arms were like twigs, my legs not much better. My skin was almost ash gray, but that could be blamed on a steady diet of bugs and no human blood to give me a healthy blush.

"What'd you expect after a decade-long nap?" I replied.

He smiled. "I seem to remember you in a similar condition the last time you got hauled up."

*...Too weak to move, too weak to breathe, but gotta breathe, gotta...*

"Yeah, I remember."

"Well, then don't worry about it. You looked fine after a while. Just gotta get some exercise, that's all."

I smiled ruefully. "You think you could spare some weights?"

His grin turned feral. "Actually, I was thinking something a bit more...aggressive."